Book #2: Haders

HADERS BY AARON MCGOWAN

The characters and events in this book are fictitious. Any similarity to real persons, living or dead, is coincidental and not intended by the author.

Visit me at facebook.com/AuthorAaronMcgowan

McGowan, Aaron.

Elpis / Aaron McGowan

Summary: A plan is formed to locate powerful Nexi stones known as Haders, crafted centuries ago for the purpose of combating the Elpis. Two unlikely teams are formed, Borely, who finds himself struggling to come to terms with what he has become—a bloodthirsty vampire and airship-pilot elf Lanek who finds himself enlisted for the other Hader-searching team.

ISBN-13: 978-0-9945522-3-5

Published by Hellfun Publishing.

# Table of Contents

*"Imagination is more important than knowledge."*

– Albert Einstein

Dear Reader,

Imagination rules the world. Everything we see and create starts from one point, the idea, and the idea is born from our imagination. Where do you see your ideas going?

I want to give my sincerest appreciation for purchasing my novel. To know that you will embark on this wonderful journey of adventure, mystery and pure creativity with the characters in Elpis motivates me more to expand this world. I hope you enjoy the detail and depth put into every personality. The world was molded from inspiration, life and ideals we can strive for.

Keep up with my manga-style comics and other books by connecting with me on social media.

You can find my growing work on: www.Elpis.wikia.com, www.hellfunpublishing.com and www.alphamanga.com. And if you love the story, please share it with others! To the start of our long journey together in imagination, thank you for your support.


  -Aaron McGowan

# 1. A BOLD GAMBIT

Lanek fought the urge to keep a hand at the hilt of his rapier. It had been some time since Rilv had last summoned him—five years now?—but he still remembered quite clearly the dangers this castle represented. Though he had a guard leading him down the posh hallway, he didn't feel any safer. Perhaps he couldn't get himself to fully trust the royal guard. Or perhaps he just couldn't trust anyone anymore.

*I'm just tense*, Lanek thought. *It's being here in this palace. This is where... she died.*

His sister, Suran. He didn't want to dwell on her senseless death—the way she slowly suffered through a malicious poison, how he had been so utterly helpless to save her, the fact he had failed to avenge her in the tumultuous battle that followed. In the end, nothing Lanek did made things better for his beloved sister. And though he felt Suran and her friend Terico were in a better place now, the fact that Suran's murderer still lived unnerved Lanek.

That boy in the smiling mask, Lynx. One of the Brotherhood's most treacherous followers. Though Lanek had spent most his days the last five years focusing on his airships, he always noted any rumors involving the Brotherhood. He still looked forward to the day when he would see Lynx again. The day Lanek would have his revenge, and Suran's soul could fully find peace.

Lanek took a deep breath. *I need to relax. I need my wits about me for this meeting.*

It was difficult to calm his nerves, when such terrible memories were so deeply engrained in this place. The pristine white walls, the polished cherrywood floors, the immaculate works of art, the smell of lavender, the crisp echo of footsteps, the colored light flowing through stained glass windows... The whole castle was steeped in eclectic elegance, meaningless magnificence.

All the power in the world was gathered at this city, and what did it avail anyone? The prestige of the royalty, the intelligence of the elite, and the energy of all four Elpis pieces—none of these things were enough to save Suran. Everything deemed great and marvelous about this world... What did it bring this world? A city stained in blood. A field littered with corpses. A thousand dreams and hopes, utterly shattered forever.

And yet, life moved on. Lanek kept the legacy of his family alive through his production of airships. Rather than work directly for the royal air fleet as Rilv suggested, Lanek continued to work alone, and with the assistance of a few mechanic-savvy elves in a small village called Oedin. He would assist Fiefs engineers from time to time, but for the most part the government had left him alone for five trying years. Work was difficult, money was hard to come by, and there just wasn't much to live for anymore.

But at least he hadn't been caught up in the tumult of world affairs. Until now.

When a group of royal guards delivered Rilv's request to attend a council meeting in Setar, Lanek had no choice but to fly his airship the eleven-hour trip it took to get there. It left him weary and nervous, and even now he felt ill-prepared for whatever news this meeting would bring him.

He wondered if he was dressed appropriately for the occasion. His dark turquoise uniform, black pants, gloves, and boots were better than his work clothes, at the very least. He kept his long, light turquoise hair tied back in a ponytail—a more efficient look than what he went with when he was younger.

The guard led Lanek to the polished doors of the council room. What this meeting entailed and who precisely would be in attendance, Lanek wasn't certain. All he knew was that it was about to begin.

Inside, Lanek found Rilv wrapping up a conversation with a couple guards. She turned to Lanek and nodded. There was no emotion in her face—apparently she still didn't have an opinion of Lanek even after five years.

"You made it on time," Rilv said. "You pass."

Not exactly the welcome Lanek was expecting.

"Wonderful to see you, too."

"Your airship is undeniably the fastest in the Fiefs Kingdom." Rilv ignored Lanek's greeting entirely. She was just as to-the-point as Lanek remembered her. She had the same sort of purple and white uniform she wore before, so he took it Rilv was still the royal head servant of the Fiefs House. Though she was now in her early thirties, she had the same sharp, thin eyes and silver hair reaching down to her shoulders. Lanek noted a deep weariness in her eyes, however. Rebuilding the government of a country surely couldn't have been easy for her, considering how the king and every royal duke in Setar was murdered during Delkol Shire's rampage.

"So my coming here was just a test," Lanek said.

"Don't worry," Rilv said. "You're welcome to remain for the meeting, and share your opinion on a couple matters that may interest you." She motioned to a long, white marble table—it was shaped like a thin triangle, and had about ten chairs running down its two longer sides. At the small third side was a slightly taller, more delicately carved wooden chair with white cushions embedded within it—clearly meant for the one who would preside in the meeting.

"Take a seat," Rilv said. "Just behave yourself, and be sure to stand when the king enters."

Lanek's eyes widened. "The king?"

Rilv turned to speak with another guard, but Lanek could tell she was smirking. She had completely taken Lanek by surprise—and she knew how Lanek worked hard to never appear flustered or worried.

He motioned a hand in front of his face and took on a cool, reposed expression. "Of course. The king. What an honor."

Lanek looked over the people already sitting at the table. They were all men, so it was difficult to decide who to sit next to.

*A bunch of aristocrats*, Lanek thought. It didn't take long for wealthy elites the whole kingdom over to come to Setar to fill the void in the capital's rulership. Of course, a new king was needed, and in the end a young man named Enlia Tehns was deemed to have the most royal blood. With the death of the previous king and Terico, there were no full-blooded Fiefs left in the kingdom. There was the Shire Kingdom's family of the same name—their ruler Augurc had enough royal blood to wield the Elpis, but there was no chance the Shires would ever be allowed to rule in the Fiefs Kingdom. Especially after the war their previous ruler insinuated, and the continued existence of Delkol's murderous organization, the Brotherhood.

These aristocrats at the table were surely involved in many of the Fiefs Kingdom's dealings both internally and with foreign nations. Though it was the monarch who had the final word, King Enlia Tehns Fiefs was only in his early twenties—Lanek's age—and relied on the experience and knowledge provided by royal councils.

It felt odd for Lanek to be here, but he kept calm as he sat patiently, letting the others at the table continue their conversations with one another.

"Good evening, Lanek."

Not recognizing the voice, Lanek turned and looked up at an eigni boy in his mid-teens. He wore a white jacket and pants, and had a black vest with the golden insignia of some kind of Nexi research team, it looked like. There was something familiar about this boy...

"Ah, you must be Kitoh," Lanek said.

Smiling at the recognition, the eigni sat down in the open chair to Lanek's right. "Glad you remember me."

"You're taller than I remember you."

"It's been five years, hasn't it?" Kitoh said. "You haven't changed much, though you don't look quite as smug as I remember you."

Lanek closed his eyes, frowned, and flicked a hand to the side. "The nerve of some people. You've sharpened your tongue over the years, I see. You're not cute at all anymore."

"Five years of intense research can really drain you," Kitoh said.

Lanek opened his eyes and smirked. "Studying Nexi stones?"

"Better. The Elpis stone."

"Really? What have you found out?"

Kitoh held up a knowing finger. "You'll see. I'll be sharing my team's findings in this very meeting."

A few more seats filled up, and Lanek glanced at the door from time to time to watch for the king. Lanek had never seen him in person, though he had seen a few drawings of him in bulletins posted at the village assembly hall.

Lanek looked over each person sitting at the table, analyzing whatever he could from their appearance, how they dressed, their subtle hand gestures, their manner of speech, the things they talked about, and the directions their eyes glanced toward. He decided that there were seven aristocrats and four others at the table—Lanek himself, Kitoh, an elf woman who specialized in ancient languages, and  a human man who probably worked as a special operative. Neither of the latter two had outright said these things in their conversations, but Lanek knew how to piece things together and deduce their hidden meaning.

He heard the doorway open and turned to find two men walking in. First entered a man in the uniform of a guard, but with a small bucket-like hat on his head—it marked him as a head colonel of the castle guard.

Beside the colonel was a young man in white clothes and silver armor. He wore a white mask with an inverted black cross over the right eye.

*The Brotherhood.*

Lanek stood up.

He realized there was more to the mask. A long, thin black smile was painted across it.

*Lynx.*

Lanek drew his sword.

While everyone reacted in surprise at the exposed rapier blade, Lanek rushed toward the one who murdered his sister.

The colonel turned and raised a green Nexi stone toward Lanek. Lynx leaped to the side and slid out a small, thin knife from the inside of his mask. Lanek rushed through the vines sprouting from the colonel's Nexi, and continued his swing straight toward Lynx.

The Brotherhood fighter dodged Lanek's attack, then leaped toward Lanek, his blade outstretched.

The knife fell out of Lynx's hand.

At the same time, Lanek's rapier slipped from his grasp.

The two weapons floated into the air, and in their moment of confusion Lanek and Lynx collided into each other. Vines immediately wrapped around them both and pulled them away from each other.

Lanek struggled to break free, but the colonel's control of the green Nexi was too strong to resist. The vines wrapped so tight it became difficult to breathe. Lanek glanced toward his sword, shocked to find it still floating in the air.

A second later the rapier fell to the floor, a couple meters away from him. The knife fell as well, clinking a safe distance away from Lynx.

Rilv walked toward them, holding a strange Nexi stone in her hands. It glowed a bright purple, but had a series of thin, dark blue swirls circling beneath its glassy surface.

"At least four of us have made a grave error," she said, as serious as always.

She looked to the guard first. "I expect better work from you, Colonel. This is a delicate situation. We can't risk anything like this happening in the presence of his majesty."

The colonel didn't lower his face or glance away. "Understood."

Rilv turned to Lanek. "I told you to behave yourself. You didn't."

"He's from the *Brotherhood*," Lanek said through clenched teeth. "He *killed* Suran!"

"If you don't calm down now, I will force you to leave," Rilv said.

"I didn't ask to come here *in the first place*," Lanek said.

"I assumed you would have an interest in bringing down the Brotherhood once and for all," Rilv said. "If I am mistaken, then you would not be of any help in our mission anyways. In which case, you should leave."

"Of course I wish to put an end to the Brotherhood," Lanek said. "What does it look like I'm doing?"

"Lynx has been assisting us for some time now, working as a double agent," Rilv said. "He has supplied valuable information regarding Augurc Shire's experiments and ambitions."

"I wouldn't believe him," Lanek said. "He could

be—"

"Enough," Rilv said, widening her eyes. She held her piercing gaze on Lanek for a few seconds, forcing him to stop in mid-sentence.

She slowly lowered her eyelids until she wore her default expression once again. She looked over to Lynx and frowned. "I have placed a great deal of trust in you, Lynx. And yet you have betrayed a bit of that trust. Did you not agree to give up all of your weapons upon entering the castle?"

There was a long silence.

"I asked a question, Lynx."

"I agreed," a muffled voice behind the mask responded.

"The fact you had a knife hidden behind your mask supports my opinion you should give up the mask."

"The mask stays," Lynx said. "You won't get any more information about the Brotherhood's movements if my identity is given away."

"Understood, but I must require your cooperation in return," Rilv said.

She folded her arms and glanced back to the colonel. "Unbind them."

The man looked uncertain.

"Lynx will sit between us, in three seats furthest from the king," Rilv said. "I trust you and your subordinates will keep any harm from befalling anyone during this meeting."

"Yes, we will keep a vigilant eye on the premises." The colonel took the rapier and knife off the ground, and proceeded to loosen the vines so Lanek and Lynx could stand. Once they were up, the colonel caused the vines to return into his green Nexi stone.

"I demand the most orderly of conduct from you both," Rilv said, glancing from Lanek to Lynx.

Lanek couldn't stand to even look at Lynx. The very idea that Rilv and the royal court was working with the one who killed Suran... It was the most outrageous proposition he could have ever imagined. Every fiber of Lanek's being wanted to strangle Lynx to death right here and now—but he knew that would just get him detained. Lynx wasn't an easy person to kill, and there was no telling how Rilv would lash out against Lanek.

*How had my weapon slipped from my grasp?* he wondered. *I was going to kill him... After all these years, this is the time and place he appears? I could have avenged Suran's death...*

For now Lanek acknowledged the wisest course of action was to cooperate with Rilv. He needed to find out what lies Lynx was feeding the royal court, and what Rilv's plans entailed regarding the Brotherhood's destruction.

But there was a fourth person Rilv said was to

blame for the present circumstances, Lanek recalled. The head servant looked to a far wall, not looking at anyone in particular.

"Perhaps all of this could have been avoided though, had I taken the proper measures to ensure a clash would not break out between you two," she said. "I was not certain Lynx was going to attend, and I failed to recall the animosity Lanek held toward him. As such, I am to blame for this disturbance."

She turned to the council seated at the table and bowed her head. "The sincerest of apologies. This will not happen again."

Lanek wondered if anyone intended to respond, but the room remained entirely silent for several seconds.

Rilv looked to Lynx and pointed to a chair. "Take a seat. I will sit to your left. The colonel will sit to your right."

The three sat where Rilv intended, and Lanek returned to his spot on the other side, between Kitoh and an elderly aristocrat with a gray goatee and slicked-back gray and black hair.

"I was worried this would turn into a dull meeting," the man said. "That was a splendid performance, Sir Elf."

"It's Lanek, and I'm not a duke."

"Ah, I didn't recognize you, so I wasn't certain what it is you do."

"I build air ships," Lanek said. "And I don't forget who my enemies are."

"Yes, I was surprised to see a Brotherhood member here too," the man said, scratching his chin. "I suspect Head Servant Rilv will explain everything soon enough."

All but three seats were filled now—the one at the end, and a seat to each side of it. The conversations around the table died down once the doors opened once more.

The king and two captains of the castle guard entered the room. Everyone stood up immediately.

There was a look of extreme disinterest on the king's face. He was certainly dressed like a king, with purple and white robes, a black cape, and a thin crown of golden vines and ruby flowers clasped across his forehead—but the way he walked across the room and to the seat at the end of the table... The young man didn't strike Lanek as very kingly. He had black curly hair, light green eyes, and a rather small frame for one his age.

Once the king sat down, the two captains of the guard sat in the seats to either side of him, followed by everyone else at the table.

"Good, everyone's here," the king said. He had a

slight country accent, though this didn't surprise Lanek. Sir Enlia Tehns had grown up in a small hamlet in the east most his life—it likely made him stick out amongst the nobility in Setar, most of whom were either from cities or country estates in the west.

"Let's deal with the most pressing business first," the king went on. He looked down to Lynx. "Where will the Brotherhood strike next?"

"Leading members of the Brotherhood have been collaborating with a group of elite vampires," Lynx said. "Plans are being made to incite an insurrection in Istal. One of Augurc's top experiments will likely assist in the operation."

"When will this transpire?" Rilv asked.

"In a matter of days, I imagine," Lynx said. "I was not able to attend the actual meeting where this operation was discussed—my information comes from second-hand sources."

"You're certain Istal is the Brotherhood's next target though?" the king asked.

Lynx nodded. "Augurc has been anxious to gain allies amongst vampires for some time now. This will likely be the Brotherhood's largest operation since Delkol's attack on Setar."

"Why would Augurc be so willing to engage in such a large-scale project for a group of vampire elites?"

Rilv asked. "How does it benefit the Brotherhood?"

"Brotherhood losses will be minimal," Lynx said. "Most of the combatants will be vampires, and the brunt of the work will be performed by one of Augurc's most powerful experiments."

From what Lanek understood, there were a number of people experimented on, essentially turning them into one-man armies—or so the rumors went. Several villages and small towns had been decimated over the last couple years, each occurrence deemed the work of the Brotherhood. In some instances, it was said to be the work of a single super-soldier.

The king clasped his hands together and frowned. "And then Augurc will gain the trust and assistance of a league of powerful vampires."

A man with dark brown hair and a green suit leaned forward, placing the fingertips of his white gloves together. Lanek felt this man was an operative who worked for Rilv.

"Four days ago, a caravan approaching the Refe Forest north of Istal was entirely massacred," the man said. "Distant witnesses only noted a handful of people who walked away from the scene. I believe this experiment spoken of was among them."

"Surely the caravan had guards," the king said. "Were they that helpless against Augurc's experiment?"

"Most Brotherhood operations of late have involved very few members," the agent said. "Ever since Delkol's war, the Brotherhood has dwindled in numbers, as support from the Shire ruling family continues to lessen with each passing month."

"Support which was never supposed to exist at all," the king said. "Not that we can expect the Shire Kingdom to keep its word."

"The Shire government is in shambles," an aristocrat spoke up. "They're barely managing to maintain power over their own people. With Augurc essentially king in name only, it's only a matter of time before the Shire family cuts off all ties from him. They're in no position to risk war with our kingdom."

"It seems increasingly apparent," the agent said, "that Augurc Shire has little interest in continuing his late brother's goals. The Brotherhood conducts acts of terrorism, but none of these procedures have gained the Shire Kingdom anything."

The old aristocrat beside Lanek spoke up. "Fear tactics. Or perhaps Augurc simply wishes to test the power of his experiments. Regardless, the Shire Kingdom will need to pay for the lives lost in our lands, and in surrounding territories."

"The Shire family's ruling council will always deny support of the Brotherhood," the king said. "Threats can be made, but troops are spread thin as it is, trying to keep this entire kingdom guarded. Launching an attack on the Shire Kingdom would be costly, and do little to stop the problem. In fact, war would likely increase the Brotherhood's numbers."

"Operatives have been tracking several groups within the Brotherhood," Rilv said. "And with the information Lynx has supplied, I feel we can begin a number of counter-operations to finally bring an end to the Brotherhood."

The king raised a hand. "First, is there any more information you can provide us, Lynx? Are there any other operations you know of within the Brotherhood's ranks?"

"There are always more being planned, but I don't know of any others that will be staged in the near future."

"Regarding Istal," Rilv said, "I have the means to warn a reliable ally of the situation. With any luck, a proper defense can be established before the Brotherhood attacks."

"But even with assistance from rebelling vampires," an aristocrat with a thin mustache said, "how could the Brotherhood hope to bring down Istal—the strongest vampire city in the world?"

"All I know is a powerful experiment will be deployed," Lynx said.

"And Augurc's experiments should not be taken lightly," Rilv said. "He has the ability to wield the Elpis, and with half of it at his disposal, there is no telling just how much power he is able to place in his test subjects."

"It's been five years since operatives have gone on the hunt for Augurc and his pieces of the Elpis," the king said. "What progress can we expect to see on this front?"

"The Elpis Research Team has made great progress over the past month," Rilv said. "Based on their findings, I have formulated a plan that will return the full Elpis to the Fiefs Kingdom and bring an end to the Brotherhood's destructive acts." She looked to Kitoh and pointed a hand toward him. "Kitoh will share with us all his team has concluded."

Kitoh unrolled a scroll and placed small metal cubes on each of the corners to hold the paper down for everyone to see. Everyone at the table leaned in a bit for a better look. From what Lanek could tell, this was a sketch of some kind of device involving the two pieces of the Elpis held in the castle. The glowing stones rested on a small triangular pedestal, in front of which lay a map of the world. There were long needles sticking out of various points on the map, which was surrounded with silver rectangles placed in seemingly random locations.

"We can not utilize the power of the Elpis," Kitoh said, "but we have created a device that analyzes the Nexi energy naturally emanating from the stones. These metal blocks contain pieces of Nexi stones placed in such a way that pins can be guided to specific spots on a map. These points on the map show us where unnaturally high levels of Nexi energy can be found."

Kitoh pointed to two spots on the map—one in Fiefs Kingdom, the other in Shire Kingdom. "The strongest Nexi energies are found here in Setar, and in this remote locale in the Shire Kingdom. We can expect these to be where we could find the two halves of the Elpis."

Once this information had sunk in, Kitoh pointed to several spots on the map. "We have been able to determine five other locations with a particularly strong level of Nexi magic. Not as strong as the Elpis fragments, but much more powerful than even the rarest of Nexi stones."

"What are they?" an aristocrat asked.

The elf woman Lanek identified as the linguist spoke up. "Based on my research of ancient texts, it's likely these are what were called *Haders*. They were created centuries ago, designed to be used by specialists in order to fight against wicked rulers who used the Elpis."

"Anti-Elpis weaponry," the operative mused.

Kitoh nodded. "When many of them are gathered together, it is believed their power would rival that of the full Elpis."

"I've never heard of them," an aristocrat said.

"Information about the Haders is difficult to come by," the linguist said. "Most texts that mention them are either in an ancient elvish or eigni language. It would appear the minds behind the Haders' inception didn't want the world at large to know of these weapons. Most are likely lost, but there may be people out there who have one. I imagine they wouldn't want people to find out the source of their power."

Rilv placed a Nexi stone on the table—it was the purple and blue one Lanek saw her with when he fought against Lynx. "Our goal over the coming weeks will be to collect as many Haders as we can. Once I managed to obtain this one, Kitoh's device was able to pinpoint more precise locations of all the rest. I will create a team to gather them for the sake of combating Augurc's Elpis-powered experiments and ultimately retrieving the full Elpis."

"How will the Elpis help now?" the aristocrat beside Lanek asked. "There is nobody left in our nation who can use it."

"I intend to destroy it," Rilv said. "There may come a time when relations of the Fiefs royal line will be able to use the Elpis, but King Enlia Tehns Fiefs has asked that we find a way to destroy the Elpis for good."

"The Haders may provide the means to do so," Kitoh said. "Once we have obtained more of them, we will be able to conduct better tests on both them and the Elpis."

The operative pointed to Rilv's stone. "So this is a

Hader, then. What does it do?"

"Telekinesis," Rilv said. "This particular Hader allows me to move objects through mental willpower."

Lanek assumed this was how his rapier flew from his hand, then. Rilv had used her Hader to force it from his grasp—and had also managed to pull the knife from Lynx's grasp at the same time.

"There is likely a cost associated with it," Rilv said, "so I will only use it when absolutely necessary. The Elpis fragments gave their users Nexi poisoning, and though the Haders are not broken, they hold a volatile power."

"So you wish to obtain all the Haders," Lanek said. "How do you plan to go about doing that?"

"I will lead a small team to each location Kitoh's device points us to," Rilv said. "We will act in such a way that the Brotherhood will not not learn of the operation."

"Is the Brotherhood searching for the Haders as well?" Lanek asked.

"Haders have never been brought up amongst the Brotherhood's ranks," Lynx said. "Augurc will rely on the Elpis and his experiments. I doubt he'll want to search for the Haders and thin his troops out even further."

"There is a town in the Shire Kingdom," Rilv said, "where there are two Haders stones. Though the Brotherhood may not be involved, there is likely someone who has these two Haders."

"Then there are a couple others spread out across the Fiefs Kingdom," Kitoh said. "One deep in the Endim Mountains, and another at the port city Limbo. There may be others, but we haven't been able to locate them."

"So there's at least five of these stones," Lanek said, "and Rilv already has one of them. How did you get a hold of it?"

"The same way we will get a hold of all the others," Rilv said. "By any means necessary."

Lanek didn't like the way Rilv answered this. Not only did she avoid a direct answer, but it implied she really was willing to go to any length for these stones. This wasn't entirely surprising, but he was hesitant to have any part in it. He gathered it was Rilv's intention to have him fly the team around in his airship, which would go along well with what Rilv said when he arrived—how he had "passed the test." Rilv wanted to obtain all the Haders as quickly as possible, before rumor of the operation spread across the continent. If hundreds of people started searching for the Haders, reliable information would be harder to come by—and the less the Brotherhood knew, the less they would be able to interfere. And the less they would be able to prepare for Rilv's strike against Augurc. Thanks to Kitoh's device, they now knew where Augurc was in the world—it was likely that he kept his Elpis fragments with him at all times.

"What if other people already have these Haders?" Lanek asked. "I doubt they'll give the stones up freely."

"We will be willing to negotiate," Rilv said, "but as you say, it is unlikely they will exchange such power for anything. Chances are we will have to take every Hader by force."

Lanek lowered his head a little and stared down at the table. He didn't want to get caught up in dangerous missions like this—not after what happened the last time he worked for Rilv. He and Suran nearly died on several occasions, and in the end Suran *was* killed.

Rilv continued. "Because of the danger involved, I will lead a small but capable team. Lanek will pilot an airship—the fastest one in the kingdom."

Lanek frowned. "You're not even going to ask me to help?"

"Feel free to say *no* if you are not up to the task," Rilv said.

Lanek stared at her a few seconds. On one hand this was a chance for him to help bring down the Brotherhood... The organization that brought his sister's death was still alive and at large. Shouldn't he do everything he could to bring it down? But on the other hand... he had doubts in trusting Rilv. She was clearly for the Fiefs Kingdom, and likely willing to give up her very life for the royal line. But how far was she truly willing to go for all this? Lanek didn't like the idea of relying on ancient magical stones again, or the idea of making an enemy of every single person or organization that possessed a Hader.

*How much of this world am I going to have to fight before this is through?* Lanek thought.

"Right," he said. "I'll help how I can." It wasn't like he really could deny the request... especially right in front of the king.

"Good," Rilv said. "You will pilot the airship, and Kitoh will accompany us."

"Me?" Kitoh asked.

"Yes," Rilv said. "You will be able to continue your tests with the Elpis and Haders as we travel. I also know both you and Lanek are capable fighters. To round off the group, I will ask that Lynx assist us."

Lanek nearly stood up to yell an objection, but Lynx beat him to it.

"What? I can't be away from the Brotherhood that long. They will suspect treason."

"Sit down and calm yourself," Rilv said. "I know what your goals are, and I intend to help you fulfill them. In return, you will assist us in putting an end to the Brotherhood."

Lynx sat back down but didn't respond.

"This is a bad idea," Lanek said. "He could stab us all in the back. If he's a Brotherhood member, he might be an experiment himself. Just look at his mask! He can't be entirely sane."

Rilv raised a hand and glared at Lanek once more. "I understand *all* the risks, Lanek. Even those you are not aware of. I intend to keep an eye on Lynx, and I imagine you will as well."

"If it were up to me, he'd be dead," Lanek said. "This very instant."

"You will have to cooperate with him," Rilv said. "For the sake of obtaining all the Haders, we will need to enter the Shire Kingdom. Lynx has information we need, and will be an invaluable help in matters concerning the Brotherhood."

"He will turn against us," Lanek said.

"If he does, you can kill him," Rilv said. "But I imagine Lynx will have no reason to do so."

"I have no intention to," Lynx said, "but I don't appreciate being thrown into an operation like this without warning."

"We can't risk the Brotherhood learning of this plan," Rilv said. "If we manage to obtain enough Haders quickly, we may begin work to bring down Augurc once and for all. At that point you will be free to live however you wish."

"I expect so," Lynx said.

Just looking at him as he said this filled Lanek with rage. The very idea that Rilv wanted to cooperate with this man... and then expect Lanek to cooperate with him! It was incredulous. Unthinkable.

"This sounds dangerous," Kitoh said. "There is no telling what the other Haders are capable of. It may be best if we just continue our studies of the Elpis, search for a way to counter Augurc's power through the fragments in our possession."

"Augurc's power is spread amongst a number of experiments capable of easily killing a hundred people in minutes," Rilv said. "He hasn't quite reached the point where he could launch a full invasion on the Fiefs Kingdom, and I would like to keep him from getting there. The hit-and-run procedures of the Brotherhood are bad enough as it is. It is my duty to serve the royal line in every way possible, and I don't intend to just let the kingdom suffer increasing casualties like this."

Kitoh nodded, but looked away from Rilv while doing so.

"Sounds like you have your team," the king said. "If there's no further points to share with me, I suggest you head to your first destination. I will discuss further items of business with the rest of the council."

"Very well," Rilv said. She stood up, then looked

to Kitoh, Lanek, Lynx, and the colonel. "Lynx will walk with me. Lanek will walk with the colonel, behind us. Kitoh will walk between us."

Everyone got up and left the room as Rilv instructed. Lanek tried to think of a way out of this crazy mission—and a way to kill Lynx—and a way to bring down the Brotherhood.

He didn't know what to think at all, it seemed. He couldn't believe he was being asked again to search for ancient Nexi stones of unspeakable power.

Was this path going to bring him even more sadness? Or could it bring him the peace and contentment deep down he was searching for?

•

Augurc walked through the town, listening in on every passing conversation. There were only about a thousand people who lived there, but many travelers passed down the wide road that ran down its center. Nobody paid him attention, and thanks to the light rain, he was able to conceal his scarred face and Nexi-covered arms with a hooded cloak.

Nobody had mentioned her yet. Nobody spoke of a disaster. Nobody even had bad news to talk about.

This was precisely what Augurc wanted to hear.

He walked the entire length of the village, and

then walked back. The preset meeting spot was in a small grove a hundred or so meters past a turnip and pumpkin farm just outside of the town.

He was pleased to find Project VI standing atop of a tree stump, waiting for him. There were only a couple bloodstains on her silver and black uniform—her work was getting cleaner.

"I didn't hear anyone speak of you," Augurc said. "Or of a murder."

"They're all dead," Project VI said. "There were no witnesses."

"And the bodies?" Augurc asked.

"Buried in the ditch," Project VI said. She stared straight through Augurc's eyes—it was as if she didn't even recognize he was there... As if she spoke to a wall.

From what Augurc could tell, there was no sound of alarm in the entire town. No commotion whatsoever.

All while twenty select people were murdered.

How long would it take before people realized what had happened? Augurc wondered. Surely by tonight, people would wonder where their husband went, where their wife went, where their child went, where their friend went, where their neighbor went. What would the authorities think when they suddenly realize twenty completely unrelated people went missing?

Would they ever find the bodies?

Augurc kept his eyes on Project VI's. "Follow me."

He walked on down the trail away from the town. Though he couldn't hear her footsteps, Augurc knew Project VI was following him. It had taken some time to make her obedient, but through the power of the Elpis, the vampire's emotions were guided just as Augurc wished.

"Your next test will be in Istal," Augurc said.

He said nothing more. He did not need to feel proud of his experiment. There was no need to thank her. Her performance met his expectations, and that was all he needed.

*If only everyone in the world was this beautifully predictable.*

•

# 2. AMONGST MONSTERS

Hidden amidst the shadows of the dim mangroves, Borely shut his eyes and listened for the approaching monster. Somewhere out there, Nivakil was watching, and Borely intended to show the old vampire his own tried and true method of taking down an enemy.

All the woods around him were silent, motionless. All Borely could hear was the slow beat of his own heart, the hallow air sifting through his lungs. After a couple minutes of sheer concentration, he realized his breathing had slowed down far more than he was used to. He was breathing at the unnaturally slow and quiet rate of a vampire in the middle of a hunt.

*Breathe normally*, Borely ordered himself. The last thing he wanted was to start acting like a vampire, even if he technically was one now.

It had been a rough five years, ever since the

culmination of the grand battle between Terico Fiefs and Delkol Shire. To keep Borely from dying at Augurc Shire's hand, Areo injected her vampiric venom into Borely's bloodstream, effectively turning him into a vampire. On one hand Borely was thankful, given that he would have died otherwise. But on the other hand, Areo had condemned him to a long, miserable life as a vampire.

The beings who killed his parents. Who turned his brother mad. Who forced him to kill his own brother. Who took away everything that was good in his life.

*Just make the best of it*, Borely thought. *Show everyone that I don't have to succumb to their methods. I can still keep being myself. I don't have to stoop to their level.*

Nivakil—the mentor who had taught Areo to fight—and his other pupil Jenba, were quick to take Borely out of the scene of the battle while Borely underwent the painful transformation of becoming a vampire. Then before Borely knew it, he was being carried on Jenba's back, taking a dark forest road toward the vampiric city of Istal. Nivakil was determined to help Borely transition to the life of a vampire, if only because it would have been what his pupil Areo would have wanted him to do. Admittedly, Borely recognized later on that he probably would have died had the old man not force-fed vials of blood down Borely's throat each day. Still, at the time, the very thought of drinking blood was a living nightmare.

There was no helping it, though. Borely couldn't help but acknowledge he had become the very thing he hated, but he was determined now to not let his transformation bring him down. He wasn't going to let the vampires win.

He heard something. The sound was barely audible, but he could tell there was something out there. It was something he felt more than heard. Was this monster approaching him, or slipping away deeper into the darkness of the thick, leafy mangroves?

Borely leaned out and slowly searched through the dense branches and undergrowth of the forest. His eyes could see well in the dark, and could spot minute details from great distances away. He noticed the slightest of movements, far to his right. Or rather, he felt there was a movement. Looking at the remote trees, he couldn't see anything out of the ordinary. Perhaps it was just a faint breeze. It could also have been Nivakil, though Borely doubted he'd be able to spot the old man—Nivakil could probably hide in an empty room if he wanted to.

Maintaining focus on the spot he sensed movement in, Borely's vision grew a little clearer, a little stronger. It wasn't something he liked to admit, but a vampire's senses were incredible, especially in tense situations such as this. Somehow Borely's body was able to heighten its abilities when it sensed danger... It only reassured him that he was on the right track. There was definitely a monster out there.

Borely glanced a bit to the left, guided by an intuition that kicked in during situations like these. A tree moved, camouflaged amongst the other trees. Branches moved in trees ahead. Borely sprinted silently toward the shuffling in the distance, convinced this was the prey Nivakil assigned to him. The old man hadn't told him what he'd be facing, but Borely was determined to take it down his own way, rather than through methods a vampire would rely on.

Careful to make as little noise as possible, Borely took long, quiet steps. He glanced up and down, keeping an eye on the faraway movement and on the ground ahead of him, cautious to keep from stepping on twigs and piles of leaves that would give away his location to the monster.

There wasn't much Borely could do to hide his scent, but if he was quick enough he'd be able to surprise the creature and land a finishing blow before it could fight back.

He spotted movement amidst the mangroves just ahead of him. A tree moved a few meters to his left. Borely slipped behind a tree and peered to the side. His heart pounded madly—he still hadn't quite seen what the creature entailed, but it was suddenly a lot closer to him than he expected.

He caught sight of a massive earthworm sliding silently across the forest floor, slipping between trees at a remarkable speed. It was long—at least twenty meters long, though it was hard to tell with it slipping away so quickly. In seconds it vanished amidst the trees, its dark segmented flesh blending perfectly with the dirt and leaves.

The creature had to be at least a few meters wide and tall, and though it took Borely a few seconds to realize it, the beast apparently had thin trees growing out of its back. The mangroves Borely thought he had seen move were just the thick leafy branches sprouting out of the giant earthworm.

Not wanting to lose it completely, Borely ran in the direction the earthworm took off toward. The monster hadn't noticed him hiding just a few meters away—Borely felt certain he'd be able to land a good hit on it from behind. But would the thick, fleshy creature die that easily? He had no idea where the vitals of such a creature would be. His best bet was to pound the beast's brains in, though Borely didn't know what means of defense the monster had. He was up against something much larger than he expected to face. It was probably Nivakil's hope that Borely would feel it necessary to rely on his claws and fangs. Borely didn't intend to fight the vampire way, however.

He ran as hard as he could, searching through the trees for any more shuffling branches, moving trees, or even any wide impressions in the dirt. Strangely, this earthworm didn't seem to leave any tracks—almost as if it were hovering a few centimeters above the ground.

Borely pushed himself faster, shifting his focus to distant sounds of rustling leaves to guide him in the right direction. He finally caught sight of movement amongst the trees, then forced himself down a path straight to the creature.

Just as he arrived within a few meters of the beast, the giant earthworm turned its lumbering body toward Borely. It had somehow sensed him, despite all of Borely's efforts to approach as quietly as he could manage. Suddenly the beast's faceless head was upon Borely, far faster than he expected. A bloody mouth ripped open, as if cut into and torn apart by force. The creature did not scream, but dozens of long red teeth emerged from all sides of the opening simultaneously.

Borely leaped forward as high as he could muster, crashing straight into the earthworm's head, just above the gaping maw. With his metal-gloved fists charged with orange Nexi energy, Borely slammed a full-powered punch against the beast's head. The creature folded back slightly as Borely rebounded off of the earthworm's thick, hard flesh. The beast immediately sprung back forward, and Borely timed his second punch into the side of the earthworm's head, keeping it from chomping Borely in half.

Borely landed back on the ground as the earthworm reeled back a few meters. It still didn't scream—it seemed incapable of making noise, strangely. How much it was damaged, Borely couldn't tell. For all he could see, the earthworm might not have even been bruised.

The trees on the creature's back—at least a dozen of them, perhaps, though it was hard to tell—each grew a little taller. The earthworm bent its middle upward, forcing the trees to stand higher, like the arched fur of a stretching cat. With a deafening series of explosive cracks, each of the trees bent in half, folding down like the arms of a praying mantis.

The giant beast slid toward Borely, silent once more. With only a second to act, Borely leaped up the branches of a nearby mangrove and turned back toward the earthworm. The beast snaked up to Borely, running its teeth through impending branches. Borely jumped past the worm's head. At the same time, the beast jabbed the folded half of a tree from its back toward him. Focusing on the Nexi energy within his fist, Borely punched through the tree, snapping it in half in a burst of sharp wood chips. Borely landed on the earthworm's back, careful to keep his footing gripped on the creature's segmented body. Immediately another folded tree on the worm's back swung down for him. Borely dodged, powered an orange Nexi, then punched into the base of the tree, knocking the whole thing off the earthworm's back.

The creature turned sharply, forcing Borely to leap away before being thrown off. A tree from the earthworm's back leered toward him. Borely jumped back, and the tree slammed against the ground. Just as Borely landed, the front of the earthworm turned and lunged toward him. Borely swiveled in place and readied another punch. He slammed a Nexi-powered fist against what he would have called the worm's chin, but the exhausting attack did little to slow the beast down. The front of the worm flopped up a bit, but in mere moments it was lunging toward Borely again.

He turned to run, but was stopped by a folded tree swinging in front of him, reaching down from the worm's back. Too tired to power his fists again, Borely activated the dark blue Nexi on the metal band across his forehead. A sharp stream of water pushed aside the thin tree, giving Borely a path to escape the worm's fang-filled maw.

*This is precisely what Nivakil wants,* Borely thought. *He wants me to get frustrated with this beast—one that's seemingly impossible to kill with my Nexi stones. He wants me to tear it apart with my claws, or to sink my fangs and disable it by injected venom into its bloodstream. But I'm not going to do it. I'm going to kill this beast my own way.*

The train of thought gave Borely an idea. He leaped against a mangrove and back onto the earthworm's back. A folded tree swung for Borely, which he dodged and quickly ran past. He couldn't afford to wear himself out from overusing his Nexi, so he barreled past the next tree, his innate senses helping him know when to pause and when to run.

The front of the worm turned again and arced toward Borely. He jumped backwards off the rampaging creature, facing the giant crimson mouth of the beast's looming head.

Borely landed on the ground and powered all the energy he could into the orange Nexi of his right metal fist.

"Come on!" Borely said, staring straight into the jaws of the monster.

Like the crack of a whip, the huge creature swung down and snapped its teeth for Borely's head. Borely stepped to the side and leaned back at the same moment, then swept a punch against one of the beast's thickest protruding fangs. The bloody ivory burst from the creature's mouth, but it did not roar in pain. Instead it turned to Borely and lunged again. Borely dived forward and rolled on the ground. The earthworm passed over him, and Borely snatched up the freed tooth in the process.

Borely leaped to his feet, dodged the swing of a folded tree, then slammed the sharpened end of the earthworm's fang into the fleshy side of the creature. Borely had to use the power of both his orange Nexi to exert the necessary strength to penetrate the beast's tough, dense skin. The earthworm slid several meters in the process, and Borely managed to slice down a great length of the creature before another tree jabbed down for him. Blood poured from the creature, but as far as Borely could tell he hadn't managed to inflict any serious damage on the beast. He needed to jab the fang into a vital region somehow.

The earthworm swung around again. Borely ran straight to the beast's head, clenching the worm's large, bloody fang tight. Faster than he expected, the creature flew forward, and in an instant the beast's gaping mouth was upon him. Borely leaped straight into the dark opening, avoiding all the creature's jagged teeth.

Once landing inside the worm's throat, Borely immediately slammed the fang into the top of the roof of the creature's insides. He powered the orange Nexi stones in his fists in order to push into the skin and through to the other side, then slide the fang forward to cut further down the creature. Still the beast was silent, but Borely forced himself to keep slicing down the length of the worm from the inside, tearing through the top of the beast and the roots of the trees within it.

The giant earthworm ripped apart, spewing all manner of liquids and organs in the process. Borely kept pushing himself until he reached the end of the worm, leaving its dissected remains a strewn, ghastly mess amidst fallen, bloodstained trees and branches.

Borely dropped the large fang and walked away from the grisly scene. He almost stumbled and fell to the ground, exhausted from his repeated use of the orange Nexi stones, but managed to keep standing when Nivakil arrived.

The vampire looked to be in his late fifties or so, but was likely hundreds of years old, as far as Borely knew. The old man was short, dressed in black, and had thick, dark rings beneath his yellow eyes. He wore a strange black hat with golden letters—a flat-topped, triangular hat that held some cultural significance to Nivakil, Borely imagined.

"So that's how you're going to be," Nivakil said. "Stubborn to the bitter end."

"I do things my way," Borely said. "You should know that by now."

Nivakil turned his head and stared blankly out toward the monster's torn-up corpse. Though the vampire was blind, he could still tell where anything was with his other senses. It was this devotion to hearing, smell, and touch that gave Areo and Jenba a unique style of fighting. Borely had gleaned some of this style from Nivakil as well, though he did everything he could to keep from using methods that were specifically vampiric in nature.

"Far too stubborn," Nivakil said. "Even more stubborn than Areo."

"Hey, I killed the monster like you wanted," Borely said.

"You killed it, but not like I wanted," Nivakil muttered.

Borely continued, "And there's no comparing me to Areo when stubbornness is concerned."

"I suppose you're right," Nivakil said, suddenly turning to face Borely. The old vampire's eyes stared straight through him. "Areo's stubbornness at least had some sense to it. Your stubbornness is only a hindrance."

Borely didn't care to respond. He didn't even wish

to think about Areo right now. Not unless they were finally going to do something about her.

"You look like you're about to pass out," Nivakil said. Before Borely could retort that Nivakil couldn't see anything, the old vampire continued, "Go drink some of that monster's blood."

"No thanks," Borely said. "I'm fine."

"You're not fine," Nivakil said. "Any vampire with a lick of sense would know to drink some of the prey's blood at the end of an exhausting monster hunt."

"I don't need to," Borely said. "I'll recover with my own strength, like a normal person would."

"You're a vampire, Borely," Nivakil said. "You have to drink blood."

"I will when I need to." Borely could never stand it when conversations with Nivakil went this direction, as they so often did. Of course Borely knew he had to drink blood—he would die otherwise. But he wasn't going to seek out opportunities to drink blood. He was never going to let himself enjoy it. It was his intent to only drink blood out of necessity, and never out of any vampiric desire.

"Do you know why I've been training you all this time?" Nivakil asked.

"For Areo's sake," Borely said.

"And why have you been training?"

"For Areo's sake. Which is why—"

"Why you should follow my instructions to the letter!" Nivakil yelled.

"It's not getting me any closer to saving Areo though, if you haven't noticed." Borely threw his arms out. "We should be out there, looking for her. We should always be out there."

"You and Jenba don't have Rite Nexi yet, and wandering aimlessly won't help anyone," Nivakil said. "Your last dozen excursions certainly didn't turn anything up, and left you near-dead every time. Lucky thing I was able to track you down and drag you back here to Istal."

"At least I've been trying!" Borely said. "She's out there somewhere, in the Brotherhood's clutches."

"We don't even know if she's alive still," Nivakil said. "There's no reason to assume she is still alive. And if she is still alive, we have no idea where to find her. Augurc is not nearly as showy as his older brother."

Borely couldn't stand the fact nobody could figure out where Augurc's whereabouts were. There was nothing Borely wanted more than to beat Augurc to a bloody pulp and rescue Areo from whatever experiments he had performed on her. And then perhaps beat Areo up too, for turning Borely into a vampire. And then thank her for saving his life. And then...

Borely wasn't sure. He couldn't really decide how to feel about her, especially when so much time had passed since he last saw her. The days were passing by quickly, and though five years didn't mean much to a vampire, it still felt miserable. Just thinking of what the Brotherhood could have done to Areo was infuriating. Was she locked up in some cage somewhere? Borely wanted to find it right now. Just break it open and get Areo out of whatever prison or facility she was being held up in. He was ready to take down every Brotherhood member that stood in his way.

"If she is still alive, we will find her," Nivakil said. "We must go about things intelligently, however. The Brotherhood is not a menace to be trifled with. They may be fewer in numbers, but Augurc has made up for the lack of quantity with quality. These super-soldiers only grow more powerful with each passing year, thanks to his experiments."

Borely could remember fighting some of Augurc's men five years ago, and during some of his nighttime searches for Areo in subsequent years. For whatever reason, many of them never responded to his questions, even when they were maimed and severely injured. Instead, they would just keep on fighting. The others— those who didn't undergo experiments to their minds— were too difficult for Borely to defeat, their fighting skills heightened in other ways.

It was a strange, unpredictable world now, and everything about it had become foreign to Borely. Even himself.

"I won't give up on Areo," Borely said. "I don't care if it's unlikely she's still alive. I'll find her, and find a way to bring her back here safely."

"She may be an entirely different person from what you remember," Nivakil said. "She may not even remember you anymore."

Borely thought this over for a bit. What if Areo was turned into a soldier for the Brotherhood as well? Would he be able to fight her?

"I'm going to save her," Borely said. "And I'll save her my own way."

"You may not get the choice," Nivakil said. "Are you willing to do anything for her?"

Borely didn't respond, and Nivakil didn't push him to answer right away.

•

Once the monster's blood was gathered in a set of vials Nivakil had brought, Borely staggered through the forest, pushing himself to get back to the city before Jenba's fight began. Jenba was probably Borely's only friend in Istal, and the only one who seemed to understand Borely's desire to rescue Areo. The vampire trained hard each day to prepare for the Rite this year, his one chance to obtain the transformative Nexi stone that would allow him to freely travel the world in the daytime.

Borely hoped Jenba would win, of course, but it was difficult to say how great Jenba's chances were. Jenba was a hard worker, the kind of fighter who never gave up, but he didn't have the sort of talent Nivakil or Areo had. Borely even thought he could take on Jenba, despite the advantage Jenba held in his many extra years of training. Though Jenba looked to be in his forties, he had lived at least twice that length in time—though that still kept him younger than Areo. Borely wasn't sure if Jenba had ever gone into hibernation though, like Areo had.

The light of the small white Nexi stones hanging from the mangroves' branches started to grow a little brighter. Not bright enough to hurt his eyes, but it was now quite a bit easier to see. The path widened, flattened, and became more stable beneath Borely's feet. The main road to the city didn't get much traffic, given that Istal was a city of vampires, but it was in much better condition than the surrounding thin forest trails.

Borely dropped off the vials of thick monster blood at his home—a small wooden one-room building he shared with Jenba. It was little more than a couple cots, a desk, and some shelves, but Borely was used to small living quarters back when he was a sailor. This house in Istal was the only place that gave him any feeling of nostalgia, though at times it left him longing for the sea. It had been so long since he had stood on a ship, feeling the sway of the ocean beneath his feet. He missed the salty air, the crisp winds, and the cry of passing gulls. There had never been much glamorous about his life as a sailor, but it was what he was meant to be. It was right for him to be traveling the seas.

Not living in a city of vampires. The beings who ruined his life. Now he couldn't even feel the warmth of the sun, or view the beauty of a sunrise or sunset. He was trapped in a cold, dark hell, where not even the light of day was real. Just the dim, artificial glow of ghostly Nexi stones.

He placed the set of vials on a shelf, alongside a few other sets he and Jenba had filled over the last week. Borely had to admit to himself he was very thirsty, but he wasn't going to let himself start drinking blood every time he felt like it. He could hold out a little longer. Perhaps after Jenba's fight, he would have a vial.

Borely pushed himself away from the shelf and walked briskly out the door. The longer he looked at the blood, the more he knew he'd desire it. It was a part of his nature now, and he hated every bit of it.

*I've got to get out of this place*, Borely thought, walking down the city street. Though even if he did escape Istal again, that wouldn't free him from being a vampire. He would still need blood to live. What if one day he went insane, like his brother had? Would he start latching onto the necks of passers-by in the woods, killing innocents, destroying families?

He wished Areo was still around. Nivakil and

Jenba did their best to help Borely out, but they only did so because that's what Areo would have wanted them to do. If Areo was still with Borely, he would have felt a little more at ease about all this. Perhaps because he had known her for a while before he was turned into a vampire? Perhaps because they had been through a crazy adventure together? Perhaps because she was the one who made the difficult decision of making him a vampire?

Perhaps because he still liked her. It was hard to say. It was hard to know.

There were a few other vampires in the area heading toward the outdoor arena where the Rite took place each year. Istal wasn't a huge city—it was more of a large town, if anything, especially when compared to the likes of Vursa or Setar. The arena only held about a thousand vampires, and it was one of the biggest events the city held each year.

Borely passed a series of wooden shops and a mansion made of stone, though obscured by the tall, tangling roots of a couple large mangroves. Ahead were the central government buildings—dark structures with golden trimming and red towers reaching toward the dizzying heights of the city's biggest mangroves. Borely had to wonder if even the trees of this forest were real, or if they were the result of some kind of Nexi experimentation. The setup worked a little too perfectly for vampires, he felt.

Down the trail a ways, Borely caught sight of a

young vampire girl in a purple dress with white frills and lacing. She was running around, getting a hoop to roll down the road with a stick she beat it with. By her long violet hair and large yellow eyes, Borely recognized her as Analicia, one of the children Jenba visited each day at the orphanage. Borely sometimes went along with him, and usually regretted it.

These child vampires were an anomaly in the city, generally humans and elves who were turned into vampires by accident, or as the result of some series of unusual events. Analicia was bitten when she was eight, and though she had lived fourteen years now, she still acted like an eight-year-old. A very feisty one, to say the least.

She grabbed her hoop and turned to grin wickedly at Borely. "Hey, take me to the arena, Borely. I want to see the Rite."

"Okay," Borely said.

"What?" Analicia yelled. "You weren't supposed to agree so easily! You weren't supposed to agree at all..."

"Don't you want to go?"

"Of course I do! But everyone always tells me *no*. I wasn't expecting you to say *yes*."

"You're old enough to watch a couple adults brutally try to kill one another, and witness a grisly murder for the sake of being able to walk outside like any normal person," Borely said, folding his arms. "And you're a vampire yourself. You should be used to bloodshed."

"I'm not allowed to kill anything," Analicia said, a hint of sadness in her voice. "I'm too little..."

Borely remembered that though she was fourteen technically, she was still eight at heart, so perhaps she would never be allowed to go on a hunt. It made sense, of course. Who would send an eight-year-old out to kill monsters? She'd just get herself killed.

Not that Borely cared, of course.

"If you say so," he said. "Probably best you stay here then." Borely walked on down the road, but didn't get far before Analicia jumped onto his back and clenched his shoulders tight. He screamed and tried to shake her off, but she dug her claws into Borely's skin to keep a firm grip on him.

"Take me to the arena!" she cried. "I'm so bored! Let me watch the fight! It's Jenba today, and I want to watch!"

"What if he dies, you little brat?" Borely yelled through clenched teeth. "Do you really want to watch him get killed?"

Analicia only cried out louder. "There's no way Jenba will lose! He's the best there ever was! Now take me to the arena! It's almost time for it to start! Hurry up, Borely!"

All Borely wanted was for her to get her claws out of his skin. "Fine! Just get off of me!"

The small girl immediately plopped back to the ground and started to walk nonchalantly down the road. "Glad to know there's at least a few brain cells in your head."

Borely gripped one of his shoulders and scowled. "Is that what you say to someone doing you a favor? I'll pound you if you attack me again."

Analicia turned around and placed her hands on her hips. "If you're hurt so badly, just drink some blood, you idiot! If you're going to cry about it you can have some of mine." She tilted her pale neck to the side and strummed her tiny fingers across it.

Borely covered his eyes and groaned. "As if I'd do something that disgusting... I'd die before I suck *your* blood."

The child lowered her eyelids and smirked, as if trying to look seductive. "Don't lie to yourself, Borely... You know you want some of this."

Borely stomped past Analicia and walked at a brisk pace down the road. "This conversation is over! Come on, we're going to be late if we don't get going."

There wasn't much Borely was looking forward to in this Rite. There was a chance his one friend in the city was going to die, for one thing. But even if Jenba did win, would Borely get any closer to finding Areo? If Borely found out anything about Areo's whereabouts, perhaps he could nab Nivakil's Rite Nexi, and then go with Jenba to save Areo.

Borely tried to take his mind off the pain of the deep incisions in his shoulders, off his growing thirst for blood, and off of Analicia's incessant chatter.

•

Jenba's Rite match was going very poorly.

Borely sat between Nivakil and Analicia—a rather uncomfortable situation in and of itself—and watched as Jenba struggled to keep up with the vampire he was pitted against. Jenba's opponent was a large man who looked to be in his thirties, dressed in a white collared suit—which remarkably hadn't been stained in any blood yet. Perhaps this was to show just how confident he was.

Jenba repeatedly attempted to attack the man with bursts of flame from his red Nexi stone, but the opponent was quick to utilize his yellow Nexi each time he was hit. The glowing energy of the yellow barrier protected him from the fire, and the man was able to fight through Jenba's defenses quite easily. The opponent's efficient use of Nexi energy was remarkable in and of itself, but the fact he was a strong, burly man and a well-trained fighter made it difficult for Jenba to combat him.

And though Jenba was well-trained also, he looked almost frail in comparison to his opponent. Jenba's brown robes and yellow sash were splattered with blood, and even his red bandana had been clawed up to keep him from covering his eyes like Areo apparently had in her Rite duel.

It was painful to watch Jenba get repeatedly clawed, punched, and kicked by this opponent. Jenba was giving his all, and pulling off some really clever moves to keep from dying—but it didn't look like it was going to be enough.

*At least, that's probably what Nivakil is thinking,* Borely thought. There was nobody more pragmatic than Nivakil, and the old man had repeatedly insisted that Jenba not go through with the Rite this soon. Jenba was too anxious to save Areo to let Nivakil stop him, however. And Borely didn't want to give up hope on Jenba—or Areo.

"Come on, Jenba!" Borely yelled. "Finish this guy off already!"

Jenba gritted his teeth and fired off a giant burst of fire. The opponent activated his yellow Nexi, continuing his charge toward Jenba straight through the ball of flames. Jenba ran forward at the same time, claws ready to tear into his enemy.

He was fast. Faster than Borely had ever seen Jenba run before. *He was running into the massive burst of fire he had just created.*

A blood-curdling scream erupted from within the smoke flames.

The opponent's body flew through the air backwards, a bleeding hole in his chest. The airborne fires dissipated, and Borely turned to find Jenba lying on the ground, a burnt, bloody heap.

The enemy clenched his gaping wound and screamed, but managed to keep standing. He staggered toward Jenba, who struggled to push himself up.

Nivakil stood up, and Analicia gasped as the enemy stomped toward Jenba, claws outstretched.

"What is happening?" Nivakil asked. It was the first time Borely had ever heard the old man ask such a thing. Nivakil prided himself on always knowing what was going on, despite his blindness.

"Jenba's trying to get up, but—"

"He got hit again? How?"

"He jumped in the flames," Borely said. "That's how he jabbed his claws into the guy's chest. It was very unexpected."

"That... that *is* unexpected," Nivakil said. "Jenba wouldn't... That much fire will kill him unless he gets blood quickly."

"It was a last-ditch effort," Borely said, "but it still

might not be enough. His opponent is—"

The man reached Jenba, who was still trying to stand up. The man swung back, ready to sever Jenba's head off with his elongated claws.

"Jenba!" Analicia screamed.

Suddenly Jenba was standing to the side of his opponent, shoving his claws straight into the man's stomach. Jenba had pretended to be nearly dead, just to get the enemy close to him.

The man stumbled backward, and Borely expected to see a second gaping hole in his body. Instead, Borely realized there was a faint yellow glow about the opponent's body. The man had activated his yellow Nexi as a precaution, just in time.

Jenba fell to his knees, screaming in agony—his claws had shattered upon impact with the man's barrier of energy. The sudden transition of feelings rushing through Borely was nauseating. One second it looked like Jenba was going to die, the next second it looked like he was going to win—and now it looked like he was going to die again. It was clear the man had been hurt by the quick and powerful blow, but Jenba's claws hadn't managed to pierce his body.

"You just... try that again!" the man yelled as his barrier faded, and he fought to catch his breath. He approached Jenba again, who now looked even worse off than he had before. It was obvious the same trick wasn't going to work again, and once the man finished Jenba off he'd be able to drink Jenba's blood and heal the gaping injury in his chest.

But before the man could get closer, screaming began to fill the far end of the arena. Borely looked across to find a large man walking past the table of startled judges. The man had a black vest, pants, and bandana, a scar across his nose, and at least a dozen green Nexi stones grotesquely implanted in his muscular arms. Vines coming from the green Nexi held several city guards tight, and held them up high enough for everyone to see. Jenba and his opponent both turned, the fight suddenly a secondary concern.

This was Augurc Shire, walking into the arena right in the middle of a Rite.

Borely and tens of others stood up.

*It's him*, Borely thought. *I'm going to get him to tell me where Areo is. And I'm going to kill him!*

Before anyone could make a move toward him, Augurc caused all his vines to squeeze the eight vampires he had captured even tighter. Drastically tighter. In a single moment, all eight of the guards were squeezed so tight they were each chopped up into a half-dozen bloody, screaming chunks.

Tens of screaming vampires leaped from the stands, rushing with claws outstretched, or Nexi stones raised. Augurc raised a hand, and Borely stood up, shocked at what he found. In Augurc's hand were two pieces of a stone, glowing bright, changing color with each passing moment.

Half of the Elpis.

"It's Augurc!" Borely said. "He has the Elpis!"

Just as Borely was about to leap down to the dirt field below, the arena filled with an overwhelming blinding white light. All the white Nexi stones of the mangroves above glowed brighter and brighter—a flash of white Nexi light that remained constant. All the vampires in the stadium were effectively blinded.

Borely shut his eyes tight, his ears ringing with the screams and groaning of a thousand vampires. He and Nivakil and Jenba would be able to get out without relying on their sight, but was this entire arena about to become a complete massacre? Augurc had just managed to overpower all of the white Nexi in the area without even batting an eye.

The sounds of dying screams filled the stands. Scraping metal accompanied bursts of fire, water, and earth. Borely could make out the sound of claws scraping against flesh. The gurgling cries of murdered innocents.

"I'll get Jenba," Nivakil said. "You watch over Analicia and find a way out of here. There's probably at least a hundred enemies here."

Borely tied a handkerchief around his eyes to help keep the increasingly blinding light from piercing through his eyelids. He heard Nivakil dash off down a stairway, then turned his focus to Analicia. The girl was screaming in pain—it had been years since she was exposed to even a fraction of this much light.

"Get on my back," Borely said, grabbing the girls arms and forcing them to drape around his neck. "Hold tight. I'm going to have to fight my way through this."

He was still exhausted from his fight with the giant earthworm. It was going to be strenuous to use more Nexi energy this soon, and any injury he'd sustain was going to hurt like crazy. He swore. If only he had taken some of the monster's blood to drink. He would have been ready for this ambush.

*I've got to at least capture a Brotherhood member*, he thought. *I've got to get answers... I've got to find out where Areo is!*

He leaped down the benches, pushing his way through frantic, fleeing vampires and huddled, shrieking children. Most of the people in the stands weren't going to be expert fighters—they were going to be slaughtered by the Brotherhood if something wasn't done. But what was Borely going to be able to do?

He reached the stairs, focusing on nearby sounds for any approaching Brotherhood members. If this was all part of Augurc's plan, then it was likely the ambush team had a way to see in the blinding light—or at least could fire large-scale attacks blindly into the stands.

Just as the thought came to Borely's mind, he sensed a series of large projectiles approaching—boulders perhaps. He sprinted down the stairs, careful to keep a hold of Analicia, who nearly flew off his back at the sudden burst of speed. Rocks exploded into the stairway behind Borely, and he struggled to listen for any other attacks. He heard footsteps everywhere—people fleeing, screaming.

The whoosh of a weapon. Borely turned and punched at what he expected to be the flat end of a blade. Instead, he bashed straight through claws. The vampire screamed and fell back—Borely continued to run, hearing the spread of flames across nearby wooden benches.

He wondered momentarily why a vampire had attacked him. He certainly had plenty of people in Istal who didn't think highly of him, but was this the opportune moment for any of them to attack him? Or were there vampires working with the Brotherhood? He remembered hearing of elites who broke away from Istal's government in past years, and how some vampires had been trained to fight in blinding conditions such as this. The vampire who fought Areo in her Rite duel was one, and his trainer one of the forerunners of a potential insurrectionist movement. Perhaps these vampires had helped Augurc and his soldiers reach Istal and bypass the city's defenses. A full-blown coup d'etat.

Borely reached the stage of the arena, where there

was a bit more room to maneuver around. Was Augurc still down there? And what about Jenba and Nivakil? There was screaming everywhere. Bursts of flame, shattering of ice, whooshing of arrows. The field had turned to sheer chaos, and Borely couldn't see any of it.

Several sets of footsteps approached Borely. He was in no condition to fight multiple vampires or Brotherhood fighters at the same time, especially with a child in tow. He blasted a jet of water from his headband's Nexi and dashed ahead, coughing up smoke from a nearby explosion of fire. He nearly stumbled, but managed to keep running. The air around him suddenly turned cold—a light blue Nexi effect. He heard icicles sprout from the ground in front of him. He leaped over them, listening for other attacks, other enemies.

Something flew through the air, spinning toward him. Toward his head.

"Lean right!" Borely yelled. Upon landing he turned to his right as hard as he could, and Analicia leaned with him. What Borely took to be a knife flew just past his left ear. Footsteps ahead marked the assailant. Borely accessed the orange Nexi energy of his fist and punched the face of the enemy. A Brotherhood mask shattered upon impact, and Borely continued to run, hearing he was being followed.

He wanted more than anything to take down everyone in this arena, and to start questioning all the Brotherhood members he could about Areo. But there just wasn't time, and he didn't have the strength to keep this up much longer. If he could stop for just a few seconds to suck blood out of an enemy, he'd stand a better chance...

Borely heard the zipping of vines, the muffled groans of struggling victims. He kept running, careful to avoid a couple nearby figures, who may or may not have been enemies. There was a scraping of claws—two vampires fighting one another.

Though utterly spent, Borely kept pushing himself toward a stadium exit. There had to be Brotherhood members or vampires keeping people from getting out. The continued exposure to this blinding light was giving Borely an infuriating headache, and carrying Analicia like this was keeping him from fighting freely.

*This might be my one chance to find out where Areo is,* Borely thought. *I've got to find Nivakil and drop this kid off.*

A wave of dirt burst out of the ground a few meters away. Borely heard the cries of several vampires, but listened for the movement of the dirt. It was approaching him. He turned toward it to face it head on. Just as the wall of earth was about to encircle him, he shot off another blast of water, weakening the hardening dirt just in front of him. He headbutted through the earth and kept running. The person who made the attack stood just ahead. Borely raised an arm and clotheslined the attacker. He heard claws lengthening out just as he did so, marking this as another vampire.

He turned toward the exit—or at least what he believed was the direction of the exit. It was difficult to be certain, when he had moved in so many directions upon reaching the fighting pit of the arena.

Three sets of footsteps ran for him from straight ahead. Borely heard the unsheathing of a sword, then a subsequent charge of energy—perhaps orange Nexi energy for the sword. At the same time, Borely made out the taut pull of a bow's string. He struggled to make out the exact location of the archer. And a moment later, the third figure rushed toward Borely in an extra burst of speed—inhuman speed a well-trained vampire was capable of.

Borely gritted his teeth and leaped to the right the moment he heard the snap of the archer's bowstring. An arrow flew to Borely's left an instant later. A moment after that, the vampire reached Borely, swinging his claws for his head. Instantly Borely forced his own claws to elongate, and sliced the enemy's hand clean off in one quick swoop. As the man screamed, Borely kicked the man in the chest and ran straight over him. Borely listened for the swordsman. Three footsteps. Borely rushed to the enemy's right. The fighter swung his blade, charged with energy. Borely turned in place and leaned forward. The blade passed beneath Analicia. Borely kept turning, then jabbed his elongated claws into the enemy. It didn't matter where he hit—Borely shoved his claws through the assailant's body and pushed past him. At the same time, the archer had readied another arrow. Borely listened for the string.

Pull. Snap. With the enemy's location certain now, Borely side-stepped the arrow and rushed head-first toward the archer. The enemy ran for it at the last moment, but Borely managed to swipe his claws through the assailant's bow and on through his chest.

Struggling to breathe, Borely ran out of the arena, noting the change in the hardness of the dirt beneath him. He kept to the road, not confident enough to make his way through the thick forest without the assistance of his eyes. Minutes passed before he reached an area in the city that wasn't lit up like a dozen suns. The power of the Elpis was a terrible thing to behold—it seemed Augurc's studies of the stone had served him well. Perhaps he had found effective ways of using the stone in a way that would not poison him or fill him with agony, as had been the case for Terico and Delkol. Where Delkol's brashness and vigor had failed him, Augurc's patience and shrewdness was paying off.

It took time for Borely's eyes to adjust back to the dim light of the city's mangroves that weren't affected by Augurc's Elpis. He kept his eyes closed and his blindfold down, relying on his other senses to guide him further through the city. There was no sound of anyone chasing him, but he had the feeling he was being hunted. Something was stalking him—he could sense it. It gave him a strange sense of deja vu, only now he was in the place of the monster. Would he suffer the same fate as that giant earthworm? He was in much worse shape than that creature had been when it fought him.

"Borely."

The sound of a voice so close to him made Borely jump, the wind knocked out of him by the sheer suddenness of the beckoning. It was only Nivakil though. Borely slowed to a stop and struggled to regain his breath. How long had he been running for?

"Good, you still have her," Nivakil said, referring to Analicia. "Let her go. You're about to collapse."

The child got off Borely's back, and the lifted weight almost sent him floating up a few centimeters—or so he felt. It took some time to breathe normally again, but he was strong enough to keep standing.

"Jenba safe?" Borely asked.

"I'm fine," Jenba said. Apparently he was right there with Nivakil.

Borely lifted his bandana and squinted at the two figures standing before him. Once his eyes adjusted enough, he saw Jenba was alive and well. Presumably Nivakil supplied Jenba with some blood so he could regenerate from the near-fatal wounds his opponent had inflicted on him.

"We're going to have to flee the city," Nivakil said. "A Brotherhood scout spotted you running down the middle of the road, and is now gathering a team to take us down."

"We can't just run," Borely said. "We have to find out where they're keeping Areo. We have to help all those people in the arena." Though they were vampires, Borely still couldn't just stand by while the Brotherhood murdered helpless civilians.

"It's too late for them," Nivakil said. "This city is being overtaken by the banished elites. There's no stopping that." He handed Borely a vial of blood. "Drink this, quickly."

Borely didn't argue, knowing he'd need the energy if another fight did break out. And he fully intended to find a way to bring down some more Brotherhood members and accompanying vampires. This was finally his chance to get some answers, and he wasn't about to let Nivakil stop him.

Borely downed the blood in a couple gulps. He hated drinking blood, hated the overwhelming satisfaction it naturally gave him. There was nothing good about the taste, but his entire body felt thoroughly rejuvenated by the dark, undead power held within the substance.

"Can you run?" Nivakil asked. Borely turned to see he was talking to Analicia. The small girl looked like what little color was left in her face had been sapped out of her. She nodded blankly, her face pained and weary. Perhaps she was still adjusting to the more normal light. At least, more normal for her.

"You can all go if you wish," Borely said. "I'm

staying to get some answers from the Brotherhood."

"Fine, go get yourself killed," Nivakil said, to Borely's astonishment. Was Nivakil seriously going to jet let him go? The fact Nivakil wasn't arguing and intended to just run for it placed the whole situation in a much darker light. Did he really see no hope at all in this situation?

"Are you serious?" Jenba asked, before Borely could. "There's way too many enemies for Borely to deal with here. Augurc is there somewhere, too. Even if all of us stayed, we wouldn't—"

"Now's not the time for us to run away," Borely said. "Jenba, don't you want to find Areo? This is our chance!"

"I do, but..." Jenba began. He glanced to Nivakil and frowned a little. He turned back to Borely. "But we should really follow Nivakil. If he feels the risk is too great, it's too great."

Borely was expecting more support than this. "Don't you care about Areo? I thought she was like a sister to you!"

Jenba grabbed Borely's shoulders, and for a moment it looked like he was going to scream something.

Footsteps approached.

Jenba turned away from Borely, just as a vampire

lunged out of a nearby tree, claws outstretched. Analicia screamed. Two more vampires followed, and just as Borely began to turn, he heard the footsteps of two others from the other side of the road. Nivakil rushed to the nearest vampire. Borely forced his claws to elongate, knowing he was near his limit for Nexi stone usage. In an instant, dozens of claws scratched against one another—a frantic cacophony of scrapes and shoves.

Nivakil lobbed off the head of one, but then found himself pushed back by a woman with long, light blue hair. Her claws tangled with Nivakil's, and she grinned into his face.

"Hidif," Nivakil said. "I see you think you're in control of this situation."

"I always find my way to the top, Nivakil," the woman responded.

Borely managed to drive back the vampire that targeted him—a boy who was caught off guard by Borely's strength. Borely took the moment to assist Jenba, who had two enemies to deal with. Jenba lashed out at a man with blood red hair and a goatee, then dodged an attack by a vampire in a top hat. The moment he had an opening, Borely tore his claws into the second man's arm, forcing him away from Jenba.

The young vampire Borely fended off earlier raised a red Nexi and released a giant ball of fire into the fray. The fighters dispersed, and Borely used the moment of confusion to rush toward the vampire he had stabbed. The man was fumbling with a vial of blood, struggling to keep from screaming from his injury. Borely sliced off the man's arm and shoved him into the ground, claws pushed against the screaming enemy's neck.

"Tell me where Areo is," Borely ordered. "Tell me now!"

A figure leaped from a tree, landing a couple meters in front of the man Borely pinned down. It was a woman in a silver and black uniform.

Areo.

*She is here? Now?*

Borely was stunned speechless. He sensed he had to get away. But how was he going to? And why? What was going on?

Areo raised an arm toward Borely and caused her fingernails to lengthen into claws. Their jagged tips rushed straight toward Borely's face.

•

# 3. CONTENTION & TENSION

•

Claws flew to Borely, and though he couldn't believe anything that was happening, his body somehow managed to react by instinct. He dropped to the ground, forcing himself to fall backwards. The claws passed over him. Borely blinked, entirely dismayed by the fact Areo had attacked him.

The claws shot down toward him, too fast to even see.

He rolled away, but still got a few claws jabbed through his left arm. Pinned down and screaming, he struggled to force his way out of Areo's grasp. The vampire Borely had beaten down scampered away, hurrying back to join the other vampires fighting Jenba and Nivakil. Borely looked up to Areo's face, finding it thoroughly void of emotion. Areo was never the most emotional person in the world, but this face was different. It looked like Areo, but there was nothing *Areo* about it.

Almost as if her very soul was torn out from her body.

Areo retracted some of her claws, then forced them back out to stab Borely in the face and chest. Nivakil and Jenba couldn't save him—they had other vampires to deal with already. Borely forced himself to his feet and pushed his body further through the claws that impaled his arm. Areo's other claws still managed to hit him, but Borely managed to keep from getting his vitals punctured. His neck was badly scraped, and there were now several claws poking out his back. He coughed up blood, his entire body in agony.

He was alive, at least for a few more seconds. There was no way he'd be able to keep this up for long.

With his free arm, he powered the orange Nexi in his fist guard and punched at some of the claws impaled in his bloody torso. To his surprise, Areo didn't attempt to bring her claws back into her fingers. Instead, she held strong, and even with Borely exerting all his strength into the punch, he didn't manage to even dent the claws that pierced him. How had her claws become so freakishly strong? A punch like that could have shattered a block of steel.

Areo didn't register any pain in her face. Her claws kept Borely in place—the slightest of movements brought him excruciating pain. And Areo still had some claws free to jab straight into Borely's face.

"Areo! It's me!" Borely yelled. "I've been... trying

to find you!"

Claws shot off toward Borely's face.

With what little energy he had left, he activated the dark blue Nexi on his forehead, releasing a burst of water at the approaching claws. They deflected slightly enough to zip by either side of Borely's head.

As soon as the thin stream of water subsided, Borely stared into Areo's eyes, which still registered no emotion. She didn't look upset or surprised. It was as if she didn't care either way if Borely lived or died—she was simply doing her job. A boring, everyday job she was just expected to do. She wasn't exerting herself. She was barely even trying.

All at once, Areo forced her claws to tear out of Borely, ripping out the sides of his body. He fell to the ground, a screaming, bloody heap.

He was dying, and there was no saving him if he didn't get any blood right away. Not that he could do anything to escape Areo at this point anyways. He couldn't even call out to her anymore, though he now realized there probably was no simple way to bring her back to her senses. Augurc had experimented on her to the point where she couldn't even realize she was killing the very person whose life she had saved—whom she was willing to give herself up for.

Areo retracted her claws back into fingernails, but

left a few centimeters of claw on her right index finger. Her arm rigid and straight, she pointed down to Borely's lifted, trembling head.

Her claw lengthened out a bit more. Borely clenched his teeth.

Nothing more happened. She didn't finish him off. Areo's claw didn't grow any nearer to Borely. She simply stared down at him.

She was hesitating.

There was no hint of sadness in her eyes, or even confusion. And yet, she wasn't killing him.

A figure flew past Borely and Areo, but neither of them moved. Borely caught a flash of light blue—was it the woman fighting Nivakil, thrown through the air? The next moment Nivakil appeared in front of Borely. The old man swung his elongated claws toward Areo, who didn't seem to notice Nivakil's arrival.

Borely leaped against Nivakil's back, bleeding and screaming, feeling as if he'd fall apart if he moved any further. Nivakil's claws barely missed Areo's neck, and Borely realized she hadn't moved a muscle. But surely she had noticed Nivakil's attack?

"You fool! What are you doing?" Nivakil screamed.

"That's my line!" Borely yelled back.

Areo turned and ran, disappearing into the dim mangroves.

"Where are you going?" came a woman's voice. The elegantly-dressed woman with light blue hair stood up and rushed wearily toward the scene. She glanced from Areo's direction and back to Borely and Nivakil, her expression changing from confused to flustered to vengeful.

Nivakil shoved Borely off him and turned to the woman. *Hidif,* Borely recalled Nivakil calling her. She had a black eye and a deep gash near her collarbone, but she looked enthusiastic to continue her brawl with Nivakil.

Borely lay on the ground, his mind in a daze, his body at the breaking point, his soul tearing at the seams. Areo had tried to kill him. But then she stopped. And then Nivakil tried to kill her. And Areo ran away.

Why did Areo try to kill him? Why did she stop? Why did Nivakil try to kill her? Why did Areo run away?

Nivakil and Hidif charged toward each other, claws raised. They were fast. Much faster than Borely had seen two vampires fight one another before. Perhaps it was partly because he was dizzy and nauseous, but Borely could hardly tell how either of them were fighting. They moved too fast for him to keep up with, their every movement either scraping against claws or nicking the opponent's skin just a scratch.

"You can't hope to win, Nivakil!" Hidif yelled between breaths. "This city is mine now!"

"Congratulations," Nivakil said. "Your first act as ruler is genocide. By the end of the week you'll probably be the only one left. Just as Augurc planned. I may be blind, but I can see plain as day just how easily manipulated you still are. I better finish you off now, and save this world from your sheer stupidity."

"You were always one to talk big," Hidif said. A couple quick claw swipes forced Nivakil to step back, but his counter attacks didn't leave any openings for her. It was like watching two fighters swinging around ten long knives, and directing each one to a specific line of attack against the opponent. How either of them kept up with one another at this speed, Borely could hardly imagine. It was literally a blur of scrapes and sparks at this point.

Borely noticed Jenba was getting overpowered by the remaining two vampires—the young boy and the red-haired man. Jenba couldn't land a good attack on either of them, preoccupied with protecting Analicia.

Hidif's claws tangled with Nivakil's, and for a split-second Hidif lunged herself forward, attempting to latch her fangs into her opponent's neck. Nivakil slipped back, practically gliding across the dirt floor.

"Now, Analicia!" Hidif yelled, her eyes still focused on Nivakil.

Borely looked back to Jenba and Analicia, unable

to get up and stop what he suddenly realized was about to happen. Analicia already had her claws out. She was already swinging them straight for Jenba's back.

Astoundingly, Jenba managed to leap over Analicia's attack without even seeing it—he apparently had heard the swing of her claws and reacted accordingly, all in the space of a single second. At the same time he dodged the jabbing of claws from the red-haired vampire.

Jenba landed just as the boy vampire raised an ice Nexi toward him. Immediately Jenba slipped out his own ice Nexi, and the two vampires each flung a jagged ice formation toward each other. The giant icicles collided with one another, and Jenba moved to attack the boy. He stopped quickly, however, realizing the red-haired vampire and Analicia were both about to attack him.

Nivakil was struggling to defend a series of Hidif's attacks, and for a couple seconds the woman managed to leave several deep cuts into him. Just when it looked like Hidif had an opening for Nivakil's face, the old man lunged a hand forward, his claws snapping back against the force of Hidif's guarding claws. She started to laugh, but suddenly found Nivakil's bloody fingers clutching her arm. Nivakil flung Hidif backwards, swinging her over his back, straight into a tree. The moment she was airborne and her claws free from his, he rushed straight at the red-haired vampire.

The man was about to swing his claws straight through Jenba's neck. In the blink of an eye, Nivakil rushed the claws of his good hand straight through the man's stomach, tearing him in half. Nivakil kept running, avoiding the shattering ice shards from Jenba's and the boy's Nexi attacks. A moment later, Nivakil had forced his claws through the boy, leaving Jenba free to turn toward Analicia.

Jenba dropped to the ground and rolled forward just as Analicia made another swing with her claws. The girl tripped over Jenba, landing flat on her face, arms stretched forward. Jenba and Nivakil both turned to where Hidif had been thrown, but she was nowhere to be found. Borely assumed she ran off to find Areo, but she might have simply decided it wasn't worth continuing to try to defeat Nivakil now that he had Jenba as back-up.

Meanwhile blood continued to flow from Borely's body, and he felt what little life was left in him begin to fade away. He couldn't speak. He could hardly breathe.

His vision was blurry, but he could tell Nivakil was kneeling beside him. The old man forced a vial of blood into Borely's mouth, and Borely begrudgingly drank the crimson liquid. Even at the brink of death, he still hated the fact he had to rely on blood like this. Would he be dead now if he weren't a vampire? How had Areo managed to slice him apart so effortlessly like that? She had always been a talented fighter, but this was on an entirely different level. And the fact it was Areo attacking him certainly didn't help matters. How could he bring himself to fight to the death with her?

The pain of flesh and muscle regenerating flowed through Borely's entire body. He struggled to keep from yelling, but it was such a sharp, all-encompassing pain. It was fortunately over in seconds, the wounds of his body healing away and replacing the pain with a dull ache and weariness.

"What were you thinking?" Nivakil yelled. "Because of your foolishness, you nearly got both of us killed." The old man took a drink from his own vial, stopping the flow of blood leaking from his fingertips.

"You were about to kill Areo," Borely said.

"She's not Areo anymore," Nivakil replied. "She's lost to us, Borely. Or do you think that was actually her wanting to kill you? Would Areo want to kill you, after all she did to save your life?"

"No," Borely said, forcing himself to his knees. "But she's still Areo, at least a little bit. She could have finished me off, but she hesitated. She's not completely under Augurc's control."

"We have no way of saving her," Nivakil said. "I imagine Augurc will keep experimenting on her, making her more and more powerful with that Elpis energy. We won't even be able to fight a monster like that."

"Now you're calling her a monster?" Borely yelled. "She's one of your precious students. Why don't you care about saving her?"

Nivakil turned away, gritting his teeth. "Of course I've wanted to save her! But now she's a killing machine. Don't you understand this, Borely? I don't want my precious student murdering hundreds of innocent civilians against her will anymore. This was probably my one chance to save her, and you ruined it!"

Borely shook his head and sighed. He shakily brought himself to his feet, his mind still in a daze. What was wrong with this old man? Nivakil was just thinking like a vampire, Borely decided. The old man naturally turned to bloodshed for an answer.

Wanting Jenba to support him at least, Borely turned to him. Before Borely could say anything though, he realized Analicia was still there, now standing beside Jenba.

"What is she still doing here?" Borely asked. "She nearly killed you, Jenba."

"I'd never kill Jenba!" Analicia said. "Get it in that thick skull of—"

Jenba placed a hand on Analicia's head to stop her. "Don't worry, Borely. Analicia was just trying to keep Hidif thinking she was on her side. Hidif was the one who made Analicia a vampire, and asked Analicia to fight for her at an opportune moment—a way to return the favor, I guess."

"I had to pretend to help her," Analicia said. "I whispered to Jenba that I would attack from behind, and he went along with it."

Borely thought it all sounded a little far-fetched, but he didn't care to argue about it. Analicia wasn't making any move to attack anyone right now—he'd just be sure to keep an eye on her a little more than he had before. She had always been a bit of a trouble-maker, but the possibility of her working for the vampire elite that helped spearhead this whole operation was more than a little alarming.

"Fine," Borely said. "But at any rate, we've got to go find Areo before that Hidif woman does. We can't let the Brotherhood keep manipulating Areo more than they already have."

"Let her go, Borely," Nivakil said. "What do you plan to do for her, exactly? Shake her back to her senses? Recount her life story to her to bring her memories back? Return her mind back to normal with a kiss?"

"I know you don't care," Borely muttered. "But Jenba, don't you want to come help me find Areo? She's *here*. Right now. In this city. This is our chance to save her."

Jenba looked to the ground and frowned. "I don't know. Saving her now... It sounds impossible."

"It might not be though," Borely said. "You have to at least try. She's your sister, Jenba!"

"I... I know," Jenba said. "I want to..."

"Now's not the time," Nivakil said. "Capturing Areo in our current state is impossible. If you still wish to retrieve Areo, I suppose I'm willing to help, but right now our priority is getting out of this forest alive. The Brotherhood and banished elite have effectively taken control of the city by this point. There's no going back there now."

"But—" Borely began.

"Areo will surely go with the Brotherhood—likely with Augurc himself—and be deployed to other locations. We will retrieve Areo at a more opportune time. Right now we're all exhausted, and we'd be severely outnumbered if we just marched back into the city."

It seemed Nivakil was trying to cooperate to some degree, and perhaps deep down he did have a little desire to try saving Areo somehow. And it was true that they had no plan for how to actually capture Areo, let alone bring her mind back to normal. Borely also knew he was in no state to fight anymore at this point. Blood could heal his wounds, but he could only keep fighting for so long.

"Okay, let's go somewhere safe for now," Borely said.

Nivakil bent down to one of the vampires he killed and rummaged through the corpse's pockets. He pulled out a pink Nexi stone.

"Check the others for Rite Nexi," Nivakil said. "You'll each want one if we're going to be on the move for a long time."

They did so, and were fortunate enough to find a Rite Nexi for Jenba, Borely, and even Analicia.

"Was hoping to actually earn this today," Jenba said.

"In your case, it was a good thing the insurrection happened when it did," Nivakil said. "Considering how you were about to be killed off by your opponent."

It was a cruel thing to say, even if it was true. Jenba looked like he was stabbed in the heart, but didn't respond to his mentor's jab.

The four headed away from the city, taking the trail further and further into the forest, where the lights of the mangroves progressively grew dimmer. The trail wound up a hill, but it was impossible to look back to the city through the mangroves. How many vampires were slaughtered at the arena that day? How many more were killed in the rest of the city? And how many was Areo forced to kill by her own hand?

Borely had never felt so powerless before. So much death, so much destruction—and he couldn't even help the woman who had saved his life.

And now he was leaving her.

*I'm sorry, Areo*, he thought. *I swear I'll find you again. I'll figure out a way to free you from Augurc's grasp. You can live your life again. And we'll do whatever we want.*

"Hold on," Nivakil said, stopping to pull a Nexi stone from his pocket. It was a teal one—one that allowed people to speak with others who had teal Nexis, even when a great distance apart from each other. Borely didn't realize Nivakil still had one, though he knew the old man had communicated with Rilv in time for him and a group of vampires to come assist Setar in fighting back Delkol's army.

"This is Nivakil."

Rilv's voice came from the stone, as if she were standing right there speaking with them.

"We have received word that Istal may be attacked by the Brotherhood in the imminent future. We ask that your city prepares accordingly."

•

Hour after hour, Lanek stared out at the sky ahead. A light blue. Some clouds here and there, every now and then. The sun above them a ways, to their left. Lanek stayed at the controls, but there really wasn't much for him to deal with at this moment. He just wanted something to focus on. To busy himself with something. To keep his mind off Lynx, sitting against the wall just a few meters behind him. The man who murdered Lanek's sister.

Meanwhile Rilv sat in the seat beside Lanek,

asleep for now. She rested silently, barely breathing. She apparently had been up the entire night making preparations for this excursion. This strange mission, which Lanek felt only vaguely connected to. Yes, he wanted to bring down the Brotherhood. But he didn't want to go searching the continent for random magical stones again. And he certainly didn't want to be working with Lynx.

Of course, Rilv had warned both Lanek and Lynx to not create any trouble on this trip. Lynx was necessary for such and such reasons, none of which Lanek really bought. But perhaps Lanek could learn everything that happened to Suran. The events leading to her death. All the details Lanek had never gotten to find out from Terico. And perhaps Rilv was right to some degree—rather than simply trusting Lynx, perhaps they could actually use Lynx in some way to deal a fatal blow to the Brotherhood. It was an organization that truly needed to be destroyed, and the world would certainly be better off without Augurc Shire in the picture.

So Lanek decided he would wait. If Lynx chose to betray them, Lanek would be sure to drive his rapier straight through the madman's heart. In the meantime though, he would have to wait for a more opportune moment. Particularly one in which Rilv wouldn't be able to fling him around with her telekinesis stone.

Lanek glanced back to Kitoh, who sat on the floor with a stack of old books and a few scrolls. Apparently he was researching some of the materials lent to him by the linguist elf woman back at the council meeting.

"Anything interesting?" Lanek asked. He didn't want to interrupt Kitoh's reading, but he was tired of hearing nothing but the hum of machinery. Over the years he had made improvements on this ship, giving it a more aerodynamic design made of lighter materials, and providing it an engine that made the ship stronger and quieter than ever before.

"I'm just trying to understand how the Haders were created," Kitoh said. "It seems a council of elves came up with the concept, and some of the most powerful eigni at that time supplied much of the energy needed to craft the stones. There are accounts of people all around the world using the Haders though, vampires and humans included. The Haders brought about new power struggles much more often than they helped defeat kings who used the Elpis cruelly."

"Makes you wonder if this search will be worth it," Lanek said. "Perhaps we'll stop Augurc from using the Elpis any more, but now there will be a bunch of Haders in our hands."

"But in the end, precisely whose hands will be holding all these Nexi?" Kitoh asked quietly. "Rilv is leading this operation. There will likely be several Haders and a full Elpis involved before this is all over. What do you think she will do with that much power?"

"She can't use the Elpis, at least," Lanek said.

"And she made it clear that she wouldn't be the only one in charge of the Haders."

"Who knows, though," Kitoh said. "My team has found some use for the Elpis. Perhaps there are other teams I don't know about. Perhaps Rilv has a plan in mind for when the four pieces of the Elpis are all gathered together. Or perhaps she just wants to use Augurc and the Elpis as an excuse to obtain a bunch of the Haders."

Lanek was worried Rilv was hearing any of this, but he watched her carefully, noting her slow breathing and the movement of her eyes—she was deep in a dream.

"Do you not trust her then?" Lanek asked.

"She has always been thoroughly loyal to the royal court, as far as I can tell," Kitoh said. "She may or may not have any ulterior motives, but either way it's dangerous for anyone to get a hold of so much power."

"It's fatal to use any of these things too much," Lanek said. "I don't think she wants to die. And neither do any of us. We'll just have to find a way to destroy the stones when we're through."

Throughout the conversation Lanek wondered if Lynx was going to comment on anything, but the masked man kept perfectly silent. Was he asleep? He sat perfectly straight, so it didn't seem likely. Lanek didn't like the fact he couldn't see Lynx's face, or know where his eyes were looking. There was no way Lanek was ever going to be able to trust him for anything on this mission.

"I guess we'll figure out what to do once it's time for us to," Lanek said. "Let's just focus on getting this first Hader for now."

•

Lanek could make out the faint, ghostly mountains in the distance. The airship continued to travel at a brisk, smooth pace, hundreds of meters above the ground. Fortunately Kitoh was handling the flight much more easily than he had when he was on *The Finest Hour*. Perhaps that was partly because the boy had some books to read through. Or perhaps the situation simply called for him to be brave. Lynx's presence certainly wasn't comforting. Rilv wasn't very cheery company, either. And admittedly, Lanek had been feeling tense the entire trip.

But how was he supposed to feel? He couldn't take this calmly. He couldn't just pretend this would all go well. A Brotherhood member was on his ship, and there was nothing Lanek could do to take his mind off the fact this masked man had killed Suran.

He tried to focus on the distant mountains. But he couldn't let himself focus too much. He had to listen. Just in case Lynx tried to attack him from behind.

*No, there's no reason for him to fight me now,* Lanek reminded himself. *I'm the only one who can fly this thing, after all.* As far as he knew, at least.

Rilv paced back and forth on the bridge, her hands behind her back, rigid and proper. It was clear she was deep in thought, planning her every move for the upcoming days. Perhaps the upcoming years, for all Lanek could tell. The woman was always calculating details in her head. Admittedly it was something she was good at—it was largely thanks to her planning that Delkol Shire was defeated, though in the end it came at a great cost. The government of Fiefs was in shambles, but Rilv somehow managed to keep things together while the dukes of the kingdom were at each others' throats over the ensuing months.

*Stability.* That was what she wanted for the kingdom, more than anything else. It was probably the word that best described herself, as well. A sharp, jagged rock sticking out of the ocean shore, immovable amidst the constant torrent of crashing waves.

Perhaps more dangerous than the waves themselves.

And to continue the analogy even further, Lanek could picture himself as a peaceful, passing boat, with no desire to get swept up in the dangerous current, and no desire to collide with the rocks.

*You can handle this,* Lanek thought to himself. *You've handled worse than this before. And we know precisely where we're going, thanks to Kitoh's device.*

The boy was setting it up again right now, placing

a map on the floor and the appropriate metal objects around it. The map was connected to a soft, thin wooden base, which allowed Kitoh to place needles into specific locations on the map. Lanek noted the silver triangular pedestal sitting in front of the map, where the two pieces of the Elpis stone were intended to rest.

"It's set," Kitoh said.

Rilv walked over and placed the two Elpis fragments into the pedestal. Apparently she had the Elpis with her all this time.

Lanek glanced back at Lynx, who continued to sit against the far wall. The masked man had one leg lying forward, the other propped up with his arm leisurely atop his knee. Was Lynx eyeing the Elpis pieces? Perhaps it was Lynx's goal to obtain the full Elpis for Augurc. Lanek didn't like the idea of Lynx being this close to the Elpis. It was quite possible that Lynx had been helping Rilv out all this time just for the chance to obtain the missing Elpis pieces for the Brotherhood.

Was this his chance? Rilv had the telekinetic Hader, and Lanek was here too. Not to mention Kitoh, who Lanek recalled could turn into a dragon when the circumstances called for it. Lynx would probably wait for a moment when he was alone with Rilv, or when everyone else was asleep. And probably when he wasn't in an airship in the middle of the sky.

Lanek had to keep an eye on him. If Augurc Shire

obtained the full Elpis, there was no telling what disasters would befall the Fiefs Kingdom.

Lynx stood up and walked toward Kitoh and Rilv. And the Elpis.

Lanek stood up, his hand on the hilt of his rapier.

"Whoa, calm down now," Lynx said, holding his hands forward a bit, making gentle wave motions. "I'm just standing up. People do it all the time."

"Don't go any closer," Lanek said. "Sit back down where you were."

"Thank you for your caution," Rilv said, "but it does not matter if Lynx stands up and walks around from time to time. He can even watch our work here if he wishes. I will simply kill him if he tries anything foolish."

"There, see?" Lynx said. "Quit worrying so much, Lanek. I'm here to help you folks out, and besides—I know better than to mess with Rilv."

Lanek's frown only deepened. He hated the way Lynx was trying to act like everyone on this ship was on friendly terms.

"You will not speak to me more than is necessary," Lanek said. "This is not some vacation amongst good pals. This is my airship, and if I tell you to stay far away from the Elpis, I suggest you follow my command."

For a moment nobody moved. The bridge turned silent, save for the hum on the engine and muffled clanking of machinery. Lanek stared at Lynx's mask, gazing straight through the thin slits the killer had to be staring through.

"No need for another fight so soon," Rilv said. "Or would you like me to fling you both to the ground again?"

"It's fine, I'll just sit back down," Lynx said. He did so, slumping back with his arm again lying atop his propped leg. "I'll just rest here until our captain has cooled down a bit."

"Don't hold your breath," Lanek said, keeping a stern gaze down at the Brotherhood fighter. "As long as you're on my ship, I don't intend to be lax about anything. One wrong move, and I finish you off once and for all."

"You've tried killing me twice now," Lynx said. "Emphasis on *tried*. Quite frankly, your threat doesn't worry me much, though I am concerned about you pestering me for the entirety of this mission."

"You will have to put up with it, Lynx," Rilv said. "I have asked Lanek to not fight you unless you force his hand. Everyone needs to place the mission above all else. We have enough worry about as it is."

"What about when the mission is over?" Lynx asked. "Let's say we find the Haders and destroy the Brotherhood. Am I going to have to put up with Captain

Elf trying to kill me the rest of my life?"

Rilv turned away from Lynx, but she didn't look toward Lanek either. "If you are cooperative for the entirety of the mission, and everything ends in success, I will guarantee your safety."

"What?" Lanek asked, forcing himself to keep from yelling. "This man murdered my sister. I will not just let him go free once this is all over."

"We will deal with this when the time comes," Rilv said.

Neither Lanek nor Lynx spoke up. With every fiber of his being, Lanek wanted to bring Lynx down. Deliver justice. Stab him through the heart. Fulfill revenge. Throw him off the ship. Anything. Anything to get rid of him. Anything to avenge Suran's death.

*What did Suran do to deserve this? What did I do to deserve this?*

Lanek was shaking, desperate—yet unable to pull the rapier from his hilt. He could kill Lynx. And if Rilv got in his way, he could kill her too.

*No, I can't go down that road*, Lanek thought. *She just wants to find these Haders. Bring down the Brotherhood. Help the Fiefs Kingdom. I just... have to go along with all this. Just for a while.*

"Sit back down," Rilv told Lanek. "Kitoh and I

are merely going to check on the location of the Haders again, to see if anyone with them is on the move."

Lanek sat down slowly and reluctantly. It was difficult to keep from shaking, but he forced himself to take long, quiet breaths. He had to stare down toward Kitoh and his map, and do all he could to keep from thinking of Lynx.

Kitoh held a needle over the map, and somehow the Elpis fragments worked in conjunction with the strange metal blocks set up around the map. The needle moved slightly in Kitoh's grip, pointing toward the location the Elpis energy designated as a location of extensive Nexi energy. With slow, careful movement, Kitoh moved the needle toward the spot unseen forces were guiding it to. Once the needle drooped back down, Kitoh pushed it into the map—this one in a spot in Fiefs Kingdom.

He repeated the process several more times, then unrolled a second map marked with Hader locations from an earlier time. Kitoh and Rilv began comparing the pinned map to the marked one.

"This can't be a coincidence," Rilv said. "We've been compromised."

"What do you mean?" Lanek asked.

Kitoh pointed to a spot with three needles in the Fiefs Kingdom. "This is where we're at right now. Two needles for the Elpis fragments, and one for Rilv's Hader."

He moved his finger to a spot with one needle in the mountains. "We're heading to this location, where there is likely another Hader." He then pointed at a spot with two needles, a ways northeast of the airship's location. "And here is someone who has what we're presuming to be two Haders."

"Could it be Augurc with two Elpis fragments?" Lanek asked.

"No, he is down in Istal," Kitoh said, pointing to two needles far to the south. "The force of the blocks is much stronger for Elpis pieces, so it's easy to tell them apart from the Haders."

"What is troubling is the fact the person with two Haders is on the move," Rilv said. "The subject is heading straight to where we're heading."

"He's definitely going in that direction," Kitoh said, "but there's no way to be sure of his final destination."

"How quickly has he been traveling?" Lanek asked.

"A speed similar to our own," Kitoh said. "He's traveled from the Shire Kingdom though, and has a bit further to go than us. We should have some time to find the exact location of the Hader before he does."

"How much time?" Rilv asked.

"Half a day. Possibly less," Kitoh said.

So even with all of Rilv's precautions, someone already knew of her mission to obtain all the Haders. But was this the Brotherhood working to find the stones, or some other enemy?

Or someone who wasn't an enemy at all, perhaps?

"Is there any chance this person with two Haders will cooperate with us?" Lanek asked.

"Unlikely," Rilv said. "There is a low chance that anyone with a Hader we encounter will cooperate with us."

Kitoh bit his bottom lip, and glanced around a bit. "But, we are planning to negotiate with the people we come in contact with, right? You said you've brought goods from the treasury to exchange with."

"Of course, we will try to reason with those who possess the Haders," Rilv said. "However, I am not confident anyone will be willing to give up such power, even for all the riches of the kingdom."

"You... you expect us to fight everyone, then," Kitoh said.

Lanek recalled Kitoh being nervous to fight the Brotherhood five years ago. He was just a child then, called to assist in a war effort at such an early age. The eigni was a strong, powerful boy, with an unparalleled link to Nexi energy. And yet he was still nervous about having to fight.

This was a good thing though, Lanek thought. It was wise to avoid a fight whenever they could. But Rilv seemed right—most people with Haders would probably react in a hostile way to any attempt to barter for the stones.

"Yes, I expect conflict in this operation," Rilv said.

"And that's where I come in," Lynx said. "You don't need to worry yourself, Kitoh. I can bring down an opponent in more ways than one, even if he's got *two* Haders."

Lanek held his tongue.

"But... what if someone has a Hader, and doesn't want to fight? And doesn't want to give it up?" Kitoh asked.

Rilv folded her arms and tilted her head a bit, considering the possibility of such an event.

"Our goal remains the same," Rilv said. "We take the Haders by any means necessary. If we have to fight, we will. Even if our opponents do not."

•

# 4. TRANQUIL HAVEN

•

It took more time than expected to navigate through the mountains, but the next day the airship came in sight of a number of small villages. Kitoh used a map of the mountain range to try to discern more specifically where they needed to go, and they ended up flying by a couple secluded elf villages in their search for the Hader in question.

Eventually Kitoh and Rilv decided the most likely location for the Hader was higher up in the mountains, and Lanek guided the airship to what turned out to be an especially small village. To Lanek's surprise, there were many farms surrounding the area, the steep hills carved into steps for the crops to grow on. The homes were small hovels, most of them made of wood. There were a couple nicer buildings made of stone, apparently carved straight into the mountainside. It was a very quiet-looking village, a place cut off from the rest of the world. The slow, wispy drifts of fog gave the fragile village a mysterious atmosphere. It was a strange, precarious place for anyone to live.

Lanek understood that the elves here had to be living a very traditional lifestyle, with a strong emphasis on the elvish culture of centuries past—long before it became commonplace for elves and humans to live together in the various cities and towns of the Fiefs Kingdom. He wasn't sure what elves of a small traditional village would be doing with a Hader. Perhaps the stone was hidden in the mountains nearby, and nobody knew it was even there. Lanek hoped this would be the case—it would make matters so much simpler. He wasn't eager to lead an attack on these people.

It was difficult to find a good place to land. There were elves working on the farms, pointing up at his airship. Lanek imagined Rilv was hoping for a less dramatic entrance, or at least one that didn't take fifteen minutes to finish. By the time Lanek found a safe spot a ways down the mountain to land at, there was quite the gathering of people at the village, watching intently. It may have been the first time any of these villagers had seen an airship. It may have been a long time since they had had visitors at all, for that matter. This was going to be a big deal, whether Rilv liked it or not.

Once the ship was landed and anchored safely, Rilv led Lynx and Kitoh outside. Lanek followed them out once he had gone through a final check to ensure everything was secured. He ran to catch up with everyone, a bit upset they didn't care to wait five minutes for him. He was concerned about leaving just Rilv and Kitoh with Lynx, even though he knew both Rilv and Kitoh could probably defend themselves... Rilv had a Hader, and Kitoh surely had some Nexi stones. But what if Lynx caught them off-guard? They seemed to trust him more than Lanek did. And Lynx was far too unpredictable to take lightly. There was no way Lanek was going to go along with the idea Lynx was truly on their side in all this.

The terrain was rocky, and the air was cold. There was little wind, and it wasn't a biting cold—but it was a solid cold, one that lingered and seeped slowly through Lanek's body. Perhaps it was the lingering fog, giving the mountaintop an extra layer of chilliness.

He caught up with the group and followed them up the thin dirt trail leading toward the village. It was a steep climb, and it was difficult to see any of the buildings from this vantage point. Lanek kept an eye on Lynx, wondering what the masked man would attempt at the small village. Perhaps the Brotherhood member would use the opportunity to take the Hader for himself, and sneak off down the mountainside. Lanek had taken precautions to make it so only he could run the airship, but he had to anticipate the possibility Lynx could still break in by force, and it was technically conceivable Lynx knew enough about airships to be able to pilot it as well.

They soon came in sight of some of the terraced fields the villagers used to farm their crops. Corn and potatoes were the main vegetables Lanek noted, but caught sight of what looked to be a vineyard further ahead. There seemed to be plenty of crops to support the small village—a level of self-reliance that wouldn't be found in much of the rest of the world, with its interconnected cities, trade routes, and shifting supplies and demands.

As the path began to level off a bit, the group came in contact with a number of farmers, taking a break from pulling weeds, it looked like.

Rilv led the team a little closer, stopping just a couple meters from where the farmers had gathered. It was just a few seconds before anyone spoke, but Lanek found the pause a bit disconcerting. Perhaps he was expecting one of the farmers to say something, but they simply looked to him, as if he should introduce everyone to them.

Before Lanek could decide how to present themselves, Rilv spoke first. "Hello. My name is Rilv, and I am the head servant of the Fiefs royal court. These are my assistants, and we come on official business."

None of the farmers responded. They looked wary, suspicious. And for good reason, Lanek thought. It wasn't likely a government airship would come to a random little village in the mountains like this without it meaning there was some kind of trouble. Some of the villagers glanced from Rilv to Lanek, their eyes shifting back and forth a couple times. Perhaps they would have preferred to speak with him, considering he was an elf like them.

"Do not be alarmed," Rilv said. "We are simply stopping here temporarily. We have been on a long journey." It seemed she was downplaying what she had just said about official business. It was important to try to get the villagers relaxed so they'd be willing to share information and cooperate, though Lanek kind of doubted Rilv would be able to actually do so...

He decided to speak up. "My name is Lanek. I've never been up these mountains before, but I've got to say, you folks have a really nice view up here. I'm surprised there are villages up this high, and so far away from any kind of big town."

"We manage well enough," a man in a patched-up coat and pants said. "You work for the government too then?"

"No, I'm just an airship pilot and mechanic," Lanek said. "I spotted this picturesque little village though, and pointed it out to Rilv here. She was so impressed, she insisted we stop by and take a look for a bit. I was kind of hoping to walk around on some stable ground for a bit anyways. It's good to get  fresh air when you can, and this seems as fresh as it gets."

Most of the villagers were smiling a little by this point.

"You flew that airship?" a woman asked. "I never imagined I'd see one here."

"Scared me half to death," a younger woman said,

"though it is kind of amazing..."

"Feel free to come up to the village proper," an old man with a cane said. "There's not much to see, though. This is no tourist destination, to say the least."

"We hardly ever get visitors at all," a small girl said. "Where are you from?"

"A small town far from here," Lanek said. "At least, when I'm building airships. When I'm traveling, I suppose the airship you saw just now is my home."

"Well, feel free to make yourself at home here," an old woman said. "If you need a place to spend the night, I'm sure we can accommodate."

"That's very kind of you," Lanek said. He decided to neither accept or reject the offer right away, and wait to see how things would play out. Glancing up the mountain trail, he noticed some more villagers approaching, though these ones looked more at ease. Perhaps they felt calmer, seeing their fellow villagers engaging in friendly conversation with these strangers. Or at least Lanek.

He decided to finish introductions. "This here is Kitoh. He is an eigni, and though he's just a boy, he's an accomplished scientist."

"Well, not really," Kitoh said. "I'm just a researcher, just studying..."

A farmer boy looked visibly impressed. "You're a

scientist? Do you not have to farm or go to school then?"

"An eigni?" a girl said to an older boy with a straw hat. "Is he…"

"Don't worry," the boy in the hat said. "Eigni are nice. And look, he's just a bit older than us. He's nice."

Lanek pointed to Lynx and added, "And this is a bodyguard. He's not allowed to speak, so don't try talking to him."

"I can speak all I want," Lynx muttered.

A few conversations continued all at once, and Lanek took the moment to turn back to Rilv and give her a slight smirk. He would have liked to see her flustered by Lanek's ability to manage the situation, but as always she refused to express any kind of interesting reaction.

Lanek shrugged and looked back to the small crowd of villagers. A young woman with light brown hair and a green and black dress approached Lanek, so he turned to speak with her.

"By the way, I was wondering what the name of this village was, Miss…?" Lanek said.

"Fenley," the woman finished. "Er, that's my name, that is. The village is Velm."

Lanek maintained the smirk he had given Rilv. "Oh? That's a lovely name."

Fenley blushed and glanced to the side. "Um... my name? Or the... village?"

"Ah, the village's name is nice too," Lanek said. "I'd like to see some more of it."

"It's... it's right this way," Fenley said, motioning toward the dirt trail. "I can show you around. You should at least see the shrine to the ancients. Well... at least if you're interested."

"That would be nice," Lanek said. "Let's go, Rilv."

Rilv stared at him with a straight face. Lanek wondered if she was upset with him to some degree, though she didn't show any displeasure in the situation. She was probably just analyzing things in her head—perhaps wondering if this shrine Fenley mentioned would hold any clue to where the Hader was. It was at least the most important building in this village, it seemed.

The villagers took the group of four up the rest of the way to the village, where small wooden structures rested a good distance from one another, with thin trails of smoke coming from small brick chimneys. Which buildings were homes and which were shops, Lanek couldn't tell. He decided he was thinking about the village structure the wrong way—what goods were sold were likely just bartered at homes, if everyone knew each other. Though the people were nervous to see visitors, they seemed like a friendly bunch. This village was probably a tight-knit group, perhaps out of necessity.

"That's my home over there." Fenley pointed at a nondescript hovel. Like all the other little buildings, this home was covered with dark wooden planks, unpainted, and lacking any kind of ornamentation. It looked sturdy and watertight, so the focus for this village was likely on practicality and resilience.

Even the shrine, as it turned out, looked very plain. It was about the size of nine village homes, three long and three wide, and made of stones mortared together. Instead of a door, it looked like there were some heavy black curtains inside the arched opening. There was a guard to either side of the doorway—elves dressed in leather armor, wielding a lance. Neither of them said anything when Fenley guided Lanek to the entrance, though she stopped before pulling the curtain back.

"Oh, I should mention only elves can come inside," she said.

A farming man with a thin mustache turned to Rilv and the others. "We can take you all to the administration building in the meantime. We have some food and drink for guests, and a fire can help you warm up."

Rilv glanced from the farmer to Lanek and back again, presumably trying to decide the best course of action. "Very well. Is this where the leader of the village lives?"

"No, but we can probably find him if you want,"

the man said. "Oh, you had business of some kind to deal with, right?"

"Nothing too big," Lanek said, before Rilv could make the situation sound grave to the villagers. "But we'd love to meet and chat with your leader, if it's not too much trouble for him."

"I doubt it'd be a problem," the farmer said. "Nullen hardly ever has anything official to deal with, as you might imagine. This'll be good for him."

Some of the villagers had dispersed at this point, perhaps to inform relatives of the arrival of visitors, while other villagers spoke quietly amongst themselves. Lanek only caught a few words here and there, but everyone seemed curious to find out what business the royal government had in mind for their little village. Perhaps it would have been good to make up a non-threatening story, but Lanek couldn't think of a good one. Hopefully Rilv would just converse with the villagers to break the ice some more before jumping straight to asking where the Hader could be.

"Sounds great," Lanek said. "Go ahead, Rilv. You and Kitoh and Lynx can go relax at the administration building a bit. I'll join you soon enough."

Rilv and the others went along with some of the villagers to the building in question—a stone building not much bigger than any of the homes in the vicinity. There was a large wooden sign nailed above the doorway though, with ancient elvish lettering intricately inscribed on it. Lanek could read elvish—not that he ever needed to use it much—but the swirling lettering on the sign seemed hundreds of years old. Despite this, the sign looked to be in pretty good condition.

"Sorry I couldn't let your friends come into the shrine with you," Fenley said, "but that's the rule. It's nothing against humans or eigni or anything..."

"It's fine," Lanek said. "I'm familiar with this sort of protocol." He was a little worried about leaving the others alone, especially with Lynx in their midst. But it seemed this was the best course of action to take—there was a chance Lanek would find something out about the Hader from this young woman, so it was important he not relinquish the opportunity to go inside the shrine.

Fenley opened the curtain to let Lanek in, as well as about a dozen villagers, most of them not much older or younger than Lanek. The inside of the shrine was surprisingly bright and spacious, the dark stone walls lit up by torches spaced just a meter or so apart. Between each torch was a work of art crafted from a thin sheet of light copper, cut into perfect circles. Lanek walked up to one and saw a depiction of a couple goddesses, surrounded by ancient elvish writing and a number of more intricate symbols. Lanek was familiar with most of the old tales of elvish religion, but he wasn't quite sure who these deities were. The other metal plates had other gods and goddesses inscribed on them, many of them holding objects that surely held significant meaning to those more pious than

Lanek.

He looked back to the center of the shrine, where a large circular pool of water rested. At the very center of the pool was a stone platform with a statue of a kneeling goddess, her arms held forward dramatically, as if she were beholding some kind of miraculous sight a ways above her.

A boy pointed at the still, clear waters of the pool. "This is divine water. It will help you feel calm and happy."

"Really?" Lanek said. "That sounds... great?"

"It *is* great," a man with light brown hair said. "A weekly rest ritual does wonders. Puts your soul at ease. Helps you see things as they are. A sort of reminder to keep things simple in life."

"Simple..." Lanek said. "I could use a little simplicity in my own life." And he genuinely meant it. Perhaps he should forget Rilv and this crazy quest, and just set up shop in this little village. It was a silly thought though, considering he'd never have access to all the necessary parts for building airships at a secluded place like this.

"You should take part in a rest ritual then!" Fenley said. "I haven't had one yet this week, and was thinking of doing it tonight. You can do it with me, if you'd like."

Lanek felt his heart beat a little faster. He didn't know what this ritual entailed, for one thing. And in a strange way he felt like he was being asked out on a date, which seemed strange, considering he had just met this girl. Not that that would be a bad thing, Lanek realized. Fenley was actually very pretty, in a homely, unassuming way. Her light brown eyes matched her hair, and she had a cute, petite frame not so different from Suran's, back in Edellerston. He wasn't quite sure how old this girl was, though.

"That sounds like a good idea," the man said, now standing beside Fenley. "Have you ever gone through a rest ritual before?"

"No," Lanek said. "Can't say I have."

"There's only a few divine pools left in the world," the man said, "so that's not so surprising. Fenley can help you out, though. She knows everything about all the rituals."

"This is my brother, by the way," Fenley said. "His name's Yalmin and he just got married a couple weeks ago! Tria, his wife—she makes the most delicious soups in the world."

"She's probably going to cook some up soon," Yalmin said. "Perhaps I can head over and see if she can make some extra? You and your friends can come over tonight if you want."

Lanek didn't want to turn down such hospitality, even if he wasn't hoping to glean information off of these people. "That sounds nice. And so does the ritual. I'll go ahead and give it a try, if it's really as nice as you say it is."

"You'll love it," Fenley said. She turned to the other villagers and looked them over for a few seconds. "You've all had a rest ritual already this week, haven't you?"

There were several nods and a couple *yes*'s, so Fenley turned back to Lanek and folded her arms. "Looks like it'll just be us then." She smiled, and Lanek couldn't help but smile a bit too. This girl—and these villagers in general—just had a sweetness that Lanek didn't find in others much anymore.

He wondered if the village's seclusion simply made the people naïve, or if the people here were as genuine as they appeared to be. Perhaps he was just over-thinking things. Perhaps he needed to not let himself get so caught up in this mission, and take the time to get to know these people just for the sake of being nice. It had been a long time since he had been able to meet new people like this.

Once everyone else left, Fenley led Lanek to the back of the room, where there were a couple of shelving units filled with stacks of folded-up clothes—all of them a light gray, it looked like. There were also a couple free-standing folding walls, apparently intended for people to change clothes behind.

"The rest ritual is a simple one, Fenley said. "You lie in the divine water, and allow the gods and goddesses to clear your mind, calm your body, and purify your soul. If you focus on one thing long enough, you'll find clarity in what it is you should do, regarding what you're thinking about."

Lanek walked to one of the shelves and picked up one of the articles of clothing. It felt very soft and silky, but was a bit stretchy. "So we change into some of these clothes?" He unfolded the clothes he held and found it to be a one-piece bathing suit for women.

"You'll want to use the other shelf," Fenley said, "but yes, you probably don't want to get your own clothes dirty. The clothes provided by the shrine represent life in this world, which is neither wholly light or dark."

Lanek returned the clothes he held and picked up a pair of shorts from the other shelf. The ritual seemed strange, and a little pointless. Not quite like going for a swim—it was really just a bath, if anything.

Though it was with some nice company, Lanek remembered.

He pulled out one of the folding walls and changed into a pair of gray swimming trunks that fit him, while Fenley changed behind the other makeshift dressing room. Lanek waited for her to come out before walking to the shrine pool, not wanting to do anything to ruin the ritual.

"Are you ready?" Fenley asked.

Lanek stepped out and nodded. Fenley was dressed in one of the plain gray bathing suits, and though her figure was shown more clearly—and was quite a bit more womanly than Lanek expected—there was still a pure look about her. She held her hands together behind her back, and looked over Lanek a few seconds. For a moment Lanek thought she was going to blush, but instead she closed her eyes and smiled.

"Ah, this might be kind of awkward for you," she said. "If you've always lived in a city, you might have never done any rituals before."

"No, I'm fine," Lanek said. "And most of my life I lived in a village called Edellerston. There weren't any shrines for ancient elf rituals there, though."

"I'm glad you're fine with this," Fenley said. "Our village hardly ever gets any visitors."

Lanek thought it was more surprising that Fenley was fine with this, but she probably felt safe since there were a couple guards just outside the entrance. Not that Lanek was planning anything—he was simply curious to see what was so special about this ritual.

Fenley led him to the waters, and pointed to the statue of the goddess with outstretched hands. "Reali will help enlighten you, though it may take a little while since it's your first time."

Though Lanek had never been very religious, he

was willing to place a little faith in this ritual for Fenley's sake. Perhaps he wouldn't find anything special about it at all, but it wouldn't be hard for him to act relaxed and edified. Lying in the water a bit would probably be nice at least, especially since there was a red Nexi at each side of the circular pool, keeping it warm.

Lanek let Fenley get into the water first so he could see if there was any specific way he needed to lie in the pool.

"Just have your hands and feet pointing toward the goddess," Fenley said. She lay down with her head propped back against the wall of the pool. Her eyes shut and her breathing slowed. Her face exuded a calmness and tranquility Lanek didn't expect to find so quickly. The pool was just deep enough to keep the rest of her body underwater, though her chest rose out a bit when she inhaled deeply. And as she had instructed, she kept her arms and legs pointed straight toward the statue kneeling on the pedestal in the pool's center. Though there was a rigidness to her position, she looked perfectly relaxed.

Lanek stepped in the pool as quietly as he could, not wanting to interrupt Fenley's concentration. The water was lukewarm—neither hot nor cold in the slightest. He assumed this was symbolic the same sort of way the plain gray clothes were.

"Feel free to speak up if you have any questions," Fenley said. "I've done this many times before, so I can regain my focus easily."

"Okay," Lanek said. He eased himself into the water and lay down beside Fenley.

She opened an eye and glanced at him, a smile spreading on her face. "You don't have to lie right next to me."

"Oh, do we need to spread out?" Lanek asked.

"No, it makes no difference," Fenley said. "I just wasn't expecting it." Some of Fenley's hair brushed against Lanek's shoulder, the water moving strands of her hair in slow, wispy motions.

"Our minds will conduct more power when we're close together," Lanek said. "And I'm a personal fellow by nature, anyways. Personable, too."

"That's good," Fenley said, to Lanek's surprise. "I sometimes wonder if people in the world are becoming more and more impersonal."

"Even in a village like this?" Lanek asked.

Fenley nodded. "Some people think it's best for everyone to mind their own business. Which... I guess is good to a degree, but..."

"People need to help each other," Lanek said. "You can't just focus on yourself all the time."

"Yes, people ought to be less selfish," Fenley said. She sighed and closed her eyes again, letting her body sink back into the water.

"Though it's good to keep your dreams in mind, too," Lanek said. "You have any big goals in life, Fenley?"

She smirked a little. "Nothing very big. I kind of just want to have a family and manage a house really well. You know... be a good wife and mother."

"Sounds like a big goal to me," Lanek said. "Those are things I'd never be able to do, at least."

Fenley opened her eyes. "What? Why's that?"

"Well, I'd make a poor wife and mother," Lanek said.

Fenley laughed a little. "I thought you were saying you'd never have a family."

"Ah, well..." Lanek paused a few seconds. "I guess I haven't given it much thought."

He also hadn't stuck with a girl long enough to begin considering anything even close to marriage, but he didn't want to bring up this aspect of his social life with Fenley. The last five years had been good for Lanek in terms of winning the hearts of lots of women, but he never tried to form a lasting relationship with any of them. None of the women who fell for him seemed to mind when Lanek moved on—most of them were just as lustful and vain as he was.

"That's right," Fenley said. "You fly an airship. I guess you wouldn't really want to be tied down to one place."

"Well, I'm usually just building airships," Lanek said. "And to be honest, I'm not anxious to be flying around for this excursion I'm on."

"It must be hectic, working for the government," Fenley said.

Lanek couldn't hold back a weak laugh. "Oh yes... In fact, a part of me would rather I just sit in this pool for the next few weeks, than continue on this... endeavor."

"I guess you can't give me details," Fenley said. "And I guess a part of you knows you have to continue it."

"Yes... a part of me knows I have to see this through to the end."

"Do you... have plans for afterward?"

It was a question Lanek wasn't expecting, and certainly wasn't one he had been thinking about ever since learning of Rilv's plan to collect the Haders. When was this mission going to be finished? Would Lanek really be able to put up with Lynx for weeks on end? Or even months? For that matter, would he even be able to put up with Rilv for that long? As Fenley said, Lanek didn't enjoy working for the government—but the fact was he inherited his parents' legacy of creating very fast airships, and this was something the Fiefs Kingdom would not be able to ignore.

Especially when the Shire Kingdom was making its own advances in the field of aviation.

"I'm not the kind of person to think very far ahead," Lanek finally said.

"Maybe this is a good opportunity to try?" Fenley said. "As the god Pilekshim said, the only person who can make you do something is yourself."

"There's always consequences to deal with afterward though."

"Yes, Pilekshim said that as well."

The girl's reliance on the ancient religion was a little peculiar to Lanek—at the very least unfamiliar—but it somehow came off as a cute quality for Fenley. Perhaps she was just that good-natured. Perhaps she was just that much like Suran.

"Fenley, if you don't mind my asking... How old are you?"

"Oh, it's kind of embarrassing... But, um, I'm seventeen."

"How is that embarrassing? That's a lovely age."

"I'm already seventeen, and still not married," Fenley said. "I guess it's been on my mind a lot lately, since my older brother just got married. But it's fine for boys to marry when they're a bit older. My relatives are worried about me, but I don't really like the boys they've tried to pair me off with."

Lanek saw this conversation going a number of ways, none of which he felt he ought to entertain right now, given that he was supposed to be focused on figuring out where the Hader was.

"I'm sorry," Fenley said. "I've ended up chatting with you, instead of letting you take part in the ritual. I'll be quiet now." She shut her eyes and repositioned her body to lie perfectly still beneath the water. Only her head remained above water, and her hair continued to slowly sway to either side of her. Lanek was surprised when she opened her mouth again. "Oh, but feel free to ask any questions if you have any, and maybe I'll be able to help you out. With what to focus your mind on, and such."

She had certainly left Lanek with plenty of things to think about. What was he supposed to focus on? He looked over to Fenley's soft, tender face, as reposed as a sleeping princess's. He watched the slight rise and fall of her breathing, and the subtle motions of her legs. Lanek imagined she was already gaining the tranquility and enlightenment this ritual offered.

He lay his head back and shut his eyes, still trying to decide what he ought to think about. Perhaps the ritual could help him figure out where the Hader was? This seemed the wisest choice, but Lanek had a feeling nothing would come of simply thinking about the Hader. Did he actually care about finding it? It wasn't his idea to go looking for the stones. And though he did have an interest in bringing down the Brotherhood, he didn't care for this method of doing so. There was no guarantee the Haders would enable them to defeat Augurc's experiments. And there was the possibility of ill side effects. Lanek wasn't about to forget what happened to Terico, who died from overuse of the Elpis fragments.

*What is it Fenley is thinking about?* Lanek wondered. Marriage was certainly on her mind, so it made sense for her to focus on that subject. What would she end up realizing? That she ought to marry Lanek? It was clear she had an interest in him.

This rest ritual was probably just wish fulfillment. People just think what they want to think. There was no reason to believe the ritual would solve anyone's problems, just by lying in the water and meditating for a little while.

It was silly, how this random girl felt Lanek could suddenly be a part of her life like this. He hardly knew her. And as soon as he found the Hader, he'd be on his way, and never see her again. Why would she care about him? He should have just been seen as a random passer-by, like any other visitor. She didn't know anything about him, save that he made and piloted airships. There was no way for her—or anyone—to know that she'd be compatible with him.

Just thinking about this was a little ridiculous, though Lanek wondered if he had been focusing on it too much. Or enough for the ritual to start to affect him. If it could affect him.

*I'll just focus on the Hader and see what happens*, Lanek decided. He forced himself to think only of the Hader hidden somewhere in or near this village. If he was going to be a part of this mission, he might as well give his all. The sooner he found the Hader, the sooner the mission would end, and the sooner the Brotherhood would come to an end. And the sooner Suran would be avenged.

It was right to do this, wasn't it? The world would be better without the Brotherhood. Safer. Augurc would be gone, and so would his devastating experiments. And his terrible followers. Lynx included. There was no way Lanek was just going to let Lynx go.

The Hader. He had to get the Hader. Lanek had to be the one to find it. He needed leverage against Lynx. The more power Lanek had, the more capable he'd be to kill Lynx.

*Where is it?*

*Where is the Hader?*

*Where is it hidden?*

*How can I obtain it?*

*How can I wield it?*

Lanek lost track of time, and even forgot he was lying in water, its gentle pushes and pulls against his body dissolving into background noise—impossible to notice as all his thoughts turned to the Hader.

He didn't know why, but he decided to open his eyes. It made no sense to do so. Wouldn't that break his concentration? And yet it came to him effortlessly, naturally, seamlessly. He stared straight above himself.

Something was hanging in the air. The goddess statue was staring up straight at it, just as Lanek was, though from a different angle. It was a glowing stone, shifting from a dull red to a bright yellow. The two colors swirled within the Nexi, radiating a light very similar to that of Rilv's telekinesis stone.

It was a Hader. Right there in the shrine, hanging from a fancy-looking white rope and some netting. How had Lanek not seen it right when he walked into the building? Perhaps it wasn't actually there, but was some kind of vision? He had focused for a good while on the Hader, but he had never felt certain he'd actually find it. It was more of a foolish hope, if anything. And yet... here it was. Just a few meters above where he lay. With the help of one of the shelving units, Lanek would be able to easily cut the rope with his rapier and take the Hader.

If it was actually there. It seemed kind of impossible for it to be there, when it had clearly not been there until now.

"I see something," he said. "There is something hanging above us. A Nexi stone of some kind."

Fenley opened her eyes and smiled. "It's the Stone of Truth. If you can see it, that means your focus has reached a conclusion. If you had a deep question in your heart, there is now an answer—a key resting in the lock, waiting for you to turn it. Just as the water calms the body and the silence calms the mind, the Stone of Truth calms the soul."

So this Stone of Truth—or rather, this Hader— had appeared once Lanek had focused on something hard enough. It was ironic that it was the Hader itself Lanek had been concentrating on. The revealing of the stone was the sign and the answer all in one.

"How do you feel?" Fenley asked.

Lanek chuckled. "Enlightened."

•

# 5. NECESSARY EVILS

The Hader and the string it was tied to disappeared before Lanek got out of the pool. He made a point of remembering precisely where it was, though it wasn't hard—he only had to look to where the goddess statue was looking. Perhaps there was a story about her finding the Hader floating in the sky—or rather a Stone of Truth, as the texts would likely put it.

Once they changed back to their old clothes, Lanek followed Fenley to the shrine doorway, his thoughts lingering on the Hader. How was he going to get it? Perhaps the guards wouldn't be around in the middle of the night, and he could just sneak in?

It felt wrong to do, of course. Everyone in this village had been nothing but kind to him so far. It wasn't right to return the favor by stealing their most precious treasure. The Hader clearly held special meaning to the villagers, and likely had many years of religious history stored up in it. It certainly held great significance to Fenley, at the very least.

Lanek doubted he'd be able to keep the Hader a secret from Rilv for long. She would find a way somehow to pin down the exact location of the stone, and would probably not be willing to leave before obtaining it.

Plus there was the possibility Lynx would get the stone. Lanek couldn't let the murderous Brotherhood member lay hands on the Hader. The consequences would be horrendous, and would put a great risk on the mission. Not to mention on Lanek himself—plus Rilv and Kitoh. Lynx was dangerous enough as it was, and there was a good chance the masked man had spearheaded this mission for the sake of getting the Haders for himself in the first place.

And Lanek remembered there was someone else approaching the village. Someone with two Haders was coming, and could very well be willing to go to any length to take the Hader in this village. It was very unlikely this enemy was on the side of the Fiefs Kingdom, at the very least.

Fenley guided Lanek from the shrine to the administration building, where presumably Rilv and the others were going to speak with the leader of the village. Lanek had noticed a bit of a spring in Fenley's step. She looked quite pleased with herself. Perhaps she was happy with the insight she gained from the rest ritual.

It worried Lanek a little. That girl likely had two things on her mind: him and marriage—and regardless of what the Stone of Truth put in that head of hers, it just wasn't going to work out.

A part of Lanek legitimately entertained the idea of a quiet village life. But it simply didn't feel right for him. How could he just hide away atop an empty mountain, leaving everything behind him? Ever since Edellerston was destroyed, ever since his parents were killed, ever since he became entangled in quests for the Fiefs Kingdom, ever since Suran was killed... there was nothing that could ever be the same. He could never really be himself again, though he had long pretended he could.

*What am I now?* Lanek wondered.

Perhaps that's what he should have thought about in the rest ritual. Maybe next week.

But there wasn't going to be a next week for him. Or for anyone. He was going to steal the Hader and be off in his airship, likely tens of kilometers away from the village before anyone caught wind of what happened.

Or maybe he wasn't. How could he live with himself after doing something like that?

*It is for the greater good,* he could imagine Rilv saying. *The Fiefs Kingdom needs the Hader more than this village does. And we can always return it once our mission is complete.*

Imagining Rilv saying this didn't make Lanek feel

any better about the prospect of stealing the Hader. In fact, it just upset him more.

Fenley knocked on the door of the administration building, which was promptly opened by a man in a white jacket and black pants. He smiled at Fenley, but raised an eyebrow at Lanek.

"Hi, Chei," Fenley said. "This is Lanek, another visitor. He just went through the rest ritual with me."

"Ah, was it your first time?" Chei asked.

"Yes," Lanek said. "I think it went well."

"Really?" Chei grinned, the tip of his tongue poking between his teeth. "It took me several months before I felt I was getting any kind of inspiration."

"Wow..." Lanek said, pretending to look shocked. "That's a long time to be sitting in the pool. Your whole body must've been covered in wrinkles."

Chei laughed so hard, Lanek and Fenley jumped back a little. "It's not like I was in there several months straight. I still just went once a week, and never longer than an hour. Can't just sit around all day, after all. Far too much work to be done."

The man led Lanek and Fenley from the entryway to a decent-sized room with several plain wooden chairs. Rilv, Kitoh, Lynx, and a couple elves sat in a circle, leaving five other chairs sitting against the far wall. There was a brick fireplace with a subdued fire going behind Kitoh and a middle-aged woman with short black hair. The only other point of notice was a rather plain green and yellow rug hanging limply behind a middle-aged man, who had a series of scars down his neck and a red scarf over the top of his head. Lanek assumed one of these elves was the village leader, since Chei didn't seem the type.

"Did you learn anything interesting?" Rilv asked, always going straight to the point. It wasn't like Lanek could just blurt out that he found the Hader though, so presumably Rilv was expecting Lanek to say something in code, or something.

"I wish I had the privilege of going through the rest ritual every week," Lanek said, deciding to not bother hinting whether or not he found out anything about the Hader. He could talk to Rilv later, when they weren't surrounded by villagers. For now, he needed to just pretend he was still trying to find out about the Hader, since he didn't want Lynx to catch on that he had found it in the shrine.

"It is a relaxing ritual," Chei said. He motioned a hand to the two elves sitting in the circle. "Allow me to introduce you to Ioliv and Neve, the village coordinator and village representative."

"Nice to meet you," Lanek said. "Does that make you the village leaders?"

"No, that responsibility falls to Nullen," Chei said.

"He should be here shortly."

"Ah." Apparently Rilv and the others hadn't even gotten the chance to speak with the leader yet. "And what's your position then, Chei?"

"Village idiot," the scarred man said.

"I've been promoted?" Chei asked.

"Don't congratulate yourself too much," the raven-haired woman said. "It's not actually a step up from village fool."

"He's actually the village greeter," Kitoh said. "And he greeted us very well."

"Everyone in this village has a title, it seems," Rilv said. "Though it appears they all farm." She looked thoroughly disinterested in the situation. She had her arms folded, one leg crossed over the other, and her head slightly tilted forward.

"Whenever we don't have visitors, at least," Chei said.

"Which isn't very often," Lanek said. "At least, that's what Fenley tells me."

Chei looked shocked for a moment, then turned to Fenley with a stern look in his eyes. "Giving away all the village's secrets, eh?"

"Well, I am the village speaker," Fenley said. This

elicited a laugh from the other two elves.

"Well, you are very good at it," the woman said.

"At speaking, that is," the man added. "Whether there are visitors or not."

Before Fenley could respond, the front door opened once more. Chei hurried to the entryway to greet who Lanek assumed to be the village leader.

Following Chei back into the sitting room was a man who looked to be in his sixties, at the very least. He had long white hair, with a series of multicolored beads strung in several of the strands hanging in front of his pointed ears. He wore robes that looked to be a strange amalgamation of different-colored robes—one sleeve was blue, the other was red, the top third was white, the middle third was gray, and the bottom third was black. And though he was an elderly man, he was also quite tall, and held a commanding presence upon entering the room.

The elves who were sitting down immediately stood up, and Lanek noticed Rilv managed to stand to attention the exact same time. Kitoh stood up a second later, upon realizing what was happening. A few seconds later, it took Rilv tapping Lynx on the shoulder to get him to stand up. Lanek wondered if he had fallen asleep—Lynx probably didn't converse with the elves the whole time Lanek was away, and it wasn't like anyone would be able to tell right away that the masked man snoozed off for a bit.

The old man chuckled as he glanced over to

Lanek, Rilv, and the others. "I assure you, we're hardly ever this formal." Everyone relaxed a bit, then sat back down one or two at a time.

"Worth a try once in a while," Chei said.

Lanek sat down in a chair beside Fenley, while Chei pulled out a chair for the village leader, who Lanek remembered was named Nullen. Everyone rearranged their chairs a bit, so Nullen sat in front, facing the village's guests.

"I hope you've enjoyed your stay so far," Nullen said. "I'm sorry I was a ways down the mountain when you arrived. I go on walks from time to time, and sometimes find myself a lot further from the village than I intend."

"He goes where the wind pushes him," the scarred elf said.

"So best hope he never stands too close to a cliff," Chei added.

Nullen frowned deeply at Chei, who simply smiled back in return.

"At any rate," Nullen said, "I hope our guests have been well received." He looked down to Kitoh for a couple seconds.

"Ah," Kitoh said, a little surprised. He probably expected Rilv to do all the talking. "I really... The elves, er, everyone here's been nice. The food was really good."

"What did you have?" Nullen asked.

"Bread and tea," Kitoh said. "The bread was really warm."

"That's how we like to eat it," Nullen said, patting his stomach. "Helps keep the fire going, though mine will probably be diminishing soon, regardless."

"Can't keep a fire going forever," the woman a few chairs from Lanek said.

"And can't keep a guest waiting forever," Nullen said. He turned to Lanek and asked, "Now, I'm kind of curious. How exactly are you all related?"

"You don't see the family resemblance?" Chei asked.

Of course, there was none, given that the group consisted of an elf, an eigni, and two humans, one of whom was masked.

"We're just all working together, you could say," Lanek said. "Rilv here is the one leading the group. She can best introduce us." He didn't want to say something wrong, given the delicacy of this operation.

Rilv gave her name, as well as Lanek's, Kitoh's, and Lynx's. "I am the head servant of the Fiefs Kingdom, and the four of us are traveling together to conduct an extensive search."

"Amazing," Nullen said. "I never expected royalty to step foot in our humble village."

"We are not royalty," Rilv said. "But our business does concern the royal court."

Nullen pointed at Lynx. "And why's he masked, exactly?"

Lynx tilted his head to the side, and held it there silently for several seconds. Lanek wondered if he was going to respond at all, but Lynx eventually cleared his throat and answered. "Well, let's just say that after I was born, my mother decided any future children in the family would need to be adopted."

Nullen and the other elves laughed, and even Kitoh laughed a little. Lanek admittedly found the joke a little amusing as well, but he was never going to let himself laugh at one of Lynx's jokes, even if the masked man was poking fun at himself.

"Well, feel free to keep it on," Nullen said. It seemed that the old man—and everyone else in the village, for that matter—didn't recognize Lynx's mask marked him as a member of the Brotherhood. Did the people in the village even know what the Brotherhood was? It was quite possible, Lanek realized, that the elves here were so cut off from the rest of the world, that they didn't know any specifics about the Brotherhood.

He couldn't let Lynx become good friends with

the people here. He would manipulate them, trick them, betray them. He didn't want anything bad to happen to these people.

And yet he was planning to steal their Stone of Truth.

Nullen and the elves got sidetracked into a discussion on masks used in some of their yearly festivals, but Lanek's thoughts were elsewhere.

Lanek couldn't stand himself. What was it he was trying to do, exactly?

*I just have to accept it*, he thought. *I just have to accept the fact these people are going to be hurt. Someone is going to be leaving the village with that Hader. I won't let it be the person who already has two of them. And I definitely won't let it be Lynx. I have to be the one that takes it. I'll do it in the middle of the night. These people will probably have us spend the night. I'll get up and steal it, then get Rilv and the others to come back with me to the airship without waking anyone up. And then... I'll just have to forget this village.*

He wasn't sure he'd be able to. He had never been to a place quite like it before.

His eyes met Fenley's for a moment, and he realized she had been looking at him. Not wanting to look as troubled as he felt, he leaned back in his chair and folded his arms, and gave her a look to show that he had caught her staring. She glanced away, but not without a smile creeping across her face.

Though he kept it to himself, Lanek regretted his continued interaction with Fenley. After tonight, there wasn't going to be any further developing of their relationship together. She was just going to be another girl who fell for his dashing good looks. Just another girl Lanek would need to leave behind and forget.

But again... he wasn't sure he'd be able to. He had never met a girl quite like her before.

Nullen and the other three elves realized they were rambling, and the village leader laughingly steered the conversation back to the matter at hand.

"Sorry, sorry," he said. He turned to Rilv, a large smile still on his face. "I should get to the point, I suppose. What is it you're looking for, that our village would have?"

"A Hader," Rilv said.

Lanek nearly slipped out of his chair. *So to the point! What is she thinking?*

"What is a Hader?" Nullen asked. The questioning look on his face looked genuine enough, but Lanek assumed that nobody in the village had connected their Stone of Truth with any of the abnormally powerful Nexi stones used in centuries past.

"Haders look something like this," Rilv said. She took the telekinesis Hader from her pocket to show to Nullen. Just as it had at Setar Castle, the stone continually gave off a swirling purple and blue glow.

"Oh!" said Fenley, accompanied by some quiet recognition from the other elves.

Except for Nullen. He stared at it curiously a few seconds before responding. "Is this a Nexi stone of some kind?"

"Yes," Rilv said. "And I take it there is another stone like it in this village, given the reactions by your fellow citizens."

"I've never seen a stone like this before," Nullen said. "And I don't recall anyone ever saying anything about a stone like this before." Nullen looked to the other elves and asked, "Have any of you ever seen one of these in the village?"

"Don't think so," the woman said.

"No," the scarred man added.

"It certainly looks nice, whatever it is," Chei said.

There was a long pause, perhaps ten seconds long. Rilv was calculating the responses, likely thinking the same thing Lanek was thinking: Nullen was lying, and the villagers were just following his lead.

But Rilv surely thought they were trying to keep secret a powerful weapon. Lanek knew the villagers saw their Hader in a completely different light—it was nothing more than an object of religious import. It somehow made a connection with their minds in some way while they rested in the shrine's pool, but they didn't seem to use it in any other way. As far as Lanek could tell, they couldn't even see it when they weren't achieving enlightenment in the pool.

Rilv looked to Fenley. "Have you ever seen a stone like this before?"

Fenley shook her head. "It's very pretty. What does it do?" She understood not to reveal anything now, but was hesitant to say an outright lie. The villagers likely felt they were justified to lie in a situation like this, to preserve their religious practices, though Fenley appeared to find it a bit more difficult. She seemed like the type of girl who probably hoped to go her whole life without lying, or doing anyone harm. And yet she managed to look calm, her face now only showing curiosity in the Hader that Rilv held.

Rilv, on the other hand, looked profoundly dissatisfied—but then again, she always did, to varying degrees.

She looked to the village leader again, and sat up even straighter than usual. For a moment Lanek thought she was going to stand up, but she retained her position. "If there is a stone like this in the village, it is of the utmost importance that I locate it. It could very well be a deciding key in the preservation of our kingdom."

"I will let you know if I see one," Nullen said.

"If you know where it may be, the kingdom will gladly assist this village in any of its needs," Rilv went on. "And, of course, you will all be substantially compensated for your assistance. I am capable of awarding the village goods with a combined value exceeding nine hundred thousand in monetary value."

"A generous offer," Nullen said, "but our village has no need for riches. We are a content, self-reliant people. I doubt any of us would feel at home in a palace of jade and gold and silk. It's best we keep things as simple as possible."

"I understand," Rilv said. "The offer to assist your village in any other way still stands, however. I work directly for the king, and am willing to procure anything you or your people desire. This could include the manpower to construct buildings and roadways, the means to produce better crops, or even a collection of ancient elvish texts that could prove invaluable to better understanding your religious beliefs."

"There is nothing we need from the government," Nullen said, surprisingly quick in his answer. "And I'm afraid nobody here knows anything about these Haders you speak of. Very few of us ever leave this village, so we tend to just know about the things we need to."

"Very well," Rilv said, pocketing her Hader. "If you don't mind, we would like to explore the surrounding area for a bit before we leave, just to make sure it isn't simply lying around somewhere."

"That's fine," Nullen said. "Just be sure to keep the peace, and don't go searching people's shops and homes without asking first."

"Of course," Rilv said.

There was another long pause. There was clearly a strange tension in the room, one that was likely difficult for everyone to pin down. Nobody had made any threats yet, but there was that clear possibility, from both Rilv and Nullen. What it was Nullen could ever do, Lanek wasn't sure. As far as he could tell, he, Rilv, Lynx, and Kitoh could probably defeat everyone in this village if a fight broke out.

The thought reminded Lanek of the couple guards at the shrine. It meant that at least some of the elves here were probably trained to fight, and surely the average citizen had access to the base Nexi stones, such as red, blue, and orange.

Also, Rilv surely saw there were guards at the shrine, and had probably already decided she would investigate the site as soon as possible. She would certainly see the possibility that the guards were protecting the Hader, rather than the sanctity of the shrine.

But she wouldn't see the Hader there—and neither would Lynx. As long as the villagers kept quiet, there was essentially zero chance of either of them locating the Hader. It was invisible, and there was no way for either of them to bump into it.

Would Rilv or Lynx force someone to tell them the precise location of the Hader? Certainly Lynx would be willing to beat the information out of someone, but Rilv would probably continue trying to keep things from escalating out of control. She was the type of woman who liked to keep everything *certain*. She likely had a plan forming in her head right now, if she didn't have one formulated already.

The elves helped Rilv and the others out of the administration building, some of them engaging in idle chatter to help deflate the tension a bit. Surely everyone was going to act as normal as they could, but chances were they were all going to be keeping a vigilant eye on the visitors—constantly. They weren't going to let anyone take the Stone of Truth.

Lanek wondered what everyone was thinking of him. They knew Fenley had taken him into the shrine and had gone through the rest ritual with him. There were only two options they could be thinking of. One: Lanek was not successful in the rest ritual, and therefore did not see the Stone of Truth. This wouldn't be so surprising, since it was his first time attempting the ritual. And two: Lanek *did* see the Stone of Truth, but had purposely chosen not to say anything. If this were the case, that would mean he was on their side. After all, he was an elf like them. That's what they'd believe.

Someone grabbed Lanek's shoulder. Before he could react, he was spun around violently, then was grabbed by the other shoulder. He found himself staring directly into Chei's eyes. They were no longer friendly eyes—they were callous, dark, morbid.

And yet his voice sounded friendly when he spoke. "By the way, how *did* your rest ritual go?" Because Lanek was turned toward Chei, Rilv and the others couldn't see Lanek's situation. In fact, it looked like everyone was leaving them behind.

"Oh..." Lanek uncharacteristically stumbled for a response. "It went well. The water was nice."

Before Chei could say more, Fenley walked over. "The ritual was thoroughly enlightening, for the both of us."

She said it calmly, without emphasizing anything—and yet the message was perfectly clear to Chei. Fenley was letting him know that Lanek had indeed seen the Stone of Truth, but had chosen not to reveal this to Rilv. The other elves likely heard this too, but Rilv, Lynx, and Kitoh wouldn't understand the hidden message. They didn't know that enlightenment in the shrine entailed seeing the Hader hanging from the ceiling.

Chei loosened his grip on Lanek slowly. He was a brave one, considering that Lanek's rapier was in plain sight all this time, and the others in Lanek's group were nearby and also armed.

"I'm glad you had a good experience," Chei said. His eyes now matched his voice again, and all was back to normal once more. It was worrisome just how quickly Chei was able to shift back and forth. Was he pretending to be a silly, jovial fellow all this time? For all Lanek knew, it was all an act.

For all he knew, everything was an act.

Was it possible that Fenley was also just pretending to be Lanek's friend? Or did she actually suspect Lanek? What was it that she really thought of him?

The village leader and his supporters guided their visitors through the town, showing each of the homes, and noting anything remotely of interest. What constituted a special site in such a small village included things like a tree that had been struck by lightning, and a small hillside with some artwork made of rocks grouped into simple patterns—apparently set by children.

Of course, there was no sign of the Hader in the short tour, which was maybe a half hour at most, even with everyone walking at a slow, careful pace, and several random villagers stopping to greet them.

Everyone was thoroughly friendly, kind, considerate. Several people offered to let the visitors spend the night at their place, but Fenley made sure to let them know Lanek had already agreed to stay at her brother's place, where they were all going to have dinner.

By the time the tour ended, Lanek could tell Rilv was growing impatient. She was surely concerned about the person with two Haders approaching. Would this person arrive tonight? Lanek felt certain it would take a while for this opponent—for this was surely an opponent—to locate this specific village, so well-hidden in the mountaintops.

The village leader and his associates split up and went about their separate ways, save for Fenley who stayed with Lanek. He noticed Nullen and the others talking with more villagers, some of them casting glances toward the visitors. Were all the villagers being told to keep an eye on them? It wouldn't take long for word to spread through the entire village that the visitors were suspicious, though Lanek recalled there was already some wariness amongst many of the people the moment they arrived.

"It's probably about time for supper," Fenley said. "I can take you and your friends over to meet my brother and his family, if you'd like."

Lanek thought it best to check with Rilv, to find out what course of action she was going to take. When he turned to her, he found she was already looking at him.

"Go ahead," Rilv said. "We will meet up with you shortly."

"Okay," Fenley said. "We live in that house, right over there." She pointed to a house in the distance, at the top of a small incline. "The one with flower boxes hanging from the window. I'm growing some red tulips in them."

Lanek kept his eyes focused on Rilv's. "Are you

sure? I don't want any trouble to start with..."

"I will have Lynx's full cooperation," Rilv said, readily understanding Lanek's concern. "We will come within a half hour—otherwise you can come find us. In the meantime, I request you... learn more about this village. And I suggest you go quickly."

She wanted Lanek to get useful information from some of the villagers before they were told to be watchful of the visitors. If the people Lanek spoke with suspected him and the others of foul deeds, they wouldn't say anything about the Hader. Of course, Lanek already knew precisely where it was, and he was pretty certain the others had no way of finding out themselves at this point.

"Got it," Lanek said.

Fenley took his hand and eagerly brought him down the path leading to her brother's home. From what Lanek could tell, nobody had gone to that house since the village officials separated, so Lanek felt safe talking with Fenley's relatives. And really, there was no reason for him to be worried. He could protect himself well enough, and Fenley would be there to keep any trouble from escalating. Lanek just had to count on Lynx not causing any strife. Or Rilv, for that matter, though for very different reasons.

"So you eat with your brother and his wife?" Lanek asked. "What about your parents?"

"They've passed away," Fenley said. "A couple years ago, they fell ill." She didn't elaborate, and though she didn't sound sad, Lanek felt bad for bringing it up.

"I'm sorry," he said. "My parents died a few years ago too. My sister as well. It's difficult to know how to go on sometimes... after something like that."

Fenley stopped a few meters from the front door of the home and looked up into Lanek's eyes. Her eyes were wet, but she wasn't quite crying. "I'm so sorry. I felt terrible... for days. And I still feel terrible at times. Even now. But I've still had my brother. And the whole village. We all support each other when anyone dies. In a way, losing a fellow villager is almost like losing a family member."

Lanek at least had Suran after his parents and friends all died in Delkol's attack, but after Suran was killed... Who did he have left? He had only himself. And there were many days where he wondered what the point of anything was. It often felt like there wasn't much reason to go on living at all.

It would have been nice if there had been someone left alive, who could have understood what he had gone through.

"I'm sorry," Fenley said. "I didn't mean to get like this all of a sudden."

"It's fine," Lanek said. "I think it's a good sign. It shows you're still attached to the ones you love."

It was just something to say. Lanek didn't really

think about it until after he finished the sentence. How much had *he* grieved these past five years?

Not very much. He didn't let himself grieve. It wasn't that he didn't want to. After his parents died, he wanted to be brave for Suran. She needed someone to support her, and Lanek was glad to be there for her. On top of this, he was thrown headfirst into a mission to help retrieve a piece of the Elpis, and then assist the nation in defending the capital against the Shire Kingdom's armies.

Then after Suran died, he felt...

It was difficult to put to words. He kept wondering how he was supposed to feel. How he was supposed to act. What he was supposed to do. Even who he was supposed to be. He was no longer a villager or student in Edellerston. He was no longer the training mechanic under his parents' tutelage. And he was no longer Suran's brother.

What was there for him? Only revenge—it was the only thing he could think of. Suran's killer still loomed at large, and so did the Brotherhood as a whole. Terico had gotten rid of the immediate threat—arguably the greater threat—but it wasn't over yet. It wasn't finished.

Fenley wiped her eyes and thanked Lanek. He was relieved to see her smile again, then knock at the door to her brother's home.

It was her brother who answered, and he showed them in to the front room of the home, which served as both a kitchen and a dining area. As Lanek expected, the house was just as humble inside as it was out, with little in the way of convenience or ornamentation. There was a thin table with four chairs, all of which looked scratched and battered over the years. And hanging near the hearth was a circular woodcarving of a number of deities, some of which looked similar to those in the shrine. Lanek tried to spot the goddess whose statue was carved in the shrine, but wasn't certain which was her.

Checking a pot in the fireplace was a woman who Lanek assumed to be the wife of Fenley's brother. She had the top of her blonde hair covered in a bandana that was half-black and half-white, and wore a fairly basic green and brown dress. She turned to Lanek and smiled.

"You must be one of the visitors," she said. "Lannick, was it?"

"His name's Lan*ek*," Fenley said. "*Eh. Eh.*"

Lanek chuckled, then glanced back to Fenley's sister-in-law. "It's good to meet you. And this soup you're cooking smells wonderful."

"Better than soup," the woman said. "This is a stew."

"By the way," Fenley's brother said, "when do you think your friends will show up?"

"Don't worry," Lanek said. "They just ate, so they're fine. They might not show up for a while, so no need to keep you waiting." Of course, if Rilv and the others took too long, he intended to check outside to see what they were doing.

In the kitchen area, an elderly couple gathered bowls and cups, and prepared a sweet-smelling tea. Though their motions were slow and weary, they were always smiling, and whispering and laughing to each other. Lanek helped bring everything to the table, while Fenley's brother helped the elderly man sit at the end of the table, and then the elderly woman sit to his right.

As Fenley's sister-in-law added some more spices to the stew, Lanek learned and relearned names—her brother was Yalmin, and his wife was Tria. The elderly couple were Tria's parents, who were the happiest old people Lanek had ever seen. Perhaps they were still in a cheerful mood from their daughter's wedding. And now that Lanek thought about it, he noticed Yalmin and Tria smiling as well. And so was Fenley. They were all simply *joyful*, and Lanek didn't feel any of it was ingenuine. They weren't just pretending to be happy in front of guests. And it made sense, Lanek realized. They all had each other. They loved each other.

Since there weren't enough chairs, Lanek and Fenley knelt on folded blankets at the end of the table, which was low enough for them to eat from comfortably. Yalmin and Tria had offered to kneel, but Lanek was quick to kneel himself, knowing they were probably tired from preparing the meal.

The food turned out to be a spicy vegetable stew, and Lanek was glad to enjoy a hot, fresh meal he didn't have to prepare himself. He wasn't a bad cook, but he felt it was nice to eat food prepared by someone else. Somehow the act of sharing a home-cooked meal could build a relationship in a deeper way that other daily interactions couldn't.

Everyone was curious to learn about Lanek and his life as an airship mechanic and pilot. He didn't give many details about his life, not wanting to ruin the light mood at the table, but he was able to tell them all the basics about airships. Everything was new and fascinating to them, and Lanek felt glad to at least provide something interesting for them to discuss with their neighbors— perhaps for the next couple weeks.

"You seem like an elf with a head on his shoulders," Tria's father said. "The village could use a few more young men like you."

"Oh yes," Tria's mother agreed. "A kind, strong man who would protect these humble hills."

Lanek held his spoon in his stew, studying it a few moments. "Well, I may have grown up in a small town, but I'm not really the type to live in a place so off-the-beaten-path. A place like this doesn't lend itself well to an airship mechanic."

"Think so?" Yalmin asked. "You're practically in the air to begin with up here. And you could always fly down the mountain to Riul to pick up whatever parts you'd need, I imagine."

"I suppose things could be worked out," Lanek admitted. "I'm just not sure what I'm doing with my life right now."

"My parents just like to voice their opinion to people," Tria said. "Only you can decide how you want to live."

"Of course," Fenley spoke up, "we *would* love to have you here."

Lanek looked over to Fenley, and her pure, bashful smile. He didn't want to look too long—he wasn't quite sure what he wanted to say about all this. He didn't like how indecisive he had become since getting to know the people of this village. Was he going to be on the village's side or on the government's side?

When he put it that way, the answer suddenly seemed rather obvious. The choices may as well have been Fenley's side and Rilv's side.

The dinner conversations turned to more trivial things, and Lanek tried to clear his mind a bit and focus on the delicious stew. But just when he was getting worried about what his teammates were up to, a knock came at the door. Yalmin got up to answer it, and Lanek looked back to see Kitoh at the entryway.

"Ah, welcome," Yalmin said. "Come in and have

some stew, if you have the time."

"Hello," Kitoh said. "I just came to give Lanek a message really quick."

"What is it?" Lanek asked.

"I... I didn't think she'd act right away," Kitoh said. "But she's going. Right now."

Lanek felt the blood drain from his face as his mind registered just what Kitoh was telling him. Rilv was already on the move. She was going to get the Hader. Right now.

He got to his feet and hurried to the door. "Sorry, I have to go." He grabbed Kitoh's hand and pulled him forward down the trail. There were voices coming from inside the house, and Lanek was pretty sure Fenley was getting up to follow him. But Lanek couldn't stop to explain anything. If Rilv had somehow figured out where the Hader was so quickly... Or perhaps was just taking drastic measures to get information out of the villagers...

"Where is she?" Lanek asked.

"Heading to the shrine," Kitoh said. "She had me make a map of the village, and we used the Elpis... She wanted me to just check that you were still at that house, but I decided to let you know the current situation while I was there."

Lanek quickened his pace, and Kitoh ran along

beside him, managing to keep up. Soon enough Lanek came in sight of the shrine, its two guards still positioned to either side of the curtain entryway. Hastily scanning the area, Lanek caught sight of Rilv and Lynx approaching the shrine from the other direction, walking at a resolute, determined pace.

*What is she doing?* Lanek thought. He slowed his pace a little in order to catch his breath, and to keep it from looking like he was running in a hostile way. Instead he jogged as if he was simply hoping to catch up and join Rilv, not wanting it to look like he was trying to stop her. It was still possible that Rilv wasn't certain the Hader was in the shrine, and at the very least there was a good chance she didn't know it was invisible.

Rilv and Lynx continued past a couple villagers who tried to greet them, made their way past a small girl playing with a jump rope, and marched straight toward the shrine entrance—and two disconcerted guards.

"I'm afraid only elves are allowed inside," one guard said, while the other lowered his lance a bit. "If you'd like, you can—"

"Set them aside," Rilv said.

Lynx leaped forward and plunged knives into each guard's neck.

"No!" Lanek screamed. He immediately sprinted forward, while Kitoh stumbled to the ground in shock at the turn of events.

Rilv scowled at Lynx, perhaps not intending for him to outright kill the two guards—but she continued to the black curtain, unperturbed by the screams and cries of villagers in the vicinity. The entire village was going to be in a panic now. Or worse—in a vengeful frenzy. Lanek had to stop this now. *Somehow.*

Rilv and Lynx were inside the shrine by the time Lanek reached the entry, and as he hoped, they didn't appear to know precisely where the Hader was. They were looking around in the large, empty room, finding nothing that stood out save for the pool and its goddess statue centerpiece.

"I can blow this place apart," Lynx suggested.

Lanek drew his rapier before Rilv could respond. She glanced back to Lanek, the way one would express displeasure at a friend's bad joke.

"We have no time for this, Lanek," Rilv said. "I apologize for Lynx's rash behavior, but we have no time left. Someone with two Haders is nearly upon us, and this operation will be severely undermined if we do not find this village's Hader before him. I suggest you tell us everything you've learned from the villagers regarding the stone's location."

"I don't know," Lanek said. "Nobody knows anything about the Hader. Now let's just get out of here and leave before you let that deranged psychopath kill any more people!"

"Tch," Lynx muttered.

"We can not leave without the Hader," Rilv said, glancing back to the entryway. There was clearly a commotion outside—villagers were gathering fast.

Kitoh ran inside, out of breath and panic-stricken.

"The Hader's not here," Lanek said to Rilv. "Everyone's going to be up in arms over this, and I'm not going to let a needless fight break out!"

"Let's hurry," Kitoh said between breaths. He pointed up in the direction of the statue, staring straight toward the Stone of Truth. "Just take the Hader and go."

*Could he see it?*

"I don't see it anywhere," Lynx said, rummaging through the shelves of gray clothing. He pushed aside the fold-out dressing walls, then started pulling off the decorative metal plates from the wall.

"It's right there, where I'm pointing," Kitoh said.

Rilv and Lynx stared right at the Hader, but they didn't show any sign of recognition. Lanek couldn't see it, and Rilv and Lynx couldn't seem to see it.

*Of course*, Lanek realized. *Kitoh is an eigni. And one with a particularly strong connection to the Nexi. He can see the stone without even going through the ritual.*

Several men rushed into the shrine, each of them

wielding a weapon and a Nexi stone.

"Get out immediately!" a middle-aged man yelled. He and the rest stopped a couple meters in front of the curtain, which was now pulled aside so other villagers could look in—many of them also armed with Nexi stones, as well as farming scythes, cleavers, and pitchforks.

"Give us the Hader, and we will leave," Rilv said.

"You will leave, or suffer the consequences!" the man replied.

A red Nexi skipped across the floor, flying straight toward the seven men.

"Get back!" Lanek yelled.

The Nexi stone exploded in a massive ball of fire, blowing up straight into two of them, and sending the rest flying backward. The curtain burned away and a good portion of the wall to the left of the entryway blasted apart in the process, eliciting cries from the elves gathered outside of the shrine.

Lanek turned to find Lynx sprinting toward the men who weren't incinerated in the powerful fire attack. Lynx had a sword raised forward in one hand, and a second red Nexi in the other. Lanek ran in front of Lynx and slipped a yellow Nexi out from his pocket.

This was his chance. This was his legitimate chance to kill Lynx. The masked man hadn't betrayed the team, but Lanek wasn't going to put up with this village slaughtering a moment longer.

"Out of my way!" Lynx yelled. He swung his sword.

Lanek leaped straight to the blade, activating the yellow Nexi just before it hit his side. The protective energy forced the blade to deflect off his clothes. Lanek slammed his shoulder against Lynx's chest, knocking them both back. Lanek recovered quickly and jabbed his rapier forward. Lynx activated his red Nexi to force Lanek's blade back. With the yellow Nexi still activated, the flames passed to either side of Lanek harmlessly.

He couldn't keep it up for long—not without tiring himself just as the fight had begun. He pushed through the flames and smoke to attack in Lynx's general direction. Lanek struck metal. Lynx let up on the red Nexi and countered, forcing Lanek to block and hold Lynx back.

"You can see the Hader, Kitoh?" Rilv asked.

"It's hanging from a string," Kitoh said. "Some kind of spell is keeping everyone from seeing it, though it's not strong enough to stay hidden from me."

"Get it and we will be on our way," Rilv said.

The men who were injured by Lynx's fire attack were on their feet again, and joined by a number of other armed villagers. There were several bystanders approaching the entryway as well, Lanek realized—civilians who would be killed quickly and easily by Lynx if Lanek didn't end this fight right away, or at least hold him back. But then there was still Rilv...

"You want to die, Lanek?" Lynx asked, blocking each of Lanek's attacks. Lynx returned a series of blows, but Lanek was quick enough to defend each swing of Lynx's blade. They were evenly matched—just as they were five years ago. Lanek had kept up his training all these years, just in hopes of being prepared for this very moment. He had to find a way to overwhelm Lynx. To take him by surprise. To get the upper hand.

Lanek managed to pull out a light blue Nexi while Lynx pushed him back with a strong swing of his sword—a heavier, thicker blade than Lanek's rapier. With a flick of his wrist, Lanek released a gust of cold air. Lynx was quick to jump to the side of the blast, but Lanek timed his motion to freeze the floor where Lynx landed. Immediately Lanek leaped forward and jabbed his blade toward Lynx's stomach, but the masked man kept from slipping on the ice, and twisted in such a way to avoid Lanek's attack.

Lynx turned his head suddenly, as if startled. Before Lanek could use the opportunity to attack, Lynx pulled out a yellow Nexi stone. A thin trail of fire exploded straight into Lynx. A burst of light, nearly too fast for Lanek to see. It enveloped Lynx in a blinding, roaring swath of flame. Past Lynx, a giant chunk of the shrine wall blew apart, but the flames remained around Lynx. It was hot—extremely hot—and Lanek had to quickly step back a ways to keep from getting burned.

He looked to where the fire attack had come from. Standing a few meters away was Chei, his eyes as fierce as they were when he had grabbed Lanek a little while ago. Chei held a red Nexi in his hand, glowing a bright, violent red. It was a fast, powerful attack, and Chei was keeping the flames going, knowing Lynx may have activated his shielding Nexi in time. If Chei could overpower Lynx's yellow barrier of energy, Lynx wouldn't last one second in such intense heat..

"Let me know when you're going to let up," Lanek said. "I'll run in and stab him the moment he deactivates his yellow Nexi." It was going to be like Lynx was underwater, holding his breath, and the moment he broke free would be the moment Lanek could attack. He simply had to time the attack for a moment when Lynx would be too weary to defend.

A giant mass of gray sludge exploded from within the fire, then flowed like a violent torrent straight for Lanek and Chei. It was swamp material from the brown Nexi, but altered in some way.

The gray Nexi, Lanek realized. The substance was poisoned, and likely lethal upon contact. The fact Lynx was able to combine the two Nexi abilities like this, and while maintaining a strong shield with a yellow Nexi... It was more than uncanny—it seemed utterly impossible.

Lanek ran out of the way of the sticky gray substance, but the material continued toward him—Lynx was somehow guiding it perfectly, even with senses obscured by flames, smoke, and screams.

There was no opening. Everywhere Lanek turned, there was more of the sludge rushing toward him. He used his ice Nexi to freeze the substance before it could reach him, then turned to check on Chei's situation. While running back from the rushing gray swamp, Chei let up on the fire pounding against Lynx. Immediately Chei released another sudden burst of fire, blasting straight through the poisoned swamp substance.

The fire around Lynx dissipated, but his yellow barrier was still barely activated when the second blast of fire slammed directly into him. This explosion sent Lynx flying straight out of the shrine, through the gaping hole that was created from the first massive fire blast.

Chei fell to his hands and knees about a meter from the settling swamp substance. He was shaking from head to toe, exhausted from Nexi use. Lanek couldn't stop to help him though, and he didn't have time to check on Lynx either. More than anything, Lanek wanted to find Lynx and skewer his heart, just to make his death definite—but the villagers were surrounding Rilv and Kitoh. The battle for the Stone of Truth was commencing, and Lanek didn't want it to last another second.

Several villagers rushed toward Rilv at once. She pulled out her Hader and activated its power, forcing the assailants to fly backwards violently. From a safe distance, one villager threw a knife, but Rilv was able to deflect this as well. At this unbelievable sight, many of the people ran away, unable to see any way to get near Rilv as long as she had the ability to effortlessly fling them back. But many of the villagers simply became riled up, and shouted for others to help them try overwhelming Rilv.

"Stop the fighting!" Lanek yelled to the stirring crowd. "We'll leave!"

"Kitoh, grab the Hader and go," Rilv said. "I will create a path for us."

The eigni boy nodded and raised a green Nexi stone, pointing it toward where Lanek knew the Stone of Truth was hanging.

A series of icicles, a couple arrows, and a spear flew toward Rilv and Kitoh. Rilv managed to deflect all of the weapons with her telekinesis Hader, but Kitoh stumbled back in surprise, the onslaught fended off mere centimeters away.

Vines flung toward where the Stone of Truth hung, which became visible the moment it was snapped off its string. The vines didn't come from Kitoh's Nexi, though. Lanek watched as the vines brought the Hader down to the village leader, standing just outside the blown-off entryway. He was accompanied by the two elves Lanek met in the administration building, each of them armed with a couple Nexi stones.

"Quickly, Lanek," Rilv called out. "Retrieve the Hader, and we will be on our way."

"No," Lanek replied. "I will not fight these people."

Rilv did not look any more upset than she usually did, and didn't seem to be surprised. More villagers were approaching her, rejuvenated by their leader's success in protecting the Stone of Truth. She turned to Kitoh, a concerned frown spread across her face. "I can not continue using my Hader so much. Fend these people off and I will retrieve the Hader myself."

"I don't want to fight these people either," Kitoh said. Lanek smiled, relieved that Kitoh at least wasn't about to turn against the village. But Lanek had hoped Nullen would call off the villagers' ambush by now. Nullen had the Hader, and there was no way Rilv was going to be able to fight off all these people by herself—right?

And yet the leader simply stood and watched, his companions ready to defend him in case Rilv did anything drastic.

"You want to die?" Rilv asked Kitoh.

A young man swung a scythe—Rilv leaped back while Kitoh ducked. At the same time, an older man released a jet of water, but missed them both entirely. Rilv punched the man with the scythe hard in the face, grabbed his scythe, and tossed it aside as he stumbled backward.

Another villager threw a spear, while two others sent waves of dirt rushing toward Rilv and Kitoh.

Lanek didn't see how he was going to stop the fighting. The people were in a frenzy, dismayed to see their beloved shrine half in ruins. After all the hospitality they had shown their visitors, it had to be unbelievable that in return their most valuable treasure was nearly stolen. He tried standing in the way of some of the villagers and yelling for them to stop, but they pushed past him, desperate to keep Rilv from taking the Stone of Truth. Lanek had to somehow convince her to give up on taking the Hader.

Which seemed about as easy as convincing a river to start flowing the other direction.

The people continued to attack Rilv and Kitoh, and a few had started surrounding Lanek as well, recognizing him as one of the visitors, but not knowing anything more of his situation. He sheathed his rapier and raised his hands, making it clear he didn't intend to fight, but the people remained in his way, reluctant to let him join up with Rilv and Kitoh.

The eigni boy wielded a dark blue Nexi, creating a large spray of water to deflect the villagers' attacks. He wasn't fighting them, but was protecting himself and Rilv. The water compacted and began swirling around the two, creating a rapid whirlpool of water in the air surrounding them. The weapons and Nexi attacks thrown at them were pushed to the side by Kitoh's power—a utilization of the water Nexi that Lanek had never heard of before, let alone seen. Water was simple enough to release from a dark blue Nexi, but it took extreme skill to maneuver it the way Kitoh was managing.

Rilv charged forward, and Kitoh ran along beside her, keeping them protected from the villagers' attacks. The villagers tried to find openings, either by timing their weapon throws to reach Rilv and Kitoh in between spurts of the rushing water, or by using Nexi attacks that could reach Rilv and Kitoh from above. However, Kitoh spotted every attack in time, and controlled the water in such a way that he was able to defend every attack and still be able to see where he and Rilv were going through the anarchy of the shrine.

They passed where Lanek and some of the villagers stood, and Lanek watched Nullen and the people outside quickly back away—nobody was certain how to get past Kitoh's defense. Lanek could hear Kitoh and Rilv speaking to each other, but he couldn't make out what they were saying. He hoped Kitoh was trying to call this whole thing off, though it didn't seem likely the boy would be able to persuade Rilv to give up on this Hader.

"Let me try to stop them," Lanek told the villagers blocking him. Before he could try to push past them though, he spotted Chei on his feet again, pointing his fire Nexi at Kitoh's barrier.

"Wait!" Lanek yelled.

A third massive burst of fire erupted from Chei's Nexi stone, slamming directly into Kitoh's rapidly circling water. The wild collision flung Rilv and Kitoh away a couple meters, throwing them against the ground. The fire dissipated before it could continue toward Rilv and Kitoh. Chei fell back to his hands and knees, breathing heavily.

Amidst the explosion and panic, Lanek slipped past the villagers and hurried outside. Most of the people outside had fled a ways, though Nullen and his supporters were a good six or seven meters away from Rilv and Kitoh.

Rilv pushed herself to her feet and pointed her Hader directly at a small girl a few meters away from everyone else—it was the girl who had been jumping rope before all this madness had escalated in the shrine.

Effortlessly, Rilv forced the girl to float in the air, higher and higher. A couple villagers ran toward Rilv, their makeshift weapons raised.

"Stop!" Lanek yelled, as other villagers began to point at the floating child. Panic spread as everyone realized Rilv was holding the child hostage. The men who were about to attack Rilv stopped, their eyes turning up to the crying girl suspended in the air, now a good ten, fifteen meters high.

"What do you think you're doing?" Nullen yelled.

Rilv spoke loudly and clearly, but resolutely. "The moment anyone attacks us will be the moment this child plummets to her death." The panicking girl was now positioned high above the shrine building, where nobody would be able to catch her if she fell.

"Now tell everyone to back away and drop their weapons," Rilv continued, staring straight toward Nullen. "Then hand me the Hader. We will leave as soon as we have that stone. The girl will be safely returned to the earth, and nobody more will have to get hurt."

The village leader stared back at Rilv a long time, perhaps trying to come up with some way to stop Rilv without having the child die in the process. A vine Nexi could be used to grab the girl, but that would take time, and Rilv could very well fling the child away if she wished. The telekinesis Hader was no ordinary Nexi, and Rilv seemed to have a good grasp for how it operated, even in this wearied state she had to be in.

"Everyone back away," Nullen said. "Set your weapons down."

The villagers complied, dropping their swords, knives, scythes, pitchforks, bows and arrows, spears, and Nexi stones. Some of them backed into the shrine, while others backed away outside, giving Rilv and Kitoh plenty of space. Lanek stayed put, remaining about four or five meters away. He was not far from what used to be the shrine entryway.

He looked over all the villagers standing outside in the distance, most of them looking frightened, the rest looking furious. Lanek spotted Fenley a ways down the trail, standing with her brother and his wife. They all looked confused and worried. What they must have thought about him right now, standing in front of the smoking, broken-down shrine...

"Let's stop this," Lanek said to Rilv. "The Hader isn't worth all this."

"I am not leaving without the Hader," Rilv said. "Do you want our kingdom to fall to Augurc's experiments? They are powered by the Elpis—even a well-trained troop of our best soldiers are slaughtered when they encounter the Brotherhood these days. We need power in order to defend the Fiefs Kingdom. I have tried reasoning with these villagers in every way I could, but they do not care about the greater good. They only care about themselves. And now they must suffer the consequences, if they refuse to cooperate. Even now, I am offering to leave without anyone more coming to harm."

She stretched her hand out toward where Nullen stood. "Hand me the Hader. Now."

Nullen gripped the stone and held it against his chest. This was the last thing he ever wanted to give up, of course. It was probably his greatest responsibility as village leader. That stone was of the greatest importance to these people.

"Now, Nullen," Rilv said. She twitched her Hader a bit, causing the hostage girl to shake in the air a little.

The child cried out, screaming for her mommy and daddy.

Villagers pointed and gasped, some of them in tears.

"Stop this, Rilv," Lanek said. "You've gone too far."

"You have ten seconds, Nullen," Rilv said, still staring at the trembling village leader.

"No," Kitoh whispered. "This is wrong."

"Stop this, Rilv!" Lanek yelled.

"I will not stop," Rilv said. "Five seconds, Nullen."

The village leader only clutched the Stone of Truth tighter. His eyes moved from the girl to Rilv, back and forth. Frantic. Desperate.

"Now, Nullen!" Rilv screamed.

"Hold it!" a man yelled, even louder.

A human leisurely walked out from behind a small hill in the other direction. He was tall, and perhaps a year or two younger than Lanek was. His hair was a violent red, short and spiky. He wore a light tan jacket, dark brown trousers, and an assortment of pouches tied to his belt, arms, and legs, all obscured by a cloak as red as his hair. There were several weapons on his person—a sword sheathed on his back, a dagger on his arm, a couple knives on his belt, and some kind of rod tied to his right leg.

"Stop," Rilv said. "I will let this child plummet if you continue."

The young man kept walking toward her, as if he hadn't heard a word she had said.

"Doubt it. I know a bluff when I see one."

He simply kept walking. Did he even know what was going on here? Who was this person?

"Don't worry, everyone," the man proclaimed to the onlookers he passed by. "I will most certainly save your village."

He grinned a long, sadistic smile at Rilv. Gripped in each of his hands was a Hader.

•

# 6. EXPLOSION

Lanek watched as Rilv stood her ground, while the stranger continued to walk toward her. He was just a few meters away now, and either didn't care for the hostage child's life or truly believed Rilv wouldn't actually kill the girl. To be completely honest, Lanek wasn't sure if Rilv was serious in her threat or not.

"Who are you?" Rilv asked.

"I am Kechi, servant of Mareba Shire," the man said, stopping a couple meters in front of Rilv. "And you will be handing your Hader to me immediately." He raised the Hader in his right hand, its swirls of light shifting between green and black.

So this man worked for Shire royalty? Lanek found it curious that Kechi didn't claim allegiance to Augurc Shire, but rather another man entirely—a noble in his fifties and wheelchair-bound, Lanek recalled reading. Mareba Shire was supposedly greatly opposed to the Brotherhood following the fall of Delkol, as all the Shire governing body claimed. The question was, was Kechi obtaining Haders just for himself, for the good of the Shire Kingdom in general, for the intent of giving Mareba Shire power over Augurc, or even for the Brotherhood specifically?

Rilv glanced at the Hader pointed directly toward her. Her own Hader was still pointed at the child she kept levitated above the battered shrine. "You can't threaten me. Any attack you send my way, I can easily push away with my own Hader."

Lanek knew she could move multiple things at the same time, but it seemed Rilv was straining herself just to keep the hostage suspended in the air. Would she actually be able to move aside Kechi's attack and still keep the child from falling to her death? And if not, would she lose control of the child the moment she was attacked? Lanek wished he was closer to where the girl was positioned, and wished the stranger was enough of a distraction to give Lanek time to reach the girl before Rilv would notice. Yet Rilv was keeping as much control over the situation as she possibly could, even when facing a confident enemy with two Haders.

"I don't need to threaten you," Kechi said, grinning wildly. "You *will* be handing your Hader to me immediately."

It was as if his words were meant to force her to just walk over and give him her Hader. Was Kechi's Hader the power to control someone's mind? Lanek watched Rilv, worried she was going to do just as Kechi ordered.

Instead she simply stood in place, frowning. If Kechi was using his Hader, it was clearly having no effect on Rilv.

A sword rose from the ground a couple meters to Rilv's right, a weapon likely forced aside earlier by Rilv's telekinesis or Kitoh's shield of water. The sword's blade turned and pointed at Kechi, who gritted his teeth. Rilv seemed to be managing just fine holding the child in the air and maneuvering the sword at the same time, and Lanek had to wonder if Kechi was going to pose a threat at all. Did he not have good control over his Haders? Or was Rilv too strong, and capable of resisting Kechi's power?

Was this Lanek's chance to try rescuing the girl above the shrine? Rilv had her mind intently focused on two things at once—this was the best chance Lanek was going to get. He spotted a green Nexi left on the ground by the villagers, and decided he could use it to save the child. He'd only get one chance at it, and he'd have to be quick. Finding a path behind some villagers just in front of what was left of the shrine wall, Lanek bolted toward the green Nexi stone, as quiet and fast as he could.

"Stop, Lanek!" Rilv yelled, jolting Lanek to a halt as he was reaching for the vine Nexi. "Despite what this man claims, I will kill this child if you or anyone else makes a move to rescue her!"

The crying child wobbled in the air a bit more, and Lanek wasn't sure if this was Rilv shaking the girl to make a point, or if Rilv was losing control with her concentration waning.

Lanek backed away from the green Nexi, trying to think of some other way to reach the child. But there was nothing...

Rilv still kept her floating sword aimed at Kechi, who continued to hold his Hader tight, still pointed at Rilv. Was he still trying to force Rilv to hand over her Hader? He almost looked like he was breaking a sweat, trying to wield his Hader's power against her.

The sword flew toward Kechi, even faster than Lanek anticipated. Kechi only had time to step back, unable to dodge quickly enough.

And yet the sword missed him entirely. By a good meter, the sword lunged to his left, flying into a hillside a ways past Kechi.

Rilv's eyes widened slightly—was this how she looked when surprised?

"I see," Kechi said. "We can't use our Haders against each other."

"I suggest you back away then," Rilv said. "If you

don't, the child will die. You have five seconds."

Kechi laughed. "You're still bluffing! But that's fine. I'll rescue the child, and just let the angry mob take you down... You're too weak to resist much longer."

A stream of red liquid rushed toward the girl in the air, far too quick for Rilv to react to in time. The child screamed, villagers screamed, people pointed and gasped, others stumbled back in surprise. Nullen knelt down, gasping for breath, and Rilv tried using her Hader to maneuver the hostage away from the strange substance. The red liquid held a tight grip on the child, as if the water had solidified to some degree.

Was this the power of Kechi's second Hader? Lanek looked and saw him with his left fist raised, a Hader glowing silver and red between his fingers.

The red liquid held the screaming girl tight, pushing against the tugs of Rilv's Hader. Rilv trembled and began to take deep breaths. She was being pushed past her limit. In one swift movement, the red liquid brought the child away from the shrine and down on the ground, a little ways in front of Fenley and her relatives. The crimson substance dropped to the ground, splattering across the dirt path like bloodstains.

Perhaps it *was* blood. And when Lanek looked over the area near the side of the shrine, where several elves had died, Lanek couldn't find any bloodstains among them.

Did Kechi gather all the blood together and maneuver it with his Hader, just as a tan Nexi could mold earth and a dark blue Nexi could mold water? Kechi's control of blood was much quicker than base Nexi abilities, however, and he seemed capable of controlling how solid or liquid the blood was. This wasn't an ability to be treated lightly.

"Quick, apprehend her!" Nullen cried out to the villagers, while pointed at Rilv. "Before she takes another child hostage!"

Tens of villagers picked their weapons off the ground and rushed toward Rilv and Kitoh. Some threw projectiles at them, but Rilv forced them all away via telekinesis. She was trembling more in the process of doing so, however. Weakened from Nexi use, Rilv wouldn't be able to use the Hader much longer.

"We have to flee!" Kitoh yelled above the cries of the encircling villagers.

"No!" Rilv replied. "Not before we've obtained the Haders!"

"It's too late..." Kitoh said.

Rilv forced aside a couple more knives and a pitchfork, but about a dozen armed villagers had gathered around the two, closing off any path of escape. Lanek considered rushing in to help Kitoh and Rilv, but Nullen specifically ordered the villagers to merely apprehend them—perhaps thinking of Lanek when he gave the order.

But at the same time, this was going exactly according to Kechi's plan. The red-haired man stood a few meters from the attacking villagers, a smug expression etched on his face. Lanek couldn't let him take all the Haders. In fact, he probably needed to be taking action against the man—but what would Lanek be able to do if Kechi could control his mind? He realized he would need a Hader himself if he were to stand a chance against Kechi. Rilv had one, and Nullen had one...

Just as a villager was about to swing a sword at Rilv, a figure rushed into the scene and stabbed the man in the stomach, then shoved him back into another villager. The rest of the villagers nearby ran away, shocked by the speed of the attack.

At the worst possible moment, Lynx had returned. Lanek had hoped to find him unconscious at the bottom of a hill, where Lanek could kill hill him once all the fighting at the shrine had ended. But it was far too late to amend anything here now. If Lanek didn't do something right away, things would likely only get worse for this village.

Lynx stood in front of Rilv, his bloody sword raised toward Nullen's direction.

"You two head to the airship," Lynx said. "I will obtain the Hader from the village leader."

He didn't realize the full situation—he had just regained consciousness and forced his way back into the fray, so he didn't know about Kechi.

Kitoh took Rilv's hand and helped her run with him down the village path. The eigni boy created a whirlwind of water around them, keeping any of the nearby villagers from attacking them. It didn't look like Rilv had the energy to resist at this point, but Lanek wondered if they were going to wait for him. Did they need him to pilot the airship? It was possible Kitoh understood how to do so—he was certainly smart enough to figure it out, at the very least.

None of the remaining villagers at the scene approached Lynx, though Nullen's guards made it clear they weren't going to let Lynx near their esteemed leader.

"Now what is the Brotherhood doing here?" Kechi screamed. "Augurc is working with the Fiefs Kingdom now?"

Lynx turned his head slightly, but whether or not he could see Kechi through the thin slits of his mask, Lanek couldn't know. But Lynx seemed aware of his presence, and perhaps the presence of two more Haders.

"So you're the man with two Haders," Lynx said. "I don't care who you work for or what your goals are, but suffice it to say I *will* be confiscating your Haders."

Kechi looked furious, gripping his Haders tighter. "Just another fool wanting all the power he can get. I'll tear you to pieces."

Blood rose from the ground near Lynx, and for a moment Lanek thought to warn him—but stopped short. Though Lanek wanted to be the one to kill Lynx, he wasn't about to get in the way of others killing Lynx for him. And a part of him wondered if Lynx really was still needed for something more, though Lanek wasn't certain if he was going to be involved in the mission for the Haders at all anymore, at this point.

Lynx avoided the burst of blood, which had formed into a long, thin needle and shot off toward his neck. The masked man was aware of Kechi's control of blood, at the very least, and was in good enough shape to be able to dodge the attack in time. Kechi forced some more blood nearby to rise from behind Lynx. The blood quickly solidified and shot off toward Lynx's back. Lynx turned and sliced his sword through the sharpening crimson projectile, forcing the blood to turn to liquid and pass around him.

A portion of blood deflected off Lynx's blade. Kechi caused this trickle of blood to gather back together while still in mid-air, and flung it at Lynx's neck. The needle of blood barely missed him, as Lynx spun while stepping to the side. Without even a moment's pause, Lynx was suddenly rushing toward Kechi, his Brotherhood weapon raised forward.

Furious, Kechi stepped back and thrust his Hader forward, forcing the stream of blood he had used earlier to rise and rush forward. The large blood splatters gathered back together and flew away from Fenley and her relatives, rushed past Kechi's left, and dashed even more quickly toward Lynx's chest. With one hand gripping his sword's hilt, Lynx slipped out a light blue Nexi with his other hand and held it forward. While aiming his blade directly for the giant blade of blood in front of him, Lynx activated his Nexi stone, forcing arctic air to rush out to either side of him. The long, thick weapon of blood split in two in front of Lynx, but Kechi immediately forced the crimson liquid to sharpen and curve back toward Lynx from the left and right. The Nexi altered the air around Lynx, and the blood instantly froze as it rushed for him from his left and right. Lynx pushed his blade through the rest of the blood and charged toward Kechi.

There was a bit more blood on the ground near where Kechi stood, and the Shire servant was quick to form it into a thin needle and fling it at Lynx's heart. Since Lynx was just finishing his push through the giant blade of blood, he had no time to swing at the small needle, aimed with an inhuman precision and speed no ordinary fighter could hope to avoid.

Lynx dropped to the ground and rolled forward, losing his sword in the process. Lanek realized that Lynx had managed to avoid the blood needle entirely, its splattered remains leaving a thin hole in an old wooden signpost.

As Lynx was getting on his feet, Kechi thrust forward his other Hader, activating its power against him. Lynx stumbled, failing to stand up all the way. For a second, it looked like Lynx was going to rush toward

Kechi and attack with his ice Nexi, but Lynx stopped himself. Or rather, it seemed Kechi was forcing Lynx to stop. Was Kechi controlling Lynx's body, then?

Gripping the Hader tight, Kechi took a careful step toward Lynx, who fell to both knees, trembling. Lynx couldn't stop shaking, and he crouched back from Kechi in fear. When Kechi took another step forward, Lynx shuffled back a bit, cowering.

This was obviously not in character for Lynx, who never expressed much emotion other than anger and sullen moodiness. And now Lynx was starting to sweat, and take shallow, frantic breaths. Kechi pocketed his blood Hader, unsheathed a knife, and took another step forward. Lynx turned and trembled further, nearly out of breath. Lanek wondered if he could take the opportunity to run over and kill Lynx for himself, but he didn't want to engage with Kechi sooner than he had to. He looked to the village leader, and saw Nullen was still clutching the Stone of Truth. Perhaps this was his opportunity to take it from him—but that would turn him into an enemy of the village. He needed the village against Kechi—not him.

Just before Kechi could force his knife into the side of Lynx's head, Lynx scampered away on his hands and knees, pushed himself to his feet, and ran away screaming. Kechi threw his knife at Lynx's back, but Lynx was too quick. The knife missed him entirely, and Lynx continued to run down the village path and out of sight, his cries muffled beneath his mask.

"Scared him... too much," Kechi muttered between deep breaths. It seemed Kechi had drained himself of a fair amount of energy by relying on the two Haders as much as he had. And it was obvious this hadn't turned out the way he planned. If this second Hader was used to control people's minds, Kechi could have simply forced Lynx to sit still while Kechi killed him. Instead, Lynx was exhibiting traits of someone who was utterly afraid. From what Lanek could tell then, Kechi's second Hader was used to heighten emotions of fear and dread in a target. This would explain Kechi's frustration when facing Rilv—he was expecting her to cower before him and give up her Hader, begging him to spare her life.

Kechi sighed and looked out to all the villagers gathered in the vicinity. Many who had run away earlier and sneaked back to watch the fight between Lynx and Kechi—they appeared relieved to see Lynx defeated. Kechi was still what he had claimed to be upon arrival in their village—a man coming to save them from the government agents.

Once he finished catching his breath, Kechi spoke out to the people. "That appears to be all of them... I only see elves left here, so I take it the village is safe now."

"Praise the gods," one villager said.

"It's finally over," another said.

"You've saved us!"

"Thank you so much..."

Some villagers were gripping each other tight, relieved the fighting had finally come to an end. Others were crying, dismayed by the deaths of their five or so fellow villagers. A few stared aghast at the destruction of their beloved shrine. And a couple others were keeping their eyes on Lanek, curious to see if he was going to do anything more. One looked like she was going to speak out against him, but stopped when Kechi spoke up once more.

"I am in a bit of a hurry, as I wish to pursue the enemies who have wrecked havoc on your village," he said. "So I ask that you allow me to borrow the tool I have come here for. In repayment for saving you village, I would like to use the Hader currently in your possession."

He stared his wide, wild eyes straight toward Nullen, who sheepishly clutched the Stone of Truth a little tighter.

"I thank you for saving the village," Nullen said. "With all my soul, I thank you. But the Stone of Truth is our most sacred relic. It must only be used for rituals of peace and righteousness. We can never allow it to leave the village, or be used for any purpose other than for the rituals it was intended for. I'm sorry, Sir Kechi, but I can't allow you to use it. We will be glad to repay you for your service any other way we can, however..."

Lanek had to admit it was rather brave of the village elder to stand up to a man who could control both blood and fear. It was obvious Kechi wasn't going to settle for anything less than the Hader, however.

"I'm afraid I must demand temporary use of your Hader," Kechi said as he began walking toward Nullen. "It's the only way to stop those government officials, and make sure they don't come back to terrorize your village."

"I'm... I'm sorry," Nullen said. "It's just not possible."

Kechi's eyes widened ever further, and he quickened his pace. "Do you not understand the situation you're in, old man?" He shoved his knife back into its sheath and took back out his other Hader, so he was holding the blood Hader in one hand and the fear Hader in the other.

"No... stop..." Nullen said, backing away. His bodyguards stood in front of him, ready to fight back Kechi—but Lanek knew they wouldn't last a second against the power of the two Haders.

"I can't stop, you fool!" Kechi screamed. "Not until I have enough Haders. Not when I'm so close to obtaining them! You will regret this lack of cooperation, old man. With two Haders, I am unbeatable. With three Haders, I will be invincible. With four Haders, I shall become omnipotent. Each and every one of my master's wishes shall be fulfilled. The world will belong to Mareba Shire!"

The two bodyguards trembled, struggling to keep standing before Kechi's approaching presence. They each dropped their weapons, unable to withstand the fear being forced upon them. Kechi immediately controlled blood from the ground nearby, and forced two stakes of blood to jab through their hearts. The blood weapons liquified and melded into the killed bodies. The bodies then burst apart from the inside, their blood controlled from within them. The corpses exploded, splattering blood on everyone around them, especially Kechi.

Villagers screamed from the sudden development. Kechi only grinned wider.

"I can't wait to test the power of three Haders on this pathetic village," he said. "The power to kill anyone and everyone I wish... It fills me with utter bliss, just thinking about it. The more I kill, the more alive I feel!"

With both Haders in one hand, Kechi stepped toward Nullen and used his free hand to pull a sword from the sheath tied to his back. As long as Nullen had the Stone of Truth, Kechi wouldn't be able to use the Haders against him. But if Lanek attacked, Kechi would easily be able to kill him.

There was no time to wait. Lanek ran toward Kechi, unsheathing his rapier. "This man only came for the Stone of Truth! He'll kill us all to get it!" Several other villagers rushed toward Kechi, who turned and forced blood from the killed bodyguards to gather together and attack them like razor-sharp tendrils. While Nullen slipped back, a few more villagers came after Kechi, brandishing weapons. Kechi drove his sword through the neck of the nearest villager, then forced a torrent of blood to erupt out of the man's severed head. The blood solidified and tore through several other villagers, providing even more blood for Kechi to utilize against the rest of the villagers who attacked alongside Lanek. There were at least a dozen other villagers who attempted to assist as well, but they all fell to their knees, cowering in fear.

Kechi caused a giant wave of blood to rush toward Lanek and the team of villagers charging with him. The blood wall blocked the projectiles thrown or shot at Kechi, and then swept up several villagers off their feet, sending them flying back. Lanek barely dodged the wide, rushing torrent of blood, and saw Kechi slicing apart several guards and villagers gathered around Nullen. There was no time to try attacking Kechi—the Stone of Truth was nearly in his grasp. If Kechi obtained a third Hader... perhaps there really would be no hope for this village.

Gritting his teeth, Lanek rushed toward Nullen. A guard turned to Lanek and raised a sword against him. Lanek didn't even need to raise his own blade, however, as a scythe-like blade of blood severed the guard's head just as Lanek reached him. Blood was rushing toward Lanek from his left. He kept running, avoiding a thin spike of blood lunging toward his chest. Lanek plowed into a villager, shoving the man aside and grabbing Nullen's hand. With no time to explain, Lanek forced the Hader out of Nullen's grasp. Lanek clenched the Hader with his free left hand and immediately turned to face a behemoth of blood, its many writhing tentacles finishing off all the other villagers all around Lanek. Kechi was screaming something, but Lanek heard nothing more as the environment all around him vanished.

He found himself in a graveyard. It was daytime, and there was nobody around him at all. It was a different location entirely, as even the mountains were gone. It was just one extensive graveyard all around him, as far as his eyes could see.

Stunned, Lanek simply stood still, trying to grasp how he ended up in a completely different place all of a sudden. He was just about to face Kechi, but now he had a Hader at his disposal—the means for him to keep Kechi from filling him with fear and turning him into an easy target to slice apart with hardened blood. How did Lanek end up in some random graveyard?

He stared down at the Hader in his hand. Did it somehow send him to this place? It was as if Lanek had traveled far across the country in an instant.

The graves around him were old and decrepit, many of them cracked, others moldy, some covered in cobwebs and leaves, and most layered in dust and grime. Everything was packed tight together, leaving very thin paths between each row of graves—if they could be called rows. It was all rather haphazardly arranged.

But what was he doing here? He needed to be at the village. Was Kechi still killing everyone at this very moment? Without the Hader he came for in sight, he would only be more furious and dangerous. And Fenley was still there. Was she locked in shock by Kechi's fear-inducing Hader? All the elves in the village had little hope against Kechi's Haders, overwhelming in their abilities, especially when utilized in twisted harmony.

"What is your name?"

Lanek nearly jumped in surprise, but instead forced himself to turn toward the speaker. He found a woman sitting on top of a large gravestone just a couple meters behind him. Where did she come from?

He had his rapier ready, but the woman didn't seem to be doing anything other than sitting there. She was an elf dressed in a black and white dress, likely in her late twenties. There was something familiar about her... Did she look like one of the villagers? Lanek felt certain he had seen this woman before.

"I'm Lanek. Who are you? And what is this place?"

"You should know me," the woman said. "You and Fenley were worshiping me not too long ago."

Lanek stepped back, but kept himself from gaping in awe once the realization set in. This was Reali, the goddess whose statue knelt in the shrine, her hands outstretched toward the invisible Stone of Truth. The goddess who enlightens the villagers' minds, helping them feel at peace, helping them feel calm with their decisions and difficulties, helping them find answers to their deepest questions.

"You... you're a goddess?" Lanek asked, unable to believe his eyes.

The woman nodded. "I am reverenced as one, at the very least."

"What do you mean?" Lanek asked.

"Well, I'm a goddess to the people of the village you're visiting," Reali said. "Not really to anyone else, though."

She faded away and vanished.

"Wait!" Lanek yelled. He walked toward the gravestone where the goddess had been sitting. "The village is in danger. Everyone needs help!"

"Don't worry," came a soft voice behind him. "I'm still here. And we are inside the Stone of Truth—a plane of reality that exists outside the confines of time. You will soon return to the exact moment you left your world."

He turned around and found Reali standing directly behind him. Lanek stumbled back a bit, gripping his rapier tighter.

"You disappeared," Lanek said, his heart racing.

"This is my power," Reali said. "To make things immaterial material, and things material immaterial. To make elements fade in and out of existence."

"Including yourself," Lanek said. "So you're like a

ghost."

"Yes," Reali said. "My power was originally used to deal with those abusing the power of the Elpis. Eventually my power became legendary amongst many of the elves, and I found myself likened to an ancient goddess. This village was the center of worship for these elves, and I likewise became a central object of their devotion."

"You enlighten everyone at that pool in the shrine," Lanek said.

"It's the least I can do," Reali said. "Turning specific thoughts and emotions immaterial, others material... If the villagers seek my help, I am happy to oblige as best I can. The ritual was set up with a system of magic that has long fallen out of use, but it will last as long as that shrine and pool exist."

"The shrine is falling apart," Lanek said. "Can you use your power to make Kechi disappear? He is killing all your people."

"I am aware," Reali said. "And I am willing to use you to save this people. If you will devote yourself solely to worthy causes, I will allow you full access to my power, Lanek."

"For now, I only want to save this village," Lanek said. "After that... I..."

He wasn't sure what to say. Did he really care for

the mission to bring down the Brotherhood? Of course he did. But was this Hader actually going to allow him to do so? And what of his more immediate goals? He wanted to kill Lynx. His goal was revenge. Was that a worthy cause? Technically he wanted to bring down the Brotherhood in revenge, as well. At least, that was a big part of it. He didn't want more innocent people like Suran to die at the hands of the Brotherhood... But he mainly just wanted Suran to be avenged.

"What else do you wish to do with my power?" Reali asked.

"My sister..." Lanek said. "She was killed."

"My power can't bring her back," Reali said.

Lanek hadn't even been considering such a possibility. That was simply too much to have ever hoped for—and he wondered if he should feel bad for having such little hope left in him.

"I know," Lanek said. "But I know the man who killed her. There is an entire organization responsible for her death. This organization is responsible for the devastation in your village as well, to some degree." At the very least, if it weren't for the Brotherhood, this mission to find the Haders would have never been conjured up.

"I will allow you to use my power as you see fit," Reali said, "though I doubt you will find gratification in revenge. The need to seek out destroying this organization is questionable, as is the need to kill the man you speak of."

"You can't say that," Lanek said. "You don't know anything."

Reali held her arms outstretched to the sides. "But of course I do.  When you rested in my waters of enlightenment, I gleaned quite a bit from the quietest stirrings of your heart."

"What do you think I should do, then?" Lanek asked. If this really was a goddess, she would know what's best for him—right? Though she was certainly real, and certainly had great power, Lanek wasn't certain if he could actually believe in her as a divine being.

Reali folded her arms and stared into Lanek's eyes a few moments, as if looking into his very soul. "You have a very intelligent mind, Lanek. You are contemplative. You know how to analyze situations. You're a decision-maker. You see a cause, and you ascertain its logical effect. In your mind, everything has its place in the world, and your moral code is based on achieving the best possible outcome in every condition you're in."

Reali smiled. "But you don't know your own place in the world anymore, do you?"

There was a long silence. Lanek didn't want to have this discussion. Not now. This wasn't the time for it. "It doesn't matter."

"It matters a great deal," Reali said. "If you don't know how you feel about your own self, how can you know how to feel about anyone else? Including people you're planning to kill?"

"I may not be much better than the people I'm planning to kill," Lanek said. "I go about my life, and this world... It's a world that took my sister away from me. And I've lost not only her... But I've lost a piece of myself as well. I don't know if I can ever get it back at this point. I thought I could replace it at least, with some feeling... Any feeling. But I'm never going to actually become whole again, am I?"

"What would your sister say if you asked her that question?" Reali said.

Lanek frowned. "She was always hopeful. She never felt it was too late for someone to change. She always saw the best in people."

"Perhaps you could afford to think of your sister a bit more," Reali said. "You've kept your memories of her alive in you—but what about her heart? I believe this is the piece of you that is missing, Lanek. And this isn't a feeling you need to go searching for. It's very much inside of you. You know what you should and shouldn't be doing. If you want to honor your beloved sister, wouldn't you want to live your life in a way that would make her smile?"

"Of course," Lanek said. "It's not such a simple thing, though... I'm still me, and I still have to make difficult decisions."

"Just give it some thought," Reali said. "Only you can choose your own path, but when the time comes to make those important decisions—remember to think with your heart, as well as your mind. You will know what to do, then."

Lanek nodded. Reali and the graveyard vanished, immediately replaced by the mountain village, the dying elves around Lanek, and the construct of blood converging upon him.

But he knew the blood couldn't touch him now. Lanek clenched his teeth, raised his rapier, and ran straight through the swarming wave of blood blades. The crimson liquid-turned-metal twisted around Lanek, who caught a glimpse of Kechi amidst the rushing streams of blood and frantic villagers. Lanek knew he wouldn't be able to use his Hader against Kechi, so it was going to be a matter of swordsmanship between them. There was no telling what Kechi would try to do though, so Lanek needed to dispose of the Shire servant as quickly as possible.

Lanek charged through the bloody waves without a single drop of the altered matter landing upon him. Kechi was controlling blood to slice apart a villager wielding a water Nexi. At the last moment, Kechi turned in time to take his sword and beat aside Lanek's jab to the heart. Lanek stumbled forward, but avoided the swing of Kechi's sword.

"Hand over the Hader!" Kechi screamed. "Hand it over, or I'll kill everyone in this village!"

Lanek swung his rapier at Kechi's neck, but the man blocked the attack, then pushed Lanek back. "You were planning on killing everyone anyways. You have no choice but to die."

A couple villagers rushed for Kechi, who activated his fear Hader to keep them from approaching any further. The courage of most of the remaining villagers in the area had dwindled at this point, and Lanek knew he wasn't going to be able to rely on overpowering Kechi through strength of numbers.

A massive fireball rushed toward Kechi—too fast to even notice until it was already upon him. It was so large, Lanek had to jump back to avoid the edge of the sphere of concentrated Nexi flames. There was an explosion of fire, blood, and bloody flames all about Kechi's location.

Lanek glanced to the shrine entrance, finding Chei lying on the floor, red Nexi stone raised forward. His arm slumped to the ground, the energy fully drained out of him. But before Lanek could go help him, he looked back as the flames slowly dissipated.

Several layers of boiling black liquid oozed to the ground, revealing Kechi in the middle of it all, covered in blood splatters and smoking patches of singed clothes and hair. He had protected himself with all the available blood in the area at the last moment. Breathing heavily, his eyes wide, and struggling a moment to stand, Kechi turned toward Chei and ran.

Lanek lunged toward Kechi and swung his rapier as hard as he could. Kechi blocked Lanek's blade, but lost his sword in the process. Lanek swung again. Kechi dodged, but Lanek kept swinging. As Kechi wearily and narrowly evaded Lanek's attacks, Kechi slipped out one of his knives with his free hands. In one sudden motion, Kechi was forcing the long blade of his knife against Lanek's rapier blade, barely spun in time to block Kechi's sweep.

A villager in front of the shrine readied a bow and arrow, but Kechi directed some of his fear Hader's power toward the aging man, who shakily pointed the arrow toward the ground. A few other villagers were attempting to rush at Kechi again, but also found themselves struggling against the Hader's power. At the very least it was whittling away Kechi's energy, though it surprised Lanek that the man was able to keep fighting in this condition so proficiently.

Lanek fought off Kechi's frantic knife swings, barely able to keep up with the madman's frenzy. Grinning wildly, Kechi began to swing faster, his zeal growing with every swoop of the blade.

"Die! Die! Die! Die!" Kechi yelled with every swing.

Lanek had to keep stepping back to keep from getting overwhelmed by Kechi's unpredictable attacks. Even without the power of the Haders, Kechi was an incredibly talented fighter. He was likely the strongest royal servant the Shire government had, considering the fact he had obtained two Haders.

Someone a ways down the village path sprinted toward Kechi. Lanek could only afford the briefest of glances to notice. Was Kechi's hold over the villagers beginning to wane?

Lanek took heart and countered Kechi's attack with one of his own. Kechi jumped back and turned to face the man rushing toward him from behind. Lanek turned and found Lynx swinging his sword at Kechi's head. Kechi held both Haders toward Lynx, but the fear Hader wasn't stopping the Brotherhood fighter anymore. Had Lynx somehow managed to overcome the artificial fear Kechi had forced upon him? The very thought that somebody could overcome the powers of a Hader through sheer willpower... It was astounding—but also unnerving, considering the source of that uncanny strength. Lanek still intended to take down Lynx as soon as Kechi was dealt with.

Kechi dodged Lynx's swing, then forced several spikes of blood to fling out of the ground in front of Lynx. Though Kechi couldn't fight Lanek with the blood, he could hold Lynx back with it—and at this point, there was plenty of it at his disposal.

Lynx dodged the solidifying strands of blood, while Lanek swung his blade at Kechi—who guarded with his knife. While fighting off Lanek, Kechi formed a wall of blood to keep Lynx back. Lynx hacked away at the blood, chopping off chunks of the shifting formation and splattering blood all about him. The pressure from two fronts was enough to force Kechi to take defensive measures against Lanek, whose anger only boiled stronger by the fact he was needing help from Lynx to get this far.

There was no chance Lanek could let up now. He had to be the one to kill Kechi. He had to be the one to obtain those Haders. If Lynx took them for himself, Lanek wouldn't be able to kill him. Lynx would flee with the power of two Haders, likely using them to further Augurc's experiments with the Elpis.

Lanek pushed against the blade of Kechi's knife as hard as he could, and Kechi stumbled backward. The Shire servant regained control and ran backward, reforming the breaking wall of blood to shift into writhing spikes that swarmed toward Lynx. Lanek leaped forward just as Kechi threw his knife at Lanek's face. There was just enough time for Lanek to reposition his rapier, deflecting the knife and flinging it to the side.

A tendril of blood flew past Lanek's side, but he ignored it and continued to run toward Kechi. Just before Lanek could jab his rapier through the man's chest, Kechi accessed control over a puddle of blood beneath his feet. The blood solidified and pushed him back, giving Kechi the boost he needed to avoid the extent of Lanek's attack.

"Lanek! Look out!" a voice cried out. It was Fenley, still standing on the village path with her brother and his wife.

Lanek turned and found the tendril of blood that had passed him by, now looming above him from a couple meters behind. At the end of the blood strand was a knife—the one Kechi had thrown at him earlier. Lanek leaped to the side just as the tendril of blood threw the knife at him with a speed even greater than that of a fired arrow.

Just as he landed, he found Kechi in front of him, throwing a second knife by hand. Lanek ducked beneath it and leaped toward Kechi, only to find Kechi was already running to the left. Lynx broke his way through the mass of blood Kechi had been controlling. Before Lynx could turn to face him, Kechi was already performing a running jump kick. Kechi hit him square in the stomach, sending Lynx flailing back to the ground several paces away. Lanek ran after Kechi, expecting the man to turn around and attack him—but instead Kechi kept running past Lynx. He wasn't trying to take Lynx down, and he wasn't doing anything to fight Lanek either. Was he trying to escape?

Lanek realized Kechi's plan just as it was too late. Kechi sprinted straight toward Fenley, likely picking her out from the crowds from when Fenley yelled her warning to Lanek. In one swift movement, Kechi punched Fenley's brother and his wife in their faces simultaneously, turned in place as he unclipped a dagger from his arm, and grabbed Fenley's arms while pushing the edge of the dagger against her neck. Other villagers nearby gasped and screamed, and several immediately ran for Kechi.

"Stop!" Kechi yelled, pushing his way back from all the villagers. "One move and she dies! It'll be easy to slit her throat. It'll be easy to kill all of you! But I don't have to, and I don't have to fight *you* anymore, *Lanek*. So stop the fighting and hand over the Hader already." He was doing the same thing Rilv did, but there was no doubt Kechi would be willing to kill his hostage. And this hostage was of direct concern to Lanek personally. There was no way he was going to let Kechi kill Fenley.

Lanek stopped a couple meters in front of Kechi and dropped his rapier to the ground. He had done enough harm to this village already... He couldn't let Fenley die, too. He couldn't let anymore of these villagers die. But he couldn't just hand over the Hader, either. Not to this madman.

"I'm not going to give a countdown like that woman did," Kechi said. "Just toss the Hader to me, and I'll let this girl go. Now."

There was no time to think of a plan. He had to act immediately. Kechi was already pushing the blade a little harder against Fenley's neck. Was he drawing blood?

No. Not Fenley. Not again. Not again!

Not again!

Lanek pulled his arm back to throw the Hader to

Kechi.

Lynx tackled Lanek to the ground before he could release the Hader.

"What are you doing?" Lanek screamed. In a jerk reaction he punched Lynx in the face, slamming his knuckles against the hard mask—much harder and sturdier than Lanek expected.

Blood streaked across Lynx's mask from Lanek's knuckles. Lynx head-butted Lanek, using his mask to inflict significantly more injury on Lanek. The pain only made Lanek angrier, and he shoved Lynx off his body, then proceeded to tackle Lynx and shove him as hard he could into the ground.

Kechi swore, and Lanek glanced to see Kechi shove Fenley to the side and drive his dagger down the length of her right leg. Fenley screamed and fell to the ground, clutching her leg, and Lanek immediately pushed aside Lynx so he could take down Kechi.

The Shire servant used the blood drawn form Fenley's leg to form a lance, which he immediately flung straight at Lanek—with a white Nexi in tow, Lanek realized. Just as the lance of blood passed Lanek by, Kechi activated the white Nexi, creating a blinding flash of light. A moment later, sharp metal slammed into Lanek's side. He fell back, screaming. It was the dagger. It hadn't punctured any vitals, but the agony was excruciating.

*He'll kill Fenley. Just as Lynx killed Suran!*

Lanek pushed himself to his feet, his eyes still adjusting from the light flare, and tore the dagger out from his side. Kechi was running toward him, sliding out the metal rod tied to his leg in the process. Some kind of weapon... At the same time, he heard Lynx approaching. Lanek instinctively reached for his sheath, and remembered he had dropped his rapier to keep Kechi from killing Fenley outright. He had already tossed the dagger aside as well, and there was no time to pick it back up.

Lynx reached Lanek first. The masked man swung his sword at Lanek. He was going for the kill—all pretenses of cooperation had vanished—he wanted the Hader for himself. At the last second, Lanek activated the power of his Hader. Lynx's sword passed straight through Lanek's neck, but Lanek felt nothing.

He had become immaterial.

The next moment, Kechi was approaching Lanek from the other side, swinging his extended pole at Lanek. Knowing his Hader wouldn't work against Kechi, Lanek leaped back, and Kechi's weapon collided with Lynx's. Kechi shoved Lynx back, but Lynx immediately forced his way upon Kechi. Lanek used the opportunity to slip out a red Nexi stone and fire it at Lynx.

Lynx dodged the blast and turned to swing his sword at Lanek. At the same time, Kechi rushed at Lanek.

To avoid Lynx, Lanek leaped into Kechi, slamming his shoulder against Kechi's chest. Kechi tried swinging his rod at Lanek, who grabbed it with his free hand and pointed the end of it toward Lynx, who was running straight at Lanek. Lynx crashed into the pole, coughing up blood, but kept on his feet and swung at Lanek once more. Kechi swung his pole against Lanek, knocking him just out of Lynx's reach.

The pain coursing through Lanek's body was all-consuming, regardless. Lanek wanted to collapse and die, but he couldn't give in—not at this critical of a moment. Not when the two men he wanted to kill most were right here, both trying to obtain the Hader.

Kechi swung his rod at Lynx, who swung his sword at the same time. An explosion accompanied the collision, the fires guided directly against Lynx. Lanek found a red Nexi stone connected to Kechi's weapon, hidden just below where he gripped the metal pole. The man could power a highly-concentrated explosion with each swing, as long as he had the energy for it.

Lynx fell back, gasping as the fire encompassed him. Water covered him nearly a moment later, as Lynx was quick and calm enough to take out a dark blue Nexi stone and douse the flames with it. Kechi was already turning toward Lanek by then. Lanek aimed his fire Nexi at Kechi, but the man was too quick for him. Kechi slammed his pole against Lanek's outstretched arm. An explosion didn't ensue—perhaps he didn't have the energy to do another one so soon—but it was still a metal pole regardless. Lanek stumbled to the side, losing the red Nexi in the process, but at least keeping a hold of the Hader. He stumbled to the ground. His arm didn't feel broken, fortunately—just badly bruised, and left with a large, stinging lump. Lynx was struggling to get back up, and Kechi was already swinging his pole down to Lanek's head.

Lanek rolled to the side, then slipped an ice Nexi out from his pocket. Just as Kechi turned, Lanek released needles of ice from his Nexi stone. Only one managed to hit Kechi, but it sunk straight into his right eye.

Kechi quickly stepped back, screaming. Lynx was suddenly upon Kechi, nearly about to drive his sword through Kechi's chest. At the last moment Kechi forced blood on the ground to erupt at Lynx, shoving him back with another violent push—straight toward Lanek. By then Lanek had pushed himself to his feet, and aimed his light blue Nexi at Lynx. As Lynx fell backward, he turned and swung his sword at Lanek, who decided at the last moment to form a shield of ice. Lynx's attack shattered the ice and knocked Lanek back, and Lynx immediately swung again. Lanek exerted what strength he had to jump back further, barely evading Lynx's swing.

"Die, both of you!" Kechi screamed.

As Lanek stepped further back from Lynx's attacks, he found Kechi had taken out a tan Nexi. The ground beneath Lanek's and Lynx's feet erupted, blowing apart into pieces and sending both of them crashing into opposite directions. Lynx rolled toward Kechi, who was already gathering more blood together into a giant wave behind him. As Lynx struggled back to his feet, the solidifying blood slammed down against him. The partly liquid mass shoved him into the earth, sending him rolling some more. Kechi didn't let up on the attack, however, and continued to shove more hardening blood against Lynx, who was still fighting to escape the trampling.

Lanek fought off his own pain as he fought to get back on his feet. Somehow Kechi still had this much energy at his disposal, even while fighting both him and Lynx. He had to focus on Kechi. He had to kill him quickly.

Despite the exhaustion of the battle, Lanek ran straight for Kechi and exerted all the energy he had on his ice Nexi, releasing as much frozen air as he could muster from the stone.

Kechi screamed at the top of his lungs, his tan Nexi glowing all the more brighter. The ground beneath Lanek's feet erupted, and Lanek leaped from rock to rising rock, forcing himself to keep from falling over. A fountain of partly solidified blood arose around Kechi, lifting him in the air a couple meters, bringing him straight toward Lanek's side. At the last second Lanek managed to turn and direct his ice Nexi energy toward Kechi. The Shire servant instantly caused most his airborne blood to transfer in front of himself, forming a shield. The wall of blood froze, and suddenly Kechi was twisting himself to the side of the shield. He had a small knife in hand, and was already throwing it at Lanek. Lanek let himself stumble over the bursting rocks in order to evade the attack, and crashed into the ground below, pain searing through his entire body.

He had to get back up. Despite the agony, he forced himself to stand—but Kechi was already returning to the ground via the mass of blood he guided himself with. With the tan Nexi in his hand, Kechi caused the earth about Lanek to break apart and weaken, causing his feet to sink into the ground. Hands of dirt formed from the ground around him, and immediately latched on to Lanek's legs before he could escape.

Kechi ran, raising his metal rod toward Lanek, the fire Nexi embedded at the end of it glowing brightly. There was no way Lanek was going to be able to dodge it, and he was too weak to escape the Nexi-strengthened earth gripping his legs. The earth continued to tighten, to the point where he felt the circulation of blood was being cut off below his knees. There was no using the Hader in this situation—the earth binding Lanek was connected to Kechi's tan Nexi, and the Hader couldn't be used against other Hader users. And Lanek didn't even have the energy to use his ice Nexi again.

A few paces away, Kechi readied his swing. Lanek took his ice Nexi and chucked it at Kechi's head as hard as he could.

The stone slammed into Kechi's forehead, and he fell down, screaming. The red Nexi in his weapon was still being powered, so it released a concentrated explosion upon impact with the ground, directly between Kechi and Lanek. The earth binding Lanek broke apart, and he was sent flying back in the furious heat of the fire Nexi blast. At the same time, Kechi was violently scraped backwards across the ground, losing his metal rod in the process. Both Lanek and Kechi had held on to their Haders, and as far as Lanek could tell, they were both still alive, shakily gasping painful liquid breaths.

Kechi was an utterly bloody mess, and Lanek imagined he didn't look much better. The sheer amount of blood involved in this fight was horrific, and it still wasn't over—not until Kechi was dead.

Lanek tried to stand up, but it had turned even more difficult to do so. The blast had battered him severely, and it was hard to tell how much more injured he was at this point. Every fiber of his being was in pain, and just the thought of fighting further was almost unbearable. And yet Lanek fought to stand.

He saw Kechi had lost control over the blood that was beating down Lynx, but the masked man hadn't gotten to his feet yet. Was Lynx dead? Lanek found it unlikely, knowing his luck. He'd have to kill Lynx as soon as Kechi was dealt with. And then... would it all finally be over? He couldn't think about it now. He had to stand up. He had to find a weapon. He had to kill Kechi.

Lanek's vision went blurry, and for a moment he wondered if he had lost consciousness. Something kicked him in the face.

He looked up and found a crimson figure standing in front of him, screaming something. Lanek couldn't make out what he was saying though. The world had turned silent for a few moments. Or had it been minutes?

"...like that?" Kechi screamed. "I'll make you pay ten-fold for these injuries you've given me!"

Blood flew across the air, and Lanek heard villagers screaming. People were running, but they weren't getting far. Lanek's vision and hearing returned, but an overwhelming nausea took its place, and he struggled to keep from throwing up. As he did so, he found villager after villager getting killed by Kechi's Hader-guided blood. There was blood everywhere, and with every villager Kechi killed, more blood became available for his disposal.

An old man was beheaded. Blood writhed from his head, its bladed tentacles slicing apart a young man a few meters away from him.

A tendril of blood wrapped around a small girl's neck, strangling her. Nearby, spikes rose from a puddle of blood beneath a teenage boy, impaling his feet and legs. The boy fell to the ground, impaling himself further on more rising spikes. The blood that burst from his back gathered together and rushed toward an older woman, bludgeoning her in the back of the head.

Thin streams of blood rushed toward a man trying to escape the carnage. The blood flowed straight into his mouth, ears, and nose. Once all of it had entered his body, he fell to his knees and began shaking uncontrollably. Kechi's Hader blood melded with the man's blood, and seconds later, the man blew apart into two halves, separated at the waist. The blood that exploded from within him soared from his body toward two women escaping down the village path. The blood ribbons formed into crimson blades and proceeded to chop off their hands and feet, then slice into their bodies at least a dozen times before finishing them off outright with slices through their necks.

And all the while, Kechi laughed. The blood covering his body vibrated with ecstatic glee. He lived for this torture. This madness. This inhumanity.

Lanek could barely grasp the sheer terror this man was inflicting. Kechi was literally a one-man army, capable of bringing an entire village to its knees with the fear Hader, and then torturing them to death with the blood Hader.

Lanek stood up, but immediately Kechi kicked him in the stomach.

"We're not done yet!" Kechi yelled. "There's still your friend here left. I'd like to deal with her personally! Let me position you in a way so you can get a good view."

Kechi wiped the blood off a nearby Nexi stone, finding it to be a green one. He pointed it at Lanek and caused vines to wrap around Lanek, binding his arms and legs together, and covering his entire body tight. The ends of the vines dug into the ground and lifted Lanek up a bit so he was standing up, staring straight toward Fenley. There was no way for him to move, especially in this weak state, and the only weapon he had on hand was the immaterial Hader. He felt some energy left in him, but he couldn't access the power of the Hader—Kechi's energy was linked to the binding vines of this Nexi stone. All Lanek could do was watch as the monstrous figure of Kechi walked over toward Fenley.

No... Not Fenley. He couldn't let him torture Fenley. He couldn't let Kechi kill her. He wanted to yell out to her—tell her to run. To just forget him. Use all her might to escape this madman.

But there she lay on the bloody earth, crying from the pain and terror her beloved village had suffered. Had all her friends and family members died? Lanek hadn't been in a state to notice who was being killed and who was escaping—if there was anyone escaping.

Kechi's fear Hader glowed a little brighter, and Fenley cowered further, her cries crumbling into barely audible whimpers.

"These weak, pathetic elves!" Kechi screamed. "Strange to think it was the elves who played the central role in creating the Haders! Not that it matters anymore. The world will come to learn the source of the greatest power the world will ever behold—the mind and strength of the royal Shire line, with Mareba Shire the star that will eternally shine brighter than all the rest! And I will forever be his most precious servant!"

Kechi knelt down beside Fenley and lifted her up so she'd lie across Kechi's lap, her back and head resting in Kechi's bloody hands. He still had his two Haders clenched in his hands.

"L... L... Lan...ek..." was all Fenley was able to get out. Whether it was concern for Lanek's safety or a plea for help, it was impossible to tell.

"You poor girl," Kechi said. "You don't need to worry about him... Let me give you something else to focus on!"

Kechi grabbed Fenley's right index finger and wrenched it back, dislocating it. Fenley screamed and writhed in pain—but could only move a little. Kechi kept a tight grip on her, and was still flooding fear into her via the green and black Hader.

"Stop..." Lanek said. It was difficult to say anything more, and he was trying to focus on breaking free of Kechi's vines. He couldn't let Kechi keep hurting Fenley... But it was too difficult to move, let alone fight.

Kechi grabbed Fenley's middle finger and wrenched it back. Fenley screamed louder, but Kechi didn't flinch. He simply smiled and moved on to the next finger. Once he broke her ring finger, he took her pinky and pulled back as hard as he could. One by one, Kechi broke each of Fenley's fingers, and her cries continued to ring more desperately across the silent, bloody village.

"Stop it, Kechi!" Lanek yelled, finding enough strength to at least struggle against the vines. Even if he somehow managed to break free, he had no idea how he'd stop Kechi. "I'll give you the Hader! Just stop!"

Kechi pointed at his still-impaled eye, the icicle dripping with blood. "You make me suffer, and I will make you suffer ten-fold! You can not stop the work of Mareba Shire, any more than you can raise a hand up to stop a waterfall from crashing down on you! Resist and suffer. Resist and perish."

Worms of blood congregated toward Fenley and Kechi from all across the bloody field. Dozens of them squirmed into Fenley's screaming, gagging mouth, while others crawled into her ears, her nose, up her dress, through her blouse, and into her eyes. At the same time, blood covering Kechi's body began to converge toward his free right hand, forming a curved, sickle-like blade.

Above Fenley's muffled cries, Kechi screamed, "As a servant of the one true power, I condemn this village and everyone who walked its grounds this day!" Kechi proceeded to carve a long, deep slice down the length of Fenley's right arm. Blood poured from her wound, forming into jagged spikes that turned and sliced across her arm in all random directions. Kechi then cut her other arm, and the process repeated.

He tore through her skirt and sliced deep into her

thigh, and on down the length of her leg. Blood poured freely—more blood for him to control, more pain for him to inflict. Still grinning, Kechi cut up her other leg, then turned her over onto her side so he could carve into her back.

Lanek screamed, his cries melding with Fenley's torturous anguish and Kechi's glee and laughter.

Suddenly the vines binding Lanek loosened. Something was cutting them from behind. Lanek didn't pause to figure out how he was being freed, or who was freeing him. He simply shoved the vines apart and sprinted toward Kechi. Though Lanek was pushed past the point of exhaustion, he willed himself to run with every fiber of his being.

Kechi's frown immediately disappeared. With the sickle of blood, Kechi quickly slit Fenley's throat and shoved her aside before turning and running away.

"No!" Lanek screamed.

Kechi killed her. He killed Fnely. And now he was running away. Why was he running away?

Kechi stumbled to the ground, his mind at a complete loss at this turn of events. He fell to his hands and knees, just in front of Fenley's limp, bleeding body.

"F... Fenley..." Lanek coughed. "Fenley... Fenley..." He crawled toward her, barely able to breathe. Her body was covered in deep, blood-filled gashes. She wasn't moving at all—not even breathing. Her eyes were filled with blood.

There was nothing left to her but a lifeless, desecrated corpse.

It was too late to save her. She was dead. There was nothing more he could do. She was gone. Lanek had wondered if he'd be able to meet with her again, even if he had to steal the Stone of Truth. Even if he had to betray her village. He still hoped he'd be able to return... To speak with her again. Explain why he had to do the things he did.

But what did any of it matter now? Just like Suran, Fenley was murdered. All because of some powerful Nexi stone. All because he had to get entangled in the world's power struggles. All because this world was filled with deranged killers.

There was blood everywhere. As far as Lanek could see, there was blood. He was covered in blood himself. This wasn't only Kechi's fault. This was his fault too. Tears filled his eyes, but he couldn't bring himself to feel any deep remorse. It was too difficult to feel anything at this point. It was all just too incredulous... As if this had all been some kind of strange, unexplainable nightmare.

But he didn't want this. He didn't want any of this.

Kechi. Rilv. Augurc. Lynx. These terrible people. These terrible, unforgivable people.

There was movement a ways behind Lanek. A

muffled cough, and the metallic ring of a sword shakily sliding into its sheath.

Turning around, Lanek found Lynx standing a couple meters away. He was a bloody mess too, quite possibly at the brink of death. No... Recalling all the injury Lynx sustained in that battle, there was no way Lynx was well-off right now. Of course, Lanek was in terrible condition as well. There was little hope for him to kill Lynx right now.

And besides... it was Lynx that freed him from Kechi's vines, wasn't it? Lanek saw a green Nexi stone in Lynx's hand, and a small knife tied to the end of the vines connected to the stone. After Lynx had been pummeled by Kechi's massive blood attack, Lynx must have somehow found the energy to use a green Nexi and control some vines with a knife tied to the end of them. Lynx cut the vines and freed Lanek, allowing him to try stopping Kechi.

Kechi ended up killing Fenley as he escaped, but had Lynx not helped Lanek... There was probably no way for Lanek to escape on his own. Kechi would have killed him once he was through with torturing Fenley, however long it was he planned on continuing that. Kechi must have run away because he saw little hope in continuing to fight both Lynx and Lanek, both of whom he may have underestimated in regards to perseverance. Kechi may have been very low on energy at that point, and didn't want to risk getting killed by a vengeful, furious Lanek and uncannily persistent Lynx.

So Kechi ran away, likely heading to his own airship, wherever it was. This technically meant Lynx had saved Lanek's life. It was infuriating to think about, but Lanek wasn't going to thank him. Lynx had tried to kill Lanek, after all. And Lynx had only helped him so that there would be two of them to fight against Kechi. Lynx was only concerned with himself. He wanted the Haders for himself. He was as selfish as he was sinister.

Was he going to try to kill Lanek now? Lanek glanced to the ground and found an abandoned knife. He picked it up and clutched it wearily, but Lynx didn't make any attempt to approach Lanek. It was difficult to tell what Lynx was thinking, of course, thanks to that mask. The smiling face was obscured with blood, as was everything else that had stood within twenty meters of Kechi's bloody rampage.

"I'm sorry," Lynx said.

And what did he mean by that? Lanek clenched his weapon tighter. There was no way Lynx was actually apologizing. It made no sense.

"I have trouble controlling myself," Lynx continued. "I need the Haders... More than anything in the world, I need them. All this blood... it triggered these emotions that have been placed in me... I really need the Haders..."

Lanek pocketed his Hader, feeling Lynx's eyes gazing at the movement of his hand. "You're the last person who needs the Haders."

More than anything, Lanek wanted to kill this man. Right here and now.

No... that wasn't true. More than anything, Lanek just wanted Fenley alive again. It was entirely wrong for her to die. If she had never met Lanek, none of this would have happened.

But it was because of people like Lynx that these tragedies kept happening. In fact, Fenley probably wouldn't have died if Lynx hadn't caused a stir in this village in the first place.

An airship was approaching. Lanek recognized the sound before he saw his ship coming. Apparently Kitoh was able to pilot it after all... And apparently Rilv still wanted to make sure they left with this village's Hader. She was coming for him, and there was going to be no way for him to resist. Lanek would have to deal with her somehow, but for now he had to figure out what to do about Lynx. He couldn't just continue this mission with Lynx as if nothing had happened.

A rope ladder lowered from the airship, and Lanek unconsciously grabbed onto it. Why was he grabbing onto it? He couldn't just leave this village now... And yet he was holding onto it. Deep down, he did want to leave. He couldn't bear to gaze at Fenley's corpse any longer. He didn't want to know who had lived and who had died amongst the villagers he had come to know and love this day. Were Fenley's relatives alive? Had Nullen survived? What about Chei? And all the other elves he had spoken with? Perhaps they were all dead now.

Lanek kept his eyes on Lynx. He didn't want Lynx to come aboard the airship too. But he didn't want to leave Lynx behind in this village, either. There were still survivors, and Lanek didn't want Lynx to kill any more of these innocent people.

Lanek started climbing, and he could feel someone climbing up after him. He didn't look down—he didn't want to see Lynx following him, like an insidious shadow.

Somehow Lanek had become part of a league of murderers, and his own airship was its base. And even after witnessing the deaths of dozens of people he cared for, he still had a desire for murder in his own heart. How much better was he than the likes of Lynx or Kechi?

●

Kechi jogged down the steep, rocky hill, cursing between heavy breaths. With his energy nearly expended, he decided it was prudent to get away from the elf and the Brotherhood member who were fighting against him. They were both formidable enemies, each of them somehow capable of fighting well after they were practically pummeled to death.

Perhaps it wouldn't have been difficult to finish them off right then and there, but Kechi couldn't afford to take any risks greater than what was necessary. He had obtained two Haders for his master—all that mattered was that he find at least two more, and bring them back to Lord Mareba Shire.

*I can't die now...* Kechi thought. *Whatever I do, I can't die yet. Once my master has four Haders... Then I can die.*

Once he was well enough away from the village, Kechi let himself sit on the ground, his whole body stinging in agony. This pain was terrible, but he knew he'd survive. This was certainly the worst off he had ever been in after a fight, but all that mattered was that he was still alive, and could continue his mission to find Haders.

*For master, I can keep going. I can keep fighting for master...*

The ice embedded in his eye had melted away, leaving behind a torn, bloody mess. The very fact the elf had managed to impale his eye like that was infuriating. Kechi had been careless. Or perhaps the elf was truly stronger than Kechi, and it was simply fortunate that he was still alive. One thing was certain—he wasn't going to underestimate the elf if they ever met again. Same with the Brotherhood member. Kechi would be sure to kill them both if they stood in the way of his Haders.

It was certainly a possibility. The uniformed woman from the Fiefs government had a Hader, and so did the elf. It seemed they were all working together, along with the Brotherhood member and the eigni boy.

Kechi looked up to the sky, trying his hardest to ignore the pain of all his injuries. His eye stung the worst, enough that he wanted to tear away at it, burn what was left of the useless organ. He would need to find a doctor to deal with it, as the pain would just hinder him in any future fights. With his good eye, Kechi spotted an airship in the distance, flying away from the village. It soon faded into the ghostly clouds, heading southeast. Kechi needed to hurry... The airship would likely be heading to another place where a Hader was located, and Kechi would need to get there before his enemies. Perhaps he could find the Hader there before them, and once they got there, he could use his three Haders to take their two Haders. Then he'd have five... The very thought of using five of the stones filled him with glee. With that much power at his disposal... there wouldn't be anything he wouldn't be able to do for his master.

Kechi's small one-man blimp was hidden further down the hill, tied to some rocks in a small enclave. As he expected, there was nobody there, and there was no sign of anyone tampering with the airship. It was a delicate vehicle, but it was fast. Once Kechi untied the ship and got the engine and appropriate Nexi stones activated, he entered through the hole in the metal floor of the ship and walked into the bridge, which was just large enough for him to sit in and operate the controls with. He didn't need anything else—the time would go by quick enough just by focusing on his mission for Lord Mareba Shire.

Once the ship was airborne, Kechi turned so he

would go in the same direction the enemy airship was heading toward. The Shire Kingdom was in that direction, and it made Kechi wonder if the next Hader was there somewhere. It would be convenient for him, considering his master was there, waiting for him.

His master was expecting to hear good news right now. It was going to be shameful to report that the enemy got away with not one, but two Haders now. Kechi took out a teal Nexi from his pocket and activated its power. He'd have just enough strength to speak to his master for a minute or two, which was all Lord Mareba Shire normally warranted anyways.

"Report, Kechi." Lord Mareba's voice was strong, vigilant. There was never any weakness in his voice, regardless of the man's age. Though Master was in his late fifties, there was no hint of frailty to him—only royal Shire pride. Unlike the quiet void that was Augurc Shire, this was a man whose very presence—whose very voice—commanded obedience and subservience.

"I apologize, Master," Kechi said. "I failed to obtain the Hader in the elf village. The enemy has escaped with it, and they still possess the telekinesis Hader."

"Follow them," Lord Mareba said. "Kill them. Take the two Haders from them. Return to me once you have finished."

"Yes, master," Kechi said.

Lord Mareba didn't say anything more. He was not a man who cared to give reprimands or rousing speeches. He simply gave orders, and expected them to be fulfilled. Kechi knew he had failed—he was filled with an overwhelming guilt for coming up short.

But it was a temporary failure. He could still succeed in the mission. He simply had to do as his master instructed. Kill the enemies. Take their Haders. Return to Master. It was simple. And all Kechi had to do was not die in the process.

It was time to restore the Shire Kingdom to its full glory. Ever since Delkol died and Augurc took his place, the kingdom had been in shambles. With the power of the Haders, Lord Mareba Shire would be able to become ruler over the land, and bring the Shire Kingdom into a new age.

*Lord Mareba Shire... You will soon rule in absolute fear and authority. With the Haders to back you up, nobody will be able to oppose you. Even Augurc with his Elpis, and his experiments, and his Brotherhood—they will all fall before you. All enemies of the Shire Kingdom will fall. The lands of Shire and Fiefs will be reunited once more, with you as the true king with true royal blood flowing through your veins. You shall be a ruler for all to look up to and reverence... for ages to come.*

*I will stop at nothing to acquire all the Haders you need, Master. I am willing to kill for your cause. I am willing to die for your cause. I need nothing more.*

# 7. SILENT REGRETS AND DREAMS

•

It was easier for Borely to readjust to the light than it was for everyone else. Out of the four of them, he had been a vampire for the least amount of time. Though Nivakil was blind, he still shuddered whenever light poked through the trees and reached his skin. And though Analicia hadn't been a vampire much longer than Borely, she was young and had more trouble handling the light, or at least was quicker to complain about it.

They had traveled the forest for about a day now, the city of Istal now far behind them, left in the hands of Augurc, Hidif, and the rest of the Brotherhood and vampire elites who overthrew it. And Areo. Borely couldn't stop thinking of her—how he had finally found her, and how he had been unable to do anything to rescue her. Her fate was worse than he had ever feared. She wasn't just a prisoner in a cage—she was a prisoner in her own body. Augurc's experimentation with the Elpis was likely responsible, and it pained Borely to think that Areo was one of Augurc's enhanced soldiers assisting in the Brotherhood's terrorism. Over the years in Fiefs Kingdom and surrounding territories, there had been many high-scale robberies, delicate assassinations, and precise acts of wanton destruction designed to inspire fear in the corrupt organization. How many of these had Areo been forced to participate in?

And all this time, Borely hadn't been able to leave Istal long enough to find her. To save her from getting so much blood on her hands. It still felt wrong to be leaving Areo behind, but he was finally part of a plan that would lead to freeing her from Augurc and the effects of the Elpis. The royal head servant of the Fiefs Kingdom—Rilv, Borely recalled—communicated with Nivakil via teal Nexi stones, informing them too late about the possibility of an attack on Istal. But fortunately, there was also a plan formulated to put an end to the Brotherhood, and at long last, Borely was going to be able to do something about it. With the fall of Istal, he was able to obtain a Rite Nexi without having to wait many years to go through the Rite, and Nivakil was finally pushed to take action.

The fact he promised to assist Borely and Jenba in rescuing Areo helped persuade him to assist the Fiefs Kingdom in its ambition to obtain materials called Haders. They were apparently powerful Nexi stones crafted for the sake of fighting against the Elpis. Precisely what Borely needed to help bring down Augurc and free Areo.

Borely knew Nivakil, Jenba, and Analicia all had doubts on this mission, and he had to admit to himself that it was going to be very risky, but he wasn't going to let Nivakil and Jenba back down now. Of course, he would have preferred Analicia stay somewhere else while they searched for the Haders, but there were no good places to leave her. Not many people would take in a vampire child, and Jenba felt it safer for her to stick with them, despite the danger they were likely walking into.

After all, they were heading to Limbo, the port city notorious for its piracy. Based on the research of Rilv's operatives and a team of Nexi researchers, one of the Haders was believed to be near Limbo. They somehow were able to tell that the Hader was moving over the sea, implying it was being used by someone who traveled on a boat. And considering how there were so many treasure-hunting pirates that docked in Limbo, it seemed likely some pirate captain had the Hader.

Borely had no qualms with taking down a pirate and apprehending the Hader from him. He had had plenty of experiences with pirates in his life before becoming a vampire. Pirates were generally just thugs that happened to be crew members on a ship. Thieves and despots, just looking for a way to stir up trouble. Whenever they went too far at the pubs Borely had frequented, he was always quick to beat some sense into them. It was going to nice to do that again.

Of course, just being in the light again was going to be nice. He and his companions were traveling through the forest, well past the artificial lighting of Istal and the surrounding area. Now bits of natural light were starting to slip in, and it was making Nivakil, Jenba, and Analicia uncomfortable.

In a physical way it was making Borely feel ill at ease—an unfortunate reminder of what he had become—but in his mind he was pleased to be approaching the daylight sun once more. He had only been in the light on a few occasions the past few years, and each time he came in contact with it, he felt a little more human again. He missed that feeling, and looked forward to getting out of this forest and taking a boat to Limbo. He hadn't been on a boat once since becoming a vampire, nor had he set eyes on the glimmering sea. Just to breathe in that crisp ocean air... Borely couldn't wait. It was going to be like stepping back into his past life. At least a little bit like it.

Everyone traveled in silence for the most part. The previous day was one long series of terrible events, and it was going to take a while for all of it to settle in their minds. They weren't going to be able to return to their homes until the Brotherhood was dealt with, and from what Borely gathered, the Fiefs Kingdom did intend to assist in freeing what was left of Istal from the banished elites. They simply needed to succeed in finding all the Haders, and then they'd have the power necessary to right all the wrongs plaguing the land at the moment.

It all felt very reminiscent to Borely's time with

Terico, Areo, Kitoh, and the others, back when they were searching for the Elpis fragments. Borely would never forget how everything ended with that life-changing adventure, but he felt things would work out better this time.

They had to. After all, how could things get worse than they already had?

•

The next day brought less trees and more light, but Borely was the only one who felt better about it. Granted, it was giving him a headache, and his body shuddered from time to time, but he felt this was progress. They were going somewhere. They were doing something about the Brotherhood, and about Areo.

Thanks to their enhanced hearing ability—particularly Nivakil's—they were able to hide whenever other travelers were approaching. Though Borely and Analicia didn't look too much like vampires yet, Jenba and especially Nivakil exhibited all the physical signs of vampirism quite clearly. Once they reached a town, Borely planned to go buy hooded cloaks for the two of them so they could avoid any trouble with passers-by.

When they were about an hour's walk away from a riverside town, traversing an open field, Nivakil heard quiet footsteps in the distance. There was no good place to hide, so there was nothing to do but travel casually and try not to bring themselves to anyone's attention. Analicia had grown used to the light enough to keep from squinting constantly (though she still complained about it), but Jenba could barely keep his eyes open at all, and Nivakil walked wearily, like a man sick with the flu. Borely hoped they would adjust to the light soon. It wasn't the first time for either of them to be out in the sunlight, after all—they were both there during Delkol's attack on Setar.

The traveler in question soon came into view, walking alone down the grassy trail. A shorter man in his thirties, wearing drab, muted clothes. A drifter, perhaps.

The man stopped in front of Nivakil, who chose to stop a few meters away. Borely and the others stopped as well, and Borely wondered if this meant they had been found out.

"You walk as quietly as Rilv informed me," Nivakil said.

"Figured that'd be the best way to let'cha know I was comin'," the man said, placing his hands in his trouser pockets. He leaned back casually, then leaned to the side, presumably cracking his back.

"She didn't mention an accent though," Nivakil said.

"Best I try to blend in when I can," the man replied. Apparently this was an operative who worked for Rilv, and was described in Rilv's conversation with Nivakil.

The man walked up to Nivakil and handed him an

envelope. "Don't spend it all in one place."

"I'll try to restrain myself," Nivakil said. He was probably the last person Borely would have pegged as an impulse spender, though. Apparently the old vampire had a bit of dry wit to him.

"Good, I'll be goin' then," the operative said.

"Rilv said you'd assist us in acquiring passage to Limbo," Nivakil said.

"An' I have," the operative said. "I'm sure you can handle the rest on your own. 'Sides, I don't really like travelin' with vampires."

Borely couldn't blame him. He watched the operative walk on down the path, nobody breathing another word.

"Let's keep going then," Nivakil said. They resumed their journey, likely none of them quite sure how to feel about the operative, or the mission in general. How much hope was being placed in them right now?

And was it just a begrudging alliance? Borely thought about his situation a little more deeply. He was a vampire now, after all. Most everyone in the world wasn't going to be looking forward to his company anymore.

He looked to Nivakil, Jenba, and Analicia. These were his lone allies right now. Just him and a bunch of vampires. A bunch of *other* vampires.

•

Once at the riverside town, they found an unassuming boat leaving for Limbo that evening. After Borely got cloaks for Jenba and Nivakil, they all boarded the vessel with a few dozen other people. Most of them were humans and elves who worked as merchants, but there were a few people planning to visit towns a ways away from Limbo. It didn't seem anyone intended to stay at the city any longer than they had to, and from what Borely could hear from conversations on deck, there were rumors of more pirate trouble than usual stirring at the port.

There were several guards aboard the ship, which itself was armed with three cannons on each side. It was a decent-sized ship, certainly larger than the one Borely ran. But despite the measures given to the ship in order for it to transfer goods successfully across dangerous waters, the traveling civilians didn't appear to feel entirely safe.

Borely wondered how much was being done to deal with these pirates. Was the Fiefs Kingdom's armed forces spread thin, needing to focus on the greater threat of the Brotherhood at this time?

It was pointless for him to worry about it, at any rate, since he was traveling to Limbo with the *intention* of finding pirates. It was likely that most of them at least knew about the Hader, and chances were good that one of them *had* the Hader. Whatever the stone did, it surely gave that pirate a great advantage over all his enemies.

Once the boat set off, Borely and most of the other civilians took the time to stand outside on deck to enjoy the brisk ocean air. Nivakil, Jenba, and Analicia were quick to go to their reserved room below deck, however, not wanting to be in any amount of light any longer than they had to. It was dark—past twilight—but they were still recovering from the journey beneath the sun, and were anxious to be in as dark an environment as they possibly could.

Borely could hear any conversation he wanted to, he realized. Back in Istal, vampires knew how to hide their voices so distant bystanders couldn't hear them. But these humans and elves didn't know Borely was a vampire—a blessing, considering how most of them would react if they did know. He didn't want to eavesdrop, so he stood by the side of the ship, resting his arms on the wall separating him from the depths of the restless sea. He focused on the sounds of the waves, angry and loud, spraying water toward his face, but never quite reaching him.

In a way, he felt like the waves, never quite able to reach what he wanted. How exactly was he going to save Areo? Rilv and the Fiefs Kingdom at large were just concerned with Augurc and the Brotherhood. And while he also hoped to put an end to their violence and cruelty, he was much more concerned with finding Areo again. Rilv probably just wanted the Haders in order to kill experiments like Areo. Most, if not all, of the royal operatives would be willing to kill Areo in a heartbeat as soon as they had the means to do so. She was an incredibly dangerous weapon now, not to mention a vampire. Borely tried not to think of how much destruction Areo must have caused in her rampage through Istal, her consciousness dulled by the Elpis, and her emotions stirred by the ambitions of the banished vampire elites and the Brotherhood.

Why was he so concerned about Areo though, in the first place?

Borely shut his eyes and thought back to all the time he spent with her. It wasn't like they ever got along that well. She had hidden the fact she was a vampire from the start, but she never sought out his blood or tried to turn him into a vampire.

Well, until he offered his blood to her. And then she did turn him into a vampire.

It was a miserable memory. The battle may have ended in victory for the Fiefs Kingdom, but it ruined Borely's life, as well as Areo's.

Borely certainly hated Augurc for everything he did in that battle, but Borely didn't feel the need to dwell on him. He just wanted to save Areo. She didn't deserve the fate handed to her. Even after what she did to Borely... Even after turning him into the thing he despised most of all.

She knew how much Borely hated vampires. But she turned him into a vampire anyways, perhaps expecting him to hate her for the rest of his life. And she was probably fine with that. She just wanted him to survive. She just wanted him to live.

And Borely was still alive, unable to change what had happened. Had she made the right decision in making him a vampire? Perhaps she wouldn't have been captured by Augurc if she hadn't taken the time and effort to inject her blood into Borely's body. Perhaps it would have been best to just let Borely die.

But everything that happened wasn't going to change.

*I just have to keep reaching*, he thought.

•

Nivakil had payed for a room with four cots, so each of them could sleep comfortably after their draining trip in the sunlight. It wasn't so comfortable for the others, but Borely felt right at home, rocked to sleep by the subtle movements of the ship.

He awoke in the middle of the night, however, when his bed shifted, rolling him from his side to his back. Something brushed up against him.

Borely opened his eyes and turned to find Analicia lying beside him, snug beneath the covers. She tried wrapping an arm around Borely's arm, at which point Borely promptly shoved her aside.

She whimpered, her eyes still closed. It was hard

to tell how awake she was, but she was able to pull the blanket around her tight—a feeble resistance.

Borely pulled the girl out of the blanket and tossed her off his bed. She landed on the floor with a loud thump, then let out a muffled whine.

"Stay in your own bed," Borely muttered.

"I'm cold," Analicia said.

"It's not that cold," Borely said. "Just go to sleep and you'll be fine."

Analicia whimpered.

"Come on," Borely said.

Analicia stood up and balled her hands into little fists. "*You* come on, you stupid pointless useless dumb lazy worthless not even worth calling a vampire totally ridiculous worthless loser!"

"Quiet, you'll wake everyone up," Borely said.

Analicia jumped onto Borely's bed, and flopped her knees down into Borely's stomach. He held back a scream, and took pained breaths as he wearily drooped his head back. Meanwhile Analicia crawled back into the covers, then scrunched her body up near Borely.

He immediately picked her up again and tossed her off the bed.

"Hey!" Analicia cried. "Why are you so mean?"

"I'm trying to sleep, obviously," Borely said. "I can't sleep with *you* lying in my bed!"

"I don't..." Analicia stopped short. She turned away and lay on the floor, gripping her legs up to her chest. She whimpered pathetically, like some kind of kicked puppy.

Borely wasn't going to fall for this charade. He rolled to his side so his back was to the child. All he had to do was ignore her, and she'd grow bored of trying to annoy him. Kids like her just enjoyed getting attention, and always had to be doing something when they were awake. And it wasn't hard for them to be awake and full of energy, even in the middle of the night.

After several minutes, her melodrama finally passed, and Borely felt himself starting to fall back asleep again.

Until his bed shifted, ever so slightly.

Borely sat up and grabbed Analicia before she could slip under the covers again.

He gripped Analicia's arms so he could stare his eyes straight into hers. "Go. To. Bed."

She turned her head away and made a pouting face. "I'm *trying* to."

Borely sighed. "How about you go bother Jenba? Don't you like him better anyways?" He didn't want Jenba to be bothered and woken up, but he couldn't put up with this girl any longer.

"He's not here," Analicia said. "He can't sleep."

Borely looked to Jenba's bed. It was more difficult for him to see in the dark than it was for everyone else, since he was the newest of the vampires. After staring for a few seconds though, Borely could get the sense that Jenba wasn't there—just a disheveled sheet.

Perhaps Jenba was on deck to get some fresh air, or was planning to sleep during the day when everyone else was up. This would make sense, since he wouldn't want to be out in the sun anyways, and didn't want people to find out he was a vampire.

Borely got up and walked out to the hall, then made his way to the stairs leading to the deck. Fortunately, Analicia didn't follow him—if he was lucky, she'd be asleep by the time he got back. And if she fell asleep in his bed, he could just take her bed.

Standing on deck were a few sailors, going about their tasks wearily. There were always things to do to keep a ship running smoothly at all times of the day and night, and Borely understood well enough what these people had to deal with. There would be only more tasks on a boat this size, and the number of people aboard the ship would require a number of people serving as guards in case some kind of trouble erupted.

Standing at the edge of the port side of the ship was Jenba, staring out at the stars reflecting off the waves of the sea. Borely stood beside him and asked how he was doing.

"Decided I could just sleep in the daytime," Jenba said.

"Don't want to be wearied by the sunlight?" Borely asked.

"Don't feel I deserve to be in the sunlight," Jenba responded.

Borely kept his eyes out on the sea and tried to imagine what was going through Jenba's head. The Rite didn't go well for him. It was admittedly likely Jenba would have been killed had Augurc not used that moment to attack the arena, while everyone's attention was on the fight. The Rite was something Jenba had worked hard toward for many years, and to fail after giving his all for such a long time... It had to be a grievous pain, and it wasn't something that was going to go away any time soon.

The fact that Jenba had failed the Rite and yet was still alive had to be disconcerting as well. Failing the Rite was supposed to entail death—Jenba probably felt like he "got off easy." On top of this, he ended up gaining a Rite Nexi, despite his failure. As long as Jenba had this Rite Nexi, he would be constantly reminded of his failure.

"Don't look at it that way," Borely said. "Everyone deserves to be in the sunlight."

"I've been a vampire a long time, Borely," Jenba said. "And I've accepted all the practices in Istal over the years. I can't just change my feelings overnight. I lost the Rite, but here I am... still living, still breathing. I shouldn't be. I should be dead. I failed myself, and my master."

Borely frowned and turned to Jenba, who kept his eyes on the waters. "Technically you didn't lose the fight. The Rite was cut short by that little invasion. The one you helped fight off, you might recall."

"I hardly contributed anything," Jenba said. "And in the end, the city fell into the hands of our enemies. I'm not strong enough of a vampire to ever play a significant role in these sorts of things. I probably never will be, despite all my best efforts."

Borely shook Jenba by the shoulder to get Jenba to glance at him. "Hey. You know that's not true. If you're going to be comparing yourself to vampires like Nivakil, then of course you'll feel incompetent. But that hardly matters—you're a lot stronger than you think. You wouldn't be as strong as you are today without all those years of hard work, after all. And if you remember, you did help out in the invasion. If you hadn't been there, I might have died, and so might have Analicia. I wouldn't call that 'hardly contributing anything.'"

Jenba closed his eyes and sighed. "I just wish...

none of this had happened."

"Same here," Borely said. "But some good will come of this. In the end, we're going to save Areo."

Jenba opened his eyes. "I hope so..." He didn't look like he believed this mission would lead to such a result. Of course, Borely wasn't certain himself if it would. He just had to hope it would.

They looked back out at the dark waters again. Borely's thoughts wandered from Jenba to Areo, and then to vampires in general, and how Borely had become a vampire. He didn't ask to become one, but he couldn't change what he was now. He needed to work as hard as Jenba, and become as strong as he could in order to save Areo. How was Borely ever going to be able to defend against Areo, when she had the power of the Elpis on her side?

"How long have you been a vampire, Jenba?" Borely asked. He was curious to know how long it took Jenba to be ready enough to participate in the Rite.

"Over forty years," Jenba said. "I hibernated on a few occasions, though not nearly as long as Areo had, of course. I've been alive as a vampire for about fifteen years."

"And you became a vampire some time in your forties?" Borely asked.

"I was thirty-nine," Jenba said. He didn't say

anything more.

Borely realized he had never found out the circumstances behind Jenba's transformation into a vampire. "Were you attacked?"

"No," Jenba said. "I was the one who wanted to attack."

"What do you mean?"

Jenba gripped the railing and pursed his lips. Perhaps it was wrong of Borely to ask a question like this, but he wanted to know more about Jenba. Maybe he'd be able to help Jenba out better if he knew what Jenba had gone through in becoming a vampire.

"When I was human, I was a farmhand in the countryside," Jenba said. "I lived a simple life. Had a wife, a son, and twin daughters. One day they were all killed."

Borely had never guessed any of this from Jenba—the man certainly never hinted at any of these things before. He wanted to ask how this happened, but he wasn't going to push Jenba to give any more details than the man wanted to.

Jenba shook his head. "It's not something I try to dwell on. It all happened in a past life, you know? And yet I can remember it all so vividly. I return home and find them all dead, blood everywhere. My entire world, gone. No warning whatsoever."

He looked to Borely for a moment. "You think it was vampires who did it?"

"It crossed my mind," Borely said.

"At the time, it crossed my mind, too," Jenba said. "There were rumors of vampires lurking in the forest, so I went straight there that very night, armed with stakes and knives. In the end I found four vampires, but I was no match for them. They beat me down and took my weapons away without me even landing a scratch on them."

"And they turned you into a vampire?" Borely asked.

"No, they told me to go home," Jenba said. "It turned out they were in the forest hunting monsters, and were searching for one in particular—a creature that could take the form of a human, or any other being. They discerned with their vampiric senses that the monster had taken my form, and went to my home on the outskirts of town while I was away. It killed my wife and children, its power strengthened with every gleeful murder."

"The vampires wanted to hunt this monster?"

"This monster's blood was very powerful," Jenba explained. "And they didn't want more innocents getting killed by it. These were vampires much more charitable than I had ever heard from the stories."

Of course, Borely knew at this point that there

were good vampires in the world, but he didn't expect this story to turn out like this. It didn't seem to make sense, considering the end result was Jenba turning into a vampire, presumably.

Jenba continued. "I asked the vampires to let me help them on this hunt. I wasn't going to just sit at home—not when this monster was still lurking in the forest, the blood of all my loved ones on its hands. Seeing how strong these vampires were, I sought their power in order to kill the monster. They were reluctant to inject any of their blood into me, since those who lack the will can die in the process, and there's always a chance the body will reject the foreign energy and go insane.

"But I persisted, and they relented, deciding they'd stand a better chance against the creature with a fifth vampire assisting. One of them bit my neck, and I received the blood that turned me into a vampire... It was painful, excruciating. But it was all worth it. I helped the vampires track down the monster, and we killed it. I had my revenge, and I vowed to become as strong as I could in order to keep others from suffering the same fate I had. Deep down, I never wished to be a vampire—but I needed that power. Without strength, I'm hopeless, and people suffer because of my inadequacies. And that's why I keep pushing myself.

And that's why I can't accept this failure of mine. The Rite was my chance to prove I had grown all these years—that I was finally capable of being the kind of vampire who could help other people. Save them from the evils of this world. And yet I've continued to fail. I couldn't protect Areo at the battle in Setar five years ago. All I did was get in the way. And now, I shouldn't even be alive, considering how much more powerful my opponent in the Rite was. I don't see how I'll be able to help save Areo in this state."

"Just keep working at it," Borely said. "Just keep struggling, keep fighting. You'll improve."

"Those words ring a little hollow from you, to be honest," Jenba said. "You're always reluctant to use your vampiric abilities."

"I use them when I must," Borely said. "I just prefer to rely on my own strength as much as I can."

"Your vampiric strength is your strength now, though," Jenba said. "One day you'll have to take Nivakil's advice to heart, and accept everything about yourself as a fighter, including your vampiric nature."

Borely didn't want to go down this road in his conversation with Jenba. He already knew all this—he just didn't want to give in to his vampire side. It was a difficult truth to swallow, even after five years, and he didn't want to be accepting of something so terrible.

"What about Nivakil?" Borely asked. "He's clearly one of the most powerful vampires there is. But there had to be a time when he became one. Some time in his fifties, it seems."

He became a vampire when he was fifty-five," Jenba said. "He's been one for over 140 years now, though again, he hibernated for some of that time."

"Do you know how he became a vampire?"

"He's never given me many details. All I know is that one day he was attacked by one, and that he had to struggle for several years in order to maintain his sanity. It was a long, hard road for him, getting to the point he's at today."

Borely doubted Nivakil would tell him any details, considering how not even Jenba had been told much. The old master was the kind of man who would tell of such things when he was good and ready to do so—which Borely supposed may not be any time soon, if ever.

"I guess everyone has had to adjust to becoming a vampire," Borely said. "I'm glad I didn't go insane, at least. I was... definitely afraid of suffering my brother's fate." He had told Jenba and Nivakil about the fateful day his brother was turned into a vampire, and how his parents were subsequently killed by his brother.

"It seems to be random, who is able to complete the transformation soundly, and who isn't," Jenba said. "And though it's possible to overcome the insanity, the intensity of the condition can vary. Your brother may have suffered a severe case of it... There was probably nothing you or anyone could have done."

"There was no reasoning with him whatsoever,"

Borely said. "He was... no longer himself. It all reminds me somewhat of Areo, actually."

There was a long silence. Borely hadn't made the connection before, but the analogy felt apt. How was Borely going to be able to free Areo's mind? Perhaps it was impossible—just as impossible as it would have been for him to save his brother.

Perhaps he was going to have to kill Areo, the same way he had to kill his brother.

"I know what you're thinking," Jenba said. "It may not have to end that way. Perhaps the Hader will be the key to freeing Areo's mind. We still have time to save her."

Borely thought over what that was going to be like. He hadn't given much thought to what he would need to do if he did somehow manage to rescue Areo from the Brotherhood, and restore her mind back to normal. Would Areo remember all the atrocities she unwittingly brought to pass? She would likely blame herself for everything— and what would Borely do then? What would he say, and what would he do for her? He wasn't even quite sure how he felt about her.

"Yeah..." Borely said. "Time isn't really the issue, though. It's more a matter of power right now. I don't think any of us can stand up to Areo at the moment."

"No," Jenba admitted. "We'll probably need the Haders in order to stand up to the Elpis, regardless of the kingdom's plans."

•

Leaving Jenba on deck, Borely walked back down to the room he and the others were staying at. Analicia was sleeping in his bed, her face tense, and her body squirming at times, as if reacting from a nightmare. Borely had to wonder if she was actually afraid. It made sense... She was still just a kid, and had just witnessed a massacre. She probably cared for Istal a lot more than Borely did, and was still recovering from the fact it had been overrun and taken over by despots. She didn't even know if any of her friends were still alive. And now she was on a boat, hardly even understanding where they were going. She probably had never been on a boat before. Everything that was happening had to be strange and unfamiliar to her.

Borely sat on Analicia's abandoned bed. He had felt it a bad idea to bring the child along—she was probably just going to get in the way of the mission. But what were they supposed to do with her? He needed to just accept that she was going to be involved from here on out.

He turned to Nivakil, who continued to sleep silently in the bed furthest away. All these years, Borely had never gotten along very well with the mentor. Nivakil always came off as a grumpy old man to Borely, too different to ever understand him. But the old man did know what it was like to turn from a human to a vampire, and even went through a period on the brink of insanity.

Nivakil's transition had to have been much worse than Borely's, at least in some ways.

And the fact was, the old master did know what he was talking about. Borely's skills as a vampire had potential, and he could feel deep down there was much more he was capable of if he didn't hold back whatsoever.

If he was going to save Areo, he was going to have to rely on every power he could obtain, be it the power of his fists, his Nexi stones, his vampiric abilities, or the Haders. He could take these strengths and make them his own, and simply leave out everything bad associated with them. He knew he could use his vampiric powers without becoming a bloodthirsty madman. He just had to take things a step further.

*I'll use all my strength to find the Hader*, Borely thought. *And then I will use that power to defeat and rescue Areo. And then... I'll find something else—some other strength or power— to restore your mind and soul.*

•

Day and night passed, and it was the middle of the next day by the time the ship reached Limbo. The city looked a lot like how Borely's companions felt—tired, beaten down, and just a mess in general. Borely, however, was excited to be in such a large port town. His ventures as a sailor never led him to Limbo very often, which was probably for the best, considering all the rumors he heard of pirates ransacking the goods of merchants. He had never had any really big trouble each time he passed through Limbo, so the rumors were likely exaggerated for the most part. But that didn't change the fact there was some piracy, and likely a number of big-name pirates who lurked in the region. The hope was that they'd find out about the one who had the Hader, be it Yeaf or some other pirate.

Of course, Borely had heard stories of Yeaf over the years. Descriptions of his appearance varied greatly, so there was no certainty even of how he looked. Even his personality seemed to change from story to story—some said he was as quiet and serious as a vengeful ghost, while others said he was as loud and wild as a raving lunatic. And then there were so many stories of his wicked deeds, it seemed he had stolen every valuable good on the continent's northern shores.

Nivakil and Jenba decided their best course of action was to start prying for information at some of the local inns and taverns, though Borely was pretty sure they mainly just wanted to get out of the sun as best they could. They wore their hooded cloaks for now, and fortunately they didn't stick out at all in this city. There were all kinds of people on the streets of Limbo, many of them poor, many of them sick, and many of them maimed in some form or another.

It was a crowded, noisy city, its docks filled with creaky boats, and its dusty streets filled with half-broken tables covered with half-broken wares. Borely's companions all seemed flustered by the crowds, but Borely found it all rather exciting.

Nivakil decided they could split up in order to get more information on the whereabouts of Limbo's most feared pirates. He'd go down one street with Jenba, while Borely would go down another with Analicia. After deciding on a time and place for them to meet back together, Borely put a hand on Analicia's back to guide her in front of him. He was going to have to keep an eye on her now, unfortunately.

As they walked down the road, Analicia asked questions about every little thing they passed by. Apparently this was her first time in a really large city. And since Istal was so much better organized and much more ancient-feeling than Limbo, everything on these jostling streets was new and intriguing to her. Borely was glad all the sights and sounds were taking her mind off her fears, but it was getting a bit tedious, putting up with all her questions. *What's that? What's that do? Why are they yelling? How much does that cost? How come they're walking so slowly? Do people actually live in that? Why are they dressed so strangely?*

They eventually found a good tavern, which brought a wave of memories crashing into Borely's mind. He always went to a pub each time he docked at a new port, and enjoyed scoping out the cities and towns in order to find the most interesting-looking ones. It was always fun to just relax, have a good drink, and play a few games with sailors like him, who were also in the mood for some new company after a long voyage.

He wasn't going to be able to enjoy any of those things now, though. He didn't have enough money to gamble with, or the time for any games. And since he was a vampire, he couldn't even enjoy any of the establishment's drinks anymore—though even if he could, this wasn't the time to get drunk. Not when he needed to find some critical information from potentially dangerous people, and not when he needed to keep an eye on Analicia. It probably wasn't a good idea to be bringing her into places like this, but things wouldn't be so bad in the daytime.

After chatting with some people in the bar, Borely got a few more vague stories about some pirates in the area, but nothing concrete about where any of them were, or when some may be coming to port.

They went to a couple more taverns, and Borely was able to learn a bit more about Yeaf. A slick, twisted man who preyed on the weak, and killed everyone he ever met. An exaggeration obviously, but it fit with the general description of a heartless criminal.

After speaking with some more people on the street, Borely was able to glean a few more stories about Yeaf and some of the other pirates in the area. Most hadn't been heard from in some time—it was only Yeaf who seemed to be making any headway in this region lately.

The sun was beginning to set by the time he found another pub—this one with many more people than the others he had visited. He was getting a little exhausted from the sunlight by this point, and for a little while had to carry Analicia to keep her going. She was very bored with this information gathering, and had to keep pestering Borely in little ways in order to entertain herself. It was getting very annoying putting up with her, but Borely forced himself to keep focused on the task at hand.

After speaking to several people in the pub, he caught wind of a few rumors of Yeaf returning to port that night. A few of the sailors looked genuinely worried, while a few others waved off the comments as groundless worries. The rest were already too drunk to really grasp what everyone was discussing.

"I think we're done," Borely told Analicia. He didn't want her to be in the restless bar any longer, and it was about time to meet back up with Nivakil and Jenba anyways.

Once they gathered back together, they shared all the information they learned.

"Yeaf is returning to Limbo in the dead of the night," Nivakil said. "It was the only specific detail I could get consistently. The sailors don't seem to have any other pirate captains worth talking about these days—most of the rest have been dealt with by government forces, apparently."

"That simplifies matters then," Borely said. "But it means we need to act right away if he'll be riding these waters tonight. Should we wait for Yeaf to arrive at the dock?"

"His ship might not actually come to port," Nivakil said. "If he's planning a heist, he won't come barging in when there are everyday people who seem to know of his presence in the area. Some of his crew will be sent in smaller boats, most likely. And we don't have a consistent description of Yeaf to go by, though I imagine he won't come to land at all. If there are no solid details about him, it means he's a secretive man, and his crew has been trained to spread a variety of conflicting tales about him. We'll have to tread carefully."

"The port is at the inside end of a long inlet," Borely said. "If his ship is to come in sight of Limbo at all, he will have to enter the inlet. If we go out in a small boat with some decent-looking goods, he may pause to confiscate our wares."

"Several sailors specifically said Yeaf preys on the weak," Jenba said. "A boat with only a few people manning it would look like an easy target."

"They would have to be goods worth his time to take, though," Nivakil said. "I suggest Borely command a small boat, while the rest of us hide in some of the barrels. Once the barrels are brought on board, we can take down Yeaf and find out if he has the Hader in question."

"You believe he has it then?" Borely asked.

"It seems likely," Nivakil said. "According to Rilv, the Hader's location is always drifting over the seas, so it has to be on a ship. It would make sense that a valuable treasure would end up in a pirate's hands, and that the Hader could be used to make said pirate very powerful. The reason Yeaf is the only pirate left in the area worth talking about may be largely because he has used the Hader to take down all of his competition."

"Makes sense," Jenba said. "So we'll all be on a small boat tonight. What will happen to Borely when Yeaf's crew steals the goods?"

"Yeaf may make Borely a slave on his ship," Nivakil said. "Or, he may simply kill Borely."

"Neither of those are very healthy options," Borely said.

"Don't worry," Nivakil said. "The better option of course is to make yourself look valuable—perhaps with your skills as a sailor—so that you'll be made a slave. When the time is right, we'll rescue you, and we'll escape the crew by taking back our boat. Or we may just kill the whole crew. They're pirates, after all."

"But what if he decides to just run me through with a blade?" Borely asked.

"You're a vampire," Nivakil said. "Just avoid a fatal blow to the heart, and you'll be fine. You can let yourself fall into the ocean, and drink a vial of blood to recover from any injuries Yeaf deals you."

It sounded very risky, but Borely wasn't about to

turn the plan down. There were a hundred things that could go wrong with it, but now was the time to act. If bringing down this pirate captain would yield him a Hader, he was going to go through with the plan, despite any of the dangers. This power could very well be just what he'd need in order to save Areo.

"Okay, let's do it then."

•

Fortunately Nivakil was given more than enough money to buy a small boat and enough goods to fill up a dozen barrels. Three of them weren't filled up all the way however, in order to leave room for Nivakil, Jenba, and Analicia to hide in. The plan was to try to get Nivakil and Jenba near Yeaf enough for them to take him down before the rest of the crew could do anything. Chances were a large fight would escalate, but Borely was confident he and Nivakil and Jenba would be able to deal with a bunch of thugs, especially after startling them with the death of their infamous captain.

The plan was to just have Analicia stay in her barrel, which she was fine with, since it would be nice and dark inside. There was no reason for her to get involved in the danger that would escalate on the pirate deck. Borely left his fighting gloves and metal headpiece with Analicia, not wanting the pirates to take them away from him. To make himself look at least a little armed though, Borely had a fire and water Nexi on his person—which he would be fine with giving up following the pirate ambush.

The barrels were filled with trinkets that looked valuable, and would prove of interest to any pirate captain. However, Nivakil made a point of placing all the goods in very ordinary food barrels, not wanting Yeaf or any of the other pirates to suspect this was a trap. If they made it blatantly obvious that a single man was transporting valuable goods across dangerous waters, it would easily give away their plan to take Yeaf by surprise. Nivakil, Jenba, and Analicia each used an inner circle of wood to keep themselves hidden beneath the pile of goods above them, so anyone opening the barrels and rummaging inside a bit wouldn't see them.

Once preparations were completed, Borely checked on each of his companions to make sure they'd be all right in case they had to be stuck in the barrels all night. They each gave a muffled okay, so Borely went ahead and launched the ship out to sea.

It didn't take long for Borely to reach the point Nivakil wanted him to guide the boat to. It was an ideal spot to watch from, but as the hours passed, Borely found himself increasingly tired. Only one ship passed by the entire time, and it was just a little one. There weren't going to be many boats leaving and entering at night, especially with talk of pirate activity in the area. Borely walked from point to point on the boat, gazing out at the thousands of waves bobbing up and down in every direction around him. There was a chance the pirate ship wouldn't come at all—rumors were nothing more than rumors, after all. But Borely really wanted to find this Yeaf character right away.

The sooner Borely got the Hader, the sooner he'd have the means to save Areo.

But in the back of his head, there was doubt. Even if he did succeed in defeating this dangerous pirate, and even if he did obtain a Hader—that didn't mean the stone's power would actually be useful in rescuing Areo. There was very little chance everything would work out as smoothly as he hoped.

Even this plan was filled with unpredictable factors. At any given moment, it could all go falling apart, and Borely could very well die. He felt capable of taking down any regular pirate—but he had no idea how powerful Yeaf could be with the Hader. Plus he and Nivakil, Jenba, and Analicia were all walking straight into enemy territory. What if Yeaf's Hader allowed him to see through their plan?

Borely focused on a speck in the far distance. Perhaps it was just some bigger waves...

*No, this is a ship approaching*, Borely realized. *And a big one.*

He hurried back to the ship wheel and maneuvered the small vessel so that it looked like his boat was leaving the inlet, just as any boat normally would. If this was the pirate ship in question, he couldn't let it look like he was just sitting there, waiting for them.

The ship flew across the water, heading straight for Borely. This was most certainly a course to intercept—

and though the ship looked very plain and ordinary, it had to be the pirate ship Borely was waiting for. He felt both nervous and excited—but mostly excited. This was his chance to finally get things moving for the mission to free Areo. He wasn't going to lose to a bunch of pirates.

As the large, tall ship loomed closer, several rowboats lowered from the closer side of the ship, each filled with three or four men. With his vampiric eyes, Borely was able to see their weapons—crossbows, Nexi stones, and swords. Once they came closer, within a normal human's sight, Borely made a point of panicking, and attempted to maneuver his boat away from the approaching pirates. As Nivakil suggested, he made a good effort of it, in hopes of getting the pirate captain to notice his seafaring skills.

Several times the shouting pirates attempted to surround him, but each time Borely made quick decisions at the helm and guided his boat through each narrow opening he could find. The pirate ship the rowboats came from had formed a wall in front of where Borely was headed, however, and though he could have kept up the struggle had he wished, he decided to give in to the pirates. He raised his hands in the air to surrender, and the capturing rowboats were quick to surround him close enough for some of the pirates to board his vessel.

The pirates didn't cheer or make a show of anything—this was simply business as usual for them. A couple of them shoved Borely to the ground and confiscated his red and light blue Nexi stones, while a few others began looking through some of the barrels.

"Rich merchant here," one of them said—a bald man in his twenties. "The captain will like this haul."

The ship brought down a series of ropes and nets to help the boarding party bring the barrels up to the deck. Once Borely's hands were tied behind his back, he too was brought up, along with each of the pirate rowboats. Borely's new boat was brought up as well—easily able fit on the giant deck of the pirate ship.

The pirates were rough with Borely bringing him up, and some suggested they just kill him here and now. A couple others voiced that the captain would be able to use Borely, however, so nobody made a move to end his life. None of them seemed to think he was a vampire yet either, and fortunately Nivakil, Jenba, and Analicia were all silent when they were brought up to the ship in their barrels.

All was going according to plan. All Borely had to do now was ascertain who on the deck was the captain, and hope that it would be Yeaf. And hope that Yeaf would reveal where his Hader was. Presumably it would be on his person, but this wasn't something Borely could count on as a certainty. And there was no way Borely could even be sure if Yeaf had the Hader. Or even if the Hader would help him achieve his goals. Or even if he would make it off this pirate ship alive.

Borely walked between two pirates onto the deck,

jabbed forward with a lot more force than he thought necessary. The men liked to make a point that there was no way out of this situation, and continually mocked Borely for being so foolish to man a small boat by himself at Limbo, of all places. Borely didn't argue with them—he'd be able to tear them apart the moment it was time to make his move. He just had to get the captain near the barrels.

The pirates guided Borely to a man hanging from a mast pole upside-down by rope, dangling a meter or so above deck. His feet were tied together, and he lurched slowly back and forth, his arms hanging limp toward the floor. He looked to be in his thirties, had short black hair, and was dressed quite nicely—almost like a seafaring aristocrat. Long black boots, purple trousers, a collared shirt, and a belted red jacket, all of which was lined with silver ornamentation. It was quite a different look from the rest of the crew, most of which were rough men dressed in shabby cloth and leather accessories.

The man glanced over at Borely and grinned, his smile looking like a twisted frown from Borely's point of view. The two pirates brought Borely right up to him, so the man's upside-down face was about a meter in front of Borely's.

"They say you've got a knack for handling a ship," the man said.

"I've been a sailor ever since I was a child," Borely said. He imagined this man was the captain, but why was he hanging upside-down?

"That's wonderful," the man said. "This ship is your new home then. Keep yourself useful to me, and I'll let you live."

A sword appeared in Yeaf's hand, the tip of the blade suddenly against Borely's neck. He flinched, but the pirates to either side of him kept him from stepping back. Borely held his breath. Where did the sword come from? It just appeared out of nowhere...

"What's your name, by the way?" the man asked.

"Rengel," Borely said, using his brother's name.

"I'm Yeaf," the man said. "You may have heard of me."

Borely chose not to respond, not wanting to reveal any fear in this situation. He simply waited for Yeaf to lift the blade from his neck. Was it the power of the Hader that allowed Yeaf to create this sword out of thin air? One moment Yeaf's hand was empty, the next moment he was holding a sword against Borely's neck. How was Borely going to deal with an opponent with that sort of power?

"Let me assure you one thing," Yeaf said. "If you ever try to leave this ship, you will be killed. In fact, if there is even an inkling of a possibility of any kind of trouble, I'll kill you."

Yeaf swung back his sword, making Borely flinch from the suddenness of the pirate captain's movement. With one swift swing of his long thin blade, Yeaf cut the rope tied to his feet. The man was quick to grab the cut end of the rope—and Borely had to blink and stare a moment to realize Yeaf grabbed the rope with the hand that had been holding the hilt of the sword... which was now gone. Vanished right before Borely's eyes. Yeaf let his feet down so he was hanging from the rope right-side up, then let himself drop onto the deck.

The man's smile faded and he untied the rope around his feet so he could walk freely. He looked over to the barrels on the other side of the deck—too far away for Nivakil and Jenba to make their surprise attack.

"I can help any way you wish," Borely said. "I can start by showing you the value in all my wares, and suggest good places where you could sell some of the items."

"Good idea," Yeaf said. "But first things first. I can never be too careful these days, considering how every operative in the kingdom wants me dead."

Yeaf raised a hand toward the barrels, and suddenly a shining purple Nexi appeared in his fist. Without any warning, all of the barrels burst apart in a blast of purple energy.

Borely gritted his teeth—Yeaf was apparently paranoid enough to blast apart the wares to check for traps.

Nivakil, Jenba, and Analicia all fell out from their hiding places, battered by the wave of purple Nexi energy targeted directly at the barrels. Pieces of wood and metal trinkets crashed about their battered frames. In one moment, the element of surprise was entirely lost, and the fighting force nullified by the painful attack of the powerful Nexi stone.

"Huh," Yeaf sighed. He spun around and swung his arm straight toward Borely's face.

The purple Nexi stone in his hand vanished, instantly replaced by a giant axe.

●

# 8. CRIMSON TIDES

Borely elongated his claws to about a half-meter long, instantly tearing through the ropes that bound his hands. As the axe descended for his face, Borely lunged forward and flung his claws at the long pole of the axe, slicing straight through it. Yeaf immediately leaped backward, stunned by Borely's inhuman reflexes.

"Vampires!" Yeaf yelled. "Kill them all!"

All the men on deck drew weapons, some of them rushing toward where Nivakil, Jenba, and Analicia lay, the rest coming to assist Yeaf against Borely.

Borely swung his claws toward Yeaf, elongating them a little further to try to take him by surprise. Yeaf leaped back again as a thick shield appeared in his hand. The captain held it so Borely's claws deflected off it, rather than slicing through it.

The two pirates who had kept Borely in check each drew weapons, but Borely had to keep his focus on Yeaf—the man's shield disappeared, only to be replaced by an ice Nexi. A long, thin icicle lurched out of the stone. Borely sliced it apart with his claws, then had to turn to the nearer of the other two pirates. With only a moment to catch the attack, Borely deflected the pirate's sword with his claws. The second man used the opportunity to run at Borely with two daggers. Borely pushed back the first pirate, turned, and flicked away both daggers from the second pirate. Yeaf lunged at Borely with a lance, which Borely had to dive away from.

Borely rolled down the deck and once back on his feet, glanced over to his companions. Jenba was on his feet, tearing apart one pirate with his right hand's claws, while shooting off a violent cloud of dust with an earth Nexi in his left hand, slowing down a few other pirates. Nivakil was struggling to get up—the old master apparently got the brunt of Yeaf's random attack with the purple Nexi. There was blood all over his chest and stomach... Fortunately Analicia didn't appear too injured, save for some bad scrapes and bruises. She had run off, carrying Borely's weapons.

Nivakil needed blood, and fortunately there was some on the deck from the shattered vials he and Jenba had brought. Once Nivakil was healed, this fight would get back under control.

"Freeze the blood!" Yeaf yelled to his crew, immediately realizing what Nivakil was about to do. The pirates acted quickly—several pulled out ice Nexi at once, and Nivakil and Jenba had to jump out of the way to avoid getting frozen. The blood-stained portions of the deck turned to ice, and the pirates kept after the two to keep them occupied, to keep them from finding a way to heal and rejuvenate themselves with any blood. Nivakil was on his feet now, but hunched over, his hand clasped over his wounded torso.

Borely turned back to Yeaf, who had a pirate to his left and another to his right. There were three other pirates approaching from the stairs leading from below deck, and then two more a ways down the deck, raising Nexi stones for some long-distance attacks. Borely glimpsed Analicia hurrying across from the opposite direction, but it was too late to wait a moment longer. He ducked beneath a blast of water, leaped forward, hacked his way through a series of vines, stepped to the side of a thrown dagger, then sprinted at the nearest pirate. The bearded man raised his sword a second too late—Borely ran his claws through the pirate's neck, beheading him.

Borely didn't stop. A second pirate was already swinging a sword at his back, and a brief glimpse showed this blade was powered by an orange Nexi. Only needing to hear the attack, Borely leaned to the side, kept his balance as the blade passed him by, then leaned back in to jab his claws through the man's chest.

A massive weapon swung toward Borely. He

leaped over it, discovering it was a ridiculously long poleaxe. It was swung by Yeaf, keeping a safe distance away from Borely. The weapon disappeared the moment it passed Borely by, only to be replaced by a brown Nexi. A large burst of swamp material flew at him, and Borely had to really push himself to avoid the entirety of the attack. The moment he escaped, an arrow flew straight for his face. He tilted his head just in time to avoid it, and wished he had his headband so he could blast the pirate away with its dark blue Nexi.

There were too many pirates to deal with all at once, and for the most part they all seemed to be competent fighters. These were the best of the best, Borely realized. The men Yeaf deemed worthy to live on his ship. And Yeaf was right there with them, using the abnormal power of the Hader to utilize virtually any weapon he wanted, whenever he wanted.

Borely knew he wouldn't be able to take down Yeaf while there were all these other pirates to deal with at the same time. He had to thin out their ranks a bit if he wanted to stand a chance against a Hader-user. Range was his greatest weakness at the moment—he had to deal with the pirate wielding a crossbow first. Borely sprinted toward the man, startling the pirate as he was readying his next shot. Another pirate got in the way with a sword, but Borely was too quick for his attack. In one swoop, Borely ripped a hole through the first pirate's side, then continued the lunge into the second pirate's neck. Borely turned, slicing the man's head off.

Another pirate came at him with two daggers. Borely flicked away one dagger from the man's grasp, then slid his other hand's claws into the enemy's face before he could even react.

But at the same time, a hand axe flew toward him from behind, and he could hear two other pirates approaching from his left. He ducked beneath the hand axe, turned to the nearer of the other two pirates, and moved his claws to block the assailant's attack. As Borely did so, he realized the other man was Yeaf, chucking a lance at him.

It was too late to get out of the way—he hadn't seen or heard the lance coming. Of course, it must have appeared in Yeaf's hand just as the man was in the process of throwing it. There was no way to prepare for Yeaf's attacks, especially when Borely was preoccupied with the man's crew.

Borely took the lance to the chest, having just enough time to avoid a blow directly through his heart. Screaming, Borely swung an arm and took off the nearer pirate's head. But before he could do anything more, a weapon slammed into the back of his right shoulder— another hand axe. The pirate who attacked from behind had a second one, apparently.

And already, Yeaf had another weapon in his hand—a yellow Nexi. And then a rapier. He could summon more than one weapon at a time. Yeaf charged at Borely with his yellow Nexi stone activated, smart enough to be cautious of Borely's claws.

Borely forced the lance out of his chest and stumbled forward, his body going into shock from the incredible pain. He couldn't just let himself fall to the floor and die, though—not at this moment, not when Yeaf was in the process of attacking him again.

Clutching his wound with one hand, and gripping the bloody lance in the other, Borely forced himself to step forward—quicker than he thought possible in this condition. Suddenly Yeaf was upon him, jabbing his rapier toward Borely's heart, fast enough to alter his movement to make up for Borely's rush. Borely lifted his arm from his wound and took the thin rapier blade directly into his hand. The rapier pierced down the entirety of his arm. The pain was excruciating, overwhelming, barely even imaginable—but Borely used the moment to slam his lance into the side of Yeaf's face. The captain's yellow barrier of energy barely held, but the impact sent Yeaf flying to the side, tumbling across the deck.

Screaming, Borely immediately turned to the pirate who had thrown a hand axe into his shoulder—the pain there barely registering when so much more agony was now coming from his arm, as well as the gaping wound in his chest. The pirate stepped back, surprised by the sight of this vampire—this monster—still standing despite all these tremendous wounds. Despite the blatant fear in the pirate's eyes, the man still managed to throw another hand axe at Borely. Standing still, Borely let the axe fly just to the right of his face. Then before the pirate could reach for a fourth hand axe from his back, Borely chucked his lance straight in the man's chest. Without the resilience of a vampire, the man simply fell to the ground, dying in a bloody heap.

With his uninjured arm, Borely reached into a pocket to pull out a vial of blood. He popped open the glass lid and downed the entirety of its contents in one gulp. It gave him the strength he needed to pull out the rapier from his arm and the hand axe from the back of his shoulder, and the wound in his chest was healed enough to keep him from dying right away. Desperate for more blood, Borely slipped out the other vial of blood he carried on his person—a strong dose of monster blood.

Two more pirates were already rushing for Borely, however, buying time for Yeaf to get back to his feet and shake off the powerful blow Borely had dealt him. Borely pocketed his vial of blood to keep from losing it, and ducked beneath a knife thrown at his head. It was painful to move his body at all, let alone to keep fighting a bunch of well-armed pirates—but they were barely leaving him time to even react to their attacks. The second pirate flung a series of icicles at Borely from one Nexi stone, and a long, thick vine from another. While Borely dodged the flying icicles and sliced away the large, heavy vine with the claws of his good arm, the other pirate sprinted toward Borely, unsheathing a thick, stocky sword in the process. It was more like a chunk of sharpened metal than an actual sword—and now it was glowing orange, powered by a Nexi stone embedded in its hilt.

Barely able to withstand the pain of his injuries, Borely lifted his mangled left arm and jabbed his claws into the running pirate's stomach and hip. The man stumbled to the ground, but forced himself back up and swung his giant blade at Borely's side. At the same time, the other pirate's vine pushed Borely back, too strong for him to withstand in his current state. Screaming again, Borely dropped to the floor so the blade passed over him. The vine was sliced by the blade in the process, and Borely had a brief moment to push himself off the ground and dash toward the pirate with the two Nexi stones. The man released a burst of freezing air just as Borely was upon him. Borely spun to the side and jabbed his claws into the back of the man's head. Borely snatched the green Nexi from the corpse's hand and flung vines at the other pirate, who was limping toward Borely. In one swift movement, Borely guided vines to wrap around the man's leg, and flung his body straight to Borely's claws, still sticking out of the front of the other man's face.

Borely ripped his claws out of the pirates and turned to Yeaf, who had formed a massive floating sphere of hardened dirt via an earth Nexi, surely summoned by his Hader.

Borely had to drink more blood—he was about to collapse from sheer pain and exhaustion. He reached for his vial of blood, but Yeaf was already launching the large ball of earth at him. It was too late to hesitate. Borely ran as hard as he could to his right, while drinking the blood at the same time. He was too weakened to use his full strength, and Yeaf's command over the tan Nexi was too superior to be taken lightly. Borely was going to be hit again.

But just before the sphere of dirt could crash into him, a strong jet of water blasted head-on into it, knocking it just to Borely's left. Borely fell to the ground, forcing himself to gulp his blood in the process. He glanced to where the stream of Nexi water had come from, and found Analicia a ways down the deck, running from a pirate. She was wearing Borely's metal headband, and had somehow managed to activate Borely's water Nexi embedded in it. There was only a second for Borely to get up again and make his next move against Yeaf, though—the captain wasn't going to be surprised by Borely's survival for very long.

On his feet again, Borely rushed toward Yeaf. The blood had reacted quickly, healing his wounds and filling himself with an intense vigor. And with the pirates in this vicinity taken down, Borely only had to concentrate on Yeaf. Unfortunately there were still a bunch of pirates fighting Jenba and Nivakil, and things weren't looking good for them in their injured state—especially for Nivakil. There was no time to assist them, though—the sooner Borely retrieved the Hader from Yeaf, the sooner they'd be able to leave the ship and escape for their lives.

Yeaf summoned a long sword in his hand and swung at Borely the moment he was within range. Borely leaped back to avoid the blade, which instantly vanished and was replaced by an armed crossbow. Yeaf fired the moment it materialized in his hand. Gritting his teeth, Borely twisted his body to avoid the arrow, barely able to use his vampiric speed and senses to keep up with the man's weaponry.

Before even another second had passed, Yeaf had replaced his crossbow with another purple Nexi, which he blasted right where Borely was stepping toward. Borely bent down, dug his long claws into the wooden deck, and pulled himself forward with all his strength. The blast of Nexi energy exploded just behind him, but by positioning himself just right, Borely used the shockwave to send himself flying toward Yeaf.

The pirate didn't look fazed, however. Instantly his purple Nexi was replaced by an ice Nexi, and before Borely had stepped back onto the deck, a thick shield of ice had formed in front of Yeaf. A giant icicle emerged from the wall of ice as Borely landed, and he had to slam his claws into the side of the sudden formation and pull himself up onto the icicle. Amidst the crackling of the growing icicle, Borely was able to hear the creeping growth of vines. Yeaf used a vine Nexi to raise himself on top of the wall of ice, but now the captain had a lance in his hand—and it was glowing a bright silver. Was that the power of a Nexi stone? What did a silver Nexi do?

Borely leaped into the wall, digging his claws into the ice to hang on. Yeaf laughed, and Borely waited for the last moment to swing himself as hard as he could, flinging himself upward and to the side of the thrown lance. A tendril of silver feathers lunged out the side of the glowing lance, digging into Borely's side. It hooked into his skin and latched on, pulling him down with the lance. Borely crashed into the deck, screaming. A couple more tendrils of silver feathers emerged from the lance, spiraling for his chest and face. Fighting past the pain, Borely pulled the lance from the deck and slammed the expanding silver formations into the wall of ice.

Already Yeaf was attacking again, now throwing knives at Borely. Barely having time to even glimpse the weapons, Borely swiped his claws at the spinning blades. Just as his claws impacted the first two knives, he realized they were powered by orange Nexi stones. The knives tore straight through his claws, breaking them. Borely pushed himself back to his feet and leaped away from the next several knives.

When was he ever going to get an opening? This pirate had an infinite disposal of powerful weaponry, and there was no way for Borely to form a plan when the weapons kept changing every half-second. Yeaf's Hader constantly gave him the element of surprise, and no matter what Borely did, Yeaf would be able to summon the perfect offense or defense to counter Borely's attacks.

Yeaf continued throwing knives at Borely, keeping him from approaching the wall of ice Yeaf stood atop of. Borely clutched the gaping wound in his side, and gritted his teeth against the stinging pain of his broken claws. It was too difficult to fight an opponent this powerful in this injured of a state. And yet he had to keep pushing himself. He knew fighting a Hader user wasn't going to be easy. Of course the road to freeing Areo wasn't going to be an easy one. And if he had to fight a dozen enemies like Yeaf, he was going to do so. He didn't even need to think about it.

A couple glances of his surroundings revealed to Borely that Yeaf had lodged about a dozen knives into the deck around Borely. The constant throwing had to be exhausting for Yeaf, but it was difficult for Borely to keep up with him as well, especially when he was out of blood to rejuvenate himself with.

"You're tiring me, vampire!" Yeaf said, continuing to throw summoned knives directly to where Borely would run toward. "It's time to bring this monster hunt to a close."

A white Nexi appeared in Yeaf's hand, and Borely realized what the captain was planning. But before he could escape, Yeaf released a flash of lightning at the knife closest to Yeaf, embedded into the deck a few meters in front of Borely. Sparkling white Nexi energy instantly connected with all the knives on deck. All the streams of Nexi lightning linked to Borely, standing in the direct center of all of Yeaf's thrown knives.

•

Pirates kept coming, and Jenba could barely keep up with them. In normal circumstances, he was certain he'd be able to take down these thugs much more easily, but he was injured and had no blood to regenerate with. Though he was able to kill several of the pirates ambushing him and Nivakil, there wasn't enough time for him to drink any of their blood. The pirates coordinated attacks from a safe distance, using Nexi stones and other weaponry to keep him constantly moving.

Jenba was also afraid to leave his master behind and just go all out against the pirates. Nivakil was very badly injured by the purple Nexi blast that blew their cover, and was having trouble standing, let alone fighting. If anyone needed blood, it was Nivakil.

And at the same time, Analicia was out there, trying to keep away from the pirates that chose to go after her. And then there was Borely, having to fight without his normal weapons, and locked in combat with the man using the Hader—presumably Yeaf.

Relying on his claws, his speed, and his sensitive senses, Jenba took down each pirate that got near him, to the point that the remaining pirates were keeping their distance, and trying to get Jenba away from Nivakil. It was up to Jenba in Nivakil's time of need to protect his master—and yet he was struggling to keep up with a group of mere pirates. He couldn't fail now. Not again. Not when he had failed his master so many times already. Not when Nivakil was truly counting on him. Perhaps for the first time in a very long time, Nivakil was truly in danger of getting killed.

Two pirates used green Nexi to send vines toward Nivakil while Jenba was occupied with a slinking snake of dirt from a third pirate's tan Nexi. Jenba clawed away at the hardened earth, wincing from the pain encompassing his entire body. Glancing back at his master, Jenba saw Nivakil was managing to avoid the Nexi plants, still capable of hearing the growing vines and sensing when they drew close to his arms and legs.

Jenba lunged toward the nearer of the two vine-wielding pirates, avoiding a burst of hardened earth in the process. The pirate unsheathed a sword, but Jenba managed to claw the man's hand off. A knife flew toward Jenba from another pirate. Jenba turned and dodged the weapon, then heard the sound of water from a dark blue Nexi. He ducked in time for the watery jet to pass over him, then rushed hunched over toward the second pirate with a green Nexi. Before the pirate could redirect some of his vines, Jenba slammed his claws into the pirate's stomach and tore through the man's side.

Jenba glanced back to Nivakil, who was being rushed by a couple other pirates. Panting but desperate, Jenba sprinted to Nivakil's position, noticing the difficulty his master had in landing an attack on the two sword-wielding pirates. They were both capable of using both an orange Nexi to power their swords with strength, and a yellow Nexi to temporarily protect themselves with a thin layer of energy. Nivakil barely managed to avoid a lunge from the nearer of the two pirates, but stumbled back when the second swung toward his neck. The old master suddenly flung himself forward and slammed his claws straight into each of their hearts, still able to tell precisely where they both were. Unfortunately he wasn't strong enough in this state to puncture through their Nexi shields, but he managed to send them crashing across the deck.

"Make noise!" a man yelled a ways away. "That vampire's blind, so he listens for our movements!"

More pirates were coming onto deck from below, and a number of them caught wind of the message. They brought up musical instruments—drums, a flute, and bagpipes—and they started playing as loud as they could, simply blaring random notes. It was an extremely noisy distraction, and one that would prove difficult for Nivakil to put up with in his current state.

Pirates armed with an assortment of weapons rushed toward Nivakil, who was shakily recovering from his exhausting attack on the two previous pirates, who were also pushing themselves back to their feet. Jenba ran in front of Nivakil and jabbed his claws at the closest approaching pirate. The man was huge, and wielded a large, thick hammer. As the man swung his giant hammer, Jenba retracted his claws to keep from losing them, realizing this man's strength was likely enough to snap them off even without the assisted energy of an orange Nexi.

As Jenba avoided the second swing of the man's hammer, a beam of hardened earth formed beside Jenba, from which flung out large rocks in random directions. Several battered against Jenba, and he was barely able to hear the snake of earth from another pirate who had been attacking him earlier. Jenba ran from the attack, checked back on Nivakil, and turned back to another pirate—this one about to land a spear directly into Jenba's face. As Jenba avoided the sharp weapon, he realized that in his brief, frantic glance of his master, the old man was struggling with ice formations rushing out of the frozen deck beneath him.

There were too many pirates to deal with all at once. Jenba had to kick things up a notch if he was going to survive this. If Nivakil was going to survive this. His master needed him to become the vampire he was trained to be. And not only Nivakil needed him, but Analicia and Borely too. Jenba was struggling so much just keeping himself alive, that he hadn't even been able to keep tabs on his partners. Was this entire mission falling apart? Did they just need to escape with their lives? What chance was there of them getting the Hader in these conditions?

Jenba focused on the situation at hand. He had to kill these pirates. He had to kill all of them. Immediately.

With all his might, Jenba launched himself at each and every pirate, avoiding their attacks, working out appropriate counter-attacks, clawing, beating, pushing, and shoving. He clawed apart one man's neck, then turned to another man and tore through his heart, not even taking the time to rely on his sight. His vampiric senses overflowed within him. He unleashed his full terror upon his enemies. There was no need to hold back. He simply had to kill, and kill, and kill.

His life was on the line, and so was Nivakil's,

Borely's, and Analicia's. Jenba couldn't keep failing everyone. He had to pull through for once. He had to use his power and succeed. He had to persevere.

A knife cut against the side of his face. He clawed at the pirate's arm, barely scraping the man's shoulder. The pirate stabbed again at Jenba, who slammed his head against the pirate's forehead. In the process of the clash, the knife didn't quite reach Jenba's heart. The moment the pirate was knocked back a bit, Jenba slammed his claws through the man's heart, then sprinted at a pirate releasing a large formation of ice at him. With his claws still through the first pirate's body, Jenba rushed through the razor-sharp ice shards, letting the corpse take the majority of the attack. It was difficult to hear where the ice-wielding pirate was amidst the overbearing noise, but Jenba could sense his location by focusing on where precisely the ice was originating from. Jenba's claws shattered through a wall of ice and punctured the stomach of the assailant.

Immediately Jenba turned to Nivakil, only to find him getting overwhelmed by dirt wrapping around him. Nivakil flung himself away from the tan Nexi attack, but the earth hardened and crushed his leg. The old man fell to the ground, screaming in agony.

"No!" Jenba screamed. He rushed toward Nivakil, but was stopped by a pirate armed with a large axe. The man was fast, and Jenba took a bad gash across his abdomen. Jenba nearly fell to the floor, but kept himself going, swiping his claws at the man's chest. The pirate dodged and swung again—Jenba used the moment to just run for it, hurrying toward Nivakil.

Blood-curdling screaming and a burst of light exploded from the other side of the deck. Jenba glanced at the scene and saw Borely getting electrocuted by a powerful white Nexi attack.

First Nivakil, and now Borely. Everyone was getting beaten. Jenba was failing them. His strength wasn't enough to save them. He wasn't fighting well enough to assist them effectively. These were just ordinary pirates, and he was failing to make a real difference. Again and again and again, he was failing the few people he cared about.

First his wife and children. Then Areo. And now everyone else who had been a large part of his life.

Jenba swiped his claws at the pirate wielding the tan Nexi stone, but the enemy was quicker than him. A tendril of dirt whipped against Jenba's back, hitting him so hard he thought his spinal cord had broken entirely. He collapsed on the ground, but immediately tried to force himself back to his feet. He had to keep fighting. Despite the pain. Despite the terrible odds.

Suddenly he was on his feet, bleeding and screaming. He couldn't let himself die yet. Not when his master needed him. For the first time in history, his master needed him! And he could not fail him!

Jenba burst through a whirlwind of dirt and sliced off the head of the pirate wielding the tan Nexi. A pirate was about to stab Nivakil in the face with a lance, but in an instant Jenba was at the man's back, ripping him in half.

Someone else was approaching. Jenba turned, only to find the captain himself, suddenly swinging a giant sword at him. He had noticed Yeaf too late—the noise of the music-players had thrown him off. Jenba leaped to the side, gasping from the strain he was forcing on his battered, bleeding body. Yeaf sliced Jenba's left arm clean off.

Jenba fell to the deck, screaming, screaming, dying, screaming.

But Yeaf now had a crossbow pointed at Jenba's head. Jenba rolled aside just before the arrow could pierce his face at point-blank range. He swiped at Yeaf's legs with his right arm's claws, but the pirate suddenly had a green Nexi, which he used to create vines that pushed himself into the air. The world turned blurry, a cacophony of agony and madness. There were more pirates. And Yeaf was somewhere else. Who was attacking whom? It didn't matter... He was dying...

Blood. He needed blood. But there was none, save for his own. He couldn't drink his own blood. And the pirates he had killed were out of his reach. And there were other pirates on deck... Not too many left, but they were much better off than he was.

No, he couldn't stop. He had to get up. He had to save Nivakil.

With his one good arm, Jenba pushed himself back to his feet, lightheaded and exhausted. He had little time left.

Nivakil screamed. Yeaf was behind him. A lance was poking out of Nivakil's chest. Nivakil spun in place, screaming, and swinging his claws at the pirate captain. Yeaf had already activated a yellow Nexi stone, and the weakened master's claws only managed to push Yeaf back, rather than tear through his torso.

Yeaf landed on his feet, an armed crossbow appearing in his hand again.

Jenba pushed Nivakil aside, taking the arrow to his own chest. Nivakil yelled something at Jenba, but he couldn't tell what the old master was saying. It was too loud, and there was too much going on, and he was losing too much blood. Yeaf was attacking again with another weapon, but Jenba couldn't tell what it was, his vision blurry and darkened.

"Sorry, master," Jenba whispered. "I always fail you."

Nivakil yelled something again, and was pulling Jenba back. The two of them tumbled to the deck. Something blew apart, releasing dirt everywhere. Something sharp and cold nicked Jenba's side. Then someone was standing in front of him and Nivakil.

It looked like Borely.

•

After his senses slipped out of the pitch black silence, Borely felt his entire body tremble uncontrollably. How long had he been knocked out by the light Nexi attack? The white lightning had jolted his heart, shocked his mind, and nearly knocked the life right out of him. Had Borely not been a vampire, Yeaf's concentrated white Nexi energy guided by the metal knives would have surely killed Borely right then and there. But how much time had passed? He had to get on his feet. He had to find the others. How was Nivakil and Jenba faring? And was Analicia still evading the pirates that were after her? Where was Yeaf?

Borely's senses came back to him all at once, overwhelming his mind, still slipping in and out of recognition of the current situation and surroundings.

"Find them," Borely told himself, his own voice sounding distant—barely audible, barely breathing. "Find them. And Yeaf. And the Hader. And Areo."

Even now he was still thinking of Areo. Was this infiltration of the pirate ship worth the effort? He could hardly think straight, and there were pirates coming. They looked surprised—no, furious. Maybe both. They wanted Borely dead—he wasn't supposed to be alive. Yeaf was somewhere else...

Borely looked past the approaching pirates and spotted Nivakil, struggling to pull Jenba away from a pirate firing a blast of water. Behind the pirate a few paces was Yeaf, summoning a long poleaxe. Borely blinked and realized Nivakil and Jenba were both injured, but it was difficult to tell how badly. Borely shoved past the pirates ganging up on him and sprinted toward his companions, ignoring the nerve-wracking earthquake splitting his mind apart. He wanted to just fall back to the ground and lie there for a few hours. The pain throughout his entire body was overwhelming, but there was no time to stop for blood. A pirate behind him was firing icicles, and it took all of Borely's might just to keep from getting impaled from behind. One of the icicles nicked one of his legs, but he managed to reach the closest pirate attacking Nivakil. Borely severed the man's head and turned to Yeaf, taking the captain by surprise. Yeaf swung his weapon, but Borely turned in time and clawed through the pole, severing it in half. Immediately Yeaf summoned a knife and jabbed the blade at Borely's neck. Borely leaned down and grabbed the blade with his teeth, then flung the knife right back at Yeaf. The captain barely managed to avoid a fatal blow to the face, but cut his ear, blood trickling down his neck.

Yeaf dove backward, summoning a sword in the process. Borely clawed at Yeaf's chest, but the captain was too quick, and Borely too tired and injured to reach him in time. However, Yeaf's sudden dive caused a golden necklace around his neck to slip out from behind his shirt and jacket. At the end of the necklace was a stone glowing a strange mix of yellow and silver, shifting back and forth like oil and water.

Borely swiped again at Yeaf, despite the man already swinging his sword straight for Borely's neck. Though weak to the brink of death, Borely pushed himself to snatch the Hader from Yeaf's control. Borely extended his claws just enough to slice through the links of Yeaf's necklace, releasing the Hader. Yeaf still had his sword, however. Borely snapped his claws together around the Hader. The stone held together tight in his grasp. Yeaf's blade reached Borely's neck.

The boat vanished beneath Borely's feet, replaced by the multicolored leaves of a bright maple-filled forest. He wasn't on the pirate ship anymore. This really was a forest. Was he dead? Or had he simply gone mad?

Collapsing into a pile of leaves, Borely lay on the forest floor, gasping slow, painful breaths. The smell of crinkly leaves was overwhelming. The stinging, shaking, resonating pain throughout every bone and organ in his body was overwhelming. Even the sunlight was overwhelming.

*I'm dead or dying*, Borely thought. He let his claws retract back into ordinary fingernails, bringing the Hader into the grasp of his hand. It continued to shift and glow, a mysterious entity emanating power of a magnitude Borely could hardly imagine. This was what he had come for— perhaps died for. Would Jenba, Nivakil, and Analicia die as well? Was it worth all that, to possibly have a chance to save Areo? Summoning weapons wouldn't actually free her mind, would it? And he wasn't even alive anymore to use it... Or had the Hader actually magically sent him to a forest somehow?

"Don't die before we've even started," a voice called out. Borely tried to lift his head, but he was simply too exhausted. The lightning attack had fried him from the inside-out. His vampire body was strong enough to survive, but not to function after such a powerful, concentrated burst of energy like that. Borely simply lay there, wondering if the voice he heard was even real.

"It seems the wielder of my power has become quite a competent fighter," the voice continued. It was a man's voice—a man Borely's age, and very normal-sounding. This wasn't a gruff pirate speaking to him, nor was it Yeaf's all-knowing, crazed tone. "You've taken quite the beating."

Borely couldn't respond. He could open his mouth, but he didn't have the strength to speak. He just wanted to slip out of consciousness and sleep... sleep until he died, and hope this dream world would bring him the results he had sought from the very beginning of this Hader search mission.

"It looks like you're a vampire," the stranger said. "A pretty recent recruit, since you're ears and skin tone haven't changed much. But it's barely noticeable."

Something cold was pushed into Borely's free hand. It felt like a large glass vial. Movement against the object implied that the man was taking off the topper to the vial.

"If you can just drink some blood to heal yourself, we can move things along quickly," the stranger said, his voice soft yet not what Borely would call kind.

It was difficult to keep a grip on the vial, but Borely managed to get it to his mouth and force hard, painful swallows of the thick blood. Where it had come from and why this random stranger in this random forest had some, Borely didn't know. Regardless, it was a powerful dose, quickly lessening the pain inflicting his body and healing the electric shock he suffered. All other injuries were patched up in a matter of seconds, Borely's regenerative body working its magic with the catalyst of the foreign blood. Within a minute or so, even his weariness felt nullified—he was more than ready to get back to the pirate ship and finish his fight with Yeaf, and all the others left in his crew.

Borely stood up and found the stranger sitting on a cleanly-cut log a few meters away. The man looked to be an elf, but what stood out most were his bright yellow eyes. He had long yellow hair—not blond, but dandelion yellow. The man was dressed in blue robes covered in shining, swirling green ivy patterns. He sat barefoot, leaning forward casually with his elbows against his knees.

"Thanks," Borely said. "But where am I, exactly?"

"In my world," the man said. "I am the Hader of Material Displacement."

"You're the Hader?"

"Yes."

Of course, this didn't make any sense. The Hader was supposed to be a Nexi stone, not an elf. And wasn't this the Hader right here, in Borely's hand? On top of this, the man's claim didn't actually explain where Borely was.

"Well, how do I get out of here?" Borely asked. "I need to return to that ship I was on."

"You don't want my power?" the elf asked. "It's unusual for someone to lay hands on the stone, and not attempt to gain access to my power."

"I don't know what you're talking about," Borely said, getting to the point. "But I really need to hurry. My friends are in danger, and need my help."

"Don't worry," the elf said. "My world exists outside of time. You're about to get your head lobbed off, though, so you'll want to be careful once you return to your reality."

"So is this just some kind of dream, or something?" Borely asked.

"Something like that." The elf stood up and formally placed his hands behind his back. "In order to access my power, you will need to prove yourself worthy of it. I can't let just anyone use the ability to summon whatever objects he pleases."

"So you're saying you're the Hader, not this

stone?" Borely asked.

"The stone provides access to magical energy, just like any Nexi stone does," the elf said. "But this stone is special. It provides access to *my* magical energy."

Borely thought this over a few seconds. "You mean you yourself are the source of this Hader's ability?"

The elf nodded. "A very long time ago, my siblings and I chose to sacrifice ourselves for the sake of protecting the world from the wicked uses of the Elpis stone. We perfected the greatest magical techniques in the world, and with the assistance of the extreme Nexi energy resources of the eigni, the Haders were created. Centuries have passed, and our essences have continued to exist within these stones."

"And you let people access this power, as long as they prove worthy of it?" Borely asked. "You let one of the worst pirates in the world use this stone, so apparently you don't care if people use the Hader for good."

"It's impossible for me to judge a person's character," the Hader said. "How much a heart will change, for better or worse, is entirely uncertain. There's no telling if you'll use my power any better than Yeaf has."

"I just want to save a friend of mine," Borely said.

"I don't care what you intend to use my power for," the Hader said. "That can change at any time, and you could end up using it for all sorts of terrible things in the long run. But I at least must ensure that you're capable of wielding the power before I grant you access to it. Otherwise you'll just get yourself and many other people killed for no reason. The power of a Hader is very difficult to contain in the hands of a weak spirit."

"So I just need to prove my strength? Is that it?"

The Hader turned and started walking away. "Defeat me in a fight, and my contract with you will be formed. You will be able to summon hundreds of physical objects that have been displaced in this invisible reality. Most of the objects are weapons, but you may find other useful items, such as that vial of blood I gave you."

"So you can summon things, just as Yeaf did," Borely said.

The Hader turned around to face Borely again, standing a good ten meters away now. "Please understand this. I am the Hader, and Yeaf's power was *my* power. Without the stone, he can no longer access my power. And though you have the stone in your hand right now, you won't be able to use it properly until you've proven yourself worthy to me. So now... I will give you five seconds to prepare yourself, and then I will begin my attack."

All at once, tens of weapons appeared around the elf, all of them floating in the air. Swords, axes, knives, crossbows, lances, and every color Nexi stone imaginable. This elf had somehow summoned well over a hundred weapons, and was able to keep them levitated. He raised an arm forward and pointed at Borely.

"One... Two..."

Was this crazy elf going to fling all these weapons at him?

"Three... Four..."

What was Borely supposed to do against so many weapons? There was no escape from something this ridiculous!

"Five."

Tens of gleaming weapons flew at Borely, all rushing toward him simultaneously. At the same time, arrows flew from crossbows and elements burst from their appropriate Nexi stones. Taking this madness head-on was impossible—Borely ran as fast as he could behind the nearest, thickest tree he could find.

Weapons slammed into the tree, pummeling it, sending splinters and strips of bark flying to either side of Borely. The ground shook beneath him, and he glanced to his left to right to find a nearly constant stream of blades and arrows flying by. The tree erupted in flames, and Borely was forced to run before dirt lurched up around his feet. He ran behind another large tree, barely quick enough to avoid the Hader's attacks in the process. In seconds this tree was destroyed as well, and Borely had to sprint to a third, despite being out of breath.

*Have to find an opening,* Borely thought. *Have to get through these weapons... Have to get to the Hader.*

He wished he had some Nexi stones he could use on his person. Something to protect himself from the summoned weapons, even if it was just for a few seconds. Or something to attack from a far distance—that would have been helpful. His metal gloves or headband would have especially been nice—good, useful weapons he had grown accustomed to over the years, nearly as familiar to him as his own limbs. But he had nothing at his disposal. Nothing but his claws and teeth, and his vampiric speed and senses. These were all very useful skills, of course, but Borely wasn't an expert at fighting as a vampire.

He didn't even want to fight as a vampire. But there was no choice at this point. He had to get to the Hader and defeat him, relying solely on his abilities as a vampire. If he was going to save Areo, he was going to have to use every power he could access.

Even if he had to become a monster—a bloodthirsty vampire, just like the ones that turned his brother mad and killed his parents.

The tree Borely stood behind split apart at the constant beating of swords, axes, and lances. He couldn't just keep hiding anymore—he had to go for it. Borely had to take down this Hader, take his power, and return to the ship prepared to defeat Yeaf and the rest of the pirates.

*I won't be able to run all the way to the Hader without*

*getting hit*, Borely thought. *But that's okay. I just need to not die.*

The rest of the tree blew apart from a burst of lightning. Borely rushed out from behind the tree, watching and listening for each and every weapon approaching him. He lifted his claws and swiped at the swords and daggers flying for him. With every open spot he could find, he took another step, swiping away at every weapon flung toward him in the process. Fire, ice, and earth converged upon him amidst the blades and arrows, and Borely had no choice but to accept getting hit by several of the attacks. His right leg burned severely, and a large rock slammed against his right shoulder. An arrow pierced his stomach, but he kept pushing his way forward. He had no time to stop to remove the arrow, as he continued to claw away at all the projectiles he could.

The Hader was still far away, constantly summoning and flinging more weapons at Borely. He needed to go faster—the Hader could just jog backward while Borely struggled through the crashing waves of weaponry.

With all the strength he could muster, Borely ran headlong into the weapons, focusing his senses as hard as he could on the movement of approaching blades and arrows. It was difficult to turn accurately amidst so much chaos, but Borely found himself getting closer to the Hader, who struggled to bring in more weapons and aim them effectively at Borely's unpredictable trajectory. Borely had to keep running, letting some of the attacks hit him. With each passing moment, the Hader had to be expecting

Borely to just collapse and give in to the overwhelming odds.

Instead, Borely kept going.

A dagger lodged into Borely's chest, just beneath his collarbone. A blast of lightning burned the side of his right arm. A lance cut through his side. An arrow shot into his right foot. Borely kept running, and kept himself from screaming. Every iota of concentration was focused on reaching the Hader, on avoiding as many of the summoned weapons as physically possible. He nearly tripped several times, but managed to recover each time and keep himself going. The Hader was closer... closer...

Borely let his vampire nature take over, not caring about the pain, knowing with a certainty he would live on. All he needed was blood. He would live on with the blood. He only needed to drink blood.

His prey stood just before him. He only needed to accept becoming the same kind of bloodthirsty monster that had destroyed his family, and altered his life forever.

More weapons hit Borely, the Hader far too capable with his summoning to slow down for even a moment. But Borely kept running, clawing away a path straight to the Hader.

*Just be a vampire*, Borely repeated in his head. *Fast and silent, merciless and ravenous. Defeat your enemy and drink his blood. Become a monster.*

He reached the Hader and latched his fangs into the elf's neck. Borely shoved the elf to the ground, oblivious to the weapons sticking out of his body. He gulped down the Hader's blood, thoroughly overpowering the elf. There was nothing the Hader could do the moment Borely began to suck his blood. The elf struggled to push Borely away, but the act of Borely latching on to his neck and drinking his blood weakened the man significantly.

Borely pulled out weapons from his body and continued drinking the Hader's blood. Borely's wounds disappeared, and an unparalleled vigor filled his very being. He could keep sucking the Hader's blood as much as he wanted. He didn't want to stop. He was a monster, and this was his victim.

Borely opened his mouth and pushed the Hader away, letting the elf drop to the ground. Borely stared down at the limp figure, blood dripping down his face. The elf was still breathing, but Borely knew he had sucked so much blood, the Hader was at the brink of death. If the Hader was as powerful as he claimed to be he would be fine, but the fact Borely had allowed himself to suck his prey's blood—just like a vampire would—was horrifying. He had nearly killed this elf, the very same way a vampire would.

He was a vampire. There was no denying it now. He had committed the unforgivable act of attacking a person and sucking his blood.

And yet, Borely didn't feel entirely despicable for it. This was his nature, now. He had become just like his brother.

How much further was he going to go, though? Would he be willing to kill people for the sake of obtaining their blood, now? Would he go mad for the blood? Would he ever want to stop drinking blood the next time the opportunity arose? He should feel terrible. He should hate himself. He should never forgive himself for letting himself become the very monster he had always despised.

It took several minutes for the Hader to regain his senses and sit up on his own. Borely sat on the log the Hader had been sitting on before the fight, waiting, watching, wondering. He had managed to keep himself from killing the Hader, but would the elf allow access to the summoning power to a monster? That was what Borely had become, and in some strange fashion he felt ashamed for not feeling horrendous for his moral downfall.

"That was surprising," the Hader said. "To think you would be so crazy as to just plow straight through my attacks..."

"I didn't see any better options," Borely said. "I couldn't just keep running away from you."

"I can't keep summoning weapons like that forever," the Hader said. "My plan is generally to intimidate the enemy and lead him into a trap before my energy wears out. Since you're a vampire, I had to lead you to the trap as quickly as I could, knowing you'd be able to outlast me. The very idea that somebody would come at me headlong is... absolutely insane!" The elf laughed. "Absolutely unthinkable! And yet you barged right through."

Borely sighed, upset to realize he didn't need to put himself through all that misery he subjected himself to. All he had to do was weather the storm of weapons a bit longer, and he would've been able to defeat the Hader through much simpler, less painful methods. "Guess that's just my style."

"You seem the headstrong type," the Hader said. "But regardless, you've most certainly proven yourself worthy of accessing my power. I hope the madness will not affect you as badly as it has Yeaf."

"What do you mean?" Borely asked.

"Access to great power can change people dramatically," the Hader said, his yellow eyes never blinking. "It can make people zealous. Overly ambitious. Proud. Arrogant. Vengeful. Hateful. Treacherous... And sometimes it just messes people up."

Yeaf certainly didn't seem all right in the head, though his paranoia proved accurate in this instance, and his unpredictable behavior did give him the element of surprise. Had he really gone mad though, from the power of the Hader? Or was he just a mad pirate to begin with?

"I just need the power to help a friend," Borely said. "Once my mission is done, I won't need your power anymore."

"If you find the means to destroy the stone, feel free to do so," the Hader said. "I have lived on long enough, and so have my brothers and sisters."

"Are you trapped in this stone, then?" Borely asked.

"I'm not even real, to be technical about it all," the Hader said. "And my concept of the passage of time is tenuous at best. Even much of my sense of self has eroded over the centuries, so there really isn't much left for me to lose. My power remains strong and vibrant, but my memories slowly fade away."

Borely nodded, feeling extremely tired from this entire surprise encounter with the being within the stone. The entire situation came and went so abruptly, it really did feel like a peculiar dream—one he wasn't quite sure he had actually experienced.

"I will let you return to the ship," the Hader said. "I suggest you take some kind of weapon or shield with you, since you're about to get your head lobbed off."

"Ah, right," Borely said. He stood up and took the Hader stone from his pocket. It glowed just the same as always, but he felt as if some kind of connection had been made between him and the smooth rock. Perhaps it was just in his head—but perhaps this entire forest and all its scattered weapons were just in his head, as well.

To his surprise, all Borely had to do was think of the item he wanted—a long, sturdy poleaxe. He had seen Yeaf use it, so Borely imagined he'd be able to summon it as well now.

And just as he hoped, the exact weapon he thought of appeared in his hands, straight out of thin air. There was no poof of smoke, or flash of light. It simply *was*.

"This will do," Borely said.

The Hader nodded. "May you find success before your journey's through."

"My journey will be through once I find success," Borely said.

The Hader looked up a bit and smiled. "Life tends to keep going, even after we've achieved a significant goal in life. Your journey in this mortal existence will be through once you've died—nothing more, nothing less. Though I imagine you will live a long time, seeing how you're a vampire."

"Thank you for lending me your power," Borely said. "I will use it well."

And with that, the forest disappeared, instantly replaced by the pirate ship Borely and his companions had boarded. And standing directly in front of Borely was

Yeaf, swinging a sword straight for Borely's neck.

Borely pushed his poleaxe against the pirate's sword, keeping the blade from reaching him. Yeaf stumbled back in surprise, clearly not expecting a weapon to appear out of thin air in Borely's hands at the exact moment the he was about to lob Borely's head off.

Before Yeaf could recover, Borely slammed the axe into the pirate's face, killing him.

There was no time to feel at ease, however. Borely pulled the axe from Yeaf's head and turned to where Nivakil and Jenba were located, still fending off a group of frenzied pirates.

Borely caught a better look at their current state. One of Jenba's arms was clearly severed, and Nivakil was impaled by a lance, square in the chest. There was no way either of them were going to survive without blood, but there was no time for them to drink any—not with so many pirates gathered around them. A blast of ice was launched at the two, and Jenba and Nivakil were struggling just to keep on their feet. At the last moment, Jenba appeared to have regained some of his strength, and managed to push the old master out of the way before the blast could overtake them. Part of Jenba's leg was frozen, but he tore it out of the ice, screaming. There were already a few more pirates with weapons charging at the two, and Nivakil looked ready to pass out.

A high-pitched scream stopped Borely in his

tracks. He turned and found Analicia, stumbling back from a couple pirates. She shot another jet of water from the dark blue Nexi on her forehead, but she missed the nearer of the two pirates, and ended up flinging herself backward in the process. It took practice to get accustomed to controlling the metal headband—something Borely doubted she had ever done before. The fact she was able to fire the stream of water at all was an impressive feat, but she was no match for these pirates, as inexperienced with combat as she was.

Borely sprinted to Analicia's position, summoning a water Nexi in the process. He shot off a jet of water at the pirate closest to Analicia, knocking the man in the side of the head hard enough to snap his neck. The other pirate turned and fired an arrow at Borely, who quickly replaced his water Nexi with a metal shield, deflecting the projectile at the last moment. Borely kept running and slammed the shield into the pirate's face, knocking him out cold.

Borely looked down to Analicia, checking to see if she was injured. "Are you all right?"

"I'm fine," Analicia said, her eyes wide, and her small body trembling. "But Jenba... And Nivakil..." The child looked as white as a sheet, noticeable even when accounting for the fact she was normally rather pale to begin with.

Borely looked across the deck and found Jenba and Nivakil surrounded even tighter by gathering pirates. A giant explosion burst from Jenba and Nivakil's location, sending several burning pirates flying around them. It looked like one of them had used a red Nexi—and then another explosion erupted, quickly followed by a third and fourth. Fire Nexis were bursting apart the ship, spreading its flames up and down the wooden planks and posts of the vessel.

Borely swore. He couldn't see through the smoke, or hear through the dying screams and crackling flames. The pirates wouldn't have been the ones to use the fire Nexi stones—it must have been Jenba or Nivakil, using last-ditch tactics to fend off the rest of the pirates.

The fires spread to Borely and Analicia's location. They had to get off this ship right away. This wasn't a mere defensive maneuver by Jenba and Nivakil—this was a final tactic to buy Borely and Analicia time to escape with the Hader.

·

Jenba set off the last of his fire Nexi, using up what little was left of his energy to spread the fires as far as possible across the ship. If Borely was smart, he'd be off the ship by now with Analicia, and swimming away to safety. The fires raged all around Jenba and Nivakil. The heat was overwhelming, but the burning paled in comparison to the pain of his injuries. He couldn't move a muscle anymore, and from what he could tell, neither could Nivakil. They had utterly wasted themselves in this battle.

Some of the pirates were trying to quell the flames with their water Nexi, but Jenba had put all his energy into those flames, spreading them all across the boat far too quickly for the remaining pirates to keep up with. Jenba wasn't sure if Borely had managed to obtain the Hader, but hopefully this fire had assisted him in some way. Borely knew about these final measures being a possibility in this mission. The fires were a signal for Borely to get out of there—even a vampire's regeneration wouldn't survive a rush through such deep, billowing flames. The body would burn and melt away in seconds.

So there was no hope for Jenba or Nivakil to survive, lying in the center of it all. Even if they had the energy to drink each other's blood, they wouldn't have been able to get through the fires.

*It's up to you now, Borely*, Jenba thought. *I hope I was able to help at least this once.*

Jenba was too weak to shut his eyes. He stared up at the stars, the world turning silent despite the roaring flames around him.

"You did well," Nivakil said, his voice barely alive, barely audible.

Jenba couldn't respond. He wasn't even sure if Nivakil had said these words. It seemed unlikely, and yet Jenba's mind had registered them. Perhaps it was just his own thoughts.

In his head, he thanked Nivakil. It was thanks to the old master that he was able to find any kind of purpose in life. He wished he could have properly repayed Nivakil for the years of training. He wished he could have saved his mentor in his hour of need.

But in the end, this was the best he could do. There was no way to know if it was enough, or if he had made any difference at all. But if Nivakil felt he had done well, that was the best Jenba could have ever hoped for.

Ever since he lost his family and became a vampire, he had hoped for some way to make up for his failures. Ever since he began training under Nivakil, he had hoped to become the type of person who used his power to save others.

*Hurry off this ship, Borely*, Jenba thought. *Keep watch over Analicia, and save Areo.*

*Finish what we started.*

•

In the end, there was no way for Borely to reach Jenba and Nivakil. The smoke was too thick, the flames too rapid and destructive. Once it was clear he wouldn't be able to find them before the ship was destroyed, Borely tried to get to the small boat he had sailed out of port, but it was already too late to access it—the fires had already spread to that part of the deck.

"What do we do?" Analicia asked.

"Can you swim?" Borely asked.

"A... a little..." Analicia said. She looked scared out of her wits.

"Hold your breath," Borely said. He grabbed the child and ran to the end of the deck, carrying her in his arms. Analicia screamed in surprise at how high of a jump this turned out to be, but remembered to take in a gasp of air before crashing into the sea. Borely sunk deep into the waters, finding it difficult to keep a hold of the child as the waves battered them around. As Borely swam toward the surface, he lost his grip on Analicia, who was spun around violently by the waves. Borely opened his eyes and searched for her, frantic and desperate.

He spotted her, floundering her way deeper into the sea, flailing her weak arms and legs without any rhythm or focus. Borely pushed himself to reach her as quickly as possible, then helped pull her up toward the surface of the waters. They both gasped for breath the moment they cleared the surface, but Borely was quick to pull Analicia with him and swim away from the burning ship, not wanting them to get pulled in with the sinking wreckage.

Analicia struggled to swim at all, let alone quickly, so Borely got her on his back and gripping his shoulders. As hard as he could, Borely swam toward the distant shore, knowing he wasn't going to reach it anytime soon. This was going to be a long, difficult swim, made all the more strenuous with having to help Analicia across as well.

Once they were a safe distance away from the ship, Borely treaded water so he could watch for any sign of Jenba and Nivakil. Analicia repeatedly asked if they were going to be okay, if they were going to get off the ship in time—but the slow, tiring minutes passed, and there was no sign of any rowboats or swimmers escaping the dying ship. The vessel soon fell apart and crumbled into the ocean, overwhelmed by the fury of the red Nexi fires.

Jenba and Nivakil never got off the boat. Borely watched intently, straining his eyes to see through the darkness, across the thousand waves of the sea. Minute after minute passed, and still he hoped that somehow Jenba and Nivakil would show up, swimming in their direction.

But it soon became too tiring for Borely to keep treading water like this, and he realized there was no way he was going to make it all the way to shore in this exhausted state. There was no sign of Jenba or Nivakil surviving, and Borely had seen the fatal injuries they had sustained. Without access to blood, they were good as dead.

"I'm sorry," he told Analicia. "They're gone."

The girl didn't respond. She simply took slow, shallow breaths, struggling to keep from sucking in salt water. Borely turned and started swimming toward shore again, quickly straining himself against the strong, constant waves. There was no way he was going to make it at this rate.

"I need some of your blood, Analicia," Borely said. It was the last thing he wanted to do, but there simply wasn't a choice in the matter. The waters were bitter cold, and he was going to wear himself out before even making it halfway to shore. He was a good swimmer, but the distance was just too far, the waves too strong.

Analicia didn't respond, so Borely treaded water and took her arm, deciding it would be easier to draw blood from there rather than try to reach for her neck. The girl didn't resist, and Borely worried for a moment if she was going unconscious or even dying. She was just overwhelmed by the series of events she had just gone through, however. Once Borely had a few gulps of blood, he repositioned Analicia and started swimming again, now able to exert much more strength and vigor.

He wasn't sure if Analicia was crying, and Borely didn't want to think about the tragedy of this mission any more than he already was. Jenba and Nivakil were gone now. It wasn't right. They were strong. They were decent vampires—great ones, in fact. They were there for him when he had no clue what to do with his life. He didn't even know if he wanted to live anymore after becoming a vampire, but they were there to help him through the harrowing transition.

And now they were dead, just when Borely had gained the power of the Hader. He had been too slow, too weak. Perhaps if he hadn't pushed for going on this mission, they wouldn't be dead now.

He kept swimming, and kept wondering if Analicia was crying. It was too hard to tell with the constant splashing of waves all about him. She was too quiet.

Eventually Borely stopped to give Analicia some of his own blood, realizing the waters were turning her deathly cold. She drank weakly from his neck, but once she got a few gulps down she was much better off. Borely had to drink some more of her blood in return, as there was still a ways to go before they reached shore.

*There's still a ways to go before we reach shore...* Borely focused on this thought. How much more would he have to go through before finally finding Areo and freeing her? Would he be able to keep fighting like this for much longer? And now without Jenba and Nivakil, the fighting force of his team had dwindled significantly.

There was nobody but himself left to save Areo now. And he wasn't sure if he had the strength to go at it alone.

•

# 9. THE WINDS SHIFT

He was stuck in a log cabin room with arguably the two most powerful fighters in the world, but Trilir wasn't worried. At least... not too worried. As long as he did as Augurc commanded, there would be no problems with him. And as long as he ensured Subject VI continued to function as expected, the Elpis-enhanced vampire would never do any harm at all. Except, of course, to those Augurc commanded.

Which, from what Trilir understood, were a great many people. From the sound of things, Subject VI was more powerful on her own than an entire platoon of Brotherhood members. And these were elite soldiers to begin with...

Right now Trilir was wrapping up an analysis of some of VI's achievements over the past week. She had managed to kill several more of the Fiefs Kingdom's top spies and assassins. The system of royal servants was a dying one at this point, and there was little hope of the Fiefs Kingdom gaining any more insight on the Brotherhood's plans. Soon enough, Augurc would likely start destroying some of the kingdom's major cities, potentially leading to a full attack on the capital of Setar.

"Subject VI is in perfect condition," Trilir said, setting down a summary of his readings and analyses. He sat at a small round table covered with papers and medical instruments. Augurc sat to his left and VI to his right.

Augurc nodded, and Trilir continued. "There isn't a single scratch on her body, and she's as healthy as a vampire can get. She is still susceptible to pain, and her mind continues to fight against your will to some faint degree. As long as you continue to give her targets to kill on a regular basis, she will continue to be a powerful servant."

"Good. The Brotherhood will soon destroy Niez," Augurc said, straightforward as always. Niez was one of the continent's largest cities, and was only about an hour's walk from this tiny village. Augurc had already directed most of the Brotherhood to gathering points closer to the city, from what Trilir understood. "VI will assist alongside all other ready subjects. It will be a final test of the Elpis's capabilities."

Of course, Subject VI was not the only successful Elpis-based experiment at this point. Subject EV had proven himself just as worthy of Augurc's approval, having taken down a whole troop of Fiefs soldiers, as well as several of the kingdom's top servant spies. As far as Trilir was concerned, there wasn't a force in the entire planet that could kill EV, even if he wasn't yet as capable of a fighter as VI.

And preparations were finally set for MI, potentially the most powerful experiment of them all. Embedding the Elpis energy necessary for Augurc to be able to summon MI was an incredible challenge, but the process went smoothly enough. It would take a while for Augurc to recover from the painful procedure, but the transfer of energy would enable Augurc to will a third experiment to destroy anyone and everyone he pleased.

"I will leave VI to you then, if that is all," Trilir said.

"Continue tests on MI's power," Augurc instructed. "If there is anything more I should know, you will convey the information to Viecint for speedy delivery."

"Yes, of course," Trilir said. He didn't care much for the Brotherhood guards Augurc had assigned to constantly breathe down his neck, making sure Trilir never performed any experiments contrary to Augurc's demands. And Trilir especially didn't care for Viecint, one of the Brotherhood's more ornery higher-ups. Of course, Trilir didn't care much for Augurc, either—but he was the man with the world's greatest Nexi energy. There was no way Trilir was going to turn down the chance to work with him.

Augurc got up to leave, and VI instinctively got up to follow him out the door. The two stationed guards locked it behind them, leaving Trilir to continue research on the Nexi seal he had placed on the center of Augurc's chest. The Elpis energy built up inside of Augurc had reached the point where the man could summon an Elpis-crafted monster potentially capable of destroying an entire city.

Or perhaps an entire country. The sky really was the limit where the Elpis was concerned. Trilir could only imagine what he could learn if he had the full Elpis.

Of course... if Augurc had the full Elpis, there probably wouldn't have been any need for Trilir. Augurc would have simply been able to do whatever he wanted. And perhaps would have destroyed the entire world ten times over by now.

Though Augurc never showed any pleasure on his face, he had made it clear that he did indeed view Trilir as the greatest mind the eigni race had ever produced. Nobody in the world had experimented with as many Nexi forces as Trilir had. And now Trilir had helped create the three most powerful beings in the world. Of course, Augurc himself was likely the most powerful being in the world, thanks to the fact he was capable of wielding half of the Elpis itself—but thanks to said Elpis fragments, Trilir had learned to enable Augurc to turn powerful beings into unstoppable ones.

Subject VI was a vampire who could kill anyone. Subject EV was an elf who couldn't be killed by anyone. And Subject MI... was a god, just waiting to be born.

And none of it would have been possible without Trilir's intellect. If it weren't for his many years of extensive research on the various Nexi energies of the world, including the Elpis, Augurc wouldn't have been able to wreak even a tenth of the havoc he had wrought since the death of his brother Delkol. The Brotherhood would have been nothing more than a dying rabble, if it weren't for Trilir. Thanks to him, Augurc and his Brotherhood was truly a force to be reckoned with.

Trilir didn't care about Augurc's goals, and frankly, he wasn't quite sure what the reticent man was actually hoping to achieve. Hundreds of people in the Fiefs Kingdom had been killed at this point (with a majority of them likely being killed by Augurc and Trilir's experiments), but there was little rhyme or reason to the destruction. The insurrection in Istal at least gained Augurc some allies amongst the scheming vampires, though Trilir questioned how much Augurc should trust any of them.

It was all none of Trilir's concern. All he really cared about was Nexi energy, and the possibilities the magical science presented him. And right now, he needed to ensure his employer would be able to keep control over the most destructive monster the world had ever seen.

•

Borely considered returning to the sea so he could retrieve Jenba and Nivakil's corpses, but he had a lot of injuries to recover from, and he didn't want to leave Analicia alone for very long. She was still worn out from the whole fiasco, but more so she was broken inside. After losing her home in Istal, she now lost the one person she had left who she'd known well. Now she was just left with Borely, and still having to travel in this strange, aimless quest. Borely felt it best they put as much ground between them and Limbo as they could, considering how any surviving pirates were probably out looking for them.

For as long as they could, they traveled in the darkness of night, slinking their way across vast fields of long grass. It was painful to travel, but Borely couldn't risk people finding him in this state. He was a vampire now, and the average night traveler would be quick to kill him at the first sign of trouble.

There was little for Borely to think about, other than Jenba and Nivakil's deaths. It didn't seem to make any sense... They were the experienced vampires. And now Borely was by himself, with nobody to help him deal with... anything. With finding the Haders. With finding Areo. With finding... himself. He had accepted the fact he was a vampire, and had to deal with life the way a vampire would need to.

But it was difficult. It was going to continue to be difficult. It wasn't something he felt ready for, but he really *needed* to be ready for it. What was he supposed to do now? He had the summoning Hader, but how was that going to help him save Areo?

He felt so tired... With so much on his mind, and with so little left in his heart, he just wanted to collapse on the ground and let a few months pass away. Perhaps this was a subconscious vampiric desire to hibernate. It still disgusted him, knowing he had these monstrous urges. A part of him still craved blood, even after the chaos that ensued aboard the pirate ship.

He had Analicia at his disposal, but he'd had enough of her blood already. He couldn't let himself lose control and suck her dry. She'd die if she lost too much blood.

Hours passed, and they walked through the countryside in moonlit silence. Borely had Analicia walk in front of him, feeling the need to keep his eye on her at all times. He certainly didn't want her around, but the fact was she was his responsibility now. She'd be helpless without him at this point, and admittedly he was at least glad that watching over her gave him something to do— something to think about other than his failures on the pirate ship, the deaths of his master and companion, and the turmoil Areo must be going through. It pained Borely to think he'd have to one day explain how Areo's master and brother figure were both killed. There was nobody left to seek out Areo but Borely now. He couldn't fail her... There was no one else to help her.

Borely could hear Analicia crying from time to time—but only a little, and in very brief spurts. The child was either trying her hardest to be strong through this tragedy, or her emotions were fried a bit. The situation had to be overwhelming for someone so young. In a way, Borely could relate, he realized... He was young when he lost everyone he loved, too.

This world of vampires was a dark, miserable one. But there was no escaping it, Borely understood. He had to simply make the world better.

Analicia stopped and sat down, her face wet and revealing just how exhausted she was. There was still a ways to go before they reached a town in the area, though Borely wasn't sure what they would do once they got there. It would probably be morning by then, though Borely would have been glad to stay at an inn for a while and sleep away some of his fatigue and misery.

Not wanting to push Analicia any harder than he had to, he sat down beside her, accepting to take a break for a few minutes. He didn't say anything, and neither did Analicia. They simply sat amidst the grass, hidden from the light of the moon, far from any trails people could be taking.

What was he supposed to do for this girl? He didn't exactly care for her—they were both simply associated with Jenba—and presumably Areo. Borely wasn't certain if Analicia had spent much time with her before.

"You going to be okay?" he asked her.

Analicia didn't respond, or even move. She just sat there, frozen in time.

"I'm sorry things turned out so badly," Borely said.

"It's not fair," Analicia said, barely loud enough to register as a whisper. She stared out blankly in front of herself, clutching her legs up to her chest.

"No... it's not," Borely said. "Sometimes you just... lose everything. That's... how it goes." This wasn't quite what he wanted to say, but he wasn't sure how to word anything better.

"Why is everyone dying?" Analicia said. It wasn't quite said like a question—it was as if she had resigned herself to this terrible fact of life. "Why didn't I..." Her words faded away, and tears began spilling out from her eyes unhindered.

Borely looked straight ahead, not wanting to watch the girl cry like this. It reminded him of all the times he had lost it all. He thought of the day he was turned into a vampire first, but his thoughts turned back to when he was a child... Just a boy on a ship, simply glad to be with his family. It only took one day to lose all of them, and suddenly his entire life was flipped upside-down. How had he moved on after that?

He simply... moved on. Just searched for something to do, something to focus on... Something to accomplish.

"It's not your fault," Borely said. "You did nothing wrong. In fact, if it weren't for you, I would've been killed." It was an embarrassing thing to admit, but Analicia did indeed save his life during his fight with Yeaf. And it would be wrong of him to not support her in her time of need in return.

The child kept crying, burying her face in her knees. She shuddered a few times, struggling against the cold of night. Borely placed a hand on her far shoulder, not sure if this was a good way to support her through this.

"If you want to leave me, you can," Borely said. "But otherwise, I'd be willing to stick with you... I'll help you get to wherever you want to go to."

"We... still need to save Areo, don't we?" Analicia said between sniffles. "That's what Jenba and Nivakil died for. And I can't just let Areo keep suffering..."

"You spent a lot of time with her?" Borely asked.

Analicia nodded. "Not as much as I did with Jenba, but Areo was always nice too."

So this mission was personal to Analicia as well. Perhaps even more so now, since there were so few vampires left that she knew at all.

"Okay," Borely said. "We'll stick together then...

We'll find a way to rescue Areo."

Analicia lifted her head and tried wiping her eyes. New tears trickled down right away, so she gave up trying to hide it.

"You're not very good at comforting people," she said. "Jenba would have done a lot better."

Borely gave a faint smile. "But I probably did better than Areo would have."

Analicia smiled a little as well. "Yeah... probably."

They sat there a few minutes longer, trying to decide where to go from there. They needed to either continue the quest for Haders, or search for Augurc and Areo. Borely wondered how he would free her with the power of this Hader he had stolen. Would he be able to defeat Augurc with the power of summoning weapons? And would that be enough to save Areo? Perhaps Rilv's team had found a Hader that would be able to free her mind from the influence of the altered Elpis energies.

Analicia pulled a stone out of a small satchel tied to the side of her dress. It was the teal Nexi stone Nivakil had used to keep in contact with Rilv.

"Nivakil gave that to you?" Borely asked. It was a bit difficult to believe.

"He wanted me to just escape in case everything went wrong with the mission," Analicia said. "If everyone else was killed in the fight, he wanted me to be able to give Rilv all the information I could about the Hader."

At the very least Borely survived, and managed to succeed in taking the Hader from Yeaf. But it turned out Nivakil's caution proved beneficial—this teal Nexi would allow Borely to find out precisely where to go next.

Analicia handed him the Nexi stone, and Borely activated its power. After speaking Rilv's name, it took a few seconds to hear Rilv's voice emanating from the stone.

"Yes, Nivakil?" she asked.

"Borely, actually..." He wasn't sure what to say next.

"What is your status?" Rilv asked.

"We've killed the pirate captain Yeaf and taken his Hader," Borely said. "Nivakil and Jenba died at the hands of Yeaf and his crew, however. Analicia and I escaped, and are a few kilometers south of Limbo."

"I'm sorry for your loss," Rilv said. Her tone was probably about as sympathetic as the woman was capable of, which wasn't much—but it was perhaps a little more than Borely expected. "What is the power of your Hader?"

"I can make weapons appear out of thin air," Borely said. "I now have an unlimited supply of weaponry."

"That will prove very useful," Rilv said. "We will meet together at the location of the next Hader, which has been on the move over the past few days. It is currently situated in a small town outside of Niev. Intelligence has informed me that there are teams of Brotherhood members in the area, so you will need to be on the lookout. Augurc is also in that region. Once you are approaching Niev, inform me, and I will give you our exact location."

"It will take at least a day to get down there by horse and carriage," Borely said. Niev was a ways south, near the border of the Shire Kingdom. "When will you get there?"

"Approximately the same time," Rilv said. "It is prudent we move as quickly as possible. A man with two Haders is currently following us, and we are still recovering from a series of incidents that have transpired. We now have two Haders ourselves. Once we reach Niev, we will work together to obtain the Hader there, giving us the cumulative power of four Haders—at which point we should be capable of defeating the man with two Haders. With six Haders, we will be able to defeat the Brotherhood, and destroy the Elpis once and for all."

"And save Areo," Borely said. He wanted to make it clear this was what he was fighting for.

"Yes," Rilv said. "Plan to meet with us by morning two days from now. I will inform you later of an exact meeting-place, possibly in one of the towns just outside of

Niev."

"Okay," Borely said. With the plans confirmed, Rilv deactivated her Hader, and the glow of the teal Nexi dimmed a bit.

"Once we reach a town, we'll have to take a horse and carriage," Borely said to Analicia. "Did Nivakil leave you with any money?"

She nodded. Even if she had just a small portion of the money Nivakil was given by the Fiefs agent, it would be easy for Borely to obtain speedy passage to Niev.

"Let's see if we can get to Niev first, then," Borely said. He patted Analicia's back and stood up.

The girl looked up at him, her face still thoroughly wearied. Borely tried to smile a little more sincerely, and bent down a bit to take Analicia's hand. She accepted, and Borely lifted her to her feet.

•

It was important to Trilir to always analyze his current situation, determine the best course of action, and be willing to change his plans at a moment's notice. He sat at his desk, looking over the many pages of notes he had taken on powerful sources of Nexi power he had learned about from hundreds of different books and scrolls over they years. The Elpis was certainly the most powerful source, particularly when it was in a whole, perfected state. But there were other stones that had been formed and improved upon over the centuries, and at the moment Trilir could only guess how these Nexi masters managed to shift the application of Nexi power so effectively.

He shut his eyes a moment and thought over his current situation. He was working for Augurc, which was perhaps the most dangerous employer he could ever have. But at the same time, this gave Trilir a great deal of protection—not to mention a great deal of information and tools for him to work with. His own survival would always be his first priority, he recognized. But after that, what mattered most was to place himself in circumstances that would enable him to access more powerful Nexi energies. All his life, he had felt there was no greater science in the world he could devote his life to. Every time he made a new discovery, he experienced nothing but pure, unblemished joy, and he wanted nothing more than to find ways to better the world with his findings.

He imagined Augurc shared some of these same feelings in some twisted form, though the Brotherhood leader was never going to show them. And it was still up in the air what Augurc wanted to accomplish precisely, though the destruction of the Fiefs Kingdom seemed to play a role in it all. But he may have only been attacking Fiefs cities in order to secretly appease the Shire governing body, receiving funds under the table for his Brotherhood—and more significantly, for his experiments.

And what wonderful experiments they were! Most were certainly in a moral gray area, but Trilir wasn't going to speak up against Augurc any time soon. Not until Trilir had the upper hand in power, at least.

What mattered most though was that Trilir was learning more about Nexi energies every day. He could only imagine what the ancient magicians must have felt when they first learned to refine Nexi stones all those millennia ago. Would he ever get to feel the same way? It would take an advancement in magic arts of an unprecedented level.

Trilir scratched at his left eye. It was tingling a bit more than usual, alerting him of potential threats. He had long ago replaced his eye with a Nexi stone designed to help keep him safe, sensing those around him who had a strong connection with Nexi energy. The stone was designed to look exactly like a normal eye, so nobody had ever suspected it to be anything but. Unfortunately, ever since Trilir found himself working with the Brotherhood, his eye was constantly throbbing ever so slightly. Fortunately he had learned to hide his discomfort somewhat while in Augurc and Subject VI's presence, whose gave Trilir a painful headache—at least until the Nexi stone eye triggered an energy to dull the pain. But Trilir had to explain it away as a twitchy eye condition to everyone else who asked about it, and Trilir could only imagine what these Brotherhood members thought of him. It was difficult to tell what any of them thought, thanks to their masks.

But now his eye was bothering him even more— enough to make him consciously notice, at least. Most every Brotherhood was an expert Nexi user, so to sense this much of an increase in Nexi competence was saying something. It meant someone especially powerful was in the area... And as Trilir's eye began to hurt even more, he realized the person in question was approaching this building. Or perhaps it was a group of people... No, it felt too concentrated. Someone was coming alone.

Trilir looked up to the door, where two masked Brotherhood guards stood. Then there was Viecint at another desk in the dimly-lit room, busy formulating battle plans while he watched over Trilir. These were some of the Brotherhood's top men, from what Trilir understood, and he always worried a little about making them mad. The last thing he wanted was a lack of cooperation on their part, making his work and research more difficult. But now he worried they wouldn't be enough for this potential threat...

"Make sure you're ready for any intruders," Trilir said, knowing he had to sound silly saying this.

"Don't worry," Viecint muttered. "You focus on your work, and we'll focus on ours."

Trilir turned back to the two guards at the door. There was something... off about them. Trilir squinted with the eye he could still see through, and realized there was something sticking out of the guards' necks.

Long, black needles... jutting straight out of the doorway, and on through the center of their necks. Two of them in each guard's neck.

Then in one motion, the needles pushed out through either side of the guards' necks, effectively severing their masked heads. The bloody corpses dropped to the ground. Trilir and Viecint stood up, Trilir stepping back while Viecint stepped forward, slipping a Nexi stone in each hand—a silver one, and a pink one.

The long black needles slid back through the door, vanishing.

Trilir and Viecint held their breath, listening with all their might for the hidden assailant. Was he still standing just outside the door? Or was he hidden somewhere else by now... invisible to their eyes?

Something scratched at the ceiling to their left. As they both looked up, something landed with a thump behind them. They both turned around, Viecint running forward to protect Trilir. Someone was there. Viecint raised an arm, which instantly turned silver, expanding with hundreds of razor-sharp silver feathers. Incredulously, he was transforming a part of his own body via the pink Nexi stone, accessing the power of the silver Nexi stone for the transformation form. Trilir had never thought someone could be capable of such a combination of high-level powers, particularly a human.

In an instant, nearly half the room filled with the fatal metallic feathers—the ultimate Nexi shield and weapon all in one.

Suddenly, Viecint stopped. He gagged, and Trilir

looked to the masked man's throat. Two long, black needles were sticking out of his neck. The next moment he was beheaded, suffering the same fate as his two companions at the door.

Trilir knew he was at the mercy of the assailant. Running would be pointless, especially when even the likes of a top Brotherhood member couldn't keep up with the enemy's speed. The needles diminished and disappeared entirely, and Trilir followed them to their source—pale, slender fingers.

A woman suddenly stood in front of Trilir. She was tall, imposing—an aristocrat with long, light blue hair.

And a vampire, Trilir realized.

"You're one of the vampires Augurc Shire assisted," Trilir said.

"I'm one of the masters, yes," the woman said. "I am Hidif. And if my sources are correct, you are Trilir, the mastermind behind Augurc's latest and greatest experiments."

There was no reason to deny the claims. "Yes... And I imagine you're not here to assist the Brotherhood, considering how you just killed a few of them."

"Very astute," Hidif said, her smile condescending.

"You haven't killed me yet, so what is it you want me to do?" Trilir asked. It seemed in his best interest to cooperate with this woman, considering there was nothing stopping her from killing him at a moment's notice.

"Something simple," Hidif said. "I saw how effective your latest experiment was... A vampire named Areo. She killed off more of my enemies in a single day than I and my associates have ever killed our entire lives."

"I see... She'd be useful for you," Trilir said.

"Maintaining hold over Istal has already proven difficult," Hidif said. "As you should well understand, the world of vampires can be an incredibly dangerous place."

"I'm afraid handing Subject VI to you is not a simple matter," Trilir said. "You would have to break her attachment to Augurc Shire first, and to do that... Well, her mind is primarily fueled by murderous rampages. You would have to get her attention in a rather... bloody way."

Hidif squinted her eyes and grinned. "Come with me then, Professor Trilir. I believe I can quite easily arrange a rather... bloody, murderous rampage."

•

The carriage ride was about as fast as Borely could hope for, though at the same time, he wished it hadn't made for such a horrendously bumpy ride. There was no way he was able to sleep the entire way, and Analicia likewise wasn't able to get any sleep. Instead she would cry curled up in the corner of her bench seat, leaving Borely anxious and frustrated. He hadn't been able to help

Analicia much through her anguish, but he supposed there simply wasn't much he could do. Anything less than bringing Jenba and Nivakil back to life would never erase the pain, after all.

The hours passed, and Borely had tried resting in every position he could to get himself to fall asleep. He didn't want to hear Analicia crying anymore, as cruel a thought as this was... Perhaps in a strange way he was jealous of the child. Jenba and Nivakil had died, and what was he concerned about? He still wanted to keep going with this mission. No time to dwell on the past.

But these were the men who helped him through his years of difficulty, as he adjusted to the miserable life of a vampire.

Borely sighed. Even now, he was still seeing it all as a miserable experience.

I've accepted what I've become... Shouldn't I be glad?

But how could he be glad, when the few people left he's cared about are either dead or might as well be dead?

The unpleasant thoughts seeped deeper into his mind. Borely didn't like focusing on any of these things. He didn't like to dwell too long on anything, really. He just preferred to keep himself busy. In the past, he busied himself with sailing, and keeping up his family's shipping

business. It felt like the right thing to do... It was his calling
in life, he had felt.

But then, he had lost his ship and become a
vampire. Nearly everything about his past self was
completely taken away from him. All he had left, it had
seemed, were his weapons. And he clung to those metal
gloves and headband as hard as he could. It was the last bit
of his identity—fighting his own way, rather than relying
on any of the vampiric fighting styles. But in the end,
fighting his own way simply wasn't enough.

Not enough to save Areo, at least. He had to be
willing to do whatever it'd take in order to save her.

And since he was forced into such a pensive
mood, he had to wonder... Why was it he had become so
focused on saving her? Was it just to pay her back for
saving his own life? Was it because this seemed to be the
first time she really needed someone to save her? Borely
recalled being saved by Areo on multiple occasions, during
their adventure with Terico, Kitoh, Lanek, and Suran.

A flood of memories came to Borely. Some of
them were good, others bad. But the main feeling Borely
got was... It was hard to pin down. It was a sublime
feeling. A feeling that he had been part of something truly
grand. Perhaps he had lost a lot of things over the course
of that adventure, but he knew he had made a difference in
the world. Thanks to Terico, Delkol and his armies were
defeated, and thousands of lives were ultimately saved.
And though Augurc and much of the Brotherhood

managed to escape, the Elpis stone was not fully taken by the enemy. In time, it was still possible for the Brotherhood to be overthrown entirely—and Borely was technically still helping out on that front. In order to save Areo, he was ultimately going to need to take down Augurc Shire.

Would the Haders be enough to defeat Augurc and the Elpis, as well as the subjects of Augurc's Elpis-powered experiments? Borely wasn't going to let himself give up. Not now. Especially not now.

He looked over to Analicia, and he could feel a little of that suffering she exuded in his own heart. How was he going to help her through all this if he wasn't even sure how he was going to get through all this himself?

Eventually the driver of the carriage stopped in a town to let the horses rest, and to allow everyone time to get something to eat. Of course, Borely and Analicia weren't about to have lunch in a diner any time soon—or ever—so they had to pretend they were on their way to one of the village's small restaurants.

Borely turned from the carriage driver to Analicia. "Where would you like to eat, Sis?" He was pretending to be her brother, to keep things as simple as possible. Borely didn't want anyone to suspect anything about them, so they wouldn't get found out as vampires. He didn't want to get caught up in any more fighting than he needed to, especially when it was likely he'd have to encounter the Brotherhood upon entering Niev.

"I'm not hungry," Analicia said.

Borely placed a hand on her back to keep her moving, his heart dropping a bit at her words. It felt like she had lost all will to live.

Borely waited a minute before saying anything more. He wanted to make sure they weren't near anyone who could hear them, but he also wanted to think through his words a bit before speaking.

"I'm sorry," he said. "I can't say everything will be okay, or if they'll even get better. But I'll try to help you, if I can."

"You don't really care about me, though," she responded.

Borely kept walking, and keeping Analicia walking.

"Why do you say that?" he asked.

"You're just sticking with me because we're all that's left of the group," Analicia said. "You never cared about me. You hate vampires. Or at least most of them."

Borely sighed. "You're right. I generally haven't liked vampires. Vampires killed my family. And the day I turned into a vampire was... a very bad day. I know now that not all vampires are bad. That's obvious... I mean, I'm trying to save Areo, since I care about her, right? And if I really hated all vampires, I wouldn't be upset about Jenba and Nivakil dying. And I wouldn't be trying to help you out, either."

Analicia pushed herself away from Borely and gritted her teeth.

"You're only helping me because... because of Areo!" she yelled.

Borely placed a hand forward to try and quiet her, but she jumped back and raised her hands in the air.

"You don't want to be with me, so just go away and do what you want!"

This didn't seem to make any sense. Wasn't she saying just a while ago how she also wanted to save Areo? So why did she suddenly want to leave him? She wouldn't last a day on her own. Granted, she was a vampire, but she was still a child. She'd get found out, and it would only be a matter of time before a group of upset villagers managed to drive a stake through her heart.

"I'm not leaving you," Borely said. "Maybe I don't care a lot about you right now. But maybe I'll care more about you over time. You told me you wanted to help save Areo. And I don't want you to come to harm—perhaps primarily for Areo's sake. But it's for your sake too."

"I don't think so," Analicia said. "You just want to stick with me to make yourself feel better. You don't really feel bad about Jenba and Nivakil dying. You don't—"

"Stop it!" Borely yelled. "Of course I feel bad

about them dying. I admit I haven't been able to do much to help you after Istal was destroyed, or after Jenba and Nivakil were killed. But I might understand how you feel, at least. At least a little. I've lost people important to me before." He had made this connection in his head, but he hadn't thought to tell Analicia about it.

The girl looked to the ground. "It doesn't matter if you know how I feel. You still don't... don't..." Her teeth clamped shut, and she looked ready to cry.

"You don't have to decide what you want to do right now," Borely said. "If you stick with me for now, that doesn't mean you have to stick with me forever. Just stay with me for a little bit. We can work together to save Areo. And then you can do whatever you want. It won't be long. But for now... I can at least give you someone to be with. And I can give you this."

He held out a hand toward her, placing his wrist in front of her face. "If you need blood, I can give you some." Borely had a few vials of blood on him, but he needed to save them for the future fights he would undoubtedly get involved in. If it would make Analicia feel better, he'd be willing to give her some of his own blood.

"I... I don't need your blood," Analicia said, her voice getting a little higher, a little softer.

"You're a vampire," Borely said. "And so am I. So I understand you want blood. It will make you feel better."

Analicia looked up at Borely, her eyes filling up

with tears. Borely could practically see the water rising up her bright, glistening eyes.

Borely glanced around, seeing nobody was in the area. He placed a hand on the back of Analicia's head, and tilted it down toward his wrist. She clamped her fangs into Borely's arm.

His eyes instinctively shutting tight, Borely focused on the flow of his blood, slowly leaking out his arm and into Analicia's mouth. She sucked quietly on Borely's wrist, her tears dripping down his forearm.

Borely kept a hand on Analicia's head, thankful the gesture was accepted. Perhaps Analicia still didn't feel Borely cared about her deep down, but she was at least willing to stay by his side...

At least a little longer.

•

The rest of the day passed slowly, despite the frantic, steady pace of the horses. Borely and Analicia both kept quiet, and eventually their sheer weariness was enough to get them both to fall asleep in the carriage. By the time Borely woke back up, it was nighttime, and the carriage was passing at a tamer pace through another small town.

Borely poked his head out the side window to speak with the carriage driver. "How close are we to Niez?"

"Not much further," the man said. "This town is just a short ways outside of Niez."

Borely thanked the driver and sat back inside the carriage. Analicia was awake now too, but didn't look happy about it.

"You doing all right?" Borely asked.

Analicia didn't respond. She wearily turned her head toward the window and stared out with her vacant, bloodshot eyes.

Perhaps it was just going to take some time for her to accept things as they were. It wasn't like one simple talk was going to be enough for her to believe Borely would actually be there for her. She was still a child, and though she was a bit older than she looked, she was still fully a child at heart.

"We'll be at Niez soon," Borely said. "And then we'll be able to move on from there." He wasn't entirely sure what he and Analicia were going to be doing next. They were going to meet up with Rilv and her team, at the very least. Hopefully she had a plan in mind. Would they be able to pinpoint the exact location of the Hader in the city?

Borely felt healed from all the injuries he went through on the pirate ship, but felt a bit drained of energy after giving up some more of his blood to Analicia. But even more so, he just felt unbelievably sore from this grueling carriage ride. It simply was not designed for comfort, especially in terms of an all-day excursion. He stuck his head out the window again and asked the driver if they could stop for a bit so he could stretch his legs and walk around. A short walk would probably be good for Analicia too, especially considering how short her attention span usually was. This carriage ride had to be rather torturous for her, even if she didn't have the burden of Jenba and Nivakil's deaths on her mind.

They got out and starting walking down the main path through town. It was a dark, drab place, but Borely wasn't really there to go sightseeing anyways. This was just a brief stop for them on their way to Niez.

Analicia was still uncharacteristically quiet, and Borely decided it best to just let her think things out while they walked around. He wanted to ponder a bit himself, glad to be walking on his own two feet and not stuck in that shaky carriage. It was easier to hold a thought in his head when he wasn't being bounced around every which way.

There was a slight gasp. It was far away... Far behind him. He stopped and heard a stifled groan. Someone was being attacked. Even with his vampiric hearing, it was the subtlest of sounds. Borely turned around and saw the carriage far in the distance. Focusing as hard as he could with his eyes, Borely could make out a figure grabbing another. It was the carriage driver, and he had turned limp in the arms of the first figure. There was another man behind him, and then two more figures slinking out from behind the trees to the side of the road.

They were stealing the carriage.

Borely sprinted toward the carriage, beckoning Analicia to keep up with him. There was no telling yet who these assailants were, but he wasn't going to leave Analicia behind at this point.

"We've taken down every Brotherhood member in the area," a man said. "Surrounding villages have also been wiped clean." It looked like he had finished sucking the blood dry of the carriage driver.

"Good," a woman said. "We'll head to our planned meeting point and move from there." She was trying to hurry a man along into the carriage.

As Borely got closer, he could see better the figures gathered at the carriage. They were vampires. And not only that—the woman was Hidif, the banished aristocrat who helped spearhead the destruction and takeover of Istal.

What was she doing here? And why would they turn against the Brotherhood now? Whatever the case, Borely couldn't just let them leave with the carriage, and get away with killing the driver like that.

"Stop it!" Borely yelled. They had surely heard his approaching footsteps already, but he wanted to make it clear he was coming to stop them.

Hidif turned to face him, and the man beside her also stopped before getting in the carriage. Borely noticed he was an eigni man, dressed in a gray robe and brown cloak. There was a pack tied to his back, and it looked like there were several large scrolls tied to it.

The other two vampires moved themselves in front of the carriage. One dropped the carriage driver on the ground, leaving his claws stretched out and bloodstained.

"Ah, this is one of Areo's friends, if I'm not mistaken," Hidif said. "Your group has diminished since last I saw you... Where's your unsightly master? I still owe him the pleasure of slicing him into pieces."

Borely stopped a few meters in front of the nearest vampires. He worked to catch his breath rather than patronize Hidif with a response, and checked to see Analicia running up to join him. She stopped just behind him to his right and began catching her breath as well.

"And it's Analicia," Hidif said, her smile broadening to a grin. "Now's the time for you to join me, my dear. You owe me that much at least, what after saving your life and giving you the one you have now."

"I'm sorry, Hidif," Analicia said. "I have to help Borely now... We need to rescue Areo."

Hidif laughed. "You silly girl. I'm already in the process of doing just that. And I'm afraid I won't allow Borely to try getting in my way."

"You're after Areo?" Borely yelled. "Somehow I

doubt you're hoping to free her out of the kindness of your nonexistent heart. Especially after it was her Rite match that led to your exile."

"Areo's no longer a person who can actually think for herself," Hidif said. "She's just a tool, and she will be best used by someone who fully understands a vampire's capabilities. She belongs in Istal, not in the hands of the Brotherhood. And once she's under my control, my world of vampires will never be able to be overthrown."

"Afraid of someone doing to you what you did yourself," Borely said. "And you're not even confident enough in your own power to protect what you've stolen. Instead you betray the people you worked with in order to greedily steal even more power."

"It's the vampire way," Hidif said. "If you can't understand that, my subordinates will be quick to give you a painful lesson in our ways."

"I've learned the ways of the vampires well these past few years," Borely said. "And of the two vampire masters I know, you're the blind one."

"I'd like to see you even attempt to lay a scratch on me," Hidif said.

Borely clenched the Hader in his hand. "As Nivakil's apprentice, and as Jenba and Areo's fellow pupils, I'll gladly be the one to bring you down."

Hidif turned to Analicia. "Are you going to let

him fight me, Analicia? I am the one who saved your life. You know where you'd still be if it weren't for me."

"I do," Analicia said. "But for now, I'm sticking close to Borely."

Hidif narrowed her eyes and glanced to the other two vampires. "Very well. Go and kill Borely. She turned to Borely and added, "And then we will see which of our vampire ways is correct."

The two vampires working for Hidif were each dressed in black slacks and suit coats, and each had a pouch at the hip for Nexi stones. The red-haired man with a goatee ran forward, extending his claws further and further. Meanwhile the older-looking man with slicked-back white hair took out two Nexi stones—a green one and a light blue one.

"Stand back!" Borely yelled to Analicia. He held forward his Hader and activated its powers.

First he summoned a long sword with a red Nexi in its hilt. The moment the red-haired man swiped his claws toward him, Borely swung his suddenly-summoned blade across the elongating claws. With the red Nexi activated, Borely sent flames rushing down the length of the man's claws, and on to the rest of his body. The man screamed first from the broken claws, and then from the fire enveloping his entire body.

At the same time, the other vampire sent vines

rushing toward Borely from the side. Just as the vines were about to surround him, sections of the vines froze and sprouted thin, jagged icicles straight for Borely. He was forcing ice Nexi energy down the vines and turning that energy into icicles from a far distance.

As Borely turned to face the icicles head-on, he caused his sword to disappear and forced a large rectangular shield to appear in its place. The icicles crashed into the shield, and Borely jumped back with their push to escape the ends of any free vines the vampire was controlling.

Borely turned and saw Hidif using a dark blue Nexi to douse the flames from the other vampire. The man's body was grotesquely charred, but Hidif was already slipping out a vial of blood to give him. He'd be back up and fighting in just a minute.

This was Borely's chance to take the older-looking vampire down. While the man was still surprised by the ability to summon weapons, Borely replaced his shield with a bow and arrow, already drawn and ready to fire. Gripping the Hader and the string of the bow, Borely aimed and fired at the vine-controlling vampire. Though Borely hadn't much experience with the bow, it wasn't a far shot. The arrow sunk into the man's chest, knocking him back to the ground. The enemy was still alive—the arrow hadn't pierced his heart.

As the man was gripping the arrow to pull it out from his chest, Borely replaced his bow and arrow with a tan Nexi. Before the man courld get on his feet, Borely used the Nexi stone to force a narrow stalagmite to jet out of the ground, piecing through the man's back and out his heart. The enemy's body turned limp, finally dead from Borely's series of attacks.

He regretted having to use the Hader so much already. The other vampire was fully healed, despite the charred remains of his clothes barely hanging over his body. Borely felt a little weak, but he knew he'd be able to take this man down. The only question was what to do once Hidif decided to enter the fight.

For now Borely concentrated on the remaining vampire. Though his wounds were healed, most of his hair had been burnt away, and the expression on his face was contorted with rage and fury. He wasn't going to be able to use his claws anymore, so Borely planned for whatever Nexi stone the man would use.

The stones were scattered on the ground, Borely realized—the fires had burned away the pouch. Just as the man hurried to grab the nearest of the Nexi stones, Borely used his tan Nexi to fling out another spike of hardened earth. The man leaped back just in time to keep from getting skewered, and the stalagmite happened to knock one of the Nexi stones toward him. He grabbed the orange Nexi and ran toward Borely. With the orange Nexi charging his entire body, the man sprinted faster than was otherwise possible.

Borely made his tan Nexi disappear and gripped

the Hader in his right fist. His metal fistpiece glowed with its own orange Nexi, and he raised his free left hand toward the enemy. Just as the vampire was upon him, Borely elongated his nails into claws, stretching out for the enemy's neck. The man leaped to the side, straight to Borely's jet of water streaming from his headband. Aided with the power of the orange Nexi, the man slinked beneath the water stream and readied his Nexi-powered punch for Borely's chest. Borely powered his fist and slammed it into the man's head, crushing it. His skull shattered, and Borely used the next moment to lob it off entirely with his already-outstretched claws. The man's remains flopped to the ground at Borely's feet, and Borely let out a sigh of relief.

He heard movement and looked up to find ten claws flinging directly toward him. He leaped to the side, but the claws stretched out far too fast for him to avoid entirely. Even from this great distance away—at least five meters—Hidif was attacking him with her claws. At the last moment Borely kept from getting beheaded or staked through the heart, but there were claws pierced through his right arm and hand, his left leg, his left shoulder, and his torso. Knowing Hidif would use these claws to tear him apart from within, Borely fought back the pain and flung himself backward, ripping his body out of the claws pinned through him.

He stumbled backward screaming, but Borely focused on his Hader, struggling to quickly access its energy. A claw flung into the Hader, knocking it out of his grasp. The claw tore open the palm of his hand in the process, and blood poured out along with the blood leaking from all the holes strewn across his body. Borely nearly fell to his knees from the overwhelming pain, but he had to watch for Hidif's claws. Several elongated further and swung for his neck—faster than he'd ever seen a vampire manage, and never at such a great distance. Borely barely managed to duck beneath the claws, but there were already several more coming for his crouched body from his left.

Borely activated the Nexi in his metal headband and blasted the claws back with a jet of water. Using the moment to get back to his feet, Borely turned and deflected back the claws from Hidif's other hand. There was no way to keep back all ten of Hidif's claws though— Borely had to run backward to get out of Hidif's range.

Hidif did not stay standing in place, however. She easily ran forward, keeping up with Borely's wincing pace. Without his Hader, there was no way to defend against all these claws, and he couldn't keep running backward for long. Hidif swung her claws at him, and Borely leaped back as hard as he could. The claws still managed to claw across his chest and stomach, and Borely felt himself going dizzy as blood stained the ground in front of him.

He stumbled backward, realizing this was it. There was no way for him to avoid the next swing of Hidif's claws.

Something stabbed him in the back.

They were claws. Tearing into his back. Borely turned and found Analicia, driving her claws back and forth into his back. Borely fell to his knees, then flat on his face. His entire body overflowed with pain, and Analicia moved closer to continue swiping into Borely's back. She was screaming something, but Borely couldn't make any of it out. He found himself unable to move entirely. Had Analicia cut into his spinal cord? He lay limp on the ground, hot blood pooling across his back. And still Analicia was slicing him up.

Why? Why now? Why did she choose this moment to betray him? Borely found it difficult to think, to put coherent thoughts together. The situation seemed to make no sense, regardless. Analicia could have joined Hidif from the start and helped her fight him. But no... Instead she chose to pretend to be on his side. She chose to wait for the opportune moment to turn against him. To stab him in the back.

Hidif retracted her freakishly long claws into regular-sized nails and took a few steps toward Analicia, now standing a few paces in front of Borely's line of view.

"I did it!" Analicia exclaimed. "Just as he was about to run away, I made my move and finished him! I wish I could've seen the look on his face!"

Hidif stared over at Borely for a few seconds. She looked disgusted, and Borely could only imagine how his remains looked in this state. He surely had to look dead at this point. He couldn't move at all. He couldn't even breathe, he realized. Was he actually dead? No... he wasn't quite dead. He wasn't breathing, and he had suffered fatal wounds, not to mention extreme blood loss... But he was a vampire, and still just barely counted amongst the living. He wouldn't last long, though.

Hidif turned to smile at Analicia and tilted her head a bit. "I must say I'm surprised you denied my invitation to join me."

"I had to keep him fooled a little longer," Analicia said. "He trusted me, and I thought I'd be able to get him if he kept thinking I was on his side."

"That's why you specifically said you'd stick by him 'for now,' then," Hidif said. "I had thought this was a hint, but I couldn't be certain. Regardless, I would have finished him off myself easily enough."

"I was just worried he'd try to escape," Analicia said. "He has a powerful Nexi stone you could use, and I didn't want him to run off with it."

So that was it, then. Had Analicia ever really been on Borely's side? When he thought back, it was possible that every time she had expressed any kind of interest in staying with him, it could have been a lie. Once Jenba was dead, she didn't have any close friends left to turn to. But there was Hidif. She was never there for her, but at least she had been the one to save Analicia's life. Granted, Hidif likely did not actually care about Analicia at all—but in Analicia's eyes, did Borely care about her at all, either?

And all this time, Borely had been hoping he had crossed some kind of bridge with the small girl. Had helped her at least a little in overcoming all these trials they had faced together. Perhaps this was simply Analicia's vampire way...

"Yes... he was somehow summoning weapons out of thin air," Hidif said. "How did that work?"

Analicia pointed to the Hader, lying on the ground a couple meters past Hidif. "It's that stone there. You'll be able to use all the weapons you want with it."

Hidif turned around and looked at the stone. "Ah, is th—"

Analicia's claws slammed through the Hidif's back, and straight through her heart.

The child pulled her claws back out as Hidif spun around, elongating her own claws. Hidif's face was livid with rage. As she crumpled to the ground, she raised her hands forward to extend her claws through Analicia's face. With one quick swoop, Analicia sliced off Hidif's hands entirely. Hidif lay back on the floor, screaming, gagging.

In seconds she was dead. Without a functioning heart, there was no way for any vampire to live—even a master like her.

Immediately Analicia turned back to Borely and began rummaging through his pockets. She found a vial of blood and forced him to drink its contents. As Borely struggled to gulp it down, she got out another vial of blood and pushed that into his mouth as well. She searched each of the fallen vampires nearby for any more vials of blood, and found several more for Borely to swallow down. He still disliked the feel of blood in his mouth, but his vampiric nature loved the taste, and he was undoubtedly thankful for all the pain of his injuries easing away. Once Borely downed a third vial of blood, he felt his back fully repaired, and his other injuries properly healed. He ached terribly and felt weak from Hader use, but he was alive and felt fully able to continue the journey to Niez again.

He sat up and looked up at Analicia, whose face was specked with sweat. She looked even paler than usual, and as worried as Borely had ever seen her.

"I... wow, that was interesting," Borely said. "Thanks, I think."

"I'm sorry I had to lie," Analicia said. "But you were about to be killed, and I thought I could trick her if I made it look like I killed you... I had to take out your lungs and spinal cord to keep you from moving... And I had to count on killing her quickly and finding blood for you before you died for good... It was really dangerous. I was... I was so scared..."

Tears were gushing down her face. "I... I killed her. She saved my life, and I killed her... She... She was such a terrible person. But she was the only one who helped me. My parents were so awful. And she was the one who was there for me, when I had nobody else. And she was evil. And she was never there for me again. And all she wanted was to use me. And I cried and cried for months. And now I've killed her... And I'm evil too. And..."

Borely stood up and placed a hand on top of Analicia's head. "Stop there. You're anything but evil, Analicia. You risked your life to save me. And made an extremely difficult decision. Something no kid should ever have to go through. I owe you my life... again."

This child had somehow managed to play the role of a double agent, killing off a vampire master in the process. And thanks to her, they were going to be able to continue their journey to save Areo... together.

Analicia pushed her face into Borely's stomach and hugged him tight. She cried, and Borely let her. He knelt down and hugged her back, just letting her weep out all the pain and sorrow bottled up in her tiny heart.

•

Borely could hear someone sitting in the carriage, trying to get the horses to move. He recalled there was an eigni person with the group of vampires, and realized the man was trying to escape. Of course, the eigni may have simply been hoping to get away from all the violence that had just ensued, but Borely wasn't going to put any foul motives past the stranger. The eigni may have been in league with Hidif and her followers.

Borely patted Analicia's head and stood up straight. "I have to check on this man up ahead. You can come with me if you wish."

Still crying, Analicia nodded. She took Borely's hand and he helped walk her toward the carriage. After picking up the Hader from the ground, Borely walked up to the right of the stagecoach, away from the corpse of the human carriage driver. The eigni man was cursing, shaking the reins up and down in an exasperated frenzy.

"That's not how you do it," Borely said. "And I wouldn't be surprised if the horses were upset, since their master has just been killed."

The eigni sighed and slumped back on the bench hanging above the horses. He glanced down to Borely with a mix of frustration and resignation in his face. "You seriously killed them all? What... are you going to kill me now, too?"

"If you intend to fight me, I will fight back," Borely said. "Otherwise we could probably get by with a conversation. I doubt I'll take up your whole day."

The eigni leaned forward a bit and clasped his hands together. "What do you want to know?"

"We'll start with introductions. I'm Borely, a vampire from Istal, which recently suffered a large-scale massacre at the hands of the Brotherhood and these vampires you were with. I'm hoping to find a friend who's been captured by the Brotherhood. What's your name?"

The eigni turned away and frowned deeply. "I'm Trilir, a scientist. I specialize in Nexi energies."

When he didn't expound any further, Borely prodded. "You worked for Hidif, and her group of elite vampires?"

"No," Trilir said, shutting his eyes. "That woman kidnapped me. I was working for the Brotherhood beforehand."

"The Brotherhood," Borely repeated. "What were you doing working for the Brotherhood?"

"A variety of experiments," Trilir said. "Many of them have involved the energies of the Elpis stone."

"You've been working with Augurc Shire?" Borely asked, his voice rising.

"Yes, he's the one with the Elpis," Trilir said. "I'd rather not work with him, but it's the chance of a lifetime. Unfortunately it's put my life at risk, what with these vampires trying to force me to work for them instead."

"What experiments were you conducting for Augurc?" Borely asked.

Trilir sighed and gazed back down at Borely. "It would take a long time to explain them all."

"Just tell me what the main objective was for the

primary experiments."

"Powerful servants," Trilir said. "The latest is a giant monster capable of destroying an entire city. Before that, a young elf who can not be killed. And before that was the experiment my vampire captors were interested in obtaining. A vampire woman with the power to kill any and all targets given her."

"Areo!" Borely exclaimed. "Where is she?"

Trilir looked worried. "I can't say where, precisely. She's with Augurc Shire, I'd imagine, and likely heading to Niez. Augurc mentioned plans to destroy Niez with his experiments."

"She's here!" Borely said. "Here in this area?"

"Yes... I..."

Trilir didn't get any more out, as Borely leaped up to the stagecoach and pulled the eigni off the bench. Borely jumped down with him and pinned him to the ground.

"Before I head off, let me get one thing straight," Borely said, his eyes ablaze with fury. "You were the one who turned Areo into the mindless killing machine she is today."

"I... I don't know who Areo is," Trilir whispered.

"The vampire woman who can kill any and all

targets given her!" Borely yelled. "That was how you put it!"

"S-subject VI," Trilir said. "She was just a test subject. I didn't know anything about her. I didn't think..."

He stopped, fear filling his face.

"You didn't think what?" Borely asked. When Trilir tried looking away, Borely shook him hard. "Keep talking!"

"I didn't think anyone would care," Trilir said. "She was a *vampire*... And apparently one of Augurc's strongest enemies. I just operated as I was instructed."

"You turned her into a murderer against her will!" Borely said. "Who in their right mind does an experiment like that? You gave her all this power so she'd be forced to kill targets for one of the most twisted leaders in history! You are no better than Augurc himself."

"I needed to l-learn about the Elpis," Trilir said. "Augurc was the only one who could use it... I have to perform experiments in order to advance society..."

"Areo was a good woman," Borely said, gripping Trilir's shoulders tighter. "She was selfless, and always quick to make the right choice. You took away everything good about her, and made her suffer in ways no person should ever have to go through. You gave her a fate worse than death!"

"It's... It's possible to save her," Trilir said. "It will take a great deal of energy though..."

"I have this," Borely said, lifting a hand off Trilir in order to hold up his Hader. "This is a Nexi stone refined to combat the Elpis."

Trilir's eyes widened. "Is that... a Hader?"

"Yes. Will that be enough energy?"

Trilir took a few slow, careful breaths. "I can't be certain. I'd have to run tests..."

"I'll assume it's enough," Borely said. If nothing else, Rilv and her people were coming with their Haders as well. Borely would be able to either ask them to assist him or force their Haders from them if he had to. He couldn't back down now, not when he was this close to finding Areo. "What else will I need to do?"

"Subject VI's mind is linked with scenes of murder and bloody violence," Trilir said. "It will take a great scene of that sort to get her attention. At that point you will have to get her to stop following Augurc's orders, either by persuasion or by force. To free her mind entirely, she will need to access the energy of the Hader to counteract the energy of the Elpis embedded within her. If that will be enough. Killing Augurc himself would sever her Elpis-enhanced link to him, but her mind would still be tainted by the desires to murder in his name. But even if you clear her mind of those Elpis-embedded desires, her mind may still be damaged..."

"Even if I do all these impossible things, her mind still might be damaged?" Borely yelled.

"I've never tried undoing the enhancements given to my experiments," Trilir said. "It's entirely possible her body won't even be able to handle the energy of a Hader, given that it barely survived the power of the Elpis..."

"This isn't good enough!" Borely said. "You don't just have a machine or something to reverse the effects of your experimentation?"

"No," Trilir said. "All my research on the Elpis is new and unpredictable. It is an energy extremely difficult to tame, and even more difficult to utilize in any fashion. Not without the royal blood Augurc has."

"So you destroyed everything Areo was," Borely said, "and you can't even propose a safe way to make her normal again."

"I'm sorry," Trilir said. "But there's..."

"I should kill you," Borely said. "I should kill you right now. You're the monster who turned Areo into a Brotherhood servant. How could I ever, ever forgive such an act?"

He gritted his teeth and used his Hader to summon a dagger in his hand. It would be easy to plunge it into the side of Trilir's head. The professor was weak, completely unable to fight back against Borely from this position.

"D-don't," Trilir gasped, tears forming in his eyes. "Please... Please don't..."

"You dare to beg for your life?" Borely asked. "What about Areo? Did she cry when you performed your experiments on her? How much pain did you put her through, Trilir? How much suffering did she have to endure, just so you could glean some more about the Elpis?"

"N-no... Please, don't..."

"How many hours of torment did you put her through? How many tears did she cry as you subjected her to the Elpis energy?"

"No, I can't die... I don't want to die..."

Borely gripped the dagger tighter, pushing the Hader hard against his palm. "How many people have died because of your experiments? How many innocent lives have you forced Areo to kill? How much blood is on your hands, all in the name of your precious science? You are the worst of murderers, Trilir! You deserve no forgiveness! Not in this life—not in any life!"

"Please! No! Don't kill me! Please! No! Help me! No! No! No!" Trilir gagged on his tears, pitifully screaming and gasping out his cries and pleas. There was no reason to give this pathetic man any degree of mercy.

And yet... Borely couldn't bring himself to finish him off. The man's crying rang in his ears, a truly pathetic face grovelling on the dirt beneath him.

Why was he faltering? Perhaps there was still reason to leave Trilir alive. The man didn't know for certain how to save Areo, but he at least had to have useful knowledge pertaining to the Elpis. But Borely didn't care about the Elpis. He just wanted to save Areo. And kill Augurc, he realized—the one truly responsible for this horrendous situation. Could Trilir help him with any of these things?

Borely couldn't stand the thought of working with Trilir. He couldn't even stand looking at the pathetic excuse of a living, sentient being.

Borely shoved him against the ground and stood up. "Stay in this town. If you leave this town, I will hunt you down and kill you. Keep yourself hidden from the Brotherhood."

If the professor stayed in this town, Borely would be able to find him again if necessary. He doubted he'd need to find Trilir again after this, though. It was time to find Areo and put this Hader to use.

Trilir lay sprawled on the floor, gasping for breath, tears still streaming. He wasn't responding to Borely's demands, but it seemed clear the eigni understood his situation perfectly well.

"I will return," Borely said as he climbed up the

carriage to the driver's bench.

"Are we really just going to leave him?" Analicia asked, following Borely up.

"Yes," Borely said. "He knows now to never experiment on people, or to assist murderous organizations. He understands now that it'll be extremely bad for his health if he were to use his knowledge of Nexi energies to harm any other living being in the entire world." He said this loud enough to ensure Trilir could hear every word.

The eigni shuddered on the floor, too afraid to sit up and look at Borely. Placing Trilir in a jail would be the best course of action, and Borely considered coming back to do just that once all this was over. But time was crucial, and the vampires had wasted enough of Borely's time as it was.

"Let's go then," Borely told Analicia. "It's time to find Areo."

•

With each passing day, Augurc had found himself growing increasingly agitated. He kept these feelings bottled up, letting them dissipate over time within him. He wasn't going to let himself become anything like his brother. The moment Augurc would be driven by blind passions, he would turn into Delkol. He would lose everything.

The darkness of the forest hid any irritation that may have slipped onto his face. He walked at a rigid pace with Subject VI and a few members of his Brotherhood. Everyone was silent. There was nothing Augurc had to discuss with these people. He only needed to focus.

Soon, many more people would get to witness the terror that was the Brotherhood. They would learn to fear Augurc, and they would learn to fear Augurc's experiments. Subjects VI and EV had proven themselves capable of fulfilling Augurc's demands, and would surely get the chance to shine here as well. And if Augurc felt he was ready, he'd be able to summon the might of Subject MI... Chances were he would save MI for the next stage of his plans, however.

Over the years, Augurc had suffered a great deal following the death of his brother. He did not mourn Delkol's death—in fact, Augurc had seen it coming, so it didn't even surprise him greatly. And in the grand scheme of things, it was best for Delkol to die when he had. The Brotherhood was formed, and Augurc had the means to conduct great experiments on a wide variety of subjects. But Delkol's death brought turmoil to the Brotherhood. Many were killed in the grand battle in Setar, and afterward there were many who defected, not trusting in Augurc to continue Delkol's mission of reuniting the continent under Shire rule.

It was true—Augurc had little reason to care for such petty aims. But he had to pretend he held his royal blood in high esteem. He had to pretend he wanted nothing more than to bring the Shire Kingdom to a new golden age. But the Shire blood meant nothing, and the Shire Kingdom meant nothing. People in general meant nothing.

People were weak. Humans, elves, eigni, vampires... They were all weak. Eternally lost in meaningless, petty squabbles. Everything people concerned themselves with was pointless. They fight over nothing, and then they die. What is the point of their lives? There is no reason for them to exist. They have minds, yet they don't use them. They lose themselves in their emotions. In hatred they kill, and when their loved ones are killed in return, they mourn in despair. An endless cycle of overwhelming feelings. It wasn't that emotion itself was entirely sinful—but as long as people were incapable of controlling themselves, there was no hope for a stable society. There was no hope for any kind of bright future, as long as people were left to do whatever they wanted.

People desire terrible things. Wasn't Delkol a perfect example of that? So was the Shire ruling body in general, for that matter.

And despite all of Augurc's efforts, the Shire royal families could never truly trust him. Most had continued to support the Brotherhood for a while to secretly encourage the disruptive acts across the Fiefs Kingdom, but it was only a matter of time before Fiefs retaliated against Shire. The majority of the Shire royalty did not wish for another war. Soon enough, they would turn against Augurc and the

Brotherhood. Funding was already trickling down, and it wouldn't be long before action would be taken against him.

He was too powerful to contain, though. It was too late for anyone in the world to withstand him. The Fiefs Kingdom had failed to find an heir with enough royal blood to wield their half of the Elpis—it was useless to them. And though the Brotherhood had dwindled in numbers, Augurc's experiments had proven themselves capable of fending off large groups of trained warriors. VI could slaughter an entire troop within minutes, and EV simply couldn't die. And MI... MI had the potential to bring down an entire nation.

The more Augurc thought about it, the more he felt it was time to go to the next stage in his plans. Wreaking havoc in Niez would avail him nothing. It wouldn't further his goals. He had already shown the Fiefs Kingdom that his Brotherhood could not be trifled with. It was time to place that same level of fear in the Shire Kingdom.

It was the perfect time to do so, Augurc realized. Niez was near the border of the Shire Kingdom, the city of Zein just on the other side of the border. Zein would be much less protected than Niez, which was expecting attacks from the Brotherhood. It would be much safer to strike against Zein, and therefore much more effective.

Once the Shire Kingdom understood that it could never turn against the Brotherhood and hope to survive, it would be simpler to receive the funds the Brotherhood needed. The experiments would continue on, and Augurc would be that much closer to reaching his ultimate goal.

For one day, he would come to know how to control the emotion of all people. Rather than a detriment leading to chaos, emotion would be contained within each individual, and utilized in the most efficient manner possible. Augurc would come to craft a people incapable of falling into the meaningless cycle of hate and despair.

There would be no weak people left in the world. There would be a little Elpis energy within every individual. Everyone would help create a stable society, a bright future.

Augurc's thoughts lingered on his hopeful visions as he reached a meeting point just outside of Niez. It was a grove with several large boulders, one of them carved flat on two sides. Perhaps it was once the site for some ancient ritual.

Once Augurc reached the site, he found dozens of bloody bodies strewn about. A violent clash. There had to be at least twenty Brotherhood corpses, and a few other corpses Augurc didn't recognize. Only one living figure remained, standing on top of the flat-edged boulder—a small boy with short black hair. His pointed ears marked him as an elf, and he wore a black and silver uniform similar to Areo's. Subject EV.

"What happened?" Augurc asked the child.

"Vampires killed everyone stationed in the city," the boy said. "I killed all the vampires. Then I brought all the Brotherhood corpses here. City guards have surely seen some of them, though. It took hours to find everyone."

The child had done well—far better than Augurc could have ever hoped for in any single follower. Looking over the boy, Augurc saw the child's uniform was riddled with holes and claw marks. The boy's body looked unharmed, but it was clear the vampires he had gone up against were very powerful. Of course, that much was clear, if just a few vampires managed to take down over twenty Brotherhood fighters.

An attack on Niez would be difficult at this point. The city would be on high alert, and troops were likely already on their way from nearby towns. And if top-tier vampires had taken down Brotherhood members here, it was possible they had done likewise in the surrounding towns as well. A terrible blow, and a serious dent in Augurc's plans. He trusted in the power of the Elpis and his two operational experiments, but even their combined might could find difficulty in taking on an entire city— especially one prepared to face them.

With Subject MI, the city would certainly fall, but there was no telling yet if MI would work effectively. Augurc intended to test it out, but he wanted to test it out on a city he knew wouldn't succeed against him in the event MI failed to summon or operate properly.

"We will go to Zein," Augurc said. "You and Subject VI will take down any and all troops on patrol in the city. Any remaining Brotherhood members in the area will join you and assist. In the meantime, I will summon Subject MI and test its capabilities."

One of the Brotherhood members who accompanied Augurc spoke up. "You wish to turn against the Shire Kingdom? You may control your experiments, but none of us will ever accept such a course of action."

"You mean to question me?" Augurc asked. "If you wish to leave, by all means. Otherwise, you may regret speaking ill of my plans."

"I... I apologize," the man said. "I will assist as the Brotherhood needs me."

"I don't understand," another Brotherhood member said. "Why are we attacking Zein? We serve to better the Shire Kingdom..."

"Precisely," Augurc said. "The Shire ruling class is not unified. The leaders of our nation do not believe in us. It is time to wake them up, and make the people in all the land truly understand what the Brotherhood is capable of."

Nobody spoke up further. Whether they agreed with Augurc's plan or not, it did not matter. If any one of them attempted to harm him, he and his two experiment bodyguards would destroy them.

The Brotherhood was in shambles at this point,

but Augurc had his experiments to rely on. The Elpis would not fail him now, like it did his brother.

It was time to usher in a new age of terror—one that would eventually lead to an eternity of strength and stability.

And it would all begin in Zein, the last place anyone would be expecting.

•

At the end of a thin alley, Shirm found herself lying on the ground, clutching her grandfather's lucky Nexi stone. Three vampires lay dead in front of her, killed by her hand.

It had all happened so fast. She had finally cornered one of them and drawn her sword, and suddenly a second vampire came from behind and attacked her. After one clawed at her back, the other leaped forward and nearly plunged his fangs into her neck. At the last moment she activated the power of the good luck stone... And somehow managed to slip away from both vampires, then kill them. Along with a third one, who seemed even stronger than the first two... It was a series of miracles. She was badly hurt from the first attack, but she was alive, and would still be able to keep fighting if necessary.

Shirm slipped off her mask so she could stare more easily into the soothing blue and gold glow of the stone. She could count on her hand the number of times she activated Grandfather's lucky Nexi. When he was alive, he had always warned to her to only use the stone in the gravest of emergencies. He said she would draw attention to herself if she used it too much, and her stone of fortune would ironically bring her a life of misfortune.

Grandfather had told her he had formed a contract with a powerful being within the stone—an ancient elf with unbelievable power, and more Nexi energy than an entire mountain full of Nexi stones. The contract enabled his descendants to use the stone, and Grandfather had chosen Shirm to be the one to have it. More than anything, Shirm wanted the Shire Kingdom to become a great, powerful nation. A land that would excel in every way possible.

She could still remember the first time she saw Delkol Shire. A man who truly had a vision for the future. There was no way she could turn down his call to join the Brotherhood—everything Delkol aspired to achieve for the Shire Kingdom was precisely what Shirm and her family had hoped for. Always hoping to keep up with her older brothers, Shirm trained for hours each and every day in order to become a respected member of the Brotherhood. She didn't hold any special position, but she could be counted on for any mission. And as long as she never brought too much attention to herself, nobody ever suspected her necklace contained an abnormally powerful Nexi stone. It was her last resort for whenever she was about to get killed, or when she absolutely needed to succeed for the sake of the Brotherhood's goals.

She wished she could have been there for her

brothers, back in the battle against Setar. Or for Delkol. Not only had her beloved leader fallen, but her brothers also died in the face of the adversary. She could never forgive the Fiefs Kingdom. And she could never let the Shire Kingdom falter further.

Which was why she always felt so uncomfortable working for Augurc. Delkol's brother was powerful, but he lacked Delkol's vision entirely. Yes, Augurc always claimed to have the Shire Kingdom's best interests in mind, but it was clear his ambitions were thoroughly personal. All Augurc cared for deep down were his experiments. The Shire Kingdom could burn to the ground, and Augurc would only be concerned about how to fund his next freakish experiment.

Shirm had never cared for Augurc's methods. Delkol was fearless, daring, heroic—a true man. Augurc was... nothing. At the very least, he wasn't the kind of man who could incite any great zeal or fervor in the hearts of the truly loyal Brotherhood members. In the end, all Augurc could really trust was his own power, and Shirm doubted the Brotherhood could last much longer under such leadership.

What was she ever going to do about it, though? She certainly couldn't oppose Augurc. Though he was no Delkol, he was still the leader of the Brotherhood, and contention would not be tolerated. She would be killed in two seconds flat, and she doubted Grandfather's lucky Nexi would change that. Augurc had the Elpis, and even in a fragmented state, there was nothing more powerful than that.

Shirm pushed herself to her feet and put her mask back on. As she slipped her way down the hidden paths of the small town, she didn't find any more vampires. She did find her Brotherhood companions torn to pieces, however. Was she the only survivor?

Eventually she worked her way to a meeting point just outside town. There was a group of Brotherhood members gathered there, and they all recognized her quickly enough. She was smaller than the average Brotherhood member, considering she was a girl in her late teens.

"Glad to see you survived, Shirm," one man said. "Vampires targeted us in every town surrounding Niez. Many of us were killed in the surprise attacks, but it seems most of them have been killed off in return. They underestimated us in the end, but we've still suffered greatly."

"What are we going to do now?" Shirm asked. "What are Augurc's plans?"

"More survivors are gathering elsewhere," the man said. "There will be three groups total, likely with a dozen or so members in each group. Augurc will be traveling ahead with his top experiments. Our task will be to take care of any citizens trying to escape the city."

"Niez, right?" Shirm asked. Everyone was

expecting Niez to be the target. It was a large city, and Augurc had been leading things up to a "grand finale" for some time now.

"No," the man said. He waited a few seconds before continuing. "We are actually targeting Zein. It will be an operation to force full cooperation between the Shire government and the Brotherhood."

Shirm nearly screamed "What?" At the last moment she bit her tongue, however, knowing that such an outburst would be read as disloyalty to the Brotherhood. Or at the very least, it would draw attention to her. She couldn't risk people finding out about her Nexi of fortune now.

"Zein..." Shirm said, hardly believing the word coming from her mouth. The very idea of the Brotherhood attacking a Shire city... One of the biggest cities on the entire continent... It was unthinkable.

And yet, she found herself marching with her Brotherhood companions toward the city, just the same. She couldn't argue about it, and she couldn't run away... She simply had to trust Augurc knew what he was doing.

Was this what she wanted to do? She never imagined the Brotherhood would turn against the very nation it was created to serve. What would Grandfather think of this? Or her brothers? Or Delkol?

Was there some reason behind this madness that she simply couldn't see? Perhaps all she needed to do was trust in Augurc, and everything would work out...

*Just obey*, Shirm thought. *Obey, and hope for the best.* She wanted to clutch her necklace, but she couldn't appear weak now. She had to keep up with the rest of the Brotherhood. She had to keep marching.

Her thoughts rested on the stone at the end of her necklace, prodding quietly against her heart. Would she find fortune or misfortune in Zein? If misfortune... would she be able to use the Nexi stone to turn the tide?

•

# 10. A GATHERING OF IMPOSSIBLE POWER

Once Borely spotted the airship descending in a distant part of the city, it was only a matter of time for Borely to lead the horses in the right direction. Fortunately Borely recognized the airship as having the same design as the one he had flown in back with Terico, Areo, and Lanek and the rest. This was definitely an airship constructed by Lanek, though this one looked in much better condition than the one Borely had been in several years ago, before he went to Istal.

It was evening, and the streets of Niez were largely deserted. Word must have got around that the Brotherhood had been gathering in the region, and people were afraid to get caught amidst the fighting between the Brotherhood and the city defense forces. Borely had noticed some Setar troops stationed in the city. The government was serious about taking down the Brotherhood once and for all, but Borely wondered if there was much hope against the likes of Areo and any other Elpis-enhanced experiments. Augurc himself also posed a considerable threat, considering he had found ways to utilize the Elpis that his brother hadn't. Unlike Delkol, Augurc had taken the time to study the limitations of the Elpis fragments, and knew how to use it without falling victim to the intense pain of its unbelievable Nexi energies.

Hopefully the Haders would be enough to defeat him and his experiments. Borely had a Hader at the very least, and he was going to combine his strength with Rilv and her team. Borely had to hope that together they would stand a chance against Augurc and his forces.

As Borely moved the horses along at a brisk pace through the city, Analicia sat beside him, hanging on to the side of the bench to keep from slipping off. Borely didn't want to delay meeting with Rilv and the others any longer than he had to—the sooner they got their plans ready, the sooner Borely would know how to go about finding Areo in this huge city. Niez and its sister city across the border, Zein, were two of the largest cities on the continent. Both were in difficult shape, but the people were resilient, hard-working citizens of their respective nations, and managed a stable trading system despite the tenuous relationship between the Fiefs and Shire Kingdoms. Borely didn't want to see these people suffer—or anyone suffer—and especially at the hands of Areo.

All Borely needed to do was free her mind, and then... Then he could decide what to do from there. He could thank Areo for saving his life, at the very least, and call things even between them. But perhaps there was more he could tell her. Perhaps there was more he needed to say.

He led the carriage to the side of the city the airship had landed at. It was an open field at the edge of the city, away from any of the major structures or areas where people lived. There were some worn-down factories in the area, but Borely didn't see many people around. Most everyone was probably at their homes at this point.

Standing a ways in front of the anchored airship were four figures. Borely was quick to recognize those nearest to him—Rilv and Kitoh. It was strange to see Kitoh this tall. The boy had grown quite a bit over the years, but he still looked about as troubled as Borely last remembered him. He wondered if Rilv's group had suffered any significant ordeals during their own search for the Haders.

Borely stopped the horses and carriage a few meters away, and raised a hand toward Rilv. She looked as professional and strict as Borely remembered her in their brief time together at Setar. She nodded at Borely, who got off the carriage and helped Analicia down after him.

"Thank you for arriving here quickly," Rilv said. "Kitoh is about to pinpoint the location of the Hader, as well as Augurc Shire's location."

"Good, we came just in time then," Borely said. He looked past Rilv and Kitoh and found Lanek approaching, carrying a few scrolls. Lanek looked much more troubled than how Borely remembered him. He had his hair in a ponytail now, and looked like he had aged at least ten years.

"How are you, Lanek?" Borely asked.

"I'll be better once this mission is completed," Lanek said. It was a terse answer, and very unlike the Lanek Borely knew. Borely felt he and Lanek had each lost a part of themselves over these past few years. Perhaps that was a large reason why they were both taking part in this mission. They both needed to restore some peace within themselves, and it was going to take something drastic to do so. Something truly meaningful.

"How about you, Kitoh?" Borely asked.

"I... I'm okay," Kitoh said. He looked more than just nervous... He almost looked ashamed to see Borely. Or could he be afraid to see Borely as he was now... a vampire?

"Don't worry, I won't bite," Borely said.

Kitoh looked up at Borely, flustered. "No, I'm not... I'm not worried about you, Borely. I'm glad to see you again. I'm just... It's just that... This mission has been..."

"It has been trying," Rilv said. "It will be over

soon, though. We have three Haders amongst all of us now, and we will soon have a fourth. And potentially a fifth and sixth, if we run into Kechi once more."

"Kechi?" Borely asked.

"A servant of Mareba Shire," Rilv explained. "A member of the Shire ruling class. Not much has been heard of him lately, but it seems he has plans to use the Haders to conquer the Shire and Fiefs Kingdoms for himself. If Kechi obtains more Haders, they may pose a greater threat than Augurc Shire and his Brotherhood."

Kitoh accepted the scrolls from Lanek and rolled one of them out on the ground. He placed small metal rectangles at various points around the map, holding it down flat. They were instruments designed for locating points of strong Nexi energy, Kitoh explained, and the map showed all the roads and important structures of Niez.

Lanek folded his arms, staring down at the map with a frown. "So this was how you pinpointed where the Hader was in Velm?"

"Yes..." Kitoh said, suddenly looking very sad. "I drew a map of the village by hand, as Rilv instructed me. The Elpis fragments didn't give a perfect reading, but it was clear the Hader was in the area of the shrine. This along with the fact the shrine was forbidden to non-elves persuaded Rilv to investigate it."

Lanek sighed. "I'm sorry you were pulled into all

this, Kitoh."

"I... I'll be okay," Kitoh said.

Rilv didn't look pleased with the conversation, but then again, she never looked too pleased, Borely recalled. She handed Kitoh the half of the Elpis Terico had gathered all those years ago. It was strange to see the shifting colors of the Elpis once more, and to see Kitoh, Lanek, and Rilv for that matter. Borely looked toward the airship and saw there was a fourth member in Rilv's group. Curious, Borely stared at the figure, trying to discern if he knew this person too.

It was a man in the clothes and armor of the Brotherhood. And the mask... It was a Brotherhood mask, but it had a smile drawn across it.

This was the man who killed Febraz and Suran. Borely was never really directly associated with either of these people, but they were important to his associates from five years ago.

"What is he doing here?" Borely asked, pointing at the masked man.

"Lynx is working for us," Rilv said. "His knowledge of the Brotherhood and its actions have been valuable, and he will continue to assist us in tracking down the last of these Haders."

"Are you serious?" Borely asked. When Rilv simply stared at him blank-faced, Borely took it as a *yes*.

He wondered if such a person could actually be trusted though—Lynx could very well be a double agent for the Brotherhood, after all. And how had Lanek managed to work with this man? Suran was his sister, wasn't she? If Borely had been in Lanek's place...

"I'm not finding anything," Kitoh said. "The Hader isn't in the city, and neither is Augurc."

"Try the next map," Lanek said. "They may be in one of the surrounding towns."

Kitoh replaced the map of Niez with a less detailed one that included Niez, various towns in the region, and Zein. The eigni moved the small Elpis-guided instruments to this map, and then began carefully holding pins above it. He placed a couple pins just outside of Zein, and a third one a little further outside Zein, coming from another direction. It looked like both the Elpis fragments and the Hader in question were heading to Zein. Kitoh then placed two pins right next to each other on a point a ways outside of Niez. It was outside of civilization, and Rilv said this would be Kechi in his small airship, which had been following them all this time.

"If we hurry, we can get to Zein at about the same time as Augurc, as well as whoever has the Hader we're after," Kitoh said.

"Will this person with a Hader..." Borely tried to formulate his words into a good question. "It just seems unlikely for it to be a coincidence this person is moving toward Zein at the same time as Augurc. This person could be in the Brotherhood."

"Or someone who wishes to oppose Augurc, perhaps," Kitoh said. "It's possible there are others who have the same idea as us."

"Will our Haders be enough to take Augurc down, though?" Borely asked. "We could also be running into trouble with this mystery person who has a Hader, as well as that man in the airship with two Haders."

"I will ensure everything goes according to plan."

Borely and the others all turned, finding the Brotherhood member suddenly standing nearby.

"I operate best under a chaotic situation," Lynx said. "I will make sure we obtain all the Haders we need tonight. I will kill everyone who opposes us, be it Kechi, this mystery enemy, or Augurc Shire."

Lanek glared at Lynx for several long seconds, and Borely wondered if the elf was going to lash out against Lynx right then and there. Perhaps Lanek was the enemy Lynx would need to worry about most, before all this was over. Lynx simply stood in place, and nobody could guess where he was staring behind that mask of his.

There was perhaps no telling who would be fighting who by the end of the day.

•

Ever since the disaster at the elf village Velm, Lanek had found himself barely able to even operate his airship. It was something that always came naturally to him... but now he simply could not get himself to care to do anything properly. It made for a shaky ride, and he had to repeatedly correct the airship's trajectory to keep it going toward Zein.

Fenley was dead. He couldn't get the image of her torture and murder out of his head. It had all happened right in front of him. The fact there were psychopaths capable of such horror... It unnerved him. He could hardly eat or sleep. He could barely even think. That small village had held so much promise, so many possibilities... The chance to escape this dark world and live a peaceful, quiet life. The chance to rekindle something in his heart that had flickered into a thin stream of smoke. The chance to be someone other than a hapless nobody unable to move on after the death of his sister.

Lanek's thoughts of Fenley's death only reminded him more of Suran. Had she died in an inhuman way, just as Fenley had? The very idea made Lanek want to strangle Lynx to death with each passing second. That madman had ruined everything for that peaceful village.

No, Rilv was to blame too. Rilv and her obsession with capturing these Haders. And destroying the Brotherhood. Yes, the Brotherhood had to fall, but did they have to stoop down to their level? Did war simply bring out the worst in everybody? Did Lanek just have to accept that there would be innocent lives lost in this struggle?

He wanted to just break down and destroy everything on the ship. Let it go crashing down in flames. Just end everything. It was painful to keep living when he had ruined so many peoples' lives. What was Lanek now? He wasn't what he was just a few days ago. And he most certainly wasn't what he was back in Edellerston. Back when he had Suran, his parents, his friends, and a peaceful village life. Though life wasn't perfect, it was at least... a semblance of a life. What did Lanek have now? Nothing but a quest that may or may not give him some degree of peace or satisfaction or vengeance or something in his heart. There was no way for him to know if anything would work out. He had a Hader. Rilv had a Hader. Borely had a Hader. And so did someone else. And Kechi had two. Lanek felt he could trust Borely to use his Hader well, but he had to admit it had been a long time since he was with Borely. The man may have changed after all these years as a vampire. As for Rilv, there was no way Lanek could count on her anymore. She was willing to do anything for her lofty goals, it seemed.

And in the midst of all this madness was Lynx, a masked man who admitted to operating best in a setting of madness. Lanek had to keep his eyes on him. If he couldn't kill Lynx right now, he had to be ready to kill Lynx the moment Lynx turned against them.

He glanced back at Lynx, sitting on the floor at the back of the bridge. What was Lynx plotting right now? Who was he watching right now? Borely and his Hader?

Rilv and her Hader? Kitoh and his Elpis fragments? At any given moment, Lynx could try killing them all off and take all this power for Augurc. Or for himself. Who knew what the madman was planning. Perhaps it wasn't Augurc or his experiments or Kechi or Mareba or any of these other enemies they truly needed to worry about...

Perhaps Lanek needed to kill Lynx right now.

He wanted to do it. He had the power to do it. With the Hader, he could make himself immaterial whenever Lynx attacked, then make himself material again and stab the masked man in the neck. Then Lanek could take that mask off and wipe that smirk off Lynx's face once and for all. At least, Lanek always imagined Lynx was smirking beneath that mask. It was hard to imagine otherwise.

"You're not piloting the airship very well," Lynx said.

Lanek gritted his teeth. He didn't want to let Lynx make him angry. Angrier than he already was. "Okay."

"You need to do a better job," Lynx said. "This is what you're supposed to be good at. You need to pilot the airship better."

"You think this is easy?" Lanek yelled. "It's not simple to pilot an airship. Especially when your mind is a little preoccupied with all the deaths at a village that were instigated by a certain masked traitor!"

"Enough," Rilv said.

She said nothing more. As if just the mere word was all that was needed to calm Lanek down. He couldn't stand this royal servant. Did she think there was any way he could just keep working with Lynx like this?

"It's not enough," Lanek said. "This is insane. You and Lynx killed a bunch of villagers."

"They failed to cooperate," Rilv said. "Following entry into the shrine, we fought in self-defense."

"We were stealing their Stone of Truth," Lanek said. "We had no right to force our way into that shrine!"

"Perhaps if you had put forth sufficient effort in obtaining it, we would not have needed to take the Hader by force," Rilv said.

"Yes," Lynx said. "Perhaps if you had worked to fulfill the mission quickly—you know, like we were supposed to—we would have gotten the Hader and left before Kechi showed up and killed half the villagers. And the rest of us would have been saved a whole lot of grief."

"Don't you dare try to blame this all on me!" Lanek said. "Those villagers were good people! Stealing the Hader from them was wrong."

"Give me the Hader, then," Lynx said. "Hand it to me, and I'll take all the blame."

"There's no way I'm giving you the Hader!" Lanek yelled. "You're the scum of the earth! The worst type of person imaginable!"

"Tell me how you really feel," Lynx said, standing up. "You know, you could at least try to picture things from my point of view. Maybe I don't want to be this type of person. Maybe I'm working with you people because I'm trying as hard as I can to be someone better. Maybe it's extraordinarily hard for me to maintain any control of who I am, because I'm a product of severe experimentation! Maybe I should rip that condescending head of yours off your neck and take that Hader away, because you certainly don't seem willing to do what is necessary to achieve our objectives."

"Okay, let's stop there, please," Kitoh whispered.

"Everyone will stop," Rilv said. "Right now."

"You feel like you have absolute authority over all of us," Lanek said, "but you don't know when to quit. You go too far, Rilv. We have no good reason to follow you. You're not worthy of our trust."

A hand fell on Lanek's shoulder. He jolted back but stopped when he saw it was just Borely.

"Let's stop," he said. "Maybe Rilv isn't the kind, wise leader we wish we had. And maybe Lynx isn't someone any of us should trust. But we have to cooperate, at least a little while longer. If we fall apart now, we won't be able to obtain the rest of the Haders. And we won't be able to defeat Augurc or his experiments. That's what you and I wish to do at least, right?"

Lanek took a few quiet, shaky breaths. This was all so much to handle, but he had to handle it... "All right."

He said nothing more, and everyone else fell into an uncomfortable silence. The small vampire girl—Analicia, Lanek had learned—was clutching Borely's leg, nervous and afraid. Kitoh also looked nervous, but he mainly just looked depressed. How much had Kitoh emotionally burdened himself with after the devastation in Velm? Meanwhile Rilv looked utterly focused on the windows looking out to the fields below, and Lynx leisurely sat back down on the floor.

How long was this silence going to last? The minutes passed, but they felt like hours. Nobody wanted to be on this airship a minute longer. The sooner they got to Zein, the sooner they could find whoever it was had the Hader there, and the sooner they'd be ready to take down Kechi and get his two Haders. It was a fragile plan, but Lanek had to count on it working. He had to count on it bringing about the end results he had hoped for from the start. He had to hope it would leave him better off than he had been before the mission started.

With Rilv pointing out upcoming city landmarks from the window, Kitoh set up another map with his Elpis-influenced instruments. "We should be close to where the person with the Hader is. Really close."

Rilv stared out the window intently, and Borely and Analicia joined her.

"There are people on that trail leading into the city," Analicia said.

"Those aren't Brotherhood fighters, though," Borely said.

Lanek couldn't see any people at all. Their vampiric vision was even more uncanny than Lanek expected.

"Wait, there's movement in that grove," Borely said. "Just beyond that hill. It's... It looked like a Brotherhood uniform!"

Suddenly there was running. Lanek turned around and saw Lynx sprinting down the hall to the back of the ship.

"Stop!" Lanek screamed, getting out of his seat. Lynx was running away... Hurrying to rejoin the Brotherhood!

"Pilot the ship, you moron," Lynx yelled back. He was already forcing open the doorway in the entry room. The moment it was open, Lynx leaped out. What was that madman thinking?

Suddenly the airship lurched hard to the right. Lanek got back to the controls and readjusted the ship to keep it from tilting too far. Lynx must have used a vine

Nexi stone to connect himself to the airship, and bring himself safely down to the ground. Lanek looked out the window to find Lynx swinging forward with vines, quickly falling down to the earth. He was heading straight to the hill Borely had spoken of.

"Traitor," Lanek muttered through clenched teeth. "He's done it now."

"We do not know that," Rilv said.

"What are you talking about?" Lanek yelled. "He ran off the moment he found his comrades. Now the Brotherhood will know everything we're planning!"

"He didn't take anything, at least," Kitoh said. "We all have the Haders and Elpis, right?"

Everyone checked to be certain. Lynx hadn't sneaked off with anything important. But now he was free to wreak whatever havoc he wanted.

"We have to take him down," Lanek said. "Before he can give anything away to the rest of the Brotherhood."

"No," Rilv said. "Continue our course to the Hader."

"It should be close to here, actually," Kitoh said. "Or maybe just inside the city..."

Lanek watched as Lynx disappeared amongst the trees. "Keep an eye on him," he told Borely and Analicia.

"We are," Borely said. "There are a couple Brotherhood fighters moving to meet up with him..."

"Wait, look out!" Analicia yelled.

A giant ball of fire launched straight toward the front of the airship.

Lanek immediately turned the airship hard to the right, and the massive fireball barely missed the canvas blimp keeping them airborne. This ship didn't have Nexi cannons, so Lanek had to make sure the airship never got hit. It was simply designed to be fast and dexterous—not to be used for combat.

A flurry of icicles flew for the airship afterward. Lanek worked the controls to send the airship diving forward, letting the jagged shards of ice shoot by just in front of the blimp.

"Hang on!" Lanek yelled. At the sight of another huge fireball, Lanek sent the ship turning hard to the left, and then raised it upward to avoid a giant jet of water that followed. There were at least three Brotherhood fighters trying to bring his ship down. From this height, it was unlikely anyone on this ship would survive if it got hit.

"Get us out of here!" Borely yelled.

"Working on it!" Lanek replied. Pulling on one of the control ropes while pushing forward several levers, Lanek sent the ship forward faster, moving it past the hill Lynx had run to. The grove of trees was now just below them, and the blasts of fire, ice, and water were passing behind the airship.

Lanek didn't let up on any of the controls, working the ship to get out of the area as fast as possible. Kitoh could rework the map later to pinpoint the Hader's location—right now they had to get away from Lynx and his Brotherhood friends. They were clearly talented Nexi users, nearly succeeding at shooting down a blimp so high above them. Such accuracy was uncanny, especially with so much power being put into the Nexi attacks.

Once Lanek brought the airship above the city of Zein, he took the time to run a series of checks on the ship, making sure it hadn't been damaged in any way from the attacks. Everything seemed to be operating just fine, so Lanek turned his attention back to the mission at hand.

"We'll have to kill Lynx if we run into him," he said. "But right now, we have to find the Hader. Can you set up the map again, Kitoh?"

"Yes, it'll take a minute..."

Before Kitoh could begin, however, a gigantic burst of light arose from the center of the city. It was a pillar of blinding white light, releasing giant sparks of electric energy from its sides, connecting the dark, clouded heavens with the city structures below. For hundreds of meters around, the center of the city filled with white, ghostly smoke.

"There's something in there," Borely said.

"It's... huge..." Analicia added.

Something had been summoned right in the middle of the city, Lanek realized.

It was a monster. A monster far larger than Lanek had ever thought possible.

Than anyone had ever thought possible.

•

It was the hugest monster Kechi had ever seen. And it was right in the middle of one of Shire Kingdom's largest cities.

"Where did that come from?" Kechi yelled, keeping his hands firmly at the controls of his one-man airship. The city looked unharmed around the smoke-covered creature, so it had to be summoned somehow... But who in the world would summon such a thing? Who in the world *could* summon such a thing?

Kechi had been just about to push his airship to the limit in order to catch up to the airship his enemies at the elf village had escaped in. But now that airship was turning away, sensibly putting some distance between themselves and the gigantic creature that had just appeared. Kechi thought to follow his enemies and obtain their Haders... but there was no time for that now. Mareba Shire would not want this monster to destroy Zein. Saving this city was Kechi's greatest priority now. He was the only one who stood a chance, with the power of two Haders at his disposal.

Using the Haders as much as he had was putting a toll on his mind, Kechi acknowledged. He recognized he had become increasingly willing to do crazy things. Perhaps he had already gone completely insane.

Perhaps willingly going against this monster was the most insane thing someone could ever do. But he was going to do it. Whether he chose to because of the Haders' influence or not, he couldn't let this beast kill off thousands of proud Shire citizens.

The smoke dissipated, and the monster was revealed a ways directly in front of Kechi's little airship. It was... nothing like Kechi could have imagined. It stood on tens of massive, scaly legs, and reached out over city buildings with tens of half-decayed, burning arms. It was an incredibly wide beast, at least fifty meters so, and its back bent at five or six points. It towered well over a hundred meters over the city, with over a dozen different heads, each filled with hundreds of teeth—each larger than a human being. The heads were flattened and contorted, deformed and rotten, oozing red and yellow goo from its many scattered, different-sized eyes. It was in every sense of the word, a monstrosity.

Within seconds it was flattening all the buildings around it. The entire city was in a panic, people screaming and fleeing in every direction. The monster hobbled over the streets faster than Kechi anticipated—it wasn't a slow, lumbering beast. It pounded homes to dust beneath its huge, decrepit feet, and swung its freakishly long, flaming arms down the streets, killing tens of people with every passing moment. The beast was in a frenzy, destroying anything and everything in its path, and anywhere remotely close to it in all directions. Jets of ooze burst from its eyes, and buildings melted in seconds. Fire from its arms flew to the piles of ooze, and explosions began bursting apart dozens of the city's central structures. Hundreds of people were dying... Bodies lined the streets, and everywhere Kechi could see from his vantage point, people struggled in vain to escape the extraordinary reach of the monster.

Kechi sent his airship toward the monster as fast as possible. He personally felt his connection to any of these people was imaginary at best—he knew none of them, and was only concerned about them because he knew Mareba Shire would be. He couldn't let his master down. He couldn't let this city perish at the hands of some enemy Kechi had not yet discerned. Whoever was behind this would surely die—Kechi would see to that. He wasn't going to let any fools have their way with Lord Mareba Shire's glorious new kingdom.

It was time for Kechi to show that nothing—not even the world's largest, most powerful monster—could stand against the might of Lord Mareba Shire.

Kechi filled the front cannon of his small airship with all the red Nexi stones the ship was equipped with. With the ship flying at its greatest speed, Kechi frantically set a trajectory toward one of the monster's many heads. As he quickly drew closer and closer, Kechi couldn't help but laugh. This was a particularly wide head—one of the central ones, as far as Kechi could tell—and it had two mouths and at least a dozen oozing eyes. It was going to go burst to pieces... and amidst the chaos, Kechi would unleash all his power and tear this beast to shreds!

He laughed, knowing this was madness. He laughed, knowing this was suicide. He laughed, knowing his master would be proud.

The ship was now mere meters from the monster's head, and Kechi had set the large fire Nexi stones to detonate on impact. He turned around and ran to the airship exit, forcing the door open and jumping out. Kechi latched vines to the bottom of the airship via a green Nexi stone, and swung himself straight toward one of the monster's other heads.

The airship crashed into the head Kechi had aimed for, and a massive explosion ensued. The monster head blew apart in a collosal fireball that took out the entire airship and snapped the neck of another of the monster's nearby heads. The fiery blast sent Kechi flying straight at another head—this one flat at the top. He swung to avoid a snakelike tongue slinking out from this face's twisted, vertical mouth. The monster then snapped its long, jagged teeth toward Kechi, who activated his fear Hader with all the might he could. The beast held back at the last second, the fear invading its animal senses just before it could devour Kechi.

Kechi landed on the beast's head and accessed the power of the blood Hader. There was an endless supply of blood on the streets far below, and Kechi found that portions of the goo leaking from the monster's eyes also contained useable blood. Kechi immediately sent dozens of metalized blood scythes and lances plunging into the monster's head. The beast lurched left and right, and Kechi used blood to create handholds atop the beast's head, keeping him from falling off amidst the creature's thrashings. Being swung left and right pounded Kechi's body, pummeling him with deep bruises, but he wasn't going to let the pain get to him.

One of the other heads twisted down toward Kechi—several times larger than he was, and it seemed to be entirely made of mouths. It was quite literally nothing but teeth.

The many roaring mouths lunged toward Kechi, who used blood to push himself out of the way and leap toward another head. One of the beast's longer, more bent and jagged teeth sliced Kechi's left side and leg in the process. While in mid-air, Kechi formed a stream of his own blood into a pole which he slammed into the long, feathered neck of one of the monster's other heads. Kechi held on as this monster head flailed about, and the flat-topped head flung its tongue at Kechi. It slammed against Kechi's chest, and for a moment he felt all the life slip out of him.

Kechi swung off his pole of blood and caused all the blood he could to fly beneath him and form a thin path connecting one head to another. Several arms reached in to grab him as he ran, and Kechi caused spikes of blood to slide out from the sides of his path, impaling each of the claw-covered arms and tentacles jerking out for him.

The head of mouths slammed down directly in front of Kechi. He activated his fear Hader to frighten it at the last moment. At the same time, a head with a massive eye surrounded by teeth lurched to the side of Kechi and released a giant blast of red and yellow ooze. Kechi leaped away and caused all the blood amidst the blast to envelop the head decked with teeth. With all the power he could muster, Kechi caused the thick monster blood to squish the freakishly jagged head. The mouth-filled face imploded from the pressure, and Kechi quickly used more blood to stabilize his path to another monster head. Some of the eye-head's ooze had splattered across Kechi's body, burning holes through his clothes and on through his skin. The pain was excruciating, but he couldn't stop now.

He landed on top of a head that had tens of burning, human-sized fingers wriggling amidst broken teeth and a boiling pocket of ooze. Kechi commanded all the blood he could to form into long swords, all of which he sent flying into the torn-apart flesh around him. Using as much blood as he was capable of controlling, Kechi made the swords of blood at least ten meters long, ensuring the head was thoroughly impaled. A few heads were down, but there were plenty more left... And Kechi wasn't even certain the beast would die if he took down all the heads.

One of the behemoth's arms swung toward Kechi. He ducked beneath it, but immediately afterward a curved bone slid out and hooked around Kechi, pulling him back. Its sharp end dug deep into his torso, and Kechi screamed from the pain. He guided a sword of blood to cut through the bone and free him, but there was already a monster head spewing another blast of ooze at him. Kechi used blood to push himself down at the last moment, and the arm melted upon impact with the burning ooze.

Kechi fell to the ground, using blood from some of the killed citizens to slow down his fall. It was still a hard crash, and Kechi felt the wind knocked out of him. The giant monster was hobbling toward him, its cacophony of randomly-sized legs and deep, endless screeches filling Kechi's mind with a pounding headache.

Fighting this beast truly was insane... But Kechi wasn't going to let it win. He wasn't so weak, that a mindless beat could defeat him. He was Lord Mareba Shire's strongest, most faithful servant. He wasn't going to fail now—not when the Shire Kingdom had yet to reach the pinnacle of its glory!

Kechi pushed himself to his feet, realizing he was moments away from being trampled beneath the closest of the gigantic beast's legs. At the last second, Kechi leaped to the side of the first leg, barely avoiding the massive claws curving out from the sides of the deformed foot. A massive foot covered in burnt fur was about to smash Kechi next—he sliced straight through it with a huge blade of blood, then ran forward through the next series of crisscrossing legs. A pile of ooze dropped down to Kechi's side, and he leaped the other way to avoid a tentacle with hundreds of vibrating claws writhing out from its sides. Once Kechi felt he was directly beneath the center of the beast, he commanded all the blood in the area to gather together and collide into a massive web of spikes and blades which Kechi caused to fly out in every direction.

"Die! Die! Die!" Kechi screamed, flinging jagged, hardened blood into every one of the beast's limbs he could reach.

Tens of the giant legs were impaled or cut apart, and the roaring beast began tripping over itself, lurching from one side to the next. Kechi was slammed in the back by a cut-off portion of one leg, then beat in the head by a small twisted foot that spiraled off another foot. His senses going in and out, Kechi forced his way through the maze of legs and piles of ooze, careful to avoid all the teeth and pillars of fire within the chaos.

Once past all the pounding legs, Kechi turned around and gathered all the blood from the streets around him, forming a giant spear of blood, nearly as wide as one of the monster's heads. The beast fell to the ground, destroying several more building in the process. But it did not slow down in its destructive course. Its arms suddenly unfolded and reached out for tens of meters—hundreds of meters. People were still screaming, running, dying.

"You dare to keep attacking my master's subjects?" Kechi screamed. "I will destroy you for your insolence!"

Tens of arms reached out for Kechi, and he immediately spun his massive weapon of blood through the air, slicing apart each of the arms. One was too fast for Kechi, however, and his left leg was impaled by an incredibly long claw. Kechi screamed and sliced apart the claw, and continued chopping away at all the other arms reaching for him. One arm decked with oozing eyes slunk toward Kechi from above, and he was nearly engulfed by its torrent of boiling pus. He realized his right arm had caught some of the spray, and his flesh was burning apart, turning somewhat gooey itself. The pain was overwhelming, but he could still keep moving. He could still keep fighting. Perhaps if Kechi didn't have the Haders affecting his mind, he would have given up long ago.

But somehow he was crazy enough to just keep going.

Kechi gripped his fear Hader tighter and accessed all the power he could grasp from it. At the same time, he gathered as much blood as possible above the writhing beast's remaining heads.

"Die, you stupid beast!" Kechi yelled at the top of his lungs. Several of the monster's heads stopped their approach toward Kechi, and the remaining arms began twitching uncontrollably. Kechi caused all his gathered blood to rush down at each of the monster's heads, hacking away at all of them at once. The beast was too afraid to fight back—it tried to flee, but the majority of its legs and arms were injured.

As Kechi sliced away at the creature's heads, he gathered together piles of the monster's blood, pushing large quantities of its ooze toward the base of its bent-up body. Through the pain pounding against every pore of his body, Kechi willed himself to keep layering the beast with more and more of the ooze. He nearly fell to his knees and keeled over, but thoughts of letting down his master kept him from giving in.

"It was nice playing with you," Kechi muttered, slipping out a red Nexi stone from one of his pouches. He threw it forward, letting a thin stream of blood guide it to the monster—right in the center of the top of its body, where all the creature's necks connected to. With what little strength he had left, Kechi caused the fire Nexi to explode.

All the monster's ooze covering its body exploded, blasting off what remained of each of its heads. The massive blast sent Kechi flying back, and for a moment it seemed all the city had erupted in a blinding, crimson light.

Kechi lay amidst a street filled with corpses, and to anyone who could see him, he had to look like a corpse himself. A half-melted bearded man lay atop his shoulder, and a small impaled girl was sprawled over his legs.

*What weak people, to let themselves get killed like that.* Kechi laughed. Here he was, nearly dead himself.

The monster had twitched for a few minutes after the blast, but Kechi listened carefully, waiting for it to stop moving entirely.

Once the street turned silent, Kechi knew the beast was dead for good. He laughed. Why had that monster been so difficult? Now Kechi couldn't even move. These bodies on top of him... He couldn't push them aside. The stench of decay all around him was nauseating. His body was filled with indescribable pain.

But it was all for Lord Mareba Shire. It was worth it. And as soon as he could, Kechi was going to stand up again. And he was going to find all those people with the Haders. And he was going to kill them too. He was going to torture them and enjoy every second of it. And then he'd have all the Haders his master needed.

It was going to be a glorious night.

•

Kitoh held on tight as Lanek violently turned the airship away from the massive monster that began crawling out of the smoke that birthed it. The sheer number of legs, arms, heads, eyes, and teeth... It was like a hundred giant monsters had been crushed into one incomprehensible, disgusting creature. The beast was clearly summoned, but Kitoh couldn't guess who would be responsible. There was Augurc Shire, of course, but what reason did he have to attack a city in his own kingdom?

At any rate, Lanek was driving the airship away

from the behemoth, while Borely and Analicia held to the window to keep on the lookout for any of the people they were searching for. Kitoh clutched the map, Elpis fragments, and instruments he was using to locate the missing Hader user. The person in question was definitely in this corner of the city, but the arrival of this monster complicated matters.

"Enemy ahead," Lanek yelled as he worked to stabilize the airship. "It's passing us."

Kitoh looked out the window and saw a small airship in the distance. It was the one Kechi had used to get to the elf village, and to follow them all the way here to this city.

"Ignore him for now," Rilv said. "Our first priority is finding the one with the sixth Hader."

"What about the monster?" Kitoh asked. "It's destroying the city... It's killing everyone!" The monster had pushed its way down the center of the city, taking out everything in its path. Its arms crushed people fleeing in every direction, and its legs trampled all the houses and shops to rubble.

"We avoid it," Rilv said. "It does not concern us."

"What?" Kitoh whispered. He understood that their mission was important, but to just let this beast kill everyone?

"Look for a place to land well outside the

creature's range," Rilv told Lanek. "Keep us out of its view entirely if possible."

"We can't just let everyone in this city get killed," Kitoh said. He was afraid to speak up to Rilv like this, but he couldn't just go along with everything she ordered anymore. He had been pushed around by her and her kind for years now... always doing every single thing he was told to do. It was that way back home in Vursa, and it was that way in Setar as well. And no matter where Kitoh was dragged to, he always found himself being forced to use his skills and knowledge in ways he didn't wish to.

And then the incident at the elf village happened. The massacre of Velm... It was something he'd never be able to forget. No matter what he did, he would never be able to undo all the deaths that transpired there. His hands were stained in blood. It wasn't something he could just pretend never happened.

And he couldn't just sit and watch as tragedy unfolded once again.

Rilv was ignoring him, so Kitoh spoke up louder. "We can't just run away. We have to confront that monster!"

Rilv turned to him and frowned a little deeper than usual. "We do not have the means to fight such a beast. Time is of the essence. As soon as we find this next Hader, we will have to confront either Kechi or Augurc. Whatever happens this night, we must be ready to destroy the Elpis once and for all. Do you have your tools?"

"Yes," Kitoh said. During the flight from Velm to Niez, Kitoh had been analyzing Rilv's and Lanek's Haders, comparing their energy signatures and the way their powers resonated under various circumstances. He combined his findings with all the research his team had conducted on the Elpis, and discerned a plausible method of destroying Nexi stones as powerful as the Haders or even the Elpis. With the residual energy of the Elpis fragments, Kitoh managed to create an instrument that would shatter the Elpis upon impact. Its properties were similar to the instruments Kitoh had created to detect high Nexi energies, but there was no way to be certain the destroying tool worked until he tested it out. Of course, Rilv didn't want Kitoh to test it out on one of their Haders, or on their half of the Elpis. Rilv was counting on Kitoh's skills and intelligence, as she always was.

As everyone always was.

The pressure was unbearable. He wasn't perfect. That much was made painfully certain, after all those people died in Velm. And now people were dying here. Should he jump out of the airship and use his transformative Nexi to become a dragon? Would he be able to take on the monster then? Or would he just get himself killed? He didn't want to separate from the rest of the group. And he needed to be there when it was time to destroy the Elpis.

Lanek found a small field to land in—a patch of

dead grass between a number of old buildings. They were a good ways from the giant creature now, which appeared to be heading in another direction through the city. People were running down the streets, crying out, searching for their loved ones... It was a state of sheer panic.

"I saw lines of soldiers moving down one of the streets east of here," Borely said. "They were all getting killed off somehow."

"I didn't see Areo there," Analicia said.

"It has to be her, though," Borely said. "I don't think anyone else is that capable of killing so many trained soldiers like that. Except maybe Augurc. And either way, I intend to go there."

Lanek operated the controls to bring the airship down for a safe landing. "Let's stick together, at least. The entire city is a madhouse, and I doubt any of us are going to be considered welcome here in the Shire Kingdom."

"The monster will assist as a distraction," Rilv said. "If we ignore the Shire troops, they should ignore us. They have much bigger problems to worry about at the moment."

Lanek got up, and Rilv turned to hurry out in front of him. She pulled out her telekinesis Hader, and Lanek and Borely followed suit with their Haders. Kitoh followed after them with Analicia.

At the door, Rilv turned to Kitoh and asked him

to set up the map and Nexi-seeking instruments one more time. Kitoh worked quickly to discern Augurc's location, which was in the region where the monster was located. Kechi was also apparently in that area, though neither Kitoh nor Rilv were certain if Kechi was involved with the monster summoning in any way. The person with the sixth Hader was inside the city, but quite a ways from their current location. This person was at the south end of the city.

"Augurc is there?" Borely said, pointing to the map. When Kitoh nodded, Borely turned to Analicia. "Are you coming with me?"

"Yeah," Analicia replied. "Where to?"

"Areo can't be far from where Augurc is," Borely said. "We'll use our vampire senses and find her."

"You can not leave us now," Rilv said. "We need to locate the next Hader."

"You and Lanek and Kitoh can handle it," Borely said. "I'll join back up with you as soon as I've rescued Areo." Borely looked to Lanek, and the elf nodded.

"Good luck," Lanek said. "I was hoping you'd stay with us, but I understand your desire to find Areo. If it were Suran... I'd want to head out there too."

"Thanks," Borely said. He leaped out the door, and Analicia ran out after him.

Kitoh had noticed Rilv clutching her Hader tightly, and even lifting it up a little when Borely ran out. She clearly didn't want the group to split up at this point, but starting a fight now would've slowed everything to a standstill.

"We must hurry," Rilv said. She held a hand out to Kitoh, and he gave her the Elpis fragments, as well as the small metal rectangles for Nexi detecting, and the larger curved block intended to destroy the Elpis with. She had told him beforehand that she would want to hold on to all these things upon arrival.

Rilv hopped down to the ground, and Lanek and Kitoh followed after her. They ran through the field and on down a dirt path through a run-down neighborhood, pushing through crowds of people hurrying away from the monster looming far in the distance. The creature's roars were terrible even from this distance—Kitoh could only imagine how traumatizing it was for all the people anywhere near the beast... Of course, anyone near it was probably in the process of being killed. And here Kitoh was, doing nothing to stop it. Perhaps he simply needed to understand that he couldn't go around saving everyone's lives, but he had a greater connection with Nexi energy than the average person—and therefore had a greater responsibility to use his power to help others in need. Terico wouldn't have wanted Kitoh to just let the people of this city perish... Even if this was a Shire city. These were still people, just like the people of any other city in the world.

It was difficult to keep up with Rilv and Lanek. They weaved through the panicking multitude, and Kitoh had to really push himself to make sure he didn't lose them.

An entire troop of Shire soldiers rushed out from between a couple large buildings ahead, and pushed their way past the crowds of civilians. Rilv, Lanek, and Kitoh suddenly found themselves caught in the midst of the troop and their weapons. None of the soldiers were attacking them specifically, but Kitoh worried they would be read as enemies at any given moment, and suddenly they'd have nearly a hundred armed men to deal with...

People began screaming. Louder. More violently. Soldiers were screaming. Kitoh turned left and right, searching for the cause of the commotion. All he could see were people running in every direction. And now Lanek and Rilv were gone... A soldier flailed backward, knocking into two other soldiers. A few meters in front of Kitoh, a screaming civilian fell over, bleeding everywhere. More soldiers were screaming, crashing into each other. The loud, screeching scrapes of metal against metal reverberated all around Kitoh.

Someone was killing all the soldiers, as well as any civilians in their midst.

Kitoh spotted Lanek, getting pushed aside by a couple soldiers. The Shire swordsmen were rushing toward the enemy, which Kitoh finally found a few meters to his left. A young boy dressed in black and silver. An elf, Kitoh realized. And the boy had long, wide blades grafted to his arms, covering them entirely on both sides.

The boy leaped toward one soldier and spun in the air. His blades sliced the man's head clean off, and immediately upon landing, the boy leaped at another soldier, stabbing him beneath the arm where there was no armor. Soldiers tried throwing knives or reaching for the boy with lances, but the boy simply dodged all the weapons. It was almost as if time was passing by more slowly for the boy, and this legion of soldiers had no hope of keeping up with him. One at a time, the boy killed each and every soldier that drew near him.

And these soldiers weren't poor swordsmen or lancers—they were wielding their weapons well. A number of them came together behind the boy and attacked him at the same time. The boy spun around and slashed away at their weapons, deflecting them. But at the same time, a swordsman slipped past some civilians that kept him hidden to the boy's right. The man swung his sword through the boy's side, and Kitoh thought it was all over.

Instead the boy sliced the man's head off, and proceeded to take down each of the other soldiers that attacked him all at once.

Lanek grabbed Kitoh's hand and tried helping him past the last of the gathering soldiers. The elf boy in black slipped past the soldiers surrounding him and began taking down the soldiers in front of Lanek and Kitoh. A couple civilians were killed in the process, and Kitoh realized this child intended to kill each and every single person in this area. Ahead, Kitoh spotted Rilv running toward them, using her telekinesis Hader to push aside a couple soldiers who rushed in front of her, likely recognizing her Fiefs royal uniform. A couple other soldiers spotted Kitoh and Lanek, and yelled out to them, curious what an eigni and elf were doing here.

Before these soldiers could reach them, however, the child with arm blades tore through a few more people and continued running straight into these soldiers, the mangled bodies of his previous victims still impaled through his blades. The child was much faster and stronger than anyone his age had any right to be. He had to be about five years younger than Kitoh... The age Kitoh was when he was first dragged into a series of terrifying adventures.

*This child is an experiment*, Kitoh realized. This was one of Augurc's Elpis-powered experiments. The very idea that Augurc would use a young boy as a weapon like this...

No, it wasn't that inconceivable. After all, how different was Kitoh? From the very beginning, he had been regarded as a powerful entity... A tool to be used by those above him. A means for achieving specific, bloody goals.

This boy was like Kitoh, but had been driven to the point of losing his mind entirely...

"Look out!" Lanek yelled. He pushed Kitoh aside

and activated his Hader. The experiment boy sliced his arm blades straight through Lanek and stumbled forward. Just in time, Lanek had made himself immaterial, saving his life.

The boy recovered instantly and took down another soldier in his way. He tore apart the man and leaped back straight to Kitoh. Immediately Kitoh slipped out a dark blue Nexi and blasted the experiment boy with an especially wide jet of water. Had it been a normal-sized attack, the boy would have easily dodged, but Kitoh knew he couldn't hold back against this opponent. And at this point, Kitoh knew there was no escaping this child. He had to defeat him...

"We need to get out of here!" Rilv yelled, pushing aside a soldier via telekinesis.

Suddenly the child was behind Rilv, about to stab her in the back.

Kitoh turned and blasted a thin, powerful jet of water at the child, careful to keep from shooting Rilv's head or shoulder. She crouched down and Kitoh expanded the blast, moving it toward the experiment boy as he turned back into the crowds.

The boy ran straight into a soldier's lance, impaling him straight through the chest.

Kitoh sighed. It wasn't the ending he wanted... He truly hoped he could have thought of a way to save the poor boy. But what hope was there, really?

The boy leaped back and tore out the lance from his chest. There was a gaping, bleeding hole in the boy's body, but he immediately began jabbing his arm blades into the soldier that dealt him the blow.

Without screaming, without stopping for a second... The boy was attacking more of the soldiers and civilians in the area. What few of them were left.

Kitoh remembered Augurc's experiments on some of his captured Brotherhood members. Back in the battle for Setar, some members of the Brotherhood were capable of fighting on and on, regardless of their injuries. But this was on a different level entirely. This boy was fighting despite wounds that should have been utterly fatal.

Amidst the boy's frenzy, Kitoh noticed the child's huge injury had healed entirely. There was a hole in his shirt, but nothing more, save for some blood that had spilled out back when there was a hole through his body.

The last of the soldiers were finished off—it was just Kitoh's group and a few injured civilians left. Kitoh slipped out his transformative Nexi stone. Would he be able to kill this boy if he had to? He didn't want to... He didn't want to stoop to that level. This boy didn't want to be killing these people. If only Kitoh knew how to save him...

Lanek used a green Nexi to send vines toward the boy. As the boy sliced apart all the vines, Rilv used telekinesis to drive a sword through the back of the boy's head, the blade sticking out the right side of the front of his face. Kitoh gasped, and the boy stumbled down to his knees.

"Good, now let us hurry," Rilv said. "We do not..."

She stopped as the boy stood back up and wrenched the sword out of his head, his arm blades scraping hard against the metal of the sword. Without even a moment's hesitation, he was rushing toward Rilv. She jumped back and used her Hader to push the boy back. He flung backward several meters, but landed on his feet. Lanek released a burst of ice Nexi energy to try capturing the boy by his feet, but the child was too quick, leaping hard to the side immediately upon landing.

There was no way to kill this boy, Kitoh realized. It was simply impossible. The Elpis was used in some way to make it so the boy would survive any painful injuries, and regenerate in the event of a fatal blow.

Rilv used her Hader to send several weapons flying at the boy from multiple directions. The boy was prepared for telekinesis now, and managed to avoid all the attacks. Lanek took out a fire Nexi and released a wave of fire at the boy, which the child leaped straight through. The boy's blade nearly lobbed Lanek's head off, but he managed to wield his immaterial Hader just as the blade cut into his neck. As the boy passed him, Lanek stumbled forward, clutching his bleeding neck.

Before the boy could turn and stab Lanek in the back, Kitoh shot off another blast of water to keep the boy back. Kitoh knew none of his attacks would actually kill the boy, or even harm him... So what was he going to do?

As the boy dodged Kitoh's water blasts, Rilv used a purple Nexi stone to create explosions of violent energy all around the enemy. The boy was pummeled back and forth, and any normal human being would have surely been killed in the process. Instead, the boy fell to the ground and immediately ran straight for Rilv.

At the last moment, Rilv caused a sword to fly in her grasp, and she plunged the blade straight through the boy's neck, severing his head entirely. The boy's body crashed into Rilv, who barely managed to avoid the ends of his blades. The sides of his weapons cut into her as they fell to the ground, and Kitoh ran over to check if she was all right. Gasping, Rilv shoved the boy's headless body aside and clutched at a deep cut in the side of her stomach, and another in her right arm.

"I will be fine," Rilv said. "I only need bandages. Check on Lanek."

"I'll live too," Lanek said quietly, still clutching his neck. "Just get me some bandages."

Kitoh had some on him in a pouch, but he felt certain this battle wasn't over yet. If the boy could survive getting impaled through the heart...

Kitoh looked to the boy's corpse. Something was growing from its severed neck... A thick, bloody mass... A portion of it turned to bone, then eyes formed, and teeth and flesh... Then all the same elements of the boy's face that existed on the boy's severed head, which was still lying on the ground. In a matter of seconds, the boy regenerated his entire head.

Fully alive and well again, the boy ran straight for Kitoh.

There simply was no way to kill him. And with Rilv and Lanek both injured...

Kitoh leaped back to Lanek and grabbed his Hader from him.

Without warning, Kitoh found himself in a different setting entirely. The street was gone, as were all the corpses, and the buildings, and the screams of the distant monster... In their place was a graveyard.

Lanek had told Kitoh about the graveyard world within the Hader... as well as the goddess who inhabited it. Reali, he had called her. One of the divine beings the elves worshiped in that village. Kitoh had not had the time to dwell too much on what any of this entailed, but now he had to decide how he was going to use the power of the Hader to stop the experiment boy. This reality existed outside of time, so Kitoh at least had the chance to think of a plan.

"Another visitor so soon," a voice said.

Kitoh looked and found an elf in a black and white dress—a woman in her twenties. She approached him slowly, cautiously.

"Hi," Kitoh said. "My friends were in trouble, so I grabbed the Hader... I was just planning to use it to defend myself against the enemy, but I ended up here. I guess anyone who wishes to use the Hader is sent here... And I take it you are Reali? My friend told me about you."

"Yes," the woman said. "Your friend said he would use my power for good purposes. Has he done so?"

"He hasn't had much chance to yet," Kitoh said. "I haven't been able to do much good yet either. Our mission has been very... difficult."

"You wish to use my power to defend yourself against an enemy?" Reali asked.

"I don't know," Kitoh said. "I mean... yes, I want to defend myself... But I don't really want to hurt this boy. He's an elf like you, but his mind's been altered by a strong Nexi power—the Elpis. He's just being used. He can't help himself..."

"He reminds you of yourself," Reali said.

Kitoh bit his lip and looked to the ground. "Yes... but I can at least choose what I wish to do. If I really try and stand up for myself... I can achieve something good with my own power."

"Your power alone is not enough to save that boy," Reali said. "Your connection to Nexi energy is great, though. Enough that you can become one with my power."

"What do you mean?" Kitoh asked.

"My power is the power to transcend realities," Reali said.

Kitoh thought over it for a minute. "So... with your power, I could slip in and out of existence... Would I be able to take others with me?"

"If you are strong enough," Reali said. "I am willing to lend my power, and let you try. Are you willing to transcend your own reality?"

Kitoh clamped his hands tight into fists. "You mean... am I willing to die..."

"That is one way of looking at it," Reali said. "The Nexi essence spans across many realities, connecting all the powers and truths a single being can come to hold and understand. Your mind is much clearer, must stronger than any other I have ever seen. If you wish to save that child, I believe you will find a way to do so."

"If not in this reality, then perhaps in another," Kitoh said.

"You may find the answers to all the questions you seek in another realm," Reali said.

Kitoh took a deep breath, and chuckled a little. It was a nervous laugh. He wasn't sure if this was the right course of action to take. Was this his path? He was born with a greater connection to Nexi energy than anyone his people had known for centuries. And yet he had never chosen anything for himself. He was always regulated to fulfilling duties for those in power, wherever that might be. Would that trend continue forever? Perhaps Lanek and Borely and the others would be able to change the world for the better. But what would Kitoh do then? Would he ever get to choose?

This was his chance to take a step forward—in a direction he chose to travel. There was nobody telling him to seek truth in another reality.

And this was his chance to save a life. And if he could save this elf boy's life, perhaps he could learn how to save the lives of everyone else experimented on by Augurc and the Brotherhood.

"I'll do it," Kitoh said. "Reali, please lend me your power. Once I transcend my reality... please resume your contract with Lanek."

"I will be curious to see how far you will go," Reali said.

She disappeared, and so did the graveyard. Kitoh found himself back in Zein, and the elf boy was leaping straight toward him, arm blade raised forward.

Kitoh stepped to the side of the arm blade and thrust his hand forward, pushing the Hader against the elf boy's chest. Immediately upon impact, Kitoh activated the power of the Hader.

His mind cleared, and his body felt light... then lifeless.

He vanished, and the elf boy vanished with him.

Kitoh found himself enveloped in white light, then darkness, then nothingness.

And then... another world. He stood in a bright, grassy field, and the elf boy lay on the ground, unconscious.

The elf boy wasn't prepared to transcend his reality—Kitoh had forced it upon him. The boy was still alive though, and Kitoh knew he could find a way to free the elf's mind. This was a reality with a much greater connection with Nexi energy... The possibilities were endless, Kitoh felt.

He smiled. He was free. For all intents and purposes, he had died...

And yet he never felt more alive.

●

As Lynx had hoped, Lanek managed to pilot the airship well enough to avoid all the Brotherhood's attacks.

Lynx had grown a little worried when Lanek had started getting sloppy with his piloting skills, but the elf fortunately pulled through in the end.

There were nine Brotherhood members gathered here, not including Lynx himself. He felt certain one of these people had the Hader that Kitoh had detected. A Brotherhood member would be strong enough to form a contract and utilize the power of a Hader. Lynx just had to keep pretending he was truly on their side.

One of the Brotherhood fighters cursed as Lanek's airship got out of range of their Nexi stones.

"Don't worry, they will land somewhere in the city," Lynx said. "We can ambush them then."

"Lynx, what is the enemy planning?" a large man asked. Lynx recognized him as a higher-up in the Brotherhood—a bald man who wielded a giant axe and went by the codename Iron.

"The enemy has obtained abnormally powerful Nexi stones they intend to use against us," Lynx said. "They believe these stones have the power to withstand the might of Augurc and the Elpis."

"Impossible," Iron said. "But regardless, we must bring them down."

"The stones do pose a threat," Lynx said. "One is capable of granting the user telekinesis, and another allows the user to become ghostlike, able to pass through solid objects. Augurc has asked me to retrieve these Nexi stones so he can study them for future experiments. He wishes to collect all Nexi stones that hold significant power, regardless of their ability." Lynx looked from one Brotherhood member to the next, to see if any of them reacted in a particular way to his words. Unfortunately everyone wore a mask, so it was difficult to read what any of them were thinking. At the very least, none of them spoke up to reveal they had a Hader.

"Understood," Iron said. "We will seek them out and retrieve their Nexi stones."

"Wait a second," one of the other Brotherhood fighters spoke up. A tall, lanky man with green hair. "If you really are Lynx, you would have been able to kill everyone in that airship and take their Nexi stones yourself."

Lynx understood he had a reputation amongst the Brotherhood as one of Augurc's top agents. Over the years he had been given many of the organization's most dangerous missions.

"I tried to take them by surprise," Lynx said, "but as I mentioned, their Nexi stones are extremely advanced. Against multiple enemies, it was simply too much to handle. I timed my attack so that if I had to, I would be able to escape and call in the assistance of other Brotherhood members. Unfortunately you all failed to shoot the airship down."

Emphasizing the power of the Haders and shifting some blame to these Brotherhood fighters seemed to accomplish what Lynx had hoped. Nobody refuted him any further.

"I recognize him as Lynx," Iron said. "If he says he was overwhelmed, then it only means we must take these enemies seriously."

"What are your current orders?" Lynx asked Iron.

"Simply to assist in the invasion on Zein," Iron said. "Augurc is instigating a central attack with his three working experiments—primarily that monster he's summoned... We were asked to take down as many people as possible escaping the city."

Augurc just wanted the Brotherhood out of the way, Lynx realized. This was a massive operation designed to push his experiments to their limit, and perhaps a test of the Brotherhood's loyalty.

"Everyone has agreed to this?" Lynx asked.

"Of course not," one of the Brotherhood members said. A smaller man with a deep voice, perhaps in his late thirties. "It makes no sense for us to attack a Shire city."

Iron turned around and unclipped his axe from his back, pointing the end of it directly in front of the mask of the man who spoke up. "If you wish to run away like all those other cowards, you best do so now. Augurc's orders are law. You may not understand the purpose of each and every mission you are given, but as a member of the Brotherhood, you must fulfill your duties absolutely as you are commanded."

"Yes..." the man said. "Of course."

Perhaps he was the one with the Hader. It made sense for someone questioning Augurc at this time to not admit to having it.

Iron turned back to Lynx. "Of course, we will make it a priority to assist you in retrieving these Nexi stones. How many of us do you require to assist you?"

Lynx looked from one Brotherhood member to the next. He couldn't just have them all come with him.

"Do any of you know or have any kind of experience with abnormally powerful Nexi stones?" Lynx asked. "Or have any knowledge of someone else in the Brotherhood who does?"

Nobody spoke up. Lynx looked to each masked member, trying to read any kind of subtle body language. One person glanced to the side a bit... Was that a sign he knew of a Hader, but didn't want to admit it?

"If anyone knows anything, it's going to be you," a man with a bow and arrow said. "What's the point of asking this? We're wasting time."

Lynx wondered if this man should be regarded as

suspicious as well. This man might be eager to get to the city so he could escape with the Hader amidst the chaos.

"We can split up into three groups," Lynx said. If it came to a fight, he felt he could take on up to three members at a time. "Three of you can come with me." He pointed to the three he felt were most likely to have the Hader, based on what extraordinarily little information he had to go off of.

The other two groups formed, with Iron leading one of them, and a small Brotherhood member with long brown hair leading the other. Lynx realized this member was a woman, which was a bit rare in the Brotherhood. There was no evidence, but she could have reason to keep a Hader secret, if she had been using it in order to get into the Brotherhood.

"We will follow the airship to where it lands," Lynx said. "Where will each of your groups go?"

"We will remain south of the monster," Iron said. "If we clear the area, we will head east."

"We will stick west of the monster," the woman said—a rather young woman, judging by her voice.

"Okay, let's go then," Lynx said. He didn't wish the other groups luck. There was a fair chance Lynx was going to be killing many of these people shortly.

He hated to give in to killing people, even if they were his enemies. It was difficult to maintain any semblance of his true self once he started killing... It had been so deeply embedded in his mind and heart that it was right to kill for Augurc, that it was right to end people's pitiful existences...

Somehow, Lynx had to free his mind. Year after year, he had struggled to even think for himself, let alone overcome the overwhelming influences on his emotions. It had taken a very long time for him to reach this point... to be capable of working against Augurc at all... He couldn't fail now. He had to obtain the Haders. Somehow he had to believe they would be powerful enough to save him. If he couldn't find a way to use the Hader to free his mind, then perhaps Kitoh could figure something out. Or even the professor Trilir, if Lynx had to hold up his facade as a Brotherhood member. What mattered was that he obtain a Hader... He had betrayed many people to reach this point—he couldn't stop now.

Lynx led the three Brotherhood members he chose into the city. There were people running as far away as they could from the monster, though some found vantage points from which to gaze in shock at the gigantic beast. As soon as some of the monster's freakishly long arms moved in their direction, they were quick to break out of their stupor and flee.

Lynx could only guess what the rest of the Brotherhood was feeling deep down. These were people they had intended to protect all their lives—people they were willing to fight for and die for. Augurc's ability to summon such an incredible monster surely left many members of the Brotherhood in a state of amazement—perhaps even worship. But for some, the monster surely represented not a wonderful power, but a terror that should have never existed in the first place. Would Augurc's actions this day weed out the unbelieving and make the Brotherhood even more zealous, even more blind and ambitious? Or would the Brotherhood finally crumble and fall, just like these city buildings?

Lynx brought his team through a crowd of soldiers, which was likewise pushing its way through a crowd of citizens. It was time to take on his teammates, one at a time... The best way to find out who had the Hader was to push him to use it.

Lynx weaved between people and sneaked behind one of his teammates. The man turned around just as he realized what was happening. Lynx slashed him across the neck with his knife.

It was unlikely this man had the Hader...

Before the other two members of the team could notice, Lynx sneaked between more people, some of them screaming upon seeing the dead Brotherhood fighter amongst them—but many of the people were screaming already anyways. Lynx spotted one of his teammates and stabbed him in the back. The man spun around and swung his sword at Lynx, who dodged, then drew his own sword to defend against the following swings. It was impressive how well the man could fight while stabbed in the back, but Lynx noted he wasn't reaching for any Nexi stones.

It took a minute to finish him off, by which point the other member of the team had spotted Lynx's betrayal. The man powered his lance with a white Nexi stone, and released a bolt of lightning. Lynx grabbed the man he fought off and used him as a shield. The corpse was shot by the lightning, and Lynx sprinted with his sword drawn forward. The man took out a green Nexi and sent vines for Lynx from multiple directions. Knowing the man would shoot another bolt of lightning at wherever the vines forced Lynx to go, Lynx threw his sword forward. It landed straight in the man's neck.

With all three down, Lynx worked quick to check all their pockets and pouches, just to make sure they didn't have the Hader. As Lynx expected, they only had a few normal Nexi stones. He hurried to where he imagined the Brotherhood group that moved to the western side of the city would be. Some of the Shire soldiers tried attacking him, witnessing Lynx's murder of the three Brotherhood members, but Lynx was too quick for them.

He ran up and down several streets, searching for any sign of Brotherhood members. He had noted where the group had run toward, but he couldn't find any places where people were getting killed off. The Brotherhood team had to be somewhere near the edge of the city, down one of the primary paths... They were probably able to kill all the civilians they wanted, and the Shire troops would be too busy fighting off Augurc's experiments to interfere. A thoroughly reprehensible operation, and yet deep down Lynx could feel some measure of glee in it all.

Wasn't life filled with suffering? The only way to enjoy life was to be the one making others suffer. It was the only to take your mind away from your own suffering...

He had already stained his blade. He could keep going. Just go along with the orders to kill as many people as possible.

No. He couldn't let himself sink to that level. Not again. He had killed enough. Enough for a hundred lifetimes. He wanted the pain to end. If it was possible for it to end.

He had to believe it could end. It was the only way for him to keep living. And he had to keep living. He had to turn his life around. Amend all his wrongs, at least to some small degree.

At last, he spotted a Brotherhood member. A figure sitting at the top of a zig-zagging staircase, leading to the fourth story of an old, weathered brick building. It was the young woman, and she was crouched down, her masked face in her hands. Where were her two companions? Lynx searched amongst the people below, and nobody appeared to be getting killed by anyone.

Lynx hurried to the stairway and ran up it. The woman stood up and turned to run.

"Wait!" Lynx yelled.

She ran across a wood board that acted as a thin bridge between two buildings. She was climbing to the roof of that building as Lynx reached the top of the stairway of the first building.

He looked to her hands and saw it. In one of her fists was a Hader, glowing blue and gold.

"Hold on!" Lynx called out. He ran onto the long wood plank, which inexplicably broke apart as he reached its center. It was thick and sturdy—why did it suddenly break now?

He fell quickly, but managed to use a green Nexi stone to latch onto a stairway railing. He wasn't fast enough to stop the fall entirely, but he landed without breaking his legs, at least. Unfortunately, the Brotherhood woman was getting further away now.

Lynx used the green Nexi to bring himself up the stairway and onto the metal slanted roof. The woman used a vine Nexi of her own to get down the other side of the roof. She ran on down a small side street, which had few people in it. Lynx followed after her, trying to decide why she was running away. Did she know he was taking down the other Brotherhood members? It wasn't very brave of her to run away, though there was sense in avoiding a fight with a much stronger opponent.

But she had a Hader. Did she not believe in her ability to use it effectively in combat? As far as Lynx could tell, she hadn't used it at all yet.

Just as Lynx was about to nab her with some of his vines, a group of people rushed out from behind a building, getting in the way. Lynx ripped the vines off his Nexi stone and continued running down the street. She was even further ahead now, and turning down another small street. Lynx pushed himself to run even faster. He wasn't given this name for nothing... He would catch up with her soon enough.

He reached the side street and bolted down after the woman. Without any warning, a stack of crates fell down on Lynx, knocking him to the ground. It was just a poorly stacked pile of boxes... but the fact they fell at that very moment was disconcerting. Was this woman setting up traps? There wasn't any time for that.

Lynx sprinted after her. "Stop a second, will you?" She only ran faster.

What was she running from? A Brotherhood member. She had done something to betray the Brotherhood. Lynx understood what had happened to the other two members of her team, now. She had killed them.

"You killed them because they were killing Shire civilians, is that right?" Lynx yelled out. "I did the same to my teammates."

The woman slowed down a bit, looking back nervously. She looked like she was considering her options a moment...

She finally slowed down to a walk, taking deep, pained breaths. Lynx caught up to her and worked to catch his breath as well.

"It's okay..." Lynx said. "I understand what you did."

"I... I've betrayed the Brotherhood," the woman said. "I can never be forgiven..."

"The Brotherhood has fallen," Lynx said. He felt he had a good idea for how this woman viewed the Brotherhood, so he had to make it sound like he shared that viewpoint. "Under Delkol, the Brotherhood had a clear vision of a grand future for the Shire Kingdom. But Augurc has squandered that vision."

"Yes," the woman said. "Delkol would never have wanted this. And neither would have my brothers."

"Your teammates were killing helpless civilians, and you lost it?" Lynx said.

The woman nodded. "I... I tried persuading them that we didn't need to kill these people. But they wouldn't listen. They just fell back to Augurc's orders. They told me to start killing people, or they would kill me... So I used the Hader and killed them. I still nearly died in the process... And when I saw you coming, I thought it was over for me... I had to run. I had to get away from this madness."

A voice in Lynx's head told him to just kill this woman and take her Hader. This was his chance to obtain a Hader. All he had to do was kill her, and it was his. He would finally be able to free his mind.

But at the same time, he felt that if he killed her... Perhaps he wouldn't be able to free his mind. Wouldn't that be giving in to Augurc's experimentation? There was no reason to kill this woman. She was willing to cooperate with him. He just needed to rejoin Rilv and the others, and bring this woman with him. They could all work together, and with four Haders all together, it was quite possible they could achieve all their goals that day.

They could kill Augurc. They could finish off his experiments. And they could restore Lynx's mind once and for all. He would finally be himself again, without any of Augurc's Nexi experimentation clouding his mind.

"We need to stop this madness," Lynx said. "We can't just run away. We have to stop Augurc."

"There's... there's no way we can fight Augurc and win," the woman said.

"I beg to differ," Lynx said. "What is your name? Not your code name, but your real name."

"It's Shirm," the woman said. "And what is your name?"

"I am not who I was when I had a real name," Lynx said. "I am Lynx right now... but I won't be for long. Before the night is through, I hope to find the strength to be who I once was. To be myself... A human being."

•

The monster was destroying buildings left and right, and people struggled to get away from the behemoth. The lumbering creature was faster than Borely expected, and scores of helpless people were squished beneath the beast's many giant feet, or torn apart by its many incredibly long arms.

Borely ran down a street leading toward the beast, looking out for any sign of Areo—or Augurc. Borely didn't want to face Augurc right now, but there was a good chance Areo was nearby him.

Pushing through the lines of rushing people was difficult. Borely had to be careful to not hurt anyone, and in turn cause a panic if people subsequently discovered he was a vampire. But perhaps this wasn't anything Borely needed to concern himself with. Who would worry about vampires when there was this massive beast wreaking havoc across the city?

"Let me know if you see her," Borely said to Analicia. He had to keep checking to make sure she was nearby. She was small and blended in with the shifting groups of people passing around her.

"Kind of hard to see anything down here," Analicia said.

Borely led the way to a more open street, careful to watch which way the monster was going. He had to assume Augurc was sticking somewhere near the monster. Would he have sent Areo in a different direction? It probably didn't make sense for Augurc to have both Areo and the monster with him. Areo wouldn't be able to kill many people with the monster right there. She was probably sent to another part of the city.

"Let's find a vantage point," Borely said. "We can get on a tall building—somewhere away from that monster—and search for Areo from there."

There weren't any tall buildings left here in the center of the city. Borely looked north and saw a few grand structures there, and the monster was traveling in another direction.

"We'll head that way," Borely said. "If we run into a really dangerous enemy though, you'll have to promise to get as far away as you can right away. Are you okay with that?"

"Of course," Analicia said.

The fact she agreed so quickly made it way too obvious it was a lie.

"I'm serious," Borely said. "There's no point to all this if you get yourself killed."

"You worry about yourself," Analicia said. "I've handled myself fine this whole time. You just make sure you defeat whatever powerful enemy it is we run into."

Borely couldn't help but smile a little. Though Analicia was a runt, he had to admit it was nice to have her around. He hoped they'd be able to find Areo safely.

But even if they did, how exactly was he going to free her mind? He still wasn't certain how he was going to go about it.

*Just find her for now*, he told himself. He just had to believe he would know what to do when the time came for him to save her.

•

As Lynx rushed to the center of the city, he watched in amazement as the monster tumbled to the earth. It continued to thrash its many arms in all directions, destroying more buildings in its vicinity—but it wasn't on its feet anymore. Why did it fall? Were the Shire soldiers actually managing to fend off the beast? Lynx understood Augurc's other working experiments had been sent out to take down all the soldiers in the city, though. The city probably wasn't prepared for an all-out attack like this, and the fact the whole city was thrown into a panic had to make the entire situation thoroughly impossible for the city guards.

So who was fighting the monster? And was Augurc nearby? Lynx was hoping to find Rilv and the others. Were they already confronting Augurc? Or were they still making their way through the city? If they got found by one of Augurc's experiments...

Lynx had to count on them pulling through. And he had to make sure he was there when Rilv made her move. He couldn't let her destroy all the Haders or Elpis fragments. He had to make sure his mind was cured first.

He searched down each street they passed, checking on Shirm from time to time to make sure she was keeping up. She still clutched her Hader, its necklace chain tied around her arm. She was on the lookout as well, instructed to yell to Lynx if she spotted anyone suspicious. Rilv and the others could be fighting the Brotherhood, or Augurc, or an experiment, or Kechi, Shire soldiers, or even the summoned monster, for all Lynx knew. Once Lynx brought Shirm and her Hader to them, they'd be able to decide what to do next.

Running up and down the streets away from the fallen monster, Lynx found nothing but rubble, burning buildings, and all sorts of people he didn't recognize. There were corpses, children crying, people stuck beneath pieces of wrecked buildings, mangled bodies screaming for help, and injured people hobbling down the broken paths, leaving trails of bloody footprints behind them.

Lynx kept running and searching. He stopped upon sighting the monster ahead, thrashing its arms against the rubble-covered streets. A giant projectile of some kind was being utilized against the roaring, screeching beast, but Lynx couldn't make out what kind of attack it was. Tens of the creature's arms were sliced apart, and Lynx could only guess what damage the monster's heads were being dealt. Someone extremely powerful was fighting the monster... Lynx thought of Kechi, and his ability to control and harden blood for massive, sweeping attacks. Was Kechi battling the monster himself?

Lynx turned at the sound of a man screaming.

He stepped back in surprise at the sight of Augurc leaping from a building, a dozen vines tearing out of his arms and bringing him down to the ground quickly but safely. Augurc didn't see Lynx and Shirm apparently, as he hurried over to the monster.

The beast exploded.

Lynx stumbled backward, and Shirm turned and shielded her eyes from the massive blast. For several painful seconds, the giant explosion rang in Lynx's ears. He struggled to peer through the fading light, finding rubble and bodies everywhere. There already was plenty of rubble and bodies everywhere, but now there was also blood and monster guts spread all up and down the street with them.

Still screaming, Augurc rushed down the broken, crimson path, using his vines to propel himself forward. He reached the site of the monster's corpse—mostly a pile of dark mush and a pyre of mangled, charred limbs.

"You can not stop now!" Augurc screamed, raising an arm in the air. The multicolored glow of the Elpis fragments shined bright from his clenched fist. "Arise and continue your rampage through this weak and feeble city!"

A pillar of light burst to the sky, enveloping

Augurc and what was left of the giant monster he had summoned.

Was he going to heal the monster with the Elpis? It had been utterly destroyed...

Augurc stood still, Elpis energy flowing from his shaking body to the remains of the fallen beast. He was bringing it back to life. Was Augurc actually going to survive such a massive transfer of Nexi energy, though?

It didn't matter, Lynx realized. This was his chance to kill Augurc. There was nothing Augurc could do right now.

"Let's go!" Lynx called to Shirm. He bolted down the street, unsheathing his sword and preparing to stab Augurc straight through the back. Augurc couldn't see it coming... All his attention was on the monster and the Elpis energy.

"Wait!" Shirm yelled.

Lynx kept running. If killing Augurc could free his mind, he would do it... And he would do it now! And if that wasn't enough, he'd use the Haders... And the Elpis... He'd take everything he had to in order to heal himself. To restore his true self. To bring himself back to life.

Lynx leaped toward Augurc and thrust his sword straight into the madman's back.

The flow of Elpis energy deflected Lynx's sword,

then knocked him backward, sending him flying hard into the ground. Shirm hurried over to him and tried helping him up, but Lynx's whole body had filled with an excruciating agony.

Was this the pain of the Elpis?

Augurc turned around, his eyes a glowing blank white. "What is this, Lynx?"

The organs of the monster were connecting back to one another, it's scattered flesh and blood flowing behind Augurc in twisting arcs and ribbons.

"You come back here only to betray me?" Augurc asked, his voice echoing, cold and emotionless. "I turned you into something useful. The very concept of betraying me should have never been a remote possibility in your mind. And yet here you are... trying to stab me in the back!"

More of the monster was flowing into the gigantic mass it had been before the explosion. Tens of legs and arms pieced themselves back together. In seconds, the bulk of its body was whole once more.

"Nobody can oppose me," Augurc said. "It is far too late for anyone to stop my glorious work."

Lynx struggled to stand up. Shirm had stepped back a ways, unnerved by the intimidating sight of an Elpis-powered Augurc. There was no way for Lynx to attack him while he was enveloped in the energy of the

Elpis.

And there was no way for him to fight an opponent with so much more power than him.

Lynx stood up and held up a knife. "Oh, there's still some time left, Augurc. If I could fight against your experimentation on my mind all these years, I can fight you too."

•

# 11. MADNESS OVERWHELMING

Still clutching his neck, Lanek watched as Kitoh disappeared right before his very eyes. He was barely keeping up with what was happening. Kitoh had grabbed the Hader from him... and at the same time, the elf boy in black was charging for them. And then Kitoh and the experiment child both disappeared.

There was nothing but corpses all around Lanek. Dozens and dozens—perhaps hundreds—of corpses. Soldiers and civilians, all of them powerless to stand against the experiment child for long. But now the boy was gone. Kitoh had somehow finished him off, and had sacrificed himself in the process.

The Hader lay on the ground a couple meters in front of Lanek. He wasn't sure why Kitoh had grabbed it from him, other than to use it against the experiment boy, of course. But it didn't look like Kitoh used it to turn immaterial. He had somehow disappeared entirely, and had taken the enemy with him.

Lanek took a light cloak from a nearby corpse and began tearing strips from it to use as bandages. He had to tend to his wounds, as well as Rilv's. They still needed to find that next Hader, as well as Augurc and Kechi and whoever else they needed to defeat. He had noticed the giant monster was roaring louder now, as if in pain. Was someone fighting it? And actually standing a chance against it? The whole city was just one great collision of madness.

Once Lanek stopped the flow of blood from his and Rilv's wounds, he helped Rilv get up on her feet again, and explained what had transpired with Kitoh and the experiment boy. Though both Lanek and Rilv were badly hurt, they decided they were still able to keep fighting. They just needed to find their next target—whoever it was that had the next Hader.

"I suspect the strength of the Haders is helping us," Rilv said. "The Nexi energy within them has an effect on our bodies... helps us keep going, despite the pain."

"I thought the Haders weren't supposed to affect the user," Lanek said. "I thought that was a major difference between them and the Elpis fragments."

"No," Rilv said. "I have not mentioned this, but I believe the Haders do influence the user in subtle ways. It is not as direct or dramatic as the Elpis. Bit by bit though, the Haders shift the user's mind. I have felt my own mind affected, the more I have used my Hader. It may have... enhanced some of my thoughts, some of my emotions. Affected my judgement. Influenced my decisions."

Lanek hadn't felt anything significant since obtaining his Hader. He hadn't used it much yet, though. Was Rilv saying that since she had her Hader for a while and had used it a fair amount, she wasn't quite in the right state of mind?

It made sense, actually. She was zealous, but Lanek wouldn't have pinned her as one willing to work with the likes of Lynx, or willing to harm innocent civilians—especially those within her own nation's borders. Or would she? It was kind of hard to tell...

Kechi was certainly a madman, and he used his Haders quite a bit. The fact he had two of them may have turned his irrationality into sheer insanity over time. Or was he just a madman in the first place? It was, perhaps, impossible to tell.

"We can't keep using these Haders then," Lanek said.

"We must," Rilv said. "Just a little longer. As soon as the Elpis is destroyed, and as soon as our greatest enemies have been defeated, we will deal with the Haders. If Kitoh's device can destroy the Elpis, it can destroy the Haders as well."

"You're willing to destroy all these weapons?"

Lanek asked. "Even though they'd give the Fiefs Kingdom a great advantage?"

"They are too much of a risk," Rilv said. "It has been made clear that there is nowhere these stones can be kept, where they can be truly safe. We even had an Elpis fragment concealed in Setar Castle itself, and still our greatest enemy was able to obtain it. For the safety of Fiefs Kingdom, I must see to it that these Nexi stones are destroyed."

Lanek and Rilv continued their way through the city, noting the movement of the monster's arms. The creature's limbs flung outward all the way to buildings near Lanek and Rilv's location, and they had to run in several instances to keep from getting injured by flying rubble.

They found themselves getting closer to the monster, despite their efforts to keep a somewhat safe distance between them and the beast. But just when they thought they were going to be directly attacked by a couple of its outstretched arms, the limbs were severed and fell to the ground in front of them with a bloody, earth-shaking thump. The beast screamed louder and louder... and then a violent explosion erupted, just a few blocks away.

Lanek and Rilv covered their ears until the explosion's roar faded away. The monster was silent, and Lanek couldn't see it trudging around anymore. Was it actually killed? A man began screaming in utter fury.

"Augurc," Rilv said. "This sounds like our

opportunity to deal with him."

It did sound like the monster had fallen, but was this the best moment to confront Augurc? There was still at least one other experiment subject out there, though Borely and his companion were supposedly dealing with her. But Augurc still had his Elpis fragments, and was clearly in a state of rage at the moment—something Lanek found unsettling, considering the man was supposedly known for going about business practically devoid of any emotion.

Lanek and Rilv worked their way down the street, slowed down by the great mounds of rubble that filled the entire area. It was dangerous just climbing over and between the jagged piles of stone, metal, and glass, but they managed to work their way through quickly.

They soon caught sight of the monster in the distance—or rather what was left of it. Amidst the many corpses layered down the street were great globs of organs and goo, its horrid stench some kind of mixture of sewage and rotten food. The entire scene was the very image of a twisted tragedy.

A figure ran to the base of what was left of the monster. He raised a hand up, and a great pillar of light enveloped both him and the creature. From this distance it was hard to tell what precisely was going on, but there were a couple other people rushing to the scene as well. And then... pieces of the monster began floating back together.

"Augurc is restoring the beast with the power of the Elpis," Rilv said, pushing herself more quickly down the street.

They had to stop him now, but as Lanek watched the scene ahead, he saw a man rush at Augurc with a sword. It looked like a masked Brotherhood member, and for a moment, Lanek thought it might have been Lynx. But that didn't make any sense...

And whatever the case, the attack failed. The man flew back upon contact with Augurc, the Elpis energy acting as an impenetrable barrier. There was no way to attack Augurc until he had finished restoring the monster.

Yet Rilv kept running, straight for Augurc. She worked her way around the reconstructing monster while Lanek climbed over an unstable stack of rubble that fell in front of him.

"Wait!" he called out to her. But she didn't stop—she just kept running.

This wasn't like Rilv to go charging in without a plan. Did she have a plan? Or was the Hader affecting her mind, turning her more irrational? Either way, it was too dangerous to go charging straight toward Augurc like this. Lanek didn't want the monster to be brought back to life, but he didn't see any way for them to attack while Augurc was protected by the Elpis energy.

Rilv pulled out the curved block Kitoh had

designed for destroying the Elpis. Upon reaching the pillar of light, she swung the device directly into the bright, swirling energy.

The light vanished. The device negated the Elpis energy, allowing Rilv to break through Augurc's barrier. The monster let out a gurgling moan, only a few of its heads partly reconstructed. Gasping for breath, Augurc stumbled back from the impact of Rilv's device against the energy he was enveloped in. Immediately Rilv used her Hader to send Augurc flying back several meters, forcing him to crash into a fallen stone wall.

The Elpis fragments fell from his grasp. Rilv caused them to fly straight to her.

"No!" Augurc screamed, pushing himself back to his feet.

Rilv slammed the end of the curved block against the two connected Elpis pieces. Upon impact, the Elpis half exploded in a burst of multicolored dust, left to scatter and vanish in the passing wind.

Several vines burst out of every green Nexi grafted into Augurc's arms, all rushing for Rilv. Lanek drew his rapier in one hand and his Hader and a fire Nexi in the other. Rushing toward Augurc from his right, Lanek released a burst of fire at the vines. Augurc turned and shot off a blast of frozen air from the light blue Nexi in the palm of his hand.

At the same time, Rilv used telekinesis to push

against all the vines whipping toward her. With Augurc distracted by Lanek, Rilv managed to redirect each of the vines to fly around her. Given an opening for a few seconds, Rilv took out her half of the Elpis.

"Stop!" Augurc shouted, realizing what was happening. "I will kill you!"

Rilv smiled.

She floated the Elpis fragments in front of her and smashed them with her Nexi-destroying instrument. Just like the first Elpis pieces, these two blew apart into dust, also left to fade away into nothingness.

The Elpis stone was destroyed. In less than a minute, all four pieces of the Elpis were completely, utterly destroyed.

But there wasn't a moment to dwell on it. Screaming, Augurc regained control of his vines and caused them all to turn back toward Rilv from behind. At the same time, Augurc sprinted forward, using his ice Nexi to create a massive spear of ice from his arm. Lanek chased after him, but he couldn't keep up with an energized Augurc—especially not when Lanek had just been running through the city for so long. He released a ball of fire from his red Nexi, but it barely missed Augurc.

Rilv forced dozens of Augurc's vines to pass to either side of her. One ripped through her hair, tearing off a large chunk of it. She stumbled back, and a vine wrapped around her left arm—the one holding her Hader. In an instant it tore her arm off. Rilv fell to her back, screaming.

Augurc reached her and shoved his lance of ice straight for her chest. Rilv grabbed the Hader from her disembodied arm and held it up directly at Augurc. With telekinesis she sent Augurc violently flying back into the air, tens of meters high. The sheer force of the blast was enough to even push Lanek back a ways, though he was several meters away.

Augurc's vines whipped at Rilv as Augurc flew away. A portion of her right leg tore off, followed by a chunk of her stomach and the entirety of her left hip. Lanek recovered from Rilv's telekinetic push and ran toward her, but a number of Augurc's vines flew in his path, forcing him to hack away at them with his rapier.

Clenching her teeth from the pain, Rilv managed to tear her Hader from the grasp of a passing vine and place it on the ground. Before another vine could grasp the Hader, Rilv slammed her curved block against the stone. Just like the Elpis fragments, the Hader burst apart into miniscule fragments too small for the eye to see once their glow faded away.

"Bring peace to... our kingdom," Rilv got out. A vine slipped around her neck and tore her head off.

Lanek screamed Rilv's name, but it was too late for him to reach her. She had run into the battlefield expecting to die. From the very beginning, her greatest concern was always the safety of the kingdom at large. And to the very end, she was willing to give up her life for that cause. In her last minutes of life, she had managed to destroy the Elpis and one of the Haders...

It was time to finish the job. Lanek turned to Augurc, who was directing his vines to the ground beneath himself. With the support of his vines, Augurc brought himself safely to the ground, standing halfway between Lanek and the two masked figures in the distance. Apparently the second Brotherhood member had grabbed Lynx and brought him a safe distance from the monster, which was struggling to stand upright. The beast gave off a series of tormented, gurgling roars, but it wasn't able to control its arms well enough to attack Lanek or anyone else.

Lanek focused on Augurc. Once the leader of the Brotherhood was taken down, perhaps this nightmare could finally come to an end. Perhaps Lanek could find some semblance of peace in his life. The two people who brought about Suran's death now stood directly in front of Lanek. Lynx, the man directly responsible for her death. And Augurc, the man ultimately responsible for her death.

"It's time for you to pay for your crimes, Augurc," Lanek said.

Augurc's vines returned into their respective Nexi stones. He stood still, silent.

"My experiments," Augurc said, his voice loud but

not screaming. "They're supposed to be perfect. Flawless. Unstoppable."

"We've already defeated one of them," Lanek said. "And your creature here has failed you too. Not even the Elpis power that created them was unstoppable. It's time for you to fall as well."

"I can not fall," Augurc said. "I am the only one who can save this world. I won't let you stop me. Not now."

"Save the world?" Lanek said. "You're even more insane than your brother."

"No!" Augurc screamed. Dozens of vines erupted from every one of his green Nexi stones, and a lance of ice at least five meters long formed on his right arm.

"Arise, Subject MI!" Augurc yelled to the monster, which was still flailing about a ways behind Lanek. "Destroy everyone and everything in this city! Show everyone that even in this state, you are a being far superior to any lifeform on this planet! Obedient and omnipotent!"

The monster lurched upward, and giant globs of yellow and red goo began pouring from all the holes and tears in the beast's tattered body.

Lanek ran from the monster, positioning himself closer to Augurc. Suddenly, Augurc flung himself straight to Lanek, propelled by tens of vines. Lanek activated his

Hader just as Augurc slammed his gigantic lance of ice through Lanek's body.

Still running, Lanek placed a few meters between himself and Augurc as the madman turned himself around, utter shock etched in his face. Lanek didn't want to give away the power of his Hader without finishing Augurc off in the process, but he only had an instant to react from Augurc's frantic attack.

Footsteps approached Lanek from behind. He turned and found Lynx, struggling to walk forward. He picked up his sword from the ground and made his way toward Lanek.

Lanek thought Lynx was coming for him, but the masked man wasn't facing Lanek. Lynx was facing Augurc.

"I'm sick of these games, Lynx," Lanek said. "You can't keep pretending you're on our side—especially not right after you betrayed us."

"Everything I've done has been either for the sake of obtaining power, or for the sake of bringing Augurc down," Lynx said. "If you're too blind by your hatred to see this, I'll be glad to knock some sense into you once this is over."

"Failed experiments must be eliminated," Augurc said. "All who oppose me must perish."

Apparently Lynx was in fact intending to fight Augurc. Lanek wasn't about to fully trust Lynx, though. If there was a chance for Lynx to kill Lanek, there was no doubt he'd take it. But for now, it was best they cooperate in order to defeat Augurc and this monster.

"How will you fight if you can barely even stand?" Lanek asked.

Lynx pointed back to the Brotherhood member standing a ways behind him. Lanek glanced back and saw the masked figure was a woman. And in her hand was a Hader.

Lynx readied his sword. "I've got Lady Luck on my side."

•

Stuck amidst the corpses, Kechi watched as Augurc Shire himself rushed into the scene. But instead of going after him, Augurc went toward the base of the destroyed monster. Kechi's vision faded in and out a bit, but he saw a pillar of light envelop Augurc and the monster... and the monster beginning to piece back together? Kechi was in no mood to deal with that beast a second time. This at least confirmed that Augurc was the one who summoned the beast, though.

*He's turned against the Shire Kingdom*, Kechi thought. *Probably wants to show everyone he's the boss. But he's not the boss. Lord Mareba Shire is the boss, and will be the one to rule this kingdom... and bring it the glory it deserves. Augurc must die now. He has to die. I will kill him. I will knife him. Chop off his fingers and toes. Then his ears. Pull out his teeth. Cut out his tongue. Tear up his arms and legs. Pull out a bone here and there. Dig into his eyes. Rip out each one of those Nexi stones in his body. Make the filthy traitor suffer!*

It sounded like a wonderful plan.

"Where are you right now, Kechi?"

It was Lord Mareba's voice. Was it just in Kechi's head? Or was he actually there? The idea of Kechi's master actually being in this city was frightening.

"I need you to come to Zein immediately," Master said.

It was Kechi's teal Nexi stone. He wearily took it out of his pocket and held it near his mouth.

"Yes, Master," Kechi said. "I am in Zein."

"Good," Master said. "What is your situation?"

"There are at least three Haders in this city, other than the two already in my possession," Kechi said. "I will obtain all the Haders you need, Master."

"I only need four in all," Master said. "Once you have them, bring them to me. I am in my mansion just outside of Zein."

Kechi knew Lord Mareba had a mansion in each of the major Shire cities, but he didn't think Master would be here in Zein.

This was terrifying.

"It is dangerous here," Kechi said. "Augurc Shire and his Brotherhood have attacked the city. And there is a giant monster..."

"I am aware," Master said. "The monster had fallen, but it appears to be coming back to life."

So Master could see the beast all the way from the mansion. It was amazing how Master could be so calm in a situation like this... While the rest of the city was entrenched in chaos, Master spoke as if everything was perfectly under control.

"I fought it off," Kechi said. "I can destroy it again if you wish."

"I do," Master said. "My heart grieves for every innocent Shire life that has suffered this day. See to it that this monster is eliminated for good. I won't settle for this travesty to last a second longer."

"I will not fail you, Master," Kechi said. "I will kill the monster... then bring you four Haders."

"As expected," Master said. And with that, the glow of the teal Nexi faded a bit. Master was done speaking.

It was time to kill that monster again.

Kechi pushed aside the corpses around him and

stood up. He nearly screamed from all the pain in his body. Normally he wouldn't have been able to get up at all, but the two Haders he wielded seemed to give him the strength to go on. He had to keep fighting. Failure wasn't an option. He couldn't let Lord Mareba down now. He couldn't let more people in this city get killed by that monster. He couldn't stop and rest until he had brought Master those four Haders he required.

Kechi saw the monster partly reconstructed, flailing about as if in extreme pain. The pillar of light was gone, and Kechi could make out a few figures in the distance. From all the vines emerging from one figure, Kechi could tell Augurc was there. The other three, Kechi couldn't make out, but it seemed they were dealing with Augurc.

It was good that someone else was keeping Augurc occupied—Kechi doubted he'd be able to kill this monster and Augurc at the same time, at least not when he was this injured. Perhaps these other people could keep Augurc busy long enough for Kechi to destroy the monster, and then Kechi could go over and finish Augurc off himself.

But for now, Kechi focused on the beast. It only had half as many legs and arms as it had before, and many of these limbs were in terrible disrepair. Much of the creature's flesh hadn't been pieced back together, so it was mostly a grotesque mass of muscles, bones, and bleeding organs. There were a few heads formed at the top of the beast, but they weren't fully healed either. Random teeth and eyes thrown about oddly-shaped heads, leaking goo from their gaping holes.

"What an eyesore," Kechi muttered. He walked toward the beast, careful to watch for its outstretched arms moving about. There wasn't much left for it to destroy here, but it didn't seem to be anxious to move to another part of the city. Apparently the beast was being directed to stay near its summoner, helping Augurc fight off the three people gathered up ahead.

Kechi used his blood Hader to gather all the blood in the area to one central spot. He wasn't going to let this monster have its way any longer. Lord Mareba Shire demanded it. And Lord Mareba Shire would not be mocked.

Blood flowed upward from hundreds of corpses. Monster blood flowed from piles of goo, as well as from the beast's own gaping wounds.

*More... more... more... more!*

Stepping aside of a monster arm half-covered with broken claws, Kechi exerted all his strength on gathering more and more blood.

With each passing second, Kechi felt increasingly nauseous. His body wanted to just fall over and die, but he wouldn't allow it. Master needed him to kill this beast. Master needed the Haders. Once these two tasks were done... Then Kechi could die.

He laughed. And laughed. And laughed. He couldn't stop laughing.

So much blood. Enough blood to fill a house. Many houses. Kechi kept forcing more blood to come together. The monster was too busy helping its master to even notice.

*I'm going to pulverize this stupid beast!*

He formed the massive blob of floating goo into a gigantic spike. It had to be at least ten stories tall, perhaps three stories wide at its base.

The second Kechi hardened the blood into a metallic substance, he sent it flying directly into the base of the monster. Straight through its heads. On through its body. Utterly impaled.

The beast screeched for only an instant. The monster blew apart in a massive display of flying blood and gore. Arms and legs slammed into piles of rubble tens of meters away. There was nothing left of the beast's heads. The torso was thoroughly destroyed.

Kechi felt his mind snap, and all his insides seemed to explode for a moment. Moving such an immense quantity of blood so quickly was far beyond what could ever be considered safe Nexi use.

But he did it! He fell to his knees and puked blood.

It felt like a stream rushing out of his mouth. So much blood, all at once. He forced his mouth shut and gulped down whatever blood was left in throat. His body shook, overwhelmed with the Nexi use.

It was going to be difficult to kill whoever had the Haders he needed. But Kechi knew he wouldn't fail. Master required two more Haders. He was going to get them. It didn't matter how far he had to push himself.

Kechi coughed up some more blood. Once he regained composure, he realized he was coughing and puking amidst bouts of laughter. He had been laughing this entire time.

He forced himself to stop. It was time to get back to his mission.

It was time to get serious.

•

Everywhere Borely went, he heard screaming. Adults and children, men and women. Screams of fear and terror. Screams of pain and agony. The cries of the dying. The suffering of the living.

And somewhere in this city, Areo was playing a role in this turmoil. There were Brotherhood members killing off groups of civilians, but Borely couldn't find her among them. She was likely working alone.

It seemed that if the Brotherhood was being used

to take down civilians, then Augurc's experiments were being used to handle the more difficult task of bringing down the city's defenses. And there was no doubt that Areo would be able to make light work of an entire troop of trained Shire soldiers. If she was used to wipe out groups of vampires in Istal, she could be used for even more devastation in Zein.

Borely had to find her and stop her. Save her from this madness. Free her from Augurc's twisted influence.

He had searched from the top of a few buildings, but hadn't caught sight of her. Was she just making her way through the city too quickly for him? Her speed was certainly enhanced by the Elpis, as was her strength and dexterity. There was little that could slow her down at this point. But how was Borely going to keep up with her if he couldn't even find her?

"You haven't found anything yet?" he asked Analicia, who was following him down another street.

"No," she said. She kept looking back at the giant monster, and Borely couldn't help but keep checking on it as well. It seemed there were people fighting it, but Borely couldn't imagine they'd be able to fend it off for long. The beast was so massive, and had the means to attack its enemies from many different directions at once. The landscape exploded around it, and buildings fell beneath its many feet. The fact Augurc could craft such a being was unsettling—about as unsettling as the fact he was able to turn Areo into the killing machine she was now.

Borely climbed his way up a brick building, this one five stories tall. He looked out to some of the streets nearby, searching for any signs of Areo. At the end of one side road he could make out a few Shire soldiers... They were all being killed.

For a half-second, he saw her. It was Areo, dressed in a black and silver uniform. She clawed through each of the soldiers in seconds, then proceeded to slip between a couple buildings, rushing out of Borely's view.

"She's over there," Borely said, pointing so Analicia could see. "She's run off in that direction."

Immediately Analicia climbed down the building, and Borely leaped down in front of her, sprinting down the street upon landing.

He pushed himself as fast as he could. This was finally his time to save Areo. He had a Hader. He had the power to save her. And thanks to that eigni professor, he knew what it was he needed to do. Rattle Areo's mind with the sight of a bloody, murderous scene. Then get her to stop following Augurc's commands—namely, stop killing all the people in this city. Then force her to access a surge of energy from the Hader. And then... hope her mind hadn't been utterly destroyed.

"Areo!" Borely yelled. It was unlikely calling her name would stop her from continuing her onslaught against the Shire forces, but perhaps he could at least get her attention. And perhaps... she could remember him a little, like she did back in Istal. Just before she was about to kill him, she stopped, as if remembering who he was. It hadn't snapped her out of her blind obedience to Augurc, but it was something. Perhaps if she got like that again, that would be Borely's chance to transfer the Hader's energy to her.

He called her name a few more times as he searched down the road he had seen her slip away to. There were more dead Shire soldiers there. He paused a moment to suck the blood of one of the killed soldiers, giving him the strength to keep sprinting down the streets after Areo. Borely could tell this soldier was just killed—Areo had to be close by.

He hurried up another building and caught sight of her just down the next street over. Borely and Analicia rushed down another side road and leaped out just a few meters in front of Areo.

Areo stopped instantly and looked over the two of them while they tried catching their breath. She was trying to decide if Augurc would want her to kill them.

"It's us, Areo," Borely said. "Borely and Analicia. You don't have to keep fighting anymore. We can leave this city, and leave behind Augurc and the Brotherhood."

He doubted just speaking to her would stop her, but if it could somehow get her mind to process some of these concepts, perhaps it would help her fight against the influence of the Elpis.

But Areo simply stared at Borely—or perhaps through him. Her eyes registered no recognition. No emotion at all.

"We just want to help you," Borely continued. "I know you don't want to keep killing people like this."

Areo's fingernails extended into claws, nearly a meter in length.

"Get back, Analicia," Borely said.

In an instant, Areo was upon Borely, swinging her claws for his neck. He activated his Hader and summoned a large, thick shield. As Areo sliced straight through the shield, Borely pushed upward against her claws, then fell back to the ground. Her claws passed directly over him, but the chunks of the shield fell onto him. He pushed them aside and stood up, extending his own claws in the process.

Areo turned and swiped her claws at Borely again. He leaped back to avoid them, but suddenly Areo was directly in front of him, swiping again. Borely summoned two Nexi stones—ice and water—and formed a wide wave of ice between him and Areo. Her claws were encased in the ice, but she was quick to tear through and rush toward Borely again.

Borely thought he'd get more than half a moment to put some space between him and Areo, but she was just too fast. She was trained to end fights in seconds—this was already a much longer fight than she was used to. The fact Borely could summon random weapons at the last instant made him more unpredictable than anyone else she ever had to deal with...

But even then, she was just too fast.

Borely switched his ice and water Nexi stones with a large orange one. He charged up his claws with extra strength and defended against Areo's next attack. She faked for one side, then was suddenly clawing at him from the other side. Borely turned and swiped his claws against Areo's.

Her claws didn't tear through Borely's, but the force of her attack sent Borely flying to the right a meter or so. He stumbled and nearly fell over, when suddenly Areo was in front of him again, jabbing her claws toward Borely's chest. He leaped back, and immediately her claws extended further. He made a frantic swipe and deflected a few of her claws, but the rest plunged through Borely's body.

He clenched his teeth and focused enough to use his Hader to summon a crossbow. Just as Areo was about to tear her claws through Borely's body, he fired an arrow, barely able to aim amidst the suddenness of the moment.

The heavy arrow shot straight below Areo's collarbone. She flew backward, bringing all her claws out of Borely's chest and abdomen. He fell to his knees while Areo fell to her back. He screamed and shakily pulled out a vial of blood, but Areo simply lay still.

"Are you okay, Borely?" Analicia yelled, standing a ways down the road.

"Stay back," Borely groaned. He got to his feet, keeping his eye on Areo. He didn't want to shoot her like that... but it was a last resort move to keep himself from getting killed.

Areo ripped out the arrow and drank a vial of blood of her own. She leaped to her feet, then took two steps to reach Borely. Just as she was about to plunge her claws through his heart, Borely used the Hader to summon a white Nexi and a yellow one. He activated both, creating a flash of blinding light, and shielding himself with yellow Nexi energy.

Areo winced, her eyes blinded by the light. Just as Borely had noticed, she wasn't fighting the way Nivakil had taught them—she was relying on her eyes too much. Jolted by the light, Areo lost her aim and concentration, her claws spreading apart and missing their target. As Borely turned to the side, the claws scraped against his body, but the yellow Nexi was enough to keep them from tearing into his flesh.

Areo flew forward, and Borely replaced the two Nexi stones with a green one. He needed to capture her and get her to witness a bloody, destructive scene... Would he need to kill a bunch of people in front of her? Would a few Brotherhood members suffice? Or would it need to be random devastation, like the kind Areo brought about? Borely couldn't bring himself to kill random people though, even if it was to save Areo... She wouldn't want that.

Areo turned around as Borely sent several vines snapping toward her legs. She clawed through all of them instantly, and reached Borely in a matter of moments. Even anticipating her speed, she was too fast for Borely to capture.

Borely sent more vines flying from his Nexi stone, but this time aimed for the ground. The vines pushed against the earth and sent Borely up in the air. Areo's claws sliced through the vines, just barely missing Borely himself. He landed behind Areo and clawed at her from behind— but the moment he landed, she was leaping forward. Borely's claws missed her completely, and Areo was already turning around again, just outside of Borely's range.

She didn't look flustered in the slightest. She wasn't upset. She was merely continuing the fight, and would continue it for as long as was necessary. There was no chance of capturing Areo—she would always find a way to claw through whatever it was that bound her, even if it was sheer Nexi energy. And Areo wasn't going to give Borely a chance to create a bloody, violent scene in front of her. And he doubted getting killed by her would count.

Areo rushed toward Borely, who used his Hader to summon a tan Nexi. As he ran backward, he created several large, thick stalagmites between him and Areo. It only slowed her down a little, and Borely quickly found this was only tiring himself out quickly.

"Analicia, go kill a bunch of people in front of Areo while we fight," Borely said.

"What?" Analicia screamed.

No, that wouldn't work. If anything, that would direct Areo's attention to Analicia. Borely didn't want to get the child killed in all this.

He had to get Areo to witness the monster's rampage. Borely realized this was a reason why Areo was directed to fight elsewhere in the city. She needed to be killing people all on her own. Seeing extreme acts of murder and terror brought about by others would distract her, and affect her mind in ways Augurc didn't wish for. Her focus would shift away from the mission at hand.

The monster was surely killing many people. Borely didn't want it to, but if he could use the situation to his and Areo's benefit, they'd be sooner able to assist everyone else in saving this city.

He focused back on Areo, who continued to slice her way through all the stone formations Borely crafted with the tan Nexi stone. It was bad to keep using Nexi energy like this. He had to get his plan rolling before Areo overwhelmed him. She wasn't using Nexi stones at all, and it was only a matter of time before Borely exhausted himself.

He turned and ran down a side street, yelling for Analicia to run down another road and watch his back from a safe distance.

Areo was quickly gaining on Borely. Immediately upon reaching the end of one side street, Borely summoned a vine Nexi and used it to latch onto the top of a tall building. He caused the vines to pull him upward, bringing him to the roof while Areo hurried up the wall via her claws, which she shortened a bit to make climbing more manageable.

She climbed really quick. Before Borely could even begin running to the other side of the building, Areo was extending her claws for Borely's head. He fell backward and began rolling down the gradual incline of the roof. He retracted his claws a bit and latched on to the roof before falling off, then swung himself away from Areo as she swiped her claws for his head once again.

Borely sprinted down the length of the roof and leaped onto the next building, heading toward the center of the city where the monster stood. The beast was roaring, and it almost sounded like it was in pain... Were people managing to fend off the creature?

Borely worked his way from building to building, using a vine Nexi to send himself flying across streets. Though Areo was freakishly fast, and she was able to make some rather incredible jumps, she couldn't make it all the way across a street or up and down tall buildings. Green Nexi wasn't his specialty, but he was competent enough to keep from getting killed off in ten seconds flat.

He was getting more and more tired, but the monster was becoming easier to see, especially when

Borely made his way up some of the taller buildings still standing in the area. At last he reached a five-story building, just a couple streets away from where the monster stood, shoving its arms through several buildings that stood dangerously close by.

Areo leaped onto the building Borely stood on, and for a moment Borely hesitated. Should he leap down from this building and let the chase continue on, or hope Areo will see a gruesome scene from this building? How long would he have to fend against her before she glimpsed something that truly shook her up? Would she ever glimpse anything at all, if she was entirely focused on fighting Borely?

Borely extended his claws, and as Areo rushed toward him he shot off a jet of water from his headband's Nexi stone. Areo dodged, and Borely swiped his claws toward where she landed. He knew her speed, and aimed right where he anticipated she'd be running from.

Amazingly, she slowed down the very instant Borely swung his claws for her. She avoided his attack and jabbed her claws at Borely's neck.

The building shook, and Borely and Areo each fell backward. Borely glanced back and watched as a colossal crimson spike slammed down into the giant monster. Waves of blood and monster guts flew up and down the street, some of it splattering all the way onto the building Borely and Areo stood on.

Areo remained where she sat, staring straight at the incredulous scene. Never in Borely's life could he have imagined such a horrifically spectacular display of unsightly death.

Areo's mind was affected by the one thing that could affect it in its current state—the terrifying sight of a gruesome, violent murder. Now Borely needed to get her to give up on the mission Augurc gave her. And the one way he was going to get her to stop killing people, he decided, was to defeat her.

Now was the time for Borely to use all the power he had.

·

As the monster flung its arms toward him, Lanek leaped to the side, knowing his rapier wouldn't be able to cut through the thick, heavy limbs. While stepping back from the giant claw at the end of another arm, Lanek took out an orange Nexi and slid it down the length of his blade. With his rapier strengthened with Nexi energy, Lanek proceeded to slice straight through the next arm that reached out for him. Meanwhile Lynx was ambushed by several arms at once, and was bashed in the torso by a thick, knotted-up tentacle. He managed to charge his own sword with orange Nexi power, and struggled to fight off the other arms rushing toward him.

Lanek didn't see how Lynx had luck on his side. But for now, Lanek had to focus on how to defeat Augurc in a situation as trying as this. The man was taking some time to recover from the injuries Rilv had given him, allowing the giant monster to fight off Lanek and Lynx.

The arms Lanek hacked away at seemed to be growing longer. The giant beast had no problem with continuing to attack Lanek with its injured arms, no matter how much Lanek cut off. The arms just kept extending toward him, their sliced ends releasing more than just blood. Thick red and yellow goo flowed out freely from every arm, and as Lanek fought back more arms, he realized other arms were releasing goo around him. He was being surrounded by the horrid-smelling material, and he wasn't certain about any of its properties.

"Get out of there!" Lynx yelled.

Lanek's first thought was this was a trick—but would Lynx want him to die at this very moment? Right now they were both needed to fight off Augurc.

Lanek activated his Hader and turned himself immaterial. In this spirit-like form, he managed to run straight through the attacking arms and the walls of goo that surrounded him. As soon as he passed through, the goo burst in a large explosion. Several arms were knocked back and blasted apart, and the ground which Lanek had stood on was turned into a smoking crater. He would have been utterly pulverized had he ignored Lynx's cry.

There wasn't time to dwell on this. As soon as the explosion passed, Lanek returned to physical form, knowing he couldn't keep using the Hader for long without growing exhausted.

Lanek rushed out from amongst the writhing arms, and immediately made eye contact with Augurc. Tens of vines launched out for Lanek, who slipped out a fire Nexi and blasted a wall of flames at the approaching plants.

Suddenly a massive spear of ice plowed straight through the fire. Lanek activated his Hader at the last moment, and both the ice weapon and Augurc himself passed directly through Lanek.

Augurc continued past Lanek and charged straight for Lynx, who was busy dodging more of the monster's arms. The beast was trying to pound a fist on Lynx with one arm, while slipping a mouth-covered tentacle toward him from behind. Lynx spun in place, his sword outstretched, and somehow managed to step directly to the side of the fist, proceed to slice through the fist, continue his attack through the tentacle of mouths, and finish off by jabbing the end of his sword directly into the end of Augurc's ice lance. The weapon of ice shattered upon impact, and the thrust sent Lynx flying back—just in time for another of the monster's arms to miss slamming into him. It was all far too unlikely for it to have all been done on purpose. It was practically a series of miracles in the span of just a few seconds. Was this what Lynx meant by having luck on his side? Was the Brotherhood woman's Hader somehow manipulating Lynx's fortune, of all things?

Augurc reformed a giant ice lance and just continued sprinting onward, leaving Lynx behind to avoid more of the monster's attacks. Lanek found another arm reaching out for him as well, and he ran to avoid it, as well as the arms that followed directly in front of him. He sliced his way through the bent-up arm that swung for him afterward, and searched for Augurc amidst the chaos of limbs and goo. The monster began lurching toward them—was it going to try trampling them, even with Augurc there?

Lanek spotted him in the distance, running straight for the Brotherhood woman. She fled, and her Hader began glowing brighter. Vines rushed out for her, but she managed to dodge each one of them as she ran away. She didn't even need to look back—she simply knew where to run to avoid all the vines.

"Don't run!" Lynx yelled. He was counting on her to use her Hader to help them.

Lynx rushed after Augurc and took out a brown Nexi stone. He blasted a burst of swamp-like material, far too fast to avoid. Augurc turned around and aimed his giant ice spear for the swamp blast, forcing it to spray off to either side of him.

The spear of ice launched off of Augurc's arm, blasting straight through the swamp material. Lynx pulled out a fire Nexi and threw it at the giant ice formation. The Nexi stone exploded, and the spear shattered into large chunks of ice directly in front of Lynx. Unfortunately, several of the jagged blocks of ice slammed into Lynx, knocking him hard into the ground.

Augurc looked back for the Brotherhood woman, but she had used Lynx's diversion to escape. Apparently even with the fortune Hader, she found the situation against both Augurc and the monster too much to deal with.

Lanek fought through a couple more arms, and noticed that Lynx wasn't getting back up. Was he dead? It was too hard to tell. It was the worst moment for him to get beaten down, though. Augurc turned to Lanek and formed another giant spear of ice over his forearm.

Continuous laughing filled the air. It sounded familiar. Lanek turned, finding the sound coming from the other side of the monster. He looked up and found a colossal spike of blood floating in the air, high above the beast. So it was Kechi who fought off the monster...

The blood hardened, forming the largest weapon that had likely ever existed. Amidst Kechi's maniacal laughter, the ridiculously huge spike plummeted into the beast. With the creature this close to Lanek, he realized he was going to get pummeled by its bursting remains.

Lanek used his Hader to render himself immaterial, allowing the giant piles of monster flesh and goo to pass through him. The collision between the blood spear and monster shook the ground beneath Lanek's feet, and the incredible noise of the impalement made him scream in pain.

The earth-shattering crash sent waves of blood and mangled organs flying up and down streets in every direction. The instant it all passed though, Lanek turned material again and ran toward Augurc. As Lanek expected, Augurc had used his spear as a shield, plunging it into the walls of gore flying toward him. Fending off such a powerful blast was forcing Augurc to take a few seconds to recover.

Lanek charged his rapier with another swipe of an orange Nexi stone. It was time to plunge through all of Augurc's defenses and bring him down, once and for all.

•

Shirm felt terrible for abandoning Lynx, but she couldn't allow herself to fight her master. Even if Augurc wasn't half the man Delkol was, she was still a member of the Brotherhood. She couldn't turn against Augurc like this. Perhaps Augurc would kill Lynx and that elf, and the Brotherhood would finish off the rest of the city, and things could resume from there... Things could return to normal somehow.

She clutched her good luck Nexi tighter and continued to run through the ruinous city. She had evaded Augurc's arm vines—a miracle in itself, considering just how quickly and precisely the man could control them. But she couldn't let herself be found by Augurc again—not any time soon. Perhaps once all this was over, she could explain that she was forced to help Lynx, and the moment she realized Augurc was in danger, she fled, not wanting him to come to harm. Would he believe her?

No... that was ridiculous. There was no way Augurc would let her live. She needed to give up on the Brotherhood. She had to leave this city—perhaps leave the Shire Kingdom entirely.

Or was there anywhere in the world that was safe for Shirm now? As long as Augurc lived, she would be in danger.

Why did she listen to Lynx? Yes, Augurc's actions here were terrible, and it was unsettling how so many in the Brotherhood were willing to join in on the acts... But it wasn't for her to decide if the destruction of Zein was right or wrong. Perhaps this city was a necessary sacrifice. Perhaps Shirm just needed to do what was expected of her... Obey, and perform her assigned duties with exactness.

She slowed down to catch her breath. Her lucky Nexi stone had weakened her significantly—she had never used it so many times in one day before. She wasn't supposed to use it so much. Now there were people who knew about its existence. Lynx, the elf, and Augurc, at the very least. Would word of her powerful Nexi stone spread further? She had put herself in grave danger. This was exactly what she was warned to try to avoid. The lucky Nexi needed to be kept a secret to everyone but her.

She sat down in a niche hidden behind some rubble, tucked in a section of wall that was still standing. The sight of so much devastation, so much death... It made her dizzy. And then there was the fact she failed to do anything to actually stop it.

What was she supposed to do now? She couldn't run, hide, or fight. Or could she? Could she use her lucky Nexi once more? Was there a way she could use it to truly change her fortune?

Someone was approaching her. She could hear footsteps. Shifting wreckage. Rubble slipping and settling.

A man stood a couple meters in front of her. In each hand he held a stone, each filled with a glow of two swirling colors. Just like her lucky Nexi stone.

"Hand over that Nexi," the man said in a hoarse, sickly voice.

The man had several bad wounds, and just one good eye—but Shirm's attention was drawn to a gash on his arm. Blood was leaking out of it... and starting to float into the air. A thin ribbon of blood, weaving toward Shirm. The end of the thin stream shifted, then gave off a metallic sheen, just like the sharpened blade of a dagger.

Shirm leaped to her feet and shoved against the broken-down wall she hid in front of. The loose bricks collapsed, and the piles of wood and stone she hid behind fell over as well. The man leaped away from the crashing rubble, and Shirm ran for it, activating her lucky Nexi once more. She had to get away. The lucky Nexi had to protect her... just a little longer. Just long enough for her to escape.

Something slammed against her hand holding the lucky Nexi. She screamed, and dropped the stone in the process. Her hand felt broken, and she realized it was a rock that was flung at her.

She turned and found the man had made several streams of blood in the air, the ends of them picking up stones and bricks from amongst the city's rubble. He was somehow controlling the blood, using it to shoot off these projectiles at her.

All at once, the man sent stones and bricks flying at her. She was too exhausted to dodge them all—she avoided the largest of the stones, but got hit in the shoulder by a brick, then got a leg scraped by another. And the man was already picking up more of the primitive weapons.

There was no fighting him in this state, and the lucky Nexi had failed to protect her. And the man wasn't going to stop until he got that Nexi stone...

She turned and ran as hard as she could. If she stayed, she would die.

She clenched her teeth, fighting back the pain as a stone slammed into her back, followed by a brick that hit her elbow. Leaving behind her lucky Nexi, the last thing she had that connected her to her family... She couldn't believe she could give it up. Even with her life at stake, she had never wanted to leave it. Especially not now. Especially when she had lost everything she had worked for all these years.

She kept running, on and on down the streets. The stranger had stopped attacking her, perhaps satisfied with obtaining the good luck Nexi. Her precious heirloom. The one thing she had left.

What had she come to this city for? What had she been working for her entire life?

She collapsed on the ground, unable to even crawl. Barely even able to breathe. Her entire body was in pain, her injuries accentuated by her extensive Nexi use... And yet she wasn't dying. She was still alive. But what for? What was there left for her to do? Was there anything left for her to even attempt at this point? And if she did try, was there any hope for her to succeed?

She couldn't change anything even when she had the stone of good fortune. How could she change anything now?

•

There wasn't much time left. Kechi could tell he was dying, and that every time he pushed himself to use a Nexi stone a little more, he was pushing a dagger deeper into his own heart.

That was okay. He only needed one more Hader.

The elf fighting Augurc had one. He just needed to let them finish duking it out, and then he could take the Hader. And then he could present four total Haders to Lord Mareba Shire. And then...

It depended on whether he survived or not. If Kechi lived, he would remain by Master's side forever, completing all the tasks given to him for the sake of a land unified under the glory of the Shire Kingdom. But if Kechi died, then that was that. He would die having fulfilled Master's wish.

Once Master had the Haders, it didn't matter what happened to Kechi. Technically, there would be nothing Master would not be able to do on his own, so Kechi wouldn't really be needed anymore.

And that was fine. Master had given Kechi a life when he had none. If by giving back his life Kechi could repay Master back even the slightest bit, it would be worth it.

It was difficult to keep walking. Though Kechi was willing to keep walking even if all his flesh was torn off, it was difficult to force his body to do that which was past its capability. The three Haders were helping. Their power was so great, they were allowing Kechi to keep going. But his mind felt clouded. As if it weren't exactly there in his head. Only a reflection of his soul remained intact. He didn't mind, but it was getting difficult to figure out where to go, or where everything was... Everywhere Kechi looked, there was nothing but rubble, blood, and corpses. It was beautiful. It was horrifying. It was Kechi's life.

He heard a commotion nearby, and looked up to two figures fighting atop a battered yet stable building. A man and a woman, both of them fighting with long needles. Or were those claws? They were vampires, Kechi realized. He had always wanted to kill a vampire.

But what surprised Kechi even more was the glow coming from the Nexi stone the man held. It wasn't just a Nexi stone—it was a Hader. Who was this vampire, and why did he have a Hader? What were the chances that yet another person in this city would also have a Hader?

Kechi wanted to kill the elf that had taken his eye from him, and he wanted to kill Augurc as well. But Kechi needed to make sure he got a fourth Hader, no matter what. That had to be the first priority. That was why he didn't push himself to kill the Brotherhood woman he stole a Hader from. If he had been able to use his fear Hader against her, it would have been a quick and easy kill. The vampire man with the Hader would also not be easy to kill. Perhaps Kechi could use his blood Hader in a way to make it easier for the woman to kill the man, and then Kechi could just use his fear Hader on the woman and kill her off.

It was too painful to laugh, so Kechi simply focused on walking to the building, and finding a way to get to the roof.

He had some vampires to kill, and a final Hader to obtain.

•

Borely fired off a jet of water from his metal headband, forcing Areo to his left. He immediately turned and swiped his claws at her, but she ducked beneath the attack and dived forward, her claws elongating further. Borely leaped above her claws and landed to Areo's left. She was already turning once Borely landed. Before she could slice through him, Borely used his Hader to create a fire Nexi, which he tossed in front of him as he leaped backward. Just before the fire Nexi detonated, Areo stopped her attack and ran.

While Areo avoided the explosion entirely, Borely was knocked back, and nearly rolled right off the building. He latched on with his claws, and forced himself back to his feet. Areo sprinted around the hole in the roof and was upon Borely in seconds. Borely used the moment to summon a lance, which he threw to Areo's right while he fired his headband Nexi's water stream to Areo's left. Areo kept running straight for Borely, who rushed forward and caused his claws to lengthen as far as he could manage. At just the right moment, Areo was unable to leap to the right or the left, and Borely's claws had grown a half-meter longer than Areo's.

Areo suddenly stopped and leaped backward, just out of range of Borely's claws. The jet of water passed by to her left and the lance passed by her to her right. Borely kept charging, but Areo was too quick. She rushed to her right, spun in place, and swiped her claws toward Borely's side. She tore deep gashes into his arm and side, but Borely kept running to keep from getting sliced up further.

He turned around and found Areo already running to him. Borely swiped his right claws toward her, and his left claws toward where he predicted she'd leap aside to. Areo's paused for the slightest second, and Borely saw his claws about to tear straight through her chest.

Then Areo was suddenly crouched to the side of Borely's right claws. Then slicing through those claws with her own claws. Then all the way past Borely's left claws. Borely stumbled forward, screaming, realizing all his claws had been sliced off. Areo's burst of speed had rendered every one of his claws useless, and she was already turning back to slice through his neck.

Still screaming, Borely turned and caused what little was left of his claws to slide back into bloody fingernails. At the same time, Borely focused all the energy he possibly could into the orange Hader of his right metal fist, which he was already winding up for a punch. Areo's claws swung at Borely's neck, and at the last moment Borely used all his strength to punch into the sides of the claws.

Rather than snapping them off as he'd hoped, he merely pushed the claws aside, spinning Areo a bit. Her attack missed Borely, and he used the moment of her forced spin to leap toward her, his fist still charged with extra strength.

Areo dropped to the ground, rolled to the side, and swung her claws up for Borely. She sliced off each of Borely's metal fists, sending the pieces flying from his grip along with the orange Nexi stones in each.

Borely ran past her, screaming in surprise. His hands were badly cut up, but not sliced off entirely, fortunately. He turned to Areo and fired a jet of water at her, but she rolled to the side and was on her feet the next instant. Borely leaped back just as Areo was swiping her claws at his face.

He nearly collapsed as blood began flowing down his face. He hadn't even felt Areo's claws dig into his skin—it was as if the force of her swing had happened directly in front of his face, and that alone was enough to leave gashes from his forehead to the right side of his jaw. The claws had missed his right eye, but his metal headband was sliced apart. The pieces of Borely's special weapon fell off, along with the dark blue Nexi embedded within it.

The pain of all these attacks was getting to Borely, but he had no time to drink blood. He had to constantly move as fast as he could to keep from getting chopped up into bits.

His weapons were gone and his claws were torn off. He had to defeat Areo with the Hader right away—but he was injured, and Areo showed no signs of slowing down.

Just as Areo was swinging her claws at his chest, Borely used the Hader to summon a purple Nexi stone, which he immediately used to create a burst of loose energy. Areo caused her claws to shorten back into fingernails to keep them from getting blown off, and she spun her body to the side of the blast, which had shoved Borely back violently. He realized he had shot off a chunk of his side off in the process, and Areo was already lunging toward Borely, her claws lengthening again and her fangs exposed.

With no time to come up with an attack or defense, and too exhausted to use the purple Nexi again so soon, Borely simply took the stone and bashed it into Areo's forehead. Her claws pierced through Borely's chest and stomach, but Borely's punch knocked her back, pushing her claws right back out. She tumbled back across the roof, her forehead leaking blood all across her face.

She shakily got back on her feet while Borely took out a vial of blood. Immediately Areo rushed for Borely, and swiped her claws straight through the vial, slicing it clean in half. Borely leaped back to avoid the next swipe of Areo's claws, and ran for it, working his way down the length of the roof.

He caught a glimpse of Areo's face at that moment of her rushed attacks. She was livid.

Borely smiled. He was getting to her. That wasn't just a blank expression of anger. That was the look Areo got specifically when she was furious.

He wasn't going to last much longer at this rate, though. He had to defeat her to end the mission Augurc gave her, and then use the Hader to cancel out the Elpis energy embedded within her.

Borely turned around to face Areo once more, knowing he wouldn't be able to put much more space between them. He readied his Hader, and Areo swung her claws. Just as Areo's claws reached Borely, he summoned a white Nexi stone and released a bolt of lightning. At the same moment, a crimson material appeared between Areo's claws and Borely's white Nexi. Borely thought it was blood, but it hardened, and the blast of lightning was spread out in multiple directions. Instead of blowing Areo's claws clean off, her claws were merely pushed back. But due to the positioning of the blood-like substance, Borely was shot in the stomach by a portion of the lightning attack. He flew backward, launched straight off the roof of the building.

He was falling, and he could barely form a thought in his head, let alone find the energy to try and save himself. The pain was overwhelming, and his chances of saving Areo seemed to shatter in front of him. Borely crashed hard against the ground, the pain in his body only increasing. He couldn't move. He couldn't even tell if he had broken his back or neck. He lay there, unmoving.

A man walked over to Borely and bent down to pull the Hader out of Borely's grasp.

"All four at last," the man whispered. He had one

good eye, and quickly looked over Borely a moment, as if trying to tell if Borely was still alive. The man pulled a knife from a holster and held it over Borely's heart. "Just to be sure."

Before the man could finish Borely off, Areo leaped down from the building, landing just behind the stranger.

"Get away from Borely!" she screamed as she swung her claws for the man's neck.

The man caused one of his Haders to glow brighter, and Areo stopped her attack. She simply stared wide-eyed at the man. It was as if she had suddenly regretted trying to kill this man.

Apparently not wanting to continue the fight, the man turned and ran for it, falling into a coughing fit as he escaped.

Borely could hardly make sense of the situation, but there was no time left to worry. Areo was right there. Was she going to finish him off right now?

She looked down at Borely for a couple seconds.

"Areo..." was all Borely could get out.

"Target down," Areo said, her voice monotone and detached.

She turned away and ran. Apparently to seek out

new targets.

Borely couldn't move. And even if he could, what would he be able to do now? He lost his weapons. His claws. And now his Hader. There was nothing he could do now.

Areo was lost to him.

•

Lanek sprinted toward Augurc, who launched off a series of vines straight for him. Lanek swung his rapier through the vines and kept running. More vines arced toward him from the left and right. Lanek spun in place and swung through the attacks. More vines rushed at him head on. He activated his Hader and leaped through them, stepped to the side, deactivated the Hader power, and continued running. Augurc redirected tens of his vines to rush at Lanek from all directions.

Instead of using his Hader again, Lanek simply charged forward, pushing himself faster, hacking away at the freakishly fast vines with every bit of his strength.

Was this for revenge? Was this for Suran? Or was this simply what he needed to do? Was it simply the right thing to do? He wasn't even certain, but he knew Augurc couldn't be allowed to continue this nightmare any further.

Lanek sliced through every vine, turning in place to face each one of them, and continuing to run every moment he had an opening. Augurc forced even more vines to burst out from his arm Nexi stones, and Lanek had to anticipate where all of them would be at every given moment.

It was draining to keep using the orange Nexi, but it was the only way to keep the vines from overwhelming him, and he needed to save the Hader for just before the finishing blow.

Lanek approached Augurc, who continued launching vines at him. As soon as Lanek was in Augurc's range, the man slammed his giant ice spear into Lanek's body—just as Lanek turned immaterial.

Lanek rushed for Augurc, running straight down the length of his huge weapon. Augurc's expression turned from slightly flustered to genuinely worried. He had no Elpis to turn to. And with Lanek in a spirit form, how was Augurc going to fight him? As soon as Augurc was within range of Lanek's rapier, Lanek was going to leap out of the ice spear, return to physical form, and slam his blade into Augurc's heart. If Augurc managed one final attack at that moment, Lanek could leap back and turn immaterial one last time, just long enough for Augurc to die, once and for all.

Lanek continued running through the long, thick weapon of ice, and kept careful watch over each of the vines arcing in the air around him. They were going to lash out at him the moment Lanek would jump out of the ice lance—he had to be ready to avoid them all as soon as he was material again.

Just before Lanek was preparing to leap out of the ice lance, Augurc brought all his vines back to him, and began surrounding himself in the vines. In seconds, a thick cocoon of vines was formed around Augurc. But was that really enough to keep Lanek's orange Nexi-charged sword from piercing through?

As Lanek leaped out and returned to physical form, he discovered the cocoon had shifted into more of a sphere, with Augurc hanging in the direct center of it. Vines slipped out the bottom of the sphere, forming long legs that raised the ball high in the air. Augurc's massive ice weapon still stuck out the side, and through a thin hole in front of him, Augurc was able to see Lanek standing several meters down below. The sphere of vines shifted easily under Augurc's control, and the man quickly twisted it in order to swing the giant ice lance down at Lanek.

Lanek leaped to the side, and the earth shattered into pieces around him as the weapon of ice came crashing down beside him. A number of vines shot out from the sphere of vines, trying to grab Lanek as he was airborne. Lanek managed to hack away at them, but by the time he landed, Augurc was already attacking with the ice lance again.

Lanek dropped to the ground, lying flat directly beneath the swing of the giant weapon.

The fact Augurc could manage such an incredibly complex application of simple Nexi stones was a testament to the madman's genius, as well as his incredible Nexi-wielding capacity. Lanek was exhausted, but it seemed Augurc was capable of continuing this fight for some time.

Augurc turned to swing his lance again, and this time there were dozens of vines arcing toward Lanek from the other direction. Lanek was going to have to use his Hader again, but he was certain that would push him to the brink of Nexi poisoning. The vines approached faster, and Lanek began swinging his rapier at them, while still watching for the approaching ice lance.

Just before it reached him, a blast of swamp material hit the side of the ice spear, keeping it from swinging into Lanek.

Lanek glanced back and saw Lynx, still lying on the ground, but able to at least hold up a Nexi stone and wield it. Once again, Lynx had saved Lanek's life.

Not because Lynx cared for Lanek, of course. He just needed Lanek to bring Augurc down, right? But then, why did Lynx want Augurc killed in the first place? Lanek couldn't understand whose side Lynx was truly on, if he was on anyone's.

"Run!" Lynx screamed.

Lanek sliced through the next few vines and ran for it. Just moments later, an explosion went off behind Lanek. Apparently Lynx had placed a fire Nexi inside the swamp stream he fired at Augurc's weapon. The ice spear shattered into pieces, and Lanek had to turn and dodge the largest of the ice chunks to avoid the same grievous injuries Lynx had suffered. Lanek was battered by a few brick-sized chunks of ice, which only left him badly bruised. As soon as the detonation passed though, Lanek was rushing toward Augurc's sphere of vines, which was tilting far backward from Lynx's explosion.

Fire was rushing up many of the vines, and Augurc was focused on disconnecting these vines from the vine ball he hid in. It gave Lanek the few seconds he needed to sprint to the thick vine legs holding the sphere up, and charge his rapier with orange Nexi energy one more time. Upon reaching the first leg, Lanek plunged his rapier straight through the vines, then tore through to sever the thick mesh of plants entirely. As soon as one leg was cut, Lanek rushed to the other and sliced through that as well.

The ball of vines fell to the earth. There was no time for Lanek to get out of the way. He was going to get flattened.

*No. This is my chance.*

He activated the Hader and ran beneath the center of the vine sphere. For one second, Lanek leaped through the air in an immaterial form. As soon as he was inside the vine sphere with Augurc, Lanek returned to physical form and plunged his rapier into Augurc's chest. The man had no time to react, or even realize what was happening—not amidst all the chaos of that moment.

Augurc screamed and swung a punch for Lanek's

head. Lanek ducked in time, then pulled his rapier back out so he could fend off the vines rushing for him from Augurc's arm Nexi stones.

He wasn't sure if Augurc was stabbed through the heart, but Lanek felt the man was at least out of the fight. Lanek used his orange Nexi-charged rapier to force an opening through the ball of vines, and ran before Augurc's new vines could strangle him or tear him into pieces.

Lanek ran back a ways and watched as the vine sphere fell apart, dissolving into a lifeless pile.

Augurc ran out of the pile, clutching the bleeding wound in his chest. Vines were wrapping around the injury, holding him together. As he ran, he looked back to Lanek and yelled, "As soon as Lynx is dead, I will come back for you! I will not be stopped by you, or by anyone in this inferior world!"

Lanek was about to run after Augurc, but the thought of Lynx dying made him hesitate. Was Lynx really dying for good? For some reason the thought was... unsettling.

He looked back to Lynx, and the sight didn't fill him with glee. If anything, the sight was pathetic. A bleeding body, covered with gashes, and impaled with ice in several places. The man lay on the ground, motionless, ready to die.

It was precisely what Lanek had wanted to see ever since he had been dragged into this Hader-searching mission. And yet... he didn't feel relieved. He felt guilty. Though this man had killed Suran, he did save Lanek's life multiple times now. What did any of this mean? Why did Lynx have a change of heart? It would have been simpler if Lynx was nothing but a traitor. Lanek would've felt no remorse.

He hurried over to Lynx and discovered the man's mask was broken apart. Only about half his face was covered. The idea that Lynx had a face was strange in itself... Lynx was supposed to be faceless. Nothing but a twisted, wicked being. Someone who wasn't actually someone.

And as soon as Lanek lifted off the rest of the mask, he realized Lynx was not just someone.

Lynx was Turan.

This was a fellow villager from Edellerston. A classmate in school. A friend of Terico and Suran. Someone Lanek had seen often. Someone Lanek *knew*.

A flood of memories rushed through Lanek's mind. He had never been particularly close to Turan, but this was someone Lanek was truly familiar with. It was as if Lanek had suddenly traveled back in time, to a time when he lived a peaceful life. He had his parents, his sister, his friends...

No kingdoms to save. No people to kill. No monsters to become.

"Why?" Lanek asked. "Why are you here, Turan? Why are you Lynx?"

Turan's eyes had trouble focusing on Lanek's. "Sorry... I couldn't help it."

"Why are you Lynx?" Lanek screamed.

When Turan couldn't respond, Lanek worked quickly to tend to Turan's wounds as best he could. He managed to remove the chunks of ice impaled in Turan's limbs and torso, then stopped the bleeding with strips of clothes Lanek could find. It seemed likely Turan was going to die though, even if Lanek had access to better first aid equipment.

"Why... Why are you Lynx?" Lanek asked again, once he felt Turan was able to talk again.

"I... was captured," Turan said. "Turned into Lynx... Nexi experiments... Lost my mind... I need my mind back... That's all I want..."

"Why couldn't you tell us this?" Lanek asked.

"Couldn't..." Turan said. "Lost my mind..."

Apparently there had been a terrible struggle going on in Turan's mind all these years. He had been trying to fight his identity as Lynx, an identity crafted by the likes of Augurc Shire. Lynx and the other Brotherhood experiments were a precursor to the Elpis-powered experiments to come, it seemed.

"Also..." Turan continued, "I didn't... I didn't want you to know... I'm so sorry..." Tears trickled out the sides of his eyes. "I'm so sorry about Suran..."

"I... I don't know what to say," Lanek said. The thought of Suran's death wasn't something Lanek could simplify. It wasn't something he could just forgive, even if the perpetrator didn't intend it. Nothing he or Turan could do would ever bring Suran back. She was lost to him.

And this whole mission... None of it had made Lanek feel closer to her.

And now that Suran's killer was dying, Lanek felt nothing but grief. Tears filled his own eyes, and he was too exhausted to hold them back. In his heart, Lanek almost felt as if he were witnessing Suran's death all over again.

"You can kill me... if you wish," Turan said. "I long wanted to kill myself... but I never could. And then I learned of the Haders... A part of me... A part of me always held on to hope. Hope that... somehow... something could work out. I wanted to be me again... I wanted to right all my wrongs... somehow."

Lanek shut his eyes and gritted his teeth. Suran wouldn't want her friend to die. Even if Turan did kill her, she wouldn't want him to die. Perhaps if Lanek had been even a little bit like Suran, he would have been able to do what was right from the very beginning. Perhaps he would have been able to move on after her death, and not suffer like this so much...

He realized what he needed to do.

"Take this," Lanek said. He placed his Hader in Turan's grasp. "If you have the desire to use this, you will enter a realm outside of time. A goddess named Reali lives there, and she will help you. If your motives truly are just... She will give you the power to turn that which exists... into a nonexistent state. I believe you will be able to take your madness and make it disappear forever."

Tears flowed freely down Turan's face. "But... I'm dying..."

"The Hader will help you live," Lanek said. "Just do as I said, and you will make it. I have to go after Augurc now, but as soon as I'm through with him, I will return here."

"Lanek... How will you fight without the Hader?"

"I've fought my whole life without one. I'll manage."

Lanek turned and ran down the path Augurc had taken. There were far too many thoughts passing through Lanek's head, and he had no time to deal with a single one of them.

He had to stop Augurc. He couldn't let that madman get away. He couldn't let another person suffer as Lynx had.

As Turan had.

•

Kechi made it to the steps of his master's mansion. It was excruciating to keep walking, but the Haders kept him going. He couldn't fail his master. He had to get the Haders to him. He made it to the mansion. He just had to give the Haders to Master. Kechi couldn't stop. He had to fulfill his master's wishes. All he had to do was hand Master the four Haders. He was there. He was opening the door. He couldn't just collapse and die now. He needed to find Master. Give him the Haders. Master needed the four Haders. And then it would be over. He couldn't fail Lord Mareba Shire.

The inside of the mansion was all a blur. Gazing out of his one good eye, Kechi trudged through rooms, down hallways, up stairs... Where was Master? All Kechi wanted was to find Master. All he wanted was to give Master the Haders. Then it would be over. Master would be pleased. That's all Kechi wanted. What purpose would Kechi have, if it weren't for Master? If he didn't fulfill Master's wishes, there wasn't a point to his existence.

There. There was Master's room. Master was sitting in his bed.

A skeleton.

Kechi stared blankly, trying to make sense of what he was seeing. In Master's bed was a skeleton.

But now that Kechi thought about it, Master had

died a while ago, hadn't he? Not long after Kechi was given his mission for seeking out the Haders. Some Shire royal had gotten Master killed, not wanting him to bring trouble to the Shire Kingdom. But little did those fools know, Lord Mareba Shire lived on in Kechi. Master was still alive in Kechi's heart. That's all that really mattered.

The skeleton sat propped up in the bed. Completely motionless. Completely silent. Staring off into nothingness.

But Kechi could see Master for who he truly was. The man who would bring the Shire Kingdom to its full glory. Nobody could stop Master's dream from coming true. Kechi had devoted his whole existence to Master. And he could still hear Master's voice, instructing him from time to time. Kechi knew what he was doing.

And now was the time for the ritual. He had four Haders. It was time to give Master all the power he needed to conquer this world and lead it in fear and justice.

Kechi set the four Hader stones on the bed, arced past Master's feet. On the wooden base at the front of the bed, Kechi painted a series of symbols with his own blood. The creators of the Haders had come up with an entire language that could manipulate the abilities of the stones. And when several of the stones were gathered together... they had powers that could rival the full Elpis itself.

In this case, four stones could be used to do all sorts of things.

Kechi lay himself down on the floor in front of Master's bed. His head lay beneath the bloody symbols, and after a couple minutes, he could begin to feel a tense energy building up in his heart. He wanted to scream, but all feeling in his body had turned numb, meaningless.

His soul split in two.

Kechi could feel a portion of it fading away. As it transferred to Master's skeleton, Kechi got on his knees and watched as Master's organs, flesh, and clothes all pieced back together. It only took a couple seconds.

Lord Mareba looked just as Kechi always remembered him. An older man, unable to walk, but commanding an aura that could bring entire nations to their knees.

"What is the situation, Kechi?" Lord Mareba asked.

"I have brought you back, Master," Kechi said.

"I know," Lord Mareba said. "I saw it happen."

"It's my soul that was split," Kechi said. "A central part of you is me now."

"And you are everything I have told you to be," Lord Mareba said. "My aspirations are your aspirations. We are one in mind."

"I will not fail you, Master," Kechi said. "I will do

whatever you ask of me. Even die, if I must."

"You are dying already," Master said. "But if you wish, you can assist in this city's cleansing."

"Yes," Kechi said. He walked over to help Master out of his bed and into his wooden wheelchair, but Master set Kechi's hand aside.

Instead, Master caused the four Haders to float over to his hands. "I have no need for the wheelchair." The four stones glowed brighter all at once. With this much energy, Master could bypass any contracts need with the beings inside the stones. He could do whatever he wished.

Master pushed aside his blanket and stood up on the bed. In his white and green uniform, Master looked like the commander of the entire world. A silver and golden glow enveloped his entire body, obscuring the features of his face.

"It is time to test my power," Master said, his voice now sounding much younger, much stronger. "I will vanquish all my enemies in this city, restore every building that fell, and then proceed to the nearest city of the Fiefs Kingdom. I will wipe Niez off the map, and then proceed to the next closest city. Once the Fiefs government surrenders, I will return to the Shire Kingdom, and take my place as ruler of the entire continent. All who resist will perish."

It sounded like a perfect plan. Lord Mareba would

not fail, and neither would Kechi.

They could not fail each other now. To fail Master would be to fail himself.

And he could not fail himself. How would Kechi exist, if he hadn't come into being?

•

# 12. THE SHATTERED FRAGMENTS OF REVENGE

Without the Hader, the pain in Borely's body built up more and more. He shut his eyes and tried to focus on anything but the pain. He wanted to get up. Find Areo again. Keep trying to save her. This was his chance to do so, but he didn't know how he was going to overpower her. She had been a talented vampire even before the Elpis experimentation. What chance did he ever have against her, even when he had the Hader?

Something nudged him in the shoulder.

"Are you dead?" It was Analicia.

Borely opened his eyes and saw the child standing

behind his head. "Not quite."

"Then get up!" Analicia said. She placed a vial of blood at Borely's mouth and forced him to drink. "Areo's getting away."

Borely gulped the blood down and felt his wounds healing, and energy returning to his body. Analicia didn't have any more blood to give him, so Borely didn't feel in perfect condition, and his claws weren't going to heal any time soon. He wasn't going to be able to fight Analicia with his claws, and he didn't have the means to fix his metal gloves or headband. And of course, the Hader was gone too. He got up and took the Nexi stones out of his broken weapons, so he could use those at least.

"I don't see how I'll be able to stop her," Borely said. "I was giving my all, and I simply couldn't keep up with her..." The only thing hopeful about his fight with Areo was the fact she had stopped the stranger from killing Borely off. There were a few possibilities for why she did so, but Borely felt that deep down, Areo had recognized him. Or at the very least, had recognized the scene of him nearly dying, and reacted in a way to keep Borely alive—just as she had before she was captured by Augurc.

"Don't give up," Analicia said. "You've been in worse pinches than this."

"I'm not so sure about that," Borely said. "I can't use my claws, or my weapons, or the Hader."

"Maybe you don't need to use those things," Analicia said. "See if you can save her some other way."

"I've already tried talking to her," Borely said.

"Try some more then," Analicia said.

"She'll just kill me," Borely said. "In her heart, she may recognize me, but she can't stop herself from fighting everyone she deems an enemy of the Brotherhood."

"Find a way to reach her without getting killed," Analicia said.

Borely looked over the Nexi stones he had. A couple orange ones, a light blue one, a green one, and a teal one. He had used the teal Nexi to speak with Rilv from a great distance away. But two Nexi stones were needed in order to communicate, as Rilv had a teal Nexi as well. Areo didn't have one, so she wouldn't be able to hear Borely's words. And the moment Borely shouted anything to her, she would sprint over to him and stab him in the heart.

Perhaps he could use the green Nexi in some way...

"I think I have a plan," Borely said. "Which way did Areo go?"

Analicia pointed. "She went a few blocks that way, and I saw a group of soldiers ambush her the next street over."

Areo would surely kill off all the soldiers, but if they slowed her down a bit, Borely would be able to catch up with her.

"Let's go, then." He ran off down the street, weaving his way through the remains of fallen buildings, while Analicia followed behind him.

After making their way down a few blocks, Analicia directed Borely to run left. Once down another street, Borely found the corpses of dozens of Shire soldiers, many of them sliced clean in half.

He searched the area for Areo, but only found more corpses. The furthest corpse was to Borely's right. He turned that way and hurried down the street, guessing this was the direction Areo must have taken.

He stopped at a crossroads, noticing a figure standing in the distance to his left.

It was Areo. She was directly facing Borely. He turned and gazed at her, and realized she was crying. Tears were streaming down her face.

Was she realizing everything she was doing? Perhaps the moment she chose to save Borely again had a deeper effect on her mind than Borely thought.

She turned and ran. She didn't want to face Borely again.

She knew that if she did, she would kill him.

Borely ran after her, pulling out his green and teal Nexi stones. If he couldn't stop her from fulfilling Augurc's requests by force, perhaps he could tell her the right words she needed to hear, and she would decide to stop on her own. Her mind had been twisted by Augurc, but it still was her mind. Deep within that Elpis-tampered body of hers was a soul that was fighting to return to who she once was. Borely had to believe in this. And he had to believe he could help her overcome those destructive emotions Augurc had enhanced in her.

He created a bit of vine from his green Nexi stone and tied the teal Nexi to the end of it. With the teal Nexi properly secured, Borely caused the vine to extend and reach out toward Areo.

Once the teal Nexi was hovering a few meters above Areo, Borely focused on the stone, directing his energy to it through the green Nexi stone, and on down the length of the long vine. Areo was running faster, placing a good ten meters between her and Borely.

But Borely wasn't going to lose sight of her. He pushed himself harder, running as fast as he could.

"Areo, it's me... Borely," he said between breaths, his voice echoing from the distant teal Nexi. "Analicia and I came to this city to find you. We're not sure if we're going about this the right way, but we really want to help you. Augurc has forced you to kill a lot of people today, but I know you don't want to be a part of this a second longer...

"I know I can't persuade you to stop. You've always had a stubborn personality, and I'm sure Augurc took advantage of that when he twisted your mind with the Elpis. But I'm stubborn too—perhaps even more so than you. I suppose most people wouldn't want to stick around someone who kept trying to kill them... but I can't give up on you. I can't just leave you behind, or let you leave me. Not again."

Areo kept running, but she seemed to be slowing down a bit. Or perhaps Borely was just starting to run faster.

"You saved my life five years ago," Borely said, still channeling his words down the vine and out the teal Nexi stone a ways above Areo, careful to keep the vine out of reach of her claws. "I wouldn't be alive if it weren't for you. I was upset about becoming a vampire, but I know now... What you did was the right thing.

"And it's time I returned the favor. At least, that's what I felt I was doing, when I finally managed to leave Istal and go search for you. But I don't think that's how it should be... I didn't go through all this just so I could feel we were even. I've been trying to find you because I want to, Areo. Our time together five years ago wasn't exactly full of happy experiences, but there was nothing wrong with you."

"Stop it," Areo said. Borely could hear her voice from his green Nexi stone, its vine connected to the teal Nexi. "Stop it. Stop it. Stop it."

"I told you, I'm never going to stop," Borely said. "I wouldn't have come all the way here and gone through so much pain just to give up now. Even if I never did stand a chance against you. I'm still willing to give my all for you, Areo."

"Go away!" Areo yelled, her pace starting to stagger and slow down a bit. "Don't come near me!"

"I'm coming," Borely said. "Whether you like it or not, I'm coming."

He ran faster, struggling to maintain his breath. He couldn't let her get away. He couldn't let himself slow down. He had to reach Areo.

"I don't want to kill you!" Areo screamed.

"I don't want you to suffer anymore!" Borely replied. "Nobody's going to kill anyone. You don't want to kill anymore. And... neither do I. I just want this all to end. I want us to be together again. I'll help you through your pain. I'll help you recover. You can count on me, Areo. I'm here for you."

Borely found himself gaining on Areo quickly. Areo slowed to a stop, and Borely brought the vine back into its Nexi stone. He pocketed the green and teal Nexi stones, and ran right up to Areo.

Just as Borely reached her, Areo turned around and extended her claws, jabbing Borely through the chest. Borely collapsed into Areo, and wrapped his arms around her.

Borely gripped her tight and whispered into her ear. "And I'm not going to let you go."

He turned his head and sunk his teeth into her neck. Areo didn't move—she simply held her position, her claws still impaling Borely's chest. Borely injected his venom into her body, and let his blood flow amongst her own.

*You know this blood*, Borely thought. It was the blood she drank just before Augurc captured her. For vampires, there was nothing that affected the senses as strongly as blood.

Borely kept his fangs in Areo's neck. He couldn't let her forget him. He couldn't let her give up on her life. Her real life.

Areo slid her claws back into her fingernails. Borely released his teeth from Areo's neck. He slumped forward, but managed to hold on to Areo's shoulders. He felt the life fading from him, but he couldn't let himself let her go.

"Drink my blood," Areo said. She forced Borely's mouth back on her neck.

Borely smiled and accepted her request. He sunk his teeth back in her neck and sucked her blood, healing the deep, fatal injuries in his chest.

Once he felt strong enough to stand on his own once more, he released his teeth from Areo's neck again. Still holding his arms around Areo, he leaned back a bit and looked into her eyes. She was crying again... and her eyes looked genuine. They were Areo's eyes.

Areo was back.

"You look better," Borely said.

"You look terrible," Areo said.

Borely laughed. His clothes were tattered, and he must have looked a few levels beyond exhausted by now. He had pushed himself far beyond what was safe. Regardless of how much blood he drank, he couldn't exert himself forever.

"First thing you tell me is I look terrible," Borely said. "You really are back to normal."

Borely was surprised Areo was in control of her mind again. He hadn't used the Hader to cancel out the Elpis energy implanted inside of her. Had Rilv, Lanek, and Kitoh managed to destroy all the Elpis pieces? Perhaps with the Elpis itself gone, Areo was able to overcome the effects of the experimentation.

Borely kept a hold over Areo. "You're really okay now, though?"

Areo nodded. "I... I think so. But everything... I can't forget. I can't forgive myself for this..."

"None of it was your fault," Borely said. "You couldn't control yourself."

"I still let myself get captured though," Areo said. "And I wasn't strong enough to overcome Augurc's experiment."

"The Elpis is the strongest Nexi power in the entire world," Borely said. "You can't blame yourself for this."

"My... mind... It hurts..." Areo said. Tears flowed from her eyes again. "I can't..."

"It's okay," Borely said. He placed a hand on the back of her head and placed her face against his shoulder. He realized it would take some time for Areo's mind to heal.

"I'll take care of you, Areo. I won't let us get separated again."

•

Everything had failed him. Everything Augurc had ever worked for... Everything, everything, everything— everything was weak. Everything was meaningless. Everything was utterly imperfect.

The Elpis, his experiments, his Brotherhood... He couldn't rely on anything.

He worked his way through the ruinous city, the

very embodiment of what had become of his every dream and ambition.

His experiments had failed him. And Augurc could blame nobody but himself. Not his father, not his brother, nor any of the Shire dukes. Not even his enemies. His experiments were supposed to be perfect. They were formed just as he intended them to be.

But they failed. From several vantage points, Augurc searched the city over, and he could find no sign of Subject VI or EV. They must have been defeated, just as MI was—the creature that was supposed to rival the power of a god, and the obedience of a flawless servant.

There was nothing Augurc could rely on. Not even himself.

He sat atop a roof of one of the only tall buildings left in the city, and found nothing but ruin and failure.

It was the cycle of hatred and despair.

Augurc shut his eyes and gripped his fists. Everything he had worked his whole life for... None of it changed a thing. If anything, his life's work only strengthened the cycle. He wanted to eradicate hatred. He wanted to extinguish despair. He wanted to break down the walls of the world's meaningless nations, and replace the meaningless peoples of the land with a superior form of life.

With years of dedicated research and the power of

the Elpis, Augurc was to bring the world into an era of thought, complacency, and unity. People would no longer hate. People would no longer despair.

But it was an impossible dream. Augurc's experiments—the most powerful beings the world had ever seen—even they weren't enough to bring a single city into submission. All the world would resist, and Augurc was helpless to change a thing.

And if even the Elpis was not strong enough for him to achieve his goals, there was no use in focusing on them any further.

What was he supposed to do with his life now? It was meaningless. Just as meaningless as every other life in the world. He couldn't break the cycle, no matter what he did. All he could do was make it more painful.

He gripped the vines holding his chest together. It was possible he was going to die, without the power of the Elpis lending him any of its healing glow.

Perhaps it was time for him to die.

"Augurc Shire."

He turned around and saw a man hovering in the air behind him. He looked to be an older man, and an aristocrat—one of the Shire noble, Augurc realized. An aura of gold and silver light glowed about him, and all color had faded from his eyes. It reminded Augurc very much of his brother, charged with the power of the Elpis.

The man dropped a large bloody canvas on the flat roof. It was not tied together, so the canvas spilled out its contents all about.

About twenty masked heads rolled out.

"These strange people were murdering Shire citizens for some reason," the nobleman said.

"You have the Elpis?" Augurc asked. He couldn't see how the man had the Elpis, considering how Augurc saw each of the fragments destroyed by the Fiefs servant woman.

"No, the Haders," the nobleman said. "Much more reliable and stable than the Elpis."

"I doubt it." Augurc had no idea what the Haders were, but he couldn't get himself to care. There was always a price to pay for such power.

"You accomplished a great deal of destruction with the Elpis," the nobleman said. "But it pales in comparison to what I can accomplish with the Haders."

"You've destroyed what was left of the Brotherhood," Augurc said. "Kill me and be done with it."

"You've given up?" the nobleman asked. "That simplifies matters. I can only hope the Fiefs Kingdom will be as weak and feeble as you!"

Augurc stood up and stared at the man. "You plan

to destroy the Fiefs Kingdom?"

"Just enough of it for the kingdom to surrender to their rightful Shire ruler. And anyone who gets in my way of becoming the ruler of this continent will likewise perish."

It was the cycle all over again. This man was making the same mistakes Delkol made.

The same mistakes Augurc made.

He formed a lance of ice on his arm and caused more vines to emerge from the Nexi stones on his arms. The nobleman floated back a bit, a long, thin grin spread across his weathered face.

"I can't let this destruction go on any longer," Augurc said. "I'll never stop the cycle of hatred and despair... And I can never hope to atone for the destruction I've inflicted on this meaningless world. But I can still do something. And in doing so... One day, perhaps I can find some meaning in it all."

•

Lanek searched the city for Augurc, catching sight of him from time to time, but never quite able to reach him. The man was looking for something. His experiments? The monster had been killed, and Kitoh had dealt with the young elf. And if all was going well for Borely, Areo was being dealt with as well. There were only the Brotherhood members Augurc could turn to now, and

Lanek hadn't seen any of them during his chase through the city.

In fact, it seemed the ambush of the city had come to a close. What exactly was going on? Did Augurc give up, and call off the attack? The defeat of his treasured experiments must have been humbling, but Augurc didn't seem the type to ever give up.

Or was he? He wasn't really like his brother Delkol, all things considered. Perhaps Augurc could be reasoned with.

At last, Lanek found Augurc again—he had made his way up another building, which was easy for him thanks to the many vine Nexi stones at his disposal. But this time Augurc was just sitting there. He wasn't searching for anything. It looked as if he just wanted to sit and think. Perhaps his mind was having trouble grasping how his experiments could have failed him. He clearly didn't foresee the Haders being used against him, and certainly not this effectively. And with his Elpis gone, his experiments defeated, and his own body critically injured, he was at the end of his line.

Someone appeared near Augurc, floating in the air. Lanek stopped, taken aback. It looked like an older man—an aristocrat, from the looks of it—and he was bathed in silver and gold light. The scene reminded Lanek very much of Terico and Delkol, when they were powered by fragments of the Elpis.

But the Elpis was destroyed. What was giving this man so much Nexi energy? It couldn't be a Hader... Could it be the combined power of multiple Haders? Yet this wasn't a man Lanek knew to have a Hader. And the only person Lanek knew to have more than one Hader was Kechi.

"Are you left breathless at the sight of my master—the omnipotent Lord Mareba Shire?"

Lanek turned and found Kechi a ways behind him, struggling to trudge down the block. He looked like he had been killed ten times over already. What happened to him, and how was he still standing? He wasn't carrying any Haders. Did he give them to the man floating in the air... Mareba Shire?

"What are you trying to do?" Lanek asked.

"I will always live for my master," Kechi said, his one good eye open wide. "I will never stop serving him. Not even death can disrupt my master's vision."

"And what would that be?" Lanek asked.

"A land as it should be," Kechi said. "A land ruled by Lord Mareba Shire."

"Even if the Fiefs Kingdom is conquered," Lanek said, "the people won't just submit themselves to your power-hungry master."

"They will have no choice but to," Kechi said.

"With the power of the Haders, nobody will be able to resist Lord Mareba's rule and glory."

"If your master was so great, he wouldn't have to force people to follow him," Lanek said.

"People are foolish!" Kechi yelled, before falling into a wretched coughing fit. "People don't understand him. They don't care for anything but themselves. They're complacent. They're afraid of change. They don't truly care for the Shire Kingdom. They just want things to stay as they are. They don't think—"

Lanek stabbed him through the heart.

Kechi slumped over the blade of Lanek's rapier. Lanek pulled the sword out and let Kechi's body collapse on the ground. Lanek had expected Kechi to attack Lanek at some point, to get revenge for the loss of his eye at least—but Kechi had become completely absorbed by his devotion to his master. Kechi wasn't able to react in time once Lanek was sprinting toward him, rapier already drawn forward.

Lanek turned to Augurc and the man Kechi called his master.

The fight was already over.

•

Augurc doubted he could fight for long. He was in poor condition to fight, and this nobleman seemed to have a power that rivaled the Elpis itself.

"You will pay for your crimes with your life," the nobleman said. He raised a hand toward Augurc and grinned.

Augurc leaped toward the nobleman and sent a series of vines rushing for him from multiple directions. Just before Augurc could slam his lance of ice into the nobleman's chest, he stopped, frozen in place. His body shook, and sweat trickled down his face. His heart felt like it was beating in his neck—his entire body filled with fear. At the same time, all of Augurc's vines missed the nobleman entirely. It was true that Augurc was in a great deal of pain, but the chances of every single one of his vines missing their target... It was unfathomable.

Why was he suddenly afraid to attack this nobleman? And how did every one of his vines happen to fly around the nobleman like that?

The nobleman laughed. "This is the future, Augurc Shire. All my enemies shall be filled with fear, and fortune will forever be on my side."

A mass of crimson liquid—blood, Augurc realized—appeared above the nobleman's head. The blood split apart into small, thin needles, which quickly hardened and turned metallic. The blood... How it was floating in the air and turning into needles, Augurc couldn't even guess.

At the same time, several swords materialized out of thin air, floating to either side of the nobleman. Augurc had never seen such power within any kind of Nexi energy before.

The ability to instill fear in enemies, have luck on your side, control blood, and summon weapons... In one moment, Augurc felt his entire understanding of Nexi power was entirely altered. What were these Haders, and how did they contain powers that were entirely unrelated to anything found within regular Nexi stones?

Augurc couldn't just let himself die. He didn't understand. There was so much he didn't understand. So much he had misunderstood. There was so much more to learn. So much more to discover. Perhaps there was still a way for Augurc to break the cycle. Perhaps there was something more for him to do in this world, even if it wasn't anything remotely similar to what he had been working for all these years.

"I'm not done," Augurc said.

The nobleman laughed. "I killed your giant monster! I can kill you too. There is nothing I can't kill. And nothing that can—"

He stopped mid-sentence, and his whole body began shaking. He gasped for air, and for a moment Augurc thought the man had been stabbed in the back. Yet there was nothing...

Augurc found the artificial fear left him, and

immediately stepped forward and slammed his spear of ice through the nobleman's heart.

"My... soul..." the nobleman coughed.

The mass of blood liquified and rained on the nobleman, and the summoned weapons fell to the roof of the building. The silver and gold glow faded away, and the nobleman fell limp over Augurc's ice spear.

Four Nexi stones fell to the floor beneath the nobleman's body. Augurc pulled his arm out of his lance and dropped it, letting the nobleman's bloody corpse flop to the side.

Each of the Nexi stones glowed with two different colors, swirling and shifting about.

*What are they?* Augurc thought. *And how should I use them?*

•

Lanek found a ladder and used it to climb to the top of the building Augurc sat upon. From what Lanek could tell, the moment he killed Kechi, it seemed Mareba Shire had suffered in some way in reaction. It looked like it was only a brief moment of weakness, but a moment was all Augurc needed to kill him.

As Lanek climbed up the ladder, he didn't hear Augurc try to run away or even move. Lanek had his rapier ready once he reached the roof, but Augurc didn't make any movement, vines or otherwise. Was Augurc too weak to fight anymore? Or was he dying?

It looked like he was still breathing. He sat hunched over, his eyes focused on some Nexi stones lying a few paces in front of him. They were Haders.

Lanek sprinted toward the Haders, expecting Augurc to grab them and use them.

But Augurc didn't move. Lanek ran up to the Haders and knelt down to pick them up. He took all four of them and walked back a few steps. Augurc still sat motionless, his gaze still focused on the spot where the Haders had been.

Lanek stood in silence, wondering what to do next. Was Augurc going to attack him or not? It made no sense for Augurc to just let Lanek take the Haders, if he understood what they were at all. With the loss of his Elpis fragments, Augurc should have been desperate to obtain these Haders.

"What do you intend to use those Nexi stones for?" Augurc asked, breaking the silence.

"The plan was to destroy them," Lanek said. "We've gotten tired of your lot using these things to wreak havoc in our kingdom."

"How pointless..." Augurc sighed. "And yet, it's just as pointless to try using them, too."

"When you fight the Fiefs Kingdom, you're going to face resistance," Lanek said. "And now you must pay for your crimes, Augurc."

Lanek pointed his rapier at Augurc, and a flood of emotions passed through Lanek's heart. This was the moment for him to avenge Suran's death, once and for all. This was the man who brought so much pain and misery to the kingdom these past five years. It was time for Lanek to find some measure of peace in his life. It was time to make this haunting mission worth something. It was time to bring this all to an end.

Someone climbed up the stairs. Lanek turned and found Borely walking onto the roof, followed by Areo.

Lanek looked back to Augurc, who still hadn't moved. Had he simply accepted death?

He kept his eye on Augurc as he spoke to the vampires. "I see you've succeeded at what you set out to do, Borely."

"I helped Areo stop following Augurc's orders," Borely said. "Unfortunately, it seems Areo's mind has been severely scarred. At first she acted and spoke like her old self, but now she's simply following me, not even aware of who I am. It might take a long time for her mind to fully heal."

"You probably would like the chance to finish off Augurc as well then," Lanek said. "He is the one responsible for your near-death five years ago, and the one who brought Areo down to this lowly state."

"I know," Borely said. He didn't say anything more for a bit, apparently thinking over his words carefully. "But Areo is alive, and I can help her through her pain. And the Elpis has been destroyed, I take it."

"It has," Lanek said. "I also have four Haders, which I intend to destroy once Augurc has been dealt with."

"Will you kill him, then?" Borely asked.

Lanek was still pointing the tip of his rapier down toward Augurc's head. The man still hadn't attempted to stop Lanek. His vines hung limp to his sides, and he didn't try to create any more weapons from his ice Nexi.

"I can not stop you," Augurc said. "I can not blame either of you in your desire for revenge. It is a central part of the human mind. I have brought you despair. It is only natural you retaliate in hatred."

Augurc bowed his head toward Lanek. He was fully accepting his fate. He was ready to die.

Lanek gritted his teeth. Why was this happening? He needed to kill this man, didn't he? Augurc had killed so many people. Brought pain and agony to so many lives. Ruined entire cities. Augurc had to pay. He was a monster. He was a monster who killed *Suran*. He couldn't be forgiven.

"I won't kill you," Borely said.

Lanek loosened his grip on his rapier. His mouth dropped open a bit, and his heart slowed its beat—it felt as if time itself had slowed down.

"Why would you say that?" Lanek asked. "You have every reason to kill this man."

"I know," Borely said. "I want to kill him... very badly. But we've already won. The Brotherhood has been defeated. The experiments have all been dealt with. The city is safe now. And the Elpis and Haders will no longer pose a threat on the Fiefs Kingdom. But the Shire government will be in an uproar over what happened today. The destruction of Zein could be used as a reason for war against the Fiefs Kingdom."

It took a few moments for Lanek to understand what the situation entailed in the political scheme of things.

"So what you're saying... is we need Augurc alive," Lanek said, the words painful to his lips.

"We can't just keep killing each other," Borely said. "Somebody has to choose peace. Otherwise... the cycle of revenge will just go on forever."

Lanek turned away from Augurc and sheathed his sword. Tears trickling down his face, he stared at Borely and took a few deep, quiet breaths.

"You're... right," Lanek said. He shut his eyes, his whole vision turning back to Suran.

Was she pleased with this decision?

Deep down, Lanek knew Suran wouldn't want him to keep walking this bloody path. Suran wouldn't want Lanek to kill people in revenge. She would just want Lanek to move on with his life, and find happiness somewhere... Create meaning in his life. Do good things for those around him. Live a dignified life. One their parents could be proud of.

"We will let the Shire Kingdom deal with Augurc as they see fit then," Lanek said.

"What if they decide to let him live?" Borely asked.

"I will only concern myself with my kingdom," Augurc said, still looking at the ground. "I have influence in my kingdom, regardless of all I have done. I will accept my punishment, and do whatever is left in my power to ensure the fighting ends between our kingdoms."

It was unlikely Augurc would be given any actual say in the government of the Shire Kingdom from this point on. But as a direct descendant in the Shire family line, he could in time come to influence the decisions of the governing court, even from the prison walls of the Shire's royal castle.

If there was even a small chance of peace, Lanek

would accept letting Augurc live. Even if Augurc was a monster who had every reason to die, Lanek recognized that Borely's decision was the better path to take. Lanek had seen enough blood over the course of this mission.

"Let's deal with this then," Lanek said. He placed the four Hader stones on the ground and took out the device Kitoh had designed to destroy the Elpis. Lanek had seen Rilv use it on her own Hader, so there was no doubt it would work on these ones as well.

With four strong whacks, Lanek destroyed the four Haders. They each burst into dust, and Lanek felt as if a great weight had been lifted with the loss of each one. The Haders were truly incredible, but it was time for them to pass on. They had served their purpose in bringing down the Elpis. The world was a much less dangerous place now.

•

Not long afterward, a troop of Shire guards arrived at the scene, led by a Brotherhood woman named Shirm. She had abandoned her mask, and apparently had turned against Augurc during the invasion of the city. She explained that she would see to it that whatever was left of the Brotherhood would be disbanded, and that any of Augurc's ongoing experiments would be brought to a halt.

The guards tied Augurc up and brought him down from the building, leading him to a prison carriage intended to head to the Shire Kingdom's capital city.

"I am probably the only Brotherhood member left in this city," Shirm said to Lanek. "There are probably only a few others spread out across the continent. Augurc had brought most all of them together for this invasion... He led us into a massacre."

"What will you do now, without the Brotherhood?" Lanek asked.

"I will act as mediator between Augurc and the royal council," Shirm said. "I failed to help the Shire Kingdom as I had always hoped to. I apparently went about it entirely the wrong way... from the very start."

"People have strong wills," Lanek said. "I think Augurc has realized this himself."

"We're not as weak as he thought," Shirm agreed.

Borely placed a hand on Lanek's shoulder, his other hand holding one of Areo's hands. "Well, we are pretty weak. We're just not the types to let that sort of thing stop us."

Lanek couldn't help but smile a little. It seemed this mission was finally over with, and though his body was still in great pain, his heart felt lighter than it had in years.

He didn't have to let his despair or hatred control him.

He could do whatever he wished.

•

After everyone took the time they needed to heal in Zein, it took a week for everything to be cleared up in Setar. With Rilv a casualty of the mission, it was up to Lanek to explain to the Fiefs royal council everything that had happened. The Elpis and Haders were destroyed, the Brotherhood disbanded, and the likes of Augurc, Mareba, and Kechi were all dealt with. Rilv, Kitoh, Nivakil, Jenba, and many civilians of the elf village Velm were all lost amidst the conflict, not to mention the many lives which perished in Istal, Zein, and a number of Fiefs towns and villages.

But at long last, the threat was thoroughly extinguished. As Lanek and Borely hoped, the Shire Kingdom's governing body learned the full story of what happened in Zein from Augurc and Shirm. Augurc took full responsibility for the lives lost there, and any potential conflict between the two kingdoms was thankfully averted. Augurc was imprisoned rather than executed, but from the sound of things it seemed the Shire leadership agreed with Augurc's assessment that more measures should be taken to ensure a stable peace between Shire and Fiefs.

Perhaps there were still those who felt the two kingdoms should be united by force, but given the bloody devastation of the last couple weeks, there didn't appear to be anyone eager to promote any further violence anytime soon.

Lanek piloted his airship to Velm, not certain

what anyone there would think of him. He brought Turan, Borely, Areo, and Analicia with him, since none of them had homes to return to at this point. The vampires could have returned to Istal now that the city was back in the hands of the citizens, Lanek supposed. But the three each had the necessary Nexi stone for them to live in the light now, and they wanted to go to this village Lanek kept telling them about.

It seemed they all wanted to find someplace peaceful to live at. All five of them had rejected the Fiefs government's honorary positions offered them in the castle, and they didn't even feel the need to accept the monetary rewards they were given. There was no need for any of that. They just wanted to go somewhere quiet.

Velm was the perfect place for them.

It took some time to explain to the villagers the full situation, and why the tragedy happened the way it did. Many of the elves were reluctant to let Lanek, Turan, or the vampires step foot in the village, but once Lanek handed the village elder the Stone of Truth, the villagers were more willing to forgive. Lanek had told the Fiefs governing body that this Hader was destroyed along with the rest of them. And since only Lanek, Turan, and the three vampires knew it was a Hader, the Stone of Truth was safe once more.

Over the following weeks, Lanek and the others helped the village in rebuilding their shrine. In a way, Lanek felt he was rebuilding his own life, and he imagined his four companions felt the same.

Turan had successfully used the Hader to clear his mind of the madness Augurc had forced upon him via raw Nexi energy. Lanek didn't know if he would always feel a little uneasy being around Turan, as Lanek still couldn't get over Suran's death. It was simply a feeling that would never leave him. But he found himself slowly becoming more accepting of Turan, who was acting more and more like his old self, rather than like Lynx did. Turan would never be as he once was, of course, but he did have his mind again. As far as Lanek was concerned, Turan was a friend, and the two had a connection with one another through their home village, Edellerston, and the times they all spent together with Terico and Suran.

Areo's mind was unfortunately much less stable. She no longer had a desire to kill anyone, and at times she seemed to have forgotten who Augurc was entirely. Lanek had tried using the Hader to try to clear her mind of madness, similar to what Turan did—but it was no use. Her mind was clear and free, but it was still damaged by the Elpis. That simply wasn't going to go away, and it was left up to Borely to help Areo. At times she would be entirely oblivious of what was going on around her, and at other times she would have terrible headaches. But then there were times where her old personality resurfaced, and Borely treasured every moment they spent together during these brief minutes.

Then again, as time passed, Borely seemed to treasure every moment he spent with Areo, regardless of her mental state. Along with Analicia, the three vampires became valued members of the elf community, and animosity between the villagers and the five newcomers slowly dissipated.

It was difficult to win everyone's trust. Beloved friends and family members had died, including a few who were killed by Turan himself. Turan apologized in every way he could, and it was made clear he was not himself at the time, thanks to Augurc's brainwashing. It was painful, but over time, the village came to accept Turan and Lanek. They worked hard, helping with a number of the village farms, and with other chores that kept many of the families busy.

Lanek visited Fenley's grave often. In some ways, she represented everything Lanek had longed for in a friend and companion. And in other ways, her personality triggered memories of all the time he spent with Suran. There was no way to bring either Fenley or Suran back. He had to accept their passing. He would never forget them, but he wouldn't let their deaths bring him to despair, either. He had to keep moving on with his life. Finding new things to do. New ways to help the people around him.

The village was a very simple, quiet place. It was difficult for everyone to move on after so much turmoil had befallen them. Perhaps there were many who would have liked to kill Lanek and Turan in revenge. And perhaps there were some who would have liked to kill Borely, Areo, and Analicia out of fear.

But nobody ever tried to hurt them. Lanek, Turan, Borely, Areo, and Analicia had all proven they would never bring any harm to the villagers. In fact, they each vowed to never let any harm befall the village at all. It was unlikely anyone would ever want to disrupt such an out-of-the-way village, but just in case—Lanek and his companions were ready to defend it. This was their home now.

Eventually the shrine was fully repaired, and it opened again for elves to enter and glean wisdom from the Stone of Truth. For several days there were constantly villagers at the shrine, eager to come to a better understanding of how to press forward with their lives. About a week passed before the shrine began having its normal, quieter flow of participation.

One cool evening, Lanek walked to the shrine entrance, passing Turan and Analicia, who happened to be serving as guards that day.

"Going for a swim?" Turan asked.

"Don't drown," Analicia added.

"I'll stay in the shallow end," Lanek replied.

He walked in and went to the back, where he could change in the gray clothes needed for the ritual Fenley had shown him. Once he was ready, he lay in the water in front of the fixed statue of the goddess Reali. She was looking up to the invisible Stone of Truth once more, and ready to help him feel at ease.

Lanek lay in the water and closed his eyes. He couldn't pretend that everything worked out perfectly. Life simply didn't work that way.

But once he was willing to let go of his hatred and despair, it was possible to find some measure of contentment.

He smiled and let the glow of the Hader give him peace.

•

The End.

# Elpis *(Elpis series book #1)*

*The Potential for Unlimited Power is revealed...*

In a world where magical abilities are utilized through the Nexi Stones, there is one stone that stands high above the rest, shrouded in myth and mystery—the Elpis. Broken into four fragments centuries in the past, the Elpis waits to be pieced back together, and to grant its user godlike powers that could reshape the world forever.

Raised in a quiet town, Terico would much rather be traveling the world and fighting monsters than working at his parents' shop and dealing with school. His life ambitions change dramatically, however, when his village is attacked and everything he holds dear is taken away from him. Delkol, leader of the feared Brotherhood and ruler of the aggressive Shire Kingdom, seeks the pieces of the Elpis, and is willing to burn Terico's village to the ground in order to find one.

When the terror has passed and Terico stands at the greatest crossroads in his life, there is only one thing on his mind—one goal that encompasses his very existence. Revenge.

Find out more at www.AlphaManga.com

# **Haders** *(Elpis series book #2)*

## *The Cycle of Hatred and Despair Continues...*

Five years have passed since the tumultuous finale of ELPIS, and though a catastrophic war has been averted between the Fiefs and Shire Kingdoms, the safety of the world is threatened by the Elpis-enhanced experiments of Augurc and his Brotherhood.

A plan is formed to locate powerful Nexi stones known as Haders, crafted centuries ago for the purpose of combating the Elpis. Two unlikely teams are formed, both of which find conflict every step of the way in their search for the Haders.

One team includes Borely, who finds himself struggling to come to terms with what he has become—a bloodthirsty vampire—the very thing he has long despised. His greatest goal is to find Areo, the one who saved his life and brought him to this state. But will the Haders enable Borely to rescue Areo from the clutches of the Brotherhood, or will he have to rely on another power in order to save her?

Meanwhile the airship-pilot elf Lanek finds himself enlisted for the other Hader-searching team, and realizes that deep down he is still suffering over the loss of his precious sister. Will finding the Haders and bringing down the Brotherhood be enough to avenge her, and finally bring peace to Lanek's aimless spirit?

**The Elpis Series**

Elpis - 2011

Haders - 2012

**Other Works By Aaron McGowan**

AslashD (Manga style comic) – 2016

Elpis #1 - The World Changes (Manga style comic) – 2016

Fantasy Foot Soliders (Manga style comic) - 2016

Find out more at www.AlphaManga.com

Please show your support and FOLLOW

# @Aaronelpis

On Twitter & Instagram

Pleaase don't forget to rate and mark as read on [Goodreads](#) or [Amazon](#).

Find out how you could become a NexiKnight @

[www.HellfunAustralia.com](#)